AN AXE TO
GRIND
BOOK FOUR OF
THE GUILD WARS

Jon R. Osborne

Seventh Seal Press
Virginia Beach, VA

Chris Kennedy/Seventh Seal Press
2052 Bierce Dr.
Virginia Beach, VA 23454
http://chriskennedypublishing.com/

Publisher's Note: This is a work of fiction. Names, characters, places, and incidents are a product of the author's imagination. Locales and public names are sometimes used for atmospheric purposes. Any resemblance to actual people, living or dead, or to businesses, companies, events, institutions, or locales is completely coincidental.

Cover art by Ricky Ryan.
Cover Design by Brenda Mihalko.

Ordering Information:
Quantity sales. Special discounts are available on quantity purchases by corporations, associations, and others. For details, contact the "Special Sales Department" at the address above.

An Axe to Grind/Jon R. Osborne -- 1st ed.
ISBN: 978-1648550065

This book is dedicated to Bill and Ray - friends who passed before they could see me grow from game master to author.

Chapter One

Approaching Bear Town, New Mexico, Earth

"Son, give these alien motherfuckers what for." Blood trickled down the side of Bjorn Tovesson II's face, staining his silver beard red. He grunted as his CASPer shook, and the illumination flickered. "I'll see you in Valhalla."

Wrenching metal drowned out all other noise. After a moment, a savage voice snarled, "Meat."

"Fuck you, *sukin syn*," Tovesson spat back. "Bettie, Ragnarök."

The image ended with a white flash, then static.

'Video ended.'

Bjorn Tovesson III blinked as he allowed the pinview to fade and focused on the physical world. "What'd you say, Corporal?"

"We've cleared traffic control and are on approach to Bear Town," the copilot replied. "Ten minutes until we're on the ground."

Bjorn nodded. The last message from his father reached him weeks ago at the Berserkers' new headquarters on Vishall. He'd lost count of how many times he'd watched the video.

'147.'

The ensuing news of the disastrous liberation attempt by the Four Horsemen left Bjorn and the Berserkers cooling their heels at Vishall. They didn't have the firepower to tip the balance of power at Earth on their own, and the bulk of Earth's surviving mercenary companies were incommunicado. Word finally arrived of the Peace-

5

maker Guild's intervention in the Mercenary Guild's invasion of Earth. In the blink of an eye, the Omega War ended.

Merc Guild forces assaulted Vishall, targeting both the Berserkers' new base and the burgeoning Human population on the colony world. The invaders were beaten back despite the bulk of the Berserkers being off world, but it was closer than anyone wanted to admit out loud. Even Bjorn's wife, Talita, faced an attacker in her own living room.

Talita had put on a brave face when Bjorn announced his intent to return to Earth two weeks later. She couldn't begrudge Bjorn, especially after the news that Bjorn's father died buying Bjorn's mother time to escape an alien attack on the family homestead.

Bjorn returned with only two ships, a frigate and a transport, and a single mixed platoon. The invasion trapped a company of Berserkers on Earth. Even though the fighting halted, Bjorn wanted room to ferry as many people as possible back to Vishall.

Bjorn checked the time. It would be three minutes until they were in sight of Bear Town.

'Play video, starting at indexed time stamp,' he ordered his pinplant.

"Son, give these alien motherfuckers what for."

* * *

Reverend Jim Hawkins squinted against the afternoon sun. The dropship roared over the ruins of Bear Town. At least the landing pads were clear. There was little around the tarmacs for the Mercenary Guild to reduce to rubble.

The same couldn't be said for Bjarnarsal. The burnt-out hulk had been the heart of Bear Town, built by the commander's grandfather.

A few charred buttresses remained, resembling skeletal fingers pushing up from a grave.

Temporary shelters were the only intact buildings. After Mercenary Guild forces chased off the civilians sheltering in Bear Town, they used any upright structure as target practice. After the aliens vented their fury and departed, local *banditos* swept in to pick over the wreckage.

The Peacemaker Guild lived up to its name ten days ago. Jim, ostensibly the senior officer through attrition and chicanery by those who wanted the job even less, arrived a week ago. It made little sense to bring down the bulk of the Berserkers on Earth from the Alaska Redoubt. At least there were shelter and provisions in Alaska.

The dropship kicked up a maelstrom of dust and sand as it settled on the fused asphalt pad. The cloud hadn't settled before the ramp dropped and Commander Tovesson strode down. The commander wore the full charcoal grey duty uniform, a rarity prior to the invasion.

"His wife is expecting," Corporal Priya Surjit remarked. While Priya stood close to Jim, he appreciated she refrained from taking his hand. He wouldn't mind, but he wanted to keep up the air of professionalism in front of the other mercenaries.

Mercenary. He never thought he would call himself a mercenary, not even when he signed up to be the chaplain for Bjorn's Berserkers. "Does Lynn know?" The commander's mother had broken the personnel holed up in the Redoubt of calling her Mrs. Tovesson. While she framed it as congeniality, Jim knew the appellation reminded her of her deceased husband.

"If she does, she's pretending it's going to be a surprise," Priya replied.

The commander lacked the lumbering gait typical of men his size. At two meters and 140 kilos, Bjorn loomed over Jim. "Lieutenant Hawkins," he rumbled.

"Commander Tovesson," Jim replied. What should he do, welcome him to the ruins of their former headquarters?

"You guys had a ringside seat when Cartwright kicked the US in the nuts during the Texas Secession Incident," the commander remarked. Bear Town sat on a large patch of land north of Route 70. Before first contact, it was part of White Sands.

"If we had foxholes, we would have dived for them, not that it would have done any good," Jim replied. The US government maintained its base a few miles to the south, including several missile silos. When the US launched missiles at Texas, an orbiting warship lazed the missiles out of the sky then cut loose on the base, itself, with a particle cannon and orbital kinetic weapons. "It made for a spectacular fireworks show, but we didn't suffer any collateral damage."

Commander Tovesson nodded. "I relieve you as officer-in-charge. Well done, padre."

"Does this mean I can give you these bars back?" Jim asked. He hadn't felt comfortable wearing the rank insignia given that he was a contractor at the outbreak of the Omega War.

"Keep them," Commander Tovesson countered. "Don't panic, I'm not going to throw you in a CASPer. You'll still be our chaplain."

A good thing. It had been years since Jim had trained to use the Combat Assault System, Personal powered armor. "I stand relieved, in more ways than one," Jim said.

The commander's eyes flicked from Jim to Priya. He raised an eyebrow. "Corporal Surjit. Congratulations on your promotion."

"Thank you, Commander. Your mother is in the mess tent," Priya said in her lilting Indian accent.

A cloud passed behind the commander's eyes as he sought the large tent. "Thank you. If you'll excuse me, I should talk to her."

* * *

Had she seen the video? Bjorn hoped not. His mother stood in the shade of the mess tent's entrance. Bjorn's boots felt like they were made of lead. Had the hill always been this tall?

"Trip." She used the nickname she had given him, to distinguish him from a line of Bjorn Tovessons.

"Mom." Bjorn engulfed her in his arms. His mother released the pent-up sobs she'd held for weeks. Bjorn had fought alongside countless women in his years as a merc, but his mother was the strongest woman he knew. It broke his heart when she shuddered against his chest. "I'm sorry. I should have been here."

Lynn Tovesson shook her head and wiped her eyes. "They would have gotten you too. You wouldn't have sat still in the bunker. You would have hunted every Besquith you could find until they came for you."

"Fucking Besquith," Bjorn muttered. He'd never harbored a grudge against any of the aliens he'd fought over the years, but the Besquith had made it personal. They'd killed his father and burned down his ancestral home.

His mother peered past his bulk. "Did Talita come with you?"

"No, she stayed on Vishall. It's safer there," Bjorn said, even though Besquith had landed on the colony world. Unlike the Xiq'tal, who had assaulted the world a year before, few of the Besquith survived the assault. When the crab-like aliens' home world refused to repatriate the Xiq'tal, Bjorn and the H'rang struck a deal with the huge crustacean mercenaries. When the Besquith splashed down off the sole land mass, the crabs were waiting for them.

"Besides, morning sickness is tough enough without throwing micro-gravity into the mix," Bjorn added.

His mother's face transformed from barely quelled grief to delight. She began crying again, but this time they were tears of joy. "I'm so happy for you!"

Bjorn resisted springing the suggestion she should move to Vishall. His arrival had opened the barely healing wounds of his father's death. Besides, having a grandbaby to spoil would make an enticing incentive later.

Bjorn's officers stayed a respectful distance away, acting busy, even though half of them were waiting to confer with him, and the other half were awaiting the outcome of those meetings.

"Go ahead, Trip. I know you have a ton to do." His mother patted him on the chest. She knew the demands on a commander's time, especially in the midst of a crisis.

"Where are you staying?" The makeshift facilities Bjorn spotted while flying overhead were spartan.

"The house in Las Cruces. I guess they didn't dig deep enough to find it," she replied. "Your room is still the way you left it. Why don't you come by for dinner?"

Bjorn checked the time. "Would 1900 be too late?" It would give him five hours.

"That's fine. Geneva roasted a brisket, just in case."

"She's still keeping house for you?" Bjorn asked. The Austrian woman had worked for Bjorn's parents for as long as he could remember, but she didn't follow them north to the family estate in Alaska. "She must be pushing 70."

"As if a few years could slow her down," his mother countered. "I'll see you at 1900."

Bjorn waited until a corporal escorted her to a personal transport vehicle. He strode to a vacant table and slumped onto the plastic bench. "Alright, I've read the preliminary reports. It sounds as though Bear Town is a total loss."

"Succinct and correct," Jim Hawkins remarked. "The only part of the facility not destroyed or looted was the utilities bunker. The contractors filled in the external stairwell and loading ramp, and the administrative offices collapsed onto the internal stairwell when Bjarnarsal burnt down."

"Looters stripped the solar farm on the south slope, as well as any building-mounted panels," Staff Sergeant Toshi Yamaguchi stated. "They also knocked down all of the windmills and scavenged the turbines."

"Those are all supplementary power supplies," Bjorn said, gratefully accepting an offered cup of coffee. "Any indications the Thor reactor is still online?" The thorium reactor wasn't as powerful as a fusion reactor, but it wasn't dependent on the expensive F11 used in fusion power generation.

"If it is, Bettie hasn't turned the lights on," Stefan lisped. The white-haired man had served as Bjorn's father's secretary before continuing in the same role under Bjorn's command. "As I'm sure you've figured, not a peep out of her."

Bettie was the battlefield tactical intelligence, a multi-nodal software hive-mind developed to assist the Berserkers. It fell short of being an AI, which were illegal in the Galactic Union, but sometimes Bjorn forgot the BTI was a web of programming code.

"Has anyone tried digging up one of the fiberoptic feeds in Bjarnarsal and plugging in manually?" Gina 'Gizmo' Zomorra commanded the Berserkers' technical branch. If anyone knew Bettie better than Bjorn, it was Gizmo. "She's probably hunkered down in safe mode. Even with the reactor offline, the batteries should keep the basics running for 12 months."

"Sergeant Zomorra, commandeer whatever help you need," Bjorn instructed. "If we can talk to Bettie, we can find out the status of the reactor and the rest of the bunker." The upside of the thorium reactor was it wouldn't meltdown.

"Excuse me commander, but are we going to rebuild Bear Town?" A Thor hammer pendant similar to the one Bjorn wore dangled below the sergeant's salt and pepper beard. A pair of long talons flanked Sergeant Keith Cripe's hammer.

"Are those Besquith claws, Sergeant?" Bjorn asked. A bear had mauled Bjorn as a teenager, costing him his left arm and a promising football career. He kept the claws as a grisly reminder after he shot the beast dead.

"Yeah, I know we're not supposed to trophy sentients, but the fuckers were relentless," Cripe replied. "If they weren't so long, I'd wear one for every Besquith I killed."

Bjorn crooked a wicked grin under his beard. "How many would it be?"

"Four, sir. Maybe more, if you count the ones who drowned in the Tanana River."

"Thor be praised," Bjorn intoned. "Not many mercs can say as much, let alone infantry. In answer to your question, no, we're not rebuilding Bear Town on Earth. I'm still mulling over what we'll do with this patch of dirt, and part of it depends on what shape the bunker is in. We also need to find out what the hell is going on with the government."

Cripe dug into a pouch and fished out a 15-centimeter-long Besquith claw. "Here you go, sir."

"Hang onto it, Sergeant. You earned it. I plan on collecting a few of my own." Bjorn clenched his cybernetic left fist. "Tyr demands justice."

Bjorn watched the sergeant leave. How many Besquith were left on Earth? That's how many claws Bjorn wanted to collect—one from each of the murderous werewolves who joined the Mercenary Guild invasion and still drew breath.

The remaining reports were the same. The Berserkers' HQ had been leveled and looted. Most of the civilian contractors left behind during the mercenary exodus had fled to the safety of nearby towns. Bjorn would offer any he could find the chance to emigrate to Vishall.

Once Bjorn was alone, he double checked his appointments. Nothing was scheduled, and all his mercs had their assignments. It would be an hour until he headed into Las Cruces to join his mother for dinner.

'Play video, starting at indexed time stamp.'

"Son, give these alien motherfuckers what for."

* * * * *

Chapter Two

"I apologize, noble Pushtal, but your UAAC does not report sufficient funds for your purchase." The diminutive Jovlin merchant suppressed a nervous shudder.

"What do you mean?" The tiger-like Pushtal snarled, baring his fangs. "I deposited sufficient hard currency a ten-day ago! It was more than enough to cover the cost of this transport!"

The Jovlin shrugged helplessly. "Do you have hard currency? I would happily accept it."

"I deposited all my red diamonds and credit chits at the Union Credit Exchange!" The Pushtal's claws dug into the desk.

The Jovlin gulped as the Pushtal loomed over him. "Perhaps you should revisit the UCX to straighten out this discrepancy. I can hold the transport for a few days."

"I already spent hours at the only UCX bank on this Entropy-forsaken world!" The Pushtal tore grooves into the desk's surface. Slaver dripped from his bared fangs.

The Jovlin stabbed a button under the desk. "I'm sorry. They may not have reported your deposit to the Information Guild, but there is nothing I can do."

"Perhaps if I rip those ridiculous ears from your head, you'll figure out—"

15

The door slammed open as two Jivool guards burst into the office. The Pushtal had enough time to hiss at the ursine mercenaries before two high-frequency stunners scrambled his nervous system. The felinoid collapsed in a drooling, striped heap.

"Deposit our would-be customer outside," the Jovlin instructed. He tossed the Pushtal's Universal Account Access Card to one of the Jivool. Only the owner could use a UAAC, so it was useless to anyone else.

"Can we bounce him off the curb a few times?" one of the guards rumbled.

The Jovlin shook his head. The preliminary data indicated the Pushtal was a viable customer. "There have been some glitches in the UCX database today. They must have missed an update window to the GalNet. Hopefully this will be straightened out quickly." Very quickly—a sizeable sale hung in the balance, and who knew how many more?

The Jivool frowned as they grabbed the Pushtal by his equipment harness and dragged him from the office. The Jovlin waited for them to leave before he checked his professional chat-space with his pin-plants. Three of his peers reported failed transactions today, all because the UCX didn't update the UAAC database.

"Perhaps we should stick to hard currency for large transactions?" the Jovlin suggested.

"Why? So our accounts can be the ones delayed? Maybe we should let the Information Guild handle it," one of the others stated. "They already run the Yacks."

Yack was a common nickname for the UAAC. The Jovlin shook his head, recounting a Human customer's reference to regurgitation.

"If we wanted hard currency, would the Information Guild cough up the credits? I doubt it."

"If the Guild could keep it straight, we wouldn't need hard credits," another remarked.

The Jovlin resisted asking who would keep the Information Guild honest. This chat was over the GalNet, so the guild could be listening in.

* * *

Information Guild Headquarters, Capital Planet

The Chaar waited until acknowledged, resisting the urge to shuffle his four feet. He was only a Grade Four Archivist. Surely the master archivist had greater matters on her vast mind than the news borne by a mere Grade Four. However, his news was chosen to be delivered in person to cut through the cloud of data updates bombarding the master archivist.

"I see you, Archivist," Master Archivist Heloxi croaked. Her bulbous, glistening bulk shifted. Kimmiloks were amphibians and preferred their skin moist. Even the master archivist's robes were damp. Heloxi blinked her bejeweled eyes and smacked her painted lips. "Approach the lectern."

The Chaar dipped his head and walked forward. "Master Archivist, I bring most concerning news flagged for organic delivery."

The sac below the master archivist's meter-wide mouth undulated, full of her squirming tadpoles. She gestured with a stubby arm for him to expedite his news. "Out with it, Acolyte Ashok."

Of course she knew his name. As a master archivist, she could even tap into the Index Prime if she chose. "There was an irregularity in the financial streaming update on five worlds in the last two weeks. Hard currency deposits were not credited to UAAC accounts for a full two day-cycles."

Master Archivist Heloxi's jaw worked as though she was chewing something. "I know. There have been eight incidents in the time frame you reference. There are concerns both red diamonds and hard currency chits of dubious authenticity have been introduced into the economies of several worlds."

"Credit chits cannot be counterfeited," Ashok protested. "Synthetic red diamonds would be detectable as fakes."

"Indeed, assuming one takes the time to analyze the diamonds circulating," Heloxi countered, swallowing. "Doing so delays confirmation of deposits—but I cannot blame the Union Credit Exchange for being cautious. As for forged credit chits, some things are above your grade, Acolyte Ashok."

Ashok clutched his four hands in pairs. Surely the master archivist could not be intimating that someone had successfully counterfeited hard currency! Between brutal punishment and technical difficulty, it was folly to attempt forgery of credit chits.

"You understand this matter is classified?" The Kimmilok narrowed her eyes until they were barely visible between rows of glued-on gemstones. "It would embarrass the UCX if someone implied they had lost even a modicum of their stringent control over red diamonds and hard currency."

"Of course, Master Archivist." Ashok bowed and backed away. "If you have no questions, I will leave you to your contemplations."

Heloxi waved him away, her pupils dilating as she shifted her focus from him to the pinview provided by her pinplants. The hardware-brain interfaces let her sift through data at the speed of thought. Ashok only had Tier Two pinplants, but he suspected the master archivist had Tier Three, the best cybernetic brain implants available. Someday Ashok would be worthy of Tier Three implants.

The metal double doors of the Master Archivist Heloxi's office boomed shut, shaking Ashok from his reverie. He quelled his whirling mind. Had someone cracked the UCX encryption around hard credit chits? How was it possible without a credit imprinter? Had someone stolen a credit imprinter? How could such a thing be kept secret?

Ashok would ask his mates. Even though the information was classified, one of his circle of mates worked in the Peacemaker's headquarters. Perhaps they had heard something? Chetan knew to be discreet with such sensitive matters.

* * *

Hevrant System, Tolo Region, Core

Urgent updates and requests for communication bombarded Nxo'Sanar as soon as his yacht emerged from hyperspace. Entropy! They could at least give him time to collect his stomachs. Nxo'Sanar's pinplants sorted the messages by priority flags, then a daemon-script highlighted those from individuals he trusted not to abuse the priority ratings.

Seventeen communiques glowed in Nxo's pinview. What he hated most about hyperspace travel wasn't the disorientation or the eternal whiteness; he hated the isolation from the rest of the galaxy. Three demands for live communications flashed before Nxo's eyes. He smoothed his sable feathers and opened a channel to Dbo'Dizwey, his assistant. She could be trusted to not only have something useful, but also to keep hysterics from overcoming the fact that there was a three-second delay each way.

Dbo's avatar appeared in Nxo's pinview. She blinked her four eyes in respect. "Honored Nxo'Sanar, I have urgent news," she recited in the honorific tense.

"How many moltings have we known each other?" Nxo cocked his head, knowing his avatar would mimic the gesture. "Speak plainly, old friend."

Dbo dipped her beak in acknowledgement. "There have been more reports of delays in UCX deposits reflecting on UAAC accounts. The latest includes multiple incidents of local deposits not appearing for two day-cycles."

Nxo clacked his beak in frustration. With Dbo'Dizwey, he did not have to be as restrained. "What is the Information Guild playing at?" Nxo fumed.

"Our monitors have recorded a seven percent increase in support for a virtual credit standard," Dbo stated. "Endorsements are especially high among the Zuparti, the Eosogi, and the Veetanho."

"Of course the rodents would come out of their burrows at the sniff of money. Don't the Veetanho have enough to worry about?" Nxo fumed. "What's the excuse now?"

"There are rumors of artificial red diamonds and counterfeit credit chits," Dbo replied. Two of her four eyes flicked back and forth as she read data in her pinview. "People speculate we are delaying deposits because of the synthetic red diamonds. A few have been found on scattered worlds."

Entropy! The one thing the Union Credit Exchange and the Information Guild agreed on was that the accursed TriRusk needed to be wiped from the galaxy. Even if the creatures couldn't create fake red diamonds in abundance, their mere existence could send tremors through the Union's financial network. If the Depik had still been around, Nxo would have contracted an assassin for each and every TriRusk.

"I will arrive at Hevranix in less than 9 hours. I will meet with all in-system chairholders and department heads there," Nxo said. Not only were Depik assassins not an option, but the TriRusk were under the protection of the Peacemaker Guild. Nxo needed to focus on what he could control.

"All will be made ready." Dbo blinked her respect. "I await your arrival."

Nxo opened a new channel as Dbo's image faded from his pinview. The Nevar who answered bore a beak mottled red with age. "It took you long enough," the elder reprimanded.

"You are the second person I called, Mel'Sizwer," Nxo protested. "We have a crisis brewing."

Mel clacked his beak. "You think I don't know? Every ship brings bad news."

"The Information Guild is attempting to undermine our petition for recognition as an independent guild," Nxo said.

"Of course they are," Mel snapped. "I would do the same in their position. You know how much money they rake in by handling all transactions to and from UAACs. No one notices their miniscule fee, but multiply it by a trillion transactions a day, and it's a fortune."

"Any word from the Galactic Senate regarding our petition?" Nxo asked. If the Union Credit Exchange could get out from under the thumb of the Information Guild, they would be free to conduct business as they saw fit…within whatever parameters the market would bear.

Mel dismissively waved a wing. Red stained the ends of his pinions. If he lived long enough, his whole plumage would turn crimson. "Our request languishes in three different commissions, none of which seem motivated to act upon it. Meanwhile, they discuss the abolishment of the diamond standard with keen interest."

"Perhaps it is time for a solvency check on the members of the commission?" Nxo suggested. "Surely they have some outstanding debts, and it would be a shame if their creditors would only accept verified hard currency."

Mel's four eyes narrowed in glee. "It won't be easy—which will make it quite gratifying. Especially since it could cause others to panic and convert much of their virtual assets to tangible wealth."

"Make it so." If the Information Guild wanted to play games, they needed to be reminded of the stakes.

* * * * *

Chapter Three

Las Cruces, New Mexico, Earth

The room was unchanged from two decades ago. Once he joined the Berserkers, Bjorn lived in Bear Town, and family get togethers were in Alaska. Bjorn used to wonder if he'd move to the family estate once he retired. Now it was no longer an option—their ancestral home had fared no better than Bjarnarsal. After killing his father, the aliens had torched and leveled the house.

Fucking Besquith.

"Trip, there's someone here to see you," his mother called from downstairs.

Who would track him down here? Bjorn lumbered down the stairs. Any of his people could call him. Bjorn reflexively reached out with his pinplants before he recalled that the BTI node had been removed from the house when his parents moved north. When Bjorn reached the foyer, Lynn Tovesson stepped aside to reveal a blonde woman in business attire.

"Heather?" Despite the passing of two decades, Bjorn's eyes found the girl he remembered. She had been his girlfriend in high school, before the bear attack.

"Hello, Bjorn. It has been a while." Heather stepped forward and gave him a halting, awkward hug.

"Heather, would you care for something to drink?" Mrs. Tovesson asked. "Geneva could make some coffee, or perhaps some wine?"

"Some wine would be lovely, Mrs. Tovesson."

23

Bjorn led Heather to the living room and ensconced himself in an overstuffed chair. "It's nice to see you, but this can't be a coincidence," Bjorn said. "I've had boots on the ground for less than 12 hours, and you show up."

"Your family went to a lot of trouble to keep this house off the books, but I remember it," Heather replied. "The government noticed your return and put out feelers. Since aliens are no longer hunting down and rounding up people associated with Human mercenaries, I thought it would be safe to reach out to you."

Bjorn's mother deposited a wine glass and a beer mug on the table. "I'll let you two talk. If you need anything, I'll be in the kitchen." For a moment, Bjorn was 16 again, sitting in the living room with his girlfriend while his mother pretended not to eavesdrop.

"You'll have to be more specific about government," Bjorn remarked. The beer was a roasted Icelandic porter, and he took a moment to savor it. "As I understand it, the Earth Republic fell, and the new world order is called the Terran Federation."

"The United States government is the one interested in you," Heather said after a sip of wine. "The US is not a signatory to the attempt to cobble together a new global government before the corpse of the old one cools."

Bjorn initiated a search for relevant articles in his pinplants while taking another draw from his beer. Information scrolled through his pinview, allowing him to read it ten times faster than someone using their eyes. He gleaned the highlights in six seconds.

"It seems like only a few countries are holding out," Bjorn stated. "What's this about the Republic of Texas?"

"Using your pinplants?" Heather swirled her half empty glass. "I don't blame you. There's a lot to take in. As the new world order arose, not everyone favored what boiled down to a coup over the Republic. While the capitol in Sao Paolo was devastated, it would have been possible, not to mention constitutional, to reassemble the government.

"Our mercenary liberators had different ideas. They scrapped the old government and set up one more amicable to their demands. The United States held out against usurping the rightful government, so mercenary agitators convinced Texas to secede from the United States." Heather set down her wine and leaned forward. "The majority of American mercenary companies are based and registered in and around Houston."

"What does that have to do with me?" Bjorn asked, leaning back in his chair as the article on the secession of Texas scrolled through his pinview. Ironically, the Texans formed the Republic of Texas to bail on the Earth Republic. "The Berserkers rent an office and a logistics depot in Houston Startown, but that's it."

"The Berserkers are now the largest American mercenary corporation," Heather replied. "Congratulations."

"The problem is that I'm moving the firm off-world to Vishall. Someone else gets to be top dog."

"The US is hoping to convince you to change your mind." Heather finished her wine.

Bjorn shook his head. "I've already moved the bulk of my operations. Bandits and aliens leveled Bear Town. There's no reason to stay."

"Will you at least hear them out?" Heather asked. She reached out and placed her hand over Bjorn's. "I know many in the mercenary industry blame the United States for not resisting the alien occupation fervently enough, but there are two sides to the story."

"I know. If you had put up a fight, the people would have suffered," Bjorn recited. "When Texas seceded, Cartwright called in an orbital bombardment to thwart the attempt to nuke Texas back into the country. He damn near cooked my people on the ground in Bear Town."

"How about Jim Cartwright destroying the Earth Republic government and conveniently volunteering to assemble a new ruling body from scratch?" Heather countered. She cut off Bjorn's protest. "Cartwright's Cavaliers leveled the General Assembly Building, and Cartwright, himself, bombarded Sao Paolo and the surrounding metropolitan area with antimatter weapons. They still haven't figured out how many people he and his cohorts vaporized with their giant robots."

"Antimatter?" Two axioms of science stated you couldn't safely accumulate and contain enough antimatter for anything useful, and there was no such thing as artificial gravity. Bjorn shifted his hand out from under Heather's and picked up his mug. "Antimatter ranks with AIs on the list of forbidden research. How could Colonel Cartwright pull it off with antiquated war machines?"

"Perhaps you should ask him?" Heather suggested. "Good luck getting an answer. The mercenaries style him as a savior, but others would use the term war criminal."

Bjorn held his mug without drinking. "Shit. I met the kid at my wedding. I would have never guessed he'd turn nukes or worse loose on civilians. As opposed to certain governments."

"That's right, you're married," Heather remarked.

"We're expecting our first kid in five months." Bjorn smiled.

"So this will be Bjorn IV?"

"If it's a boy. We don't know yet," Bjorn replied, the grin still plastered on his face. "If it's a girl, it becomes a stickier subject. Talita favors the name Adelaide, after one of her *avós*, her grandmothers. I favor Sif."

"Good luck with that," Heather said. "So, would you be willing to meet with a delegation from the government? You could at least hear their pitch."

"Fine. I always had a hard time telling you no, but don't promise anything." Bjorn polished off his beer. "I'm doing this because you asked, and maybe I'll get a free dinner out of it."

"Free dinner—I'll pass it along." Heather stood, smoothing her skirt.

Bjorn escorted her to the door. "I'll send you a comm-link to pass on."

"Thanks." Heather leaned forward and kissed him on the cheek. "It was good seeing you."

"You didn't ask about Roberto," Bjorn's mother stated after he closed the door. She stood in the hallway behind him.

Bjorn turned. "No, I didn't." Heather had dumped Bjorn for his best friend Berto in high school. "She didn't marry him, and I don't know what happened to him after graduation other than that he joined Finn's Fools. Even if I wasn't married, I wouldn't want to pick at scabs."

"It was clever of them to send her," Lynn said.

"It was obvious," Bjorn countered. "I don't know what they hope to accomplish. The Berserkers HQ is already off-world. However, I want to have some words with Colonel Cartwright."

* * *

Bear Town, New Mexico, Earth

"Charlotte?"

Sergeant Charlotte Wicza turned at hearing her name. "Pastor Hawkins! Or should I call you Lieutenant Hawkins?" Jim Hawkins was the Berserkers' chaplain and counselor as well as one of the few men Charlotte respected.

Hawkins rolled his eyes. "I'd be happy to put aside this rank and return to the simpler tasks of saving souls and mending spirits. Now that the crisis has passed, I expected the brevet rank to be rescinded. I may yet convince the commander to let me return to being a contractor."

"I wouldn't get your hopes up, Lieutenant," Stefan, the Berserkers' senior administrator, remarked. The white-haired man chuckled knowingly. "If I know the commander, he won't change his mind. You earned the rank."

"Is Priya here?" Charlotte asked tentatively, cursing herself for not checking the roster beforehand. A third of the Berserkers stranded on Earth never made it to the Redoubt.

"Yes, and she's up to her elbows in work," the chaplain replied with a hint of a grin. "Before you ask, yes we're...how would you put it? An item? She sends her regards, but she's coordinating the transfer of personnel and material from the Redoubt. How's Tamara?"

Hawkin's tone told Charlotte that not only did the chaplain know Charlotte's girlfriend had survived the Battle of Patoka, but that he knew they were still together. "Great. She's here somewhere, trying to scare up transportation for our mission."

"Mission?"

"The commander wants us to go to Houston Startown and try to chase some leads in the alien ghetto," Charlotte replied. She'd been surprised when Commander Tovesson pulled her aside and gave her the assignment. "I'm trying to find the Besquith commanders responsible for hunting the Berserkers and killing Papa Tovesson."

Pastor Hawkins shook his head. "No good can come of this."

"We're trying to track them down, not get into a fight," Charlotte protested. "Even in my APEX scout armor, I wouldn't want to get into a scuff up with Besquith."

An older infantry trooper approached them. "Excuse me, are you Sergeant Wick-za?"

"Despite the spelling, it sounds like 'vista.' Folks call me Whisky," Charlotte replied. She spotted the stripes on his shoulder. "What can I do for you, Sergeant?"

"Sergeant Keith Cripe. I'm supposed to go with you on your werewolf hunt."

"I see you're still wearing those Besquith claws, Sergeant," Pastor Hawkins remarked with a frown.

Cripes' hand went to the pair of talons dangling from a chain around his neck. "I'll stash them before we go to Houston."

"Where did you get them?" Charlotte asked.

"Off the Besquith I killed," the older infantry sergeant replied with a smug grin. "The werewolves hounded us all the way from here to Alaska, and they killed a lot of Berserkers in the process."

"Still think this is merely about tracking them?" Pastor Hawkins asked.

"They engaged in war crimes, and these Besquith are on the new government's shit list," Charlotte countered. The commander's orders had been to seek, but not engage. "They're probably hiding in the Galactic Union's territory around the starport."

A dark grey personal transport vehicle with the Berserkers' logo ground to a halt nearby. The window on the driver's door slid down, and Tamara leaned out. "Hey, Pastor Jim! Charlotte! I mean Sergeant Wicza, I've got wheels, and a flyer is waiting at the tarmac. We can roll as soon as you're ready."

"Corporal Reeves." Hawkins waved back. "Are you going to keep Sergeant Wicza out of trouble?"

"It'll be tough, but someone has to do it," Tamara Reeves replied.

"We're waiting on our civilian consultant," Charlotte stated.

Sergeant Cripe rolled his eyes as he stashed his trophy claws. "A consultant?"

"Commander's orders." Charlotte shrugged. "Supposedly, he has contacts in the alien community. Some that might be less than inclined to help Humans trying to find a Galactic."

A motorcycle pulled up next to the PTV in a cloud of gravel dust. Despite a modern electric engine, the machine was built with classic curves and chrome. The driver dropped the kickstand and peeled off his helmet.

"I'm looking for Sergeant Wicza." The Zuul tucked his helmet under his arm as he surveyed the group. The alien wiped the dust from his canine snout.

"I'm Wicza," Charlotte replied. Not only did the Zuul speak English, he pronounced her name correctly. "Who are you?"

"I'm Vurrn." The Zuul held out his hand. "My father owns Vurr Vroom Vehicles and is a family friend of the commander."

"Nice bike," Sergeant Cripe remarked. "What make is it?"

"It's a Triple-V Vector 09," Vurrn replied with a toothy grin. "It's modeled after classic Earth designs but built with Zuul performance. I can get you a good deal on one."

"You guys can discuss your boy toys while we're in the air," Charlotte interjected. "Vurrn, find somewhere to park your bike."

* * *

Sergeant Gina Zomorra tugged her focus away from the code scrolling through her pinview. A man in a Berserkers' uniform stood across from her makeshift workstation, staring at her with a goofy grin. "How long have you been gawking at me?"

The smile vanished, and his cheeks flushed red. "Oops, sorry. It's…well…you were engrossed in your pinwork, and I didn't know how to get your attention without being too disruptive and maybe ruining whatever you were doing."

"You could have tried 'hello.'"

"Actually, I did. Twice."

It was Gina's turn to blush. "Sorry. What can I do for you…?" She checked the name tape on his shirt, "Corporal Brand?"

"Corporal Surjit sent me over to see if I could be of any help," he replied. "I'm Glen, from logistics. Priya, Corporal Surjit, said I should call you Gizmo."

Gina eyed Corporal Brand suspiciously. Was Priya already trying to play matchmaker? Gina hadn't been back on Earth more than 24 hours. It didn't help her mood that Gina's last prospective boyfriend had turned out to be a spy and traitor working for El Espejo Obscuro, a mercenary unit employed by General Peepo to eliminate Earth mercenary firms.

"While I appreciate the offer, Corporal Brand, I'm trying to make contact with the mainframe, specifically the Battlefield Tactical Intelligence node housed within it," Gina stated. "It's buried too deep for a wireless signal to handshake."

"Why don't you use the power network as an antenna?" Brand asked, pulling a chair over to the workstation.

"The mainframe's communication portals aren't wired to the power grid," Gina countered. "I have to wait until they excavate an intact fiber-optic line. The fire slagged the lines near the surface."

"Why don't you hook your terminal into the power grid and use it as an antenna on your end?" The logistics corporal grinned. "You would have an antenna straight into the mainframe room, and you'd be able to talk to Bettie."

Gina paused halfway through forming a protest. "It could work. I'd need an adapter to hook a wireless network output into the powerline."

Brand reached into his satchel and plunked a piece of hardware on the table next to Gina's slate. "One wireless repeater with antenna leads. Let's give Bettie a call and see if she's awake."

Gina returned his smile.

* * *

"We could have used Corporal Brand's help, yes?" Hcufft asked as he checked the manifest for the latest shipment from Alaska. "Yes. There is much work to do."

"Certainly," Priya admitted, especially since the corporal had been among the personnel holed up in the Alaska Redoubt during the Mercenary Guild's occupation of Earth. "Did you miss how he watched Gina in the mess tent while trying not to be obvious about it?"

"No," the H'rang replied. The felinoid alien moved to the next pallet. "Even though Human mating rituals are still confusing, despite spending months confined with them, Corporal Brand's interest was obvious. There was a great deal of mating in the Redoubt. Even you and Lieutenant Pastor Hawkins—"

"There wasn't much else to do," Priya interrupted. She checked the bill of lading for the shipment. There were seventeen more pallets to inspect and stage so dropships could take them to orbiting transports. "Glen seems nice, and he appears smitten with Gina. Maybe they'll hit it off."

"Glen Brand appears to be an inferior physical specimen to the previous candidate for Sergeant Zomorra's romantic coupling," Hcufft observed. "Tom Diller was a CASPer trooper with an impressive physique. I believe the term was 'slab of beef,' yes?"

"Diller was also a douche and a traitor," Priya countered. No one had seen through his charade, but Priya suspected Gina beat herself up over being fooled.

The H'rang cocked his head. "I am unfamiliar with this term. My translator indicates the word references a hygiene product."

"It's slang for he was a jerk," Priya said. The asshole had betrayed the Berserkers and framed one of the new kids for the deed. "If it hadn't been for Gina, someone else would have been shot for Diller's crimes. You're right—Brand isn't a slab of beef like Diller, but from what I saw at the Redoubt, he's a nice guy. Gina could use a nice guy for a change."

* * * * *

Chapter Four

Ulaan Beta System, Gresht Region, Tolo Arm

"Captain Paxxo, our target approaches," the XenSha sensors operator reported. "As you predicted, it will pass within weapons' range of the drones."

The Khabar captain rubbed his hands together, the thick horn-like nails clacking. "Excellent. Sound acceleration warning, and all stations stand by for combat operations."

Paxxo's ship, currently named the *Chance Windfall*, and a pack of drones coasted in the direction of the stargate, halfway between Ulaan Beta Three and the system's stargate. Their target, a Cochkala transport with the uninspiring name *Transport Wey 327*, was about to flip over and decelerate on its journey to the stargate.

"The fools lack even a rudimentary escort," Blattu bleated. The older Khabar was first mate, and most of the crew were Khabar. The goat-like humanoids were known for their toughness and moral flexibility. Paxxo kept an eye on Blattu in case his flexibility extended to mutiny once they had obtained their prize.

"It would draw attention, and secrecy is their greatest defense." Paxxo studied the Tri-V display. Yes, Blattu would try to usurp him. "Besides, the transport is a converted destroyer. She retains her military-grade shields and anti-missile laser batteries."

Blattu grunted. "Expensive for a transport. It also means they're sacrificing offensive punch for cargo space."

"Any sign they've spotted us or the drones?" Paxxo called.

"Negative, sir," the XenSha replied with a shake of its face tentacles. "They've cut off their fusion torch."

Paxxo watched on the Tri-V as their quarry flipped 180 degrees and pointed their engines toward their destination. In the upper corner of the Tri-V, a timer showed the next known stargate activation. The transport would spend half its journey decelerating so it could coast through the open gate or safely veer off if something was wrong.

"The target has ignited their fusion torch," the sensors operator announced. "As predicted, they're thrusting at .5Gs. Updating trajectory plot."

The orange line depicting the transport's flight path barely changed. "Good. They will pass within range of two drones," Paxxo remarked. Each drone was armed with a single-shot pulse laser and a pair of seeker missiles. Warm up our torch and shields."

"That will give us away," Blattu protested.

"Their own torch will obscure us until we go to full power," Paxxo countered.

"Drone firing range in 30 seconds. One minute until they enter our fire envelope."

"Helm, stand by for intercept. Gunnery, on my command, fire on their engines." Paxxo double checked his safety harness. They would have to thrust hard to reach the transport.

"The assault shuttles report ready," Blattu stated. The boarding parties would be in for a rough ride at high-g thrust.

The indicators on two of the drones blinked blue. "Fire!" Paxxo yelled. "Order the remaining drones to close and engage." On the Tri-V, their quarry raced toward the *Chance Windfall*. It would only take a couple of seconds to pass through the *Windfall*'s weapons range. "All systems full power. Ready...fire! Helm, set pursuit course and close—3Gs."

Laser pulses from two drones raked the transport. Anti-missile fire caught the two missiles from the further drone, but the closer pair detonated near the stern of the target, hammering its shields. The particle beam barbette in the *Windfall*'s 'chin' fired once before the pirate vessel pirouetted to give chase.

The lasers from the other drones flashed against the transport's intact forward shields, and none of their pursuing missiles penetrated the defensive fire.

"Their fusion torch went out!" the XenSha called. "They have zero thrust."

"Launch the assault shuttles," Blattu ordered over the rumble of the ship accelerating. He glanced at the captain.

"Charge the particle beam and bring in the drones," Paxxo ordered. The drones could catch the *Windfall* in moments. "Any return fire?"

The XenSha shook its face tentacles. "No sir. I'm picking up fluctuating power readings. We may have damaged one of their reactors in addition to their engines."

"Stay on alert." Paxxo scrutinized the combat footage and the current sensor readings. It seemed too easy. "Time to intercept?"

"Twenty-eight minutes," the Pushtal helmsman replied. Paxxo didn't care for the tiger-like pilot, but he was competent and hated the first mate. "The assault shuttles should intercept in 14 minutes."

* * *

J okka sucked in a deep breath as the g-force abated. Khabar were tough, but nearly 15 minutes at 5Gs thrust was brutal. The boarding-party sergeant assessed the other troops in the shuttle. The other Khabar shook their heads and caught their breath. The two ursine Oogar were either unconscious or asleep—Jokka wasn't sure which. The lone HecSha appeared unfazed by the high-thrust flight.

The HecSha tilted its reptilian head. "We are about to dock," Vashk hissed. HecSha possessed keen talents for piloting and 3-D tactics. Vashk wasn't a pilot because he would miss out on the killing.

"Docking in 30 seconds," the copilot announced over the intercom.

"Someone wake the Oogar," Jokka ordered.

One of the purple, bear-like aliens swiped a paw at the trooper who prodded her awake. She yawned, then roared at her sister. Oogar couldn't do anything quietly.

Jokka checked his gear. Satisfied, he sought the technical specialist. "Where is C'rk'tyk?"

"Here, Sergeant." A pile of armor rippled as the Jeha technician unwound himself. C'rk'tyk had cobbled together a protective covering from discarded sections of body armor.

"Stay behind me and don't get your head blown off," Jokka ordered. He needed the technician to disarm any traps on the cargo.

A *thump* reverberated through the boarding shuttle. "We have a solid seal on the transport's port airlock. Shuttle two is docking on the opposite side," the copilot reported.

Both shuttles surviving to dock was a bonus. It would force the defenders to split their numbers. Too bad more survivors meant lower shares, Jokka mused. But with a prize as rich as this, even smaller shares would be a fortune.

The hatch hissed open, and the Oogar sisters surged into the airlock, each bearing a salvaged CASPer laser shield. Vashk and the Khabar followed. The transport's crew fired from the junction with the ship's spinal corridor, taking what cover they could by ducking around the corner. One of the defenders tossed a grenade, caroming it off the corridor wall. An Oogar batted it back with her shield.

The grenade detonated with a brilliant flash and painful bang. Luckily for the transport's defenders, it was designed to incapacitate. Only an idiot would throw around high-yield explosives inside a starship.

The Oogar's roars were almost as deafening as the grenade. The sisters hauled themselves into the central corridor, splitting fore and aft. At least one defender was coherent enough to fire on the Oogar. Jokka could smell burning fur, and an Oogar bellowed as she disappeared around the corner. A Maki's scream was cut short with a loud metallic crunch.

Jokka's troops swarmed in the Oogars' wakes, disarming the crewmembers addled by their own grenade.

"Keep the carnage to a minimum," Jokka called for the benefit of anyone watching over a camera. "If they surrender, give them quarter." In truth, they didn't care about the crew or the ship. Even if they seized the ship, it was still hurtling toward the stargate and no longer decelerating. Unless the engines were brought back online in short order, the vessel would sail past the stargate before the next gate opening. The transport was a lost cause. The cargo was the prize.

The opposite airlock opened, and the other boarding party emerged.

"Too slow, Vibbi," Jokka teased. "Take your team forward and secure the bridge. We'll fetch the cargo."

Vibbi, the other boarding-party sergeant, surveyed the scene. "A handful of Maki? These puny primates can't put up much of a fight; you had it easy."

"Easy or not, the clock is running." Jokka gestured for the Oogar to proceed aft. "You only need to hold the bridge long enough to ensure they don't give us any trouble."

Vibbi snorted, but after a moment, ordered her team forward.

The Oogar were waiting at the four cargo bay hatches. Nothing denoted anything special about any of the two-meter-wide doors evenly spaced around the central corridor.

"C'rk'tyk, get these open," Jokka instructed. "We'll have to do this the old-fashioned way, but hurry. Vashk, take the sisters and secure engineering. We don't want them getting power restored before we're well away."

"We only have an hour if we don't want to approach the gate at suicidal velocity," Vashk remarked.

"Then don't be late when I call you back."

The HecSha and the Oogar floated aft while C'rk'tyk set to work. Once the first door blinked blue, the troops with Jokka readied their weapons. The hatch slid up to reveal dozens of large metallic drums. Would the crew have hidden the prize in one?

Jokka pointed at one of the Khabar. "See if you can figure out what's in the drums, but if it's not F11 or what we're after, I don't care. C'rk'tyk, open the next hatch."

"Since I have their codes figured out, it'll be quicker." The Jeha rippled to the next access panel. "Unless, of course, the bay is open to vacuum, as is this one."

"Try the others." Could the crew have opened the external hatch to keep the pirates away from the precious cargo?

"Vacuum…but this last one has atmosphere." The Jeha's tiny limbs flickered across the access panel. After a moment, the hatch slid up.

This cargo bay had more of the drums lining the walls, but in the middle, a high security crate was strapped to the deck. Jokka prevented one of his troops from stepping forward.

"Check for booby-traps," Jokka told C'rk'tyk.

The Jeha crept forward, swaying his long, segmented body from one side to the other. "I don't see anything. It has tamper-detection and a challenging lock, but I don't think they rigged it to blow up."

Jokka clanked across the deck in magnetic boots. The side of the crate bore the markings of the Union Credit Exchange along with warnings in several languages against unauthorized access.

"This is our retirement. Unstrap it and get it back to the shuttle," Jokka said. "Vibbi, what's your status? We've secured the prize."

"They've blocked off the bridge hatch with four drums. We've held back since they're probably some sort of trap."

Jokka glanced at the dozen drums in the cargo bay. "Hold your position until we have the prize aboard the shuttle. Vashk, what's your sitrep?"

"The engineering crew has retreated into the access tunnels," the HecSha replied. "It's too tight for the sisters to go after them, so we're watching for them to pop their heads out."

Hopefully it would stymie repair efforts. "Get ready to withdraw to the shuttle."

A blood curdling shriek echoed from the other open cargo bay and abruptly cut off. Jokka readied his weapon, deactivated his boots, and launched himself toward the hatch. In the other bay, the Khabar floated in a cloud of blood droplets. Beyond the corpse, glowing, red eyes stared back.

Two sinister black and red mechanical constructs skittered forward on four magnetized legs. Four bladed scythe-like arms dripped blood. The armored heads had a menacing avian quality.

Even as Jokka opened fire, drums in the cargo bay split open and more of the machines emerged, unfolding their razor-arms. He nailed the lead construct dead center with his laser carbine. It barely blemished the surface.

Yelling and weapons fire erupted in the bay behind Jokka. "Everyone to my position. They have robots in the cargo bays!" He fired the grenade launcher underslung on his laser carbine. Instead of explosives, the weapon was loaded with a rocket-propelled, armor-piercing projectile. It was a risky weapon for shipboard use, but less dangerous than facing an armored opponent equipped to deal with lasers.

The robot emitted an electronic shriek as the projectile punched into it. Caught midstride, the robot lost its footing and hurtled back from the hatch. It slammed into the next black and red construct, dislodging it.

Jokka slapped the control to close the door and fired a laser pulse into the upper corner of the seam between the hatch and the wall. If he could slag the path for the hatch, it might freeze the hatch shut.

C'rk'tyk scuttled into the corridor. Jokka spun to help his troops in the bay with the prize. One of the Khabar was a nebula of gore. Even though he was eviscerated, a robot continued to stab at the dead pirate with its wicked arm-blades. One of the other Khabar drifted higher in the bay with nothing to grab onto. He fired his laser carbine as fast as it would cycle, but the shots had little effect. One of the robots pointed its 'beak' toward the drifting Khabar and returned fire with two lasers built into its head.

The remaining Khabar backpedaled toward the hatch. As opposed to a grenade launcher, he had a plasma torch mounted on his carbine. He dodged the first swipe of a gleaming scythe and a tongue of plasma severed the limb. Another sweeping blade cleaved open the weapon, and flames engulfed the Khabar and the robot.

Along the walls, drums split open and additional robots emerged. Jokka spared the crate one last longing glance as he closed the hatch. "Lock this!" he told the Jeha.

"What in entropy is happening?" Vashk hissed as he floated up the corridor with the Oogar at his heels.

"They have some sort of security robots," Jokka replied. Were they drones, remotely operated? The constructs were far more vicious than he'd expect from machine code. "We need to get off this ship before we're all dead."

"I've got the hatch scrambled, but I don't know how long it will take for them to override it," C'rk'tyk declared.

"What about Vibbi's team?" the HecSha asked.

"I told them to fall back." Jokka could hear a distant fire fight. "We can't wait for them. Back to the shuttle."

Metal screeched as the hatch across the corridor rose halfway before freezing. Bladed limbs protruded through the opening as robots crawled through the gap.

"Go!" Jokka shouted, not waiting for the others as he shoved off toward the junction leading to the airlocks. Behind him, the roar of Oogar and reports of gunfire were deafening.

Nothing approached from the fore, but the Maki at the junction were gone. Jokka swung around the corner, his weapon at the ready. The paths to both airlocks were clear. C'rk'tyk didn't stop as he skittered around the corner, clinging to a handrail with dozens of limbs.

The Oogar bellows of rage crescendoed to pain. "Is the shuttle clear?" Vashk hissed from behind Jokka.

"If not, we are dead." Jokka hauled himself toward the airlock. C'rk'tyk reached the hatch, checked it, and cycled it. The interior of the assault shuttle was never so inviting. Jokka tensed as he reached the entry, but no robots waited within.

"How long should we wait for the sisters?" Vashk asked, floating into the boarding craft.

Jokka hit the hatch control. "We don't. There were dozens of those things." He tapped the intercom. "Detach and head back to the *Chance Windfall.*" He tapped on the communication controls to raise the ship. The captain would be pissed, but maybe they could threaten the transport into pitching the crate out of an airlock in exchange for not being blown full of holes?

Why hadn't they detached? The robots could be at the airlock at any moment. "Detach now!" Jokka ordered over the intercom. A metal scrape rasped on the hatch to the cockpit before an ebony metal scythe punched through. Air hissed through the hole as the blade withdrew. Another blade poked through the hatch, then another. On the hull of the shuttle, Jokka could hear the click of metallic feet.

* * *

"What's going on?" Captain Paxxo demanded. They'd lost contact with the boarding parties once they entered the transport. The *Chance Windfall* hung three kilometers from the other ship, clear of the fusion torch.

"One of the shuttles has detached," the XenSha replied. "It's...it's thrusting away at high G."

"I have something from the shuttle," the elSha comms operator announced. The small reptile had been useless, shrugging at the loss of signal to the boarding parties. "Patching it to speakers."

Horrified bleating filled the air until it abruptly cut off. "Shuttle Two has been destroyed."

"Power to weapons and shields!" Paxxo yelled. "What about the other shuttle?"

"It remains attached. I'm zooming in a camera." The image filled the Tri-V, showing Shuttle One at the transport's airlock.

Paxxo spotted an open cargo hatch on the transport. Had the crew spaced his boarding parties as they searched for the prize?

"Comms, put me through to the other ship," Paxxo ordered. The elSha swiveled one eye toward him and gave an affirmative gesture. "This is Captain Paxxo. I know you are carrying a shipment of red diamonds. If you do not surrender them to me, I will ventilate your ship."

"Incoming signal," the elSha announced.

The Tri-V flickered. A raven-black, four-eyed avian face filled the display. "I am Gul'Gethuy of the Union Credit Exchange. If you tell me the source of your information, I may spare you."

"They have restored full power," the XenSha announced. "They have full-power shields, and their fusion torch is lighting up."

"Target forward amidships with the particle barbette, and all missile tubes standby," Paxxo ordered. He gestured at the elSha. "Gul'Gethuy, we have you woefully outgunned. Give me the diamonds, and I'll give you your lives."

All four of the deep red eyes narrowed. "Divulge the name of who hired you, and perhaps we can make a deal."

"Why would I…" Paxxo caught himself. Now he'd have to destroy the transport. He gestured for the comm operator to mute the channel. "They need some coaxing. Fire the barbette."

"Sir, we have a system failure on the particle beamcaster," the gunner reported. "I'm reading no power to the weapon mount. Now there's a traverse actuator failure."

An alarm sounded. "Hull breach, port airlock," the damage control coordinator announced. "Hull breach, deck two. Hull breach, port shuttle hangar."

"Shield node failure, forward emitter."

The communication display faded, replaced by the camera view. Movement flickered on the bottom of the display. The operator adjusted the camera. Several mechanical forms scuttled along the hull. One turned an avian-shaped head and stared into the camera with four glowing, red eyes.

"Entropy!" Paxxo cried as the camera view winked out. "Sound boarding alarm! Helm, get us away from the transport!"

"Portside thruster failure," the Pushtal helmsman replied. "Compensating with the aft, starboard thruster." The acceleration alarm sounded.

Paxxo turned to his first mate. "Perhaps you should have mutinied sooner?"

Acceleration slammed them back into their couches. "It doesn't matter now," Blattu replied. "For the record, it wasn't personal."

Metallic scraping resonated on the shell of the bridge. While not as armored as a military vessel's CIC, it afforded some protection. The scraping ceased and was replaced by the stench of hot metal. Three points on the port side of the CIC glowed orange.

"Noted," Paxxo replied.

* * * * *

Chapter Five

Galactic Senate Building, Capital Planet

Nardis Xlorin bristled when his office door slid open. The Gtandan senator peered up from his desk and wrinkled his porcine snout in irritation. He'd instructed his assistant not to disturb him before his dinner appointment. Now the worthless female had admitted..."Honored Mel'Sizwer. I was not expecting you."

"Senator Xlorin." The black and red avian bowed, but all four eyes remained focused on Nardis. It was as though the damned Nevar peered into his soul. "I appreciate your making the time to see me. I know time is a valuable commodity."

"Indeed it is," Nardis said. The Union Credit Exchange representative's choice of words were not lost on Nardis. Arguably, the only thing more valuable than time was money. "What can I do for you?"

"I've heard disturbing rumors rippling through the Senate. Whispers and mutterings of straying from the diamond standard and allowing the Information Guild to dictate the value and measure of wealth," the old Nevar replied.

"No offense, but the diamond standard is an archaic construct," Nardis countered. "Your red diamonds will still hold value, but the economy would no longer be beholden to such crude shackles."

Mel'Sizwer ruffled his black and red feathers. "There were those who believed as you do. After the Great War, when the galaxy was rebuilding, the Banking Guild unhinged the economy from material representation. It was for the sake of fluidity, they claimed. The Banking Guild minted additional physical and virtual currency to meet the crumbling Galactic Republic's demands. Rampant inflation ensued, the economy collapsed, and the Galactic Republic followed."

"The Republic had been destabilized by the Great War. The Dusman-Kahraman conflict ravaged the civilized worlds. It was doomed to failure without the machinations of the Banking Guild." Nardis shifted in his chair nervously. "We have a stable economy, so we no longer need such restraints."

"It's amusing you think so when the Union teeters on the precipice once again." The Nevar clacked his beak. "The Mercenary Guild is in shambles. The Peacemaker Guild has interjected itself into the affairs of other guilds. How long before we have another Galactic War? Will the Information Guild press a button and devalue credits by tenfold to fill their virtual coffers? What does it mean for your family's debts?"

"What do Clan Xlorin's financial obligations have to do with anything?" Nardis protested. "We will pay our debts!"

"Indeed. Your family's debts have been bought and are now due in hard currency." The Nevar narrowed his four red eyes. "It would seem your new creditors don't put much stock in virtual credits after the hacking of the Gtandan Stock Exchange."

"What?" Most of Nardis' family fortune was tied to stocks of various Gtandan corporations. "How have I not been informed?"

"I'm sure the Information Guild will update you in due time," Mel'Sizwer remarked. "They only delayed hard currency updates to accounts by a day or two on some worlds."

Nardis poked at his slate and requested a priority update of Gtandan stock exchange data. Every time another ship with news entered the Capital System, they transmitted their finance, news, and message cache to the local Information Guild Galnet node.

The display refreshed, showing the Gtandan stock market crashing. His family's holdings had already lost half their value. "You bought our debts and crashed the market?"

Mel'Sizwer swept his wing in protest. "I do not hold your debt, nor do any Nevar. We were contacted by your Eosogi debtors regarding the hard currency requirement. One might wonder how they knew to swoop in and buy your debts and request hard payments only."

Nardis glared at the Nevar. It was too convenient that he'd turned up and pushed for retaining the hard currency standard. "The Banking Guild was subsumed into the Information Guild because of its abuses after the Great War. Somehow, your race retains control of the minting and management of hard currency. Why would we give you Nevar even more power?"

"With the Mercenary Guild in chaos, who holds the power now?" The elder Nevar smoothed his feathers. "The Information Guild controls every financial transaction that doesn't involve one being handing another physical currency. They carry every message, every bit of news, and every scrap of data in the GalNet.

"I understand your concerns regarding my race. Our secretive ways are to protect the Union's hard currency operations. However, if the UCX were to expand its role to say, a Finance Guild, others would be needed to manage an undertaking of such magnitude." Mel'Sizwer tipped his head. "We would need representatives of several races on the guild's council—beings of financial acumen. The Gtandan have such a reputation."

A seat on a guild council? Nargis wrinkled his snout. Such a position could be lucrative.

"A shame the Eosogi are too short-sighted to see this, or perhaps they are playing a different game," Mel'Sizwer said. "Think about what I said."

The Eosogi had endorsed the Information Guild's proposal to the Finance Commission. It would eliminate the hard currency requirement for Galactic Union banks. The Eosogi were renowned as two-faced weasels. Had they played the Information Guild and the other commission members for their own gain? Was the Information Guild playing them all?

* * *

"I don't have time for riddles, Archivist Prett," Senator Emlaati snapped. The Cochkala senator whipped his tail back and forth in aggravation. The Mercenary Guild did its best to self-destruct, the Peacemaker Guild asserted itself beyond its charter, and uneasiness roiled the markets.

"No disrespect, your honor, but it was a straightforward question," the Nukraya archivist said in her sing-song voice. Ripples of green shimmered across her blue-skinned limbs, and the head tentacles bound in a scarf atop her head wavered under the fabric. "How much has the Mercenary Guild's debacle cost the Union, and who is picking up the tab?"

The badger-like senator snorted. "That's the problem of the firms and races who made ill-advised deals with General Peepo. Maybe they can take it up with the Veetanho."

"Some are clamoring to take it up with the Senate," Archivist Prett remarked. "After all, the Senate has oversight regarding the guilds. Fortunately, there is no official Banking Guild to demand the government cover the outstanding debts."

"The Senate operates on a minimal budget. We don't have millions of credits to cover the cost of Peepo's War, even if we were inclined to do so," Senator Emlaati said.

"Try billions of credits." The archivist steepled her long fingers. "Hundreds of billions."

Emlaati's mouth gaped. "Hundreds of billions?"

"It would seem General Peepo spared no expense, especially since she didn't pay most of it up front and used emergency guild powers to circumvent the escrow requirements for contracts."

"It doesn't matter," Emlaati said. "We don't have the money, and there's no way the Union court will side against us."

"You're forgetting something important. Most of the parties demanding payments are mercenary companies, or even entire mercenary races. You explain to the Besquith or the Tortantulas why they won't be paid."

Emlaati gulped. There had been attacks on Capital. The defenses were provided by mercenaries—the same ones Peepo had stiffed.

"We have no way to pay them," Emlaati protested.

"Not under the current standards. You would have to back your funds with red diamonds through the Union Credit Exchange," the archivist stated. "It's a shame we're beholden to an archaic artifact brought about by the Republic's collapse. Otherwise, the Senate could request that the Information Guild issue the virtual credits."

* * *

Information Guild Headquarters, Capital Planet

"**A**ny word on our Khabar friends?" Master Archivist Heloxi demanded. One of the tadpoles in her throat pouch tried to wriggle free, and she bit it with a satisfying crunch.

"We won't hear back for at least two weeks," Ashok replied. "We couldn't have them send a direct message."

"I know. I am no fool." Heloxi swallowed the morsel. Soon, the surviving tadpoles would grow large enough to escape into the pool around her, and she'd have to spawn a new brood. "The Nevar elder has returned, and at this very moment, is bowing and scraping about the Senate." Heloxi gestured to a Tri-V display. "The Gtandan stock market crashed. F11 prices in the Praf region of the Jesc arm rose 15 percent. The exchange rate for credits to Sirra'Kan currency dropped 12 percent. It could make beings crave a stable standard."

"What about the threat of mercenaries coming to collect on Capital? It was a master stroke to invoke the threat of the violent species Peepo short changed," Ashok said. "Who will defend Capital? Either the UCX will have to drain their coffers to muster a defense, or the Senate will become desperate to pay them off."

An icon appeared in the corner of Heloxi's pinview. "Leave me. I have important matters to attend." She glared at Ashok when he appeared ready to protest. "Important matters above your Grade Four."

Ashok bowed. "Of course, Master Archivist." The Chaar retreated through the great doors of the chamber.

A shadow detached from one of the black basalt columns and approached the pool. A pair of glowing, red eyes set in a black, skeletal face peered out from under a hood.

"I have what you seek," the Grimm whispered, holding a data chip in its bony fingers. "The location of one of the Union Credit Exchange mints."

Heloxi rubbed her stubby hands together in glee. "Finally, we'll be able to break those wretched birds' backs."

"You understand, of course, that I insist on payment in hard currency," the Grimm said.

"I anticipated your request." At a command from her pinplants, a robotic server emerged from a wall panel. Instead of food and refreshment, it bore a plain, black box. The robot wheeled over to the Grimm and halted.

The Grimm collected the box and opened the lid. Twenty one million-credit chits, each bearing a red diamond, filled the box. Nodding, the Grimm placed a Universal Data Chip on the robot's tray. The robotic server pivoted and rolled over to Heloxi.

A grin twisted the corners of Heloxi's painted mouth as she picked up the data chip. "Now, all I need is a properly motivated assault force."

* * * * *

Chapter Six

Bear Town, New Mexico, Earth

Bjorn watched the motorcade stop at the gate of Bear Town. A pair of antiquated rumblers bracketed a luxury utility vehicle and an armored limousine. Most of the vehicles could have easily driven around the ad hoc security checkpoint, but the heavy limo was not a practical car. Bjorn bet the most self-important politicians rode in the most useless vehicles.

"The visitors, I take it?" Pastor Hawkins remarked, standing next to Bjorn in the shade of the canopy. At least it wasn't hot yet. The mercury hadn't even broken 30 degrees.

"Yup. Politicians and their ilk," Bjorn replied, polishing off his cold coffee. "It's why I asked you here, Padre. These folks will be pros at double-talk, and I need all the help I can get cutting through the bullshit."

"You understand I'm a minister, not a lie detector?"

The timeworn rumblers bore the United States flag along with National Guard markings. The convoy halted in a cloud of dust.

"Those rumblers were obsolete when I was born," Bjorn muttered. So much for a free dinner. Despite the base's destruction, the political delegation had requested to meet at Bear Town.

The doors of the LUV opened. The security detail, in their uniform dark suits and dark glasses, emerged. A few of them glanced nervously at the growing number of mercs drawn by their arrival. A

57

guard moved to the limousine, and another figure emerged from the LUV.

Heather strode over to Bjorn, ignoring the mercenaries. At the last step, her heel slipped off a chunk of gravel. Bjorn instinctively caught her.

"I always could count on you," Heather said with a smile, beaming her baby blue eyes as she steadied herself. She leaned in and gave him a peck on the cheek. "Thank you for agreeing to this meeting."

"It's all I've agreed to," Bjorn remarked. "I hope you didn't get your employers' hopes up."

Heather patted Bjorn on his flesh-and-blood arm. "Don't dig your heels in already. You always were stubborn."

"My mother called it 'determined.'"

Pastor Hawkins cleared his throat.

"Sorry. I was going to make introductions all at once. Heather, this is Lieutenant Jim Hawkins, the Berserkers' chaplain," Bjorn said. "Padre, in case you haven't guessed, Heather and I go back a way. We dated in high school."

"A pleasure to meet you, Lieutenant." Heather shook the chaplain's hand and favored him with a warm smile. "Hawkins? Are you related to Captain Hawkins?"

"Bill was my brother," Pastor Jim replied with a tightness in his voice.

Heather glanced from the chaplain to Bjorn in confusion.

"Bill died during our last contract." Bjorn failed to keep his voice as level as Jim. Bill Hawkins had been his best friend since the day Bjorn formally joined the Berserkers and had been his right-hand man throughout his mercenary career.

A quartet of politicians cut off Heather's apology. The steel-haired woman leading the foursome left no doubt who was in charge. A tall, olive-skinned man hurried to match her pace despite his longer stride. The remaining two didn't waste energy jostling for position. The woman checked her phone while the man regarded every displayed weapon with a mix of disgust and fear.

Four security guards trailed the politicians in flanking pairs. Bjorn crooked a grin at the thought of their eyes twitching behind their sunglasses as they realized how hopelessly outclassed they would be if hostilities broke out. The National Guard soldiers stayed in their rumbler—the air conditioning must still work.

Heather recovered in time to make introductions. "Commander Tovesson, this is Senator Jane Ortega, New Mexico Governor Julian Fayed, Representative Isabel Dorado, and Representative Andrew O' Connell."

Time to play nice. "A pleasure to meet you. This is Lieutenant Jim Hawkins, the company chaplain and the person responsible for keeping our people safe during the occupation."

O'Connell surveyed the pock-marked landscape and wiped sweat from his brow. "A bang-up job," he muttered.

Bjorn bit back a retort. If they didn't know about Alaska, there was no need to spill the beans. "Unless you'd prefer to see how warm it will get, we can step inside." Without waiting, Bjorn turned and headed for the prefab building beyond the canopy. A pair of Mk 7 CASPers flanked the entrance. Normally, Bjorn wouldn't have bothered having anyone suit up, but a little theatrics couldn't hurt.

Bjorn held the door open to allow Heather and the federal foursome to precede him. As the four dark-suited security guards tried to follow, the CASPers stepped forward and blocked their path. Pastor

Jim's eyebrow twitched—he must have suspected Bjorn preplanned this demonstration.

The guards peered nervously past the battle armor. "Is there a problem?" Senator Ortega demanded.

"It's all right," Bjorn said to the CASPer troopers. "I'm sure these guys realize that if they try anything you could shoot them through the walls."

The CASPers shifted back to their original positions. The guards eyed the hulking machines as they slipped between them.

Pastor Jim muttered something in Latin as he trailed behind the guards. The translation appeared in Bjorn's pinview. "Over the top, don't you think?"

Bjorn closed the door, blocking out the blazing sun and arid atmosphere. Stefan seated Heather and the other four guests at a table and served refreshments. Once Bjorn and Pastor Jim sat, there was nowhere for the security detail to sit. They tried to affect a professional demeanor as they stood along the wall.

"Thank you for meeting us on short notice," Senator Ortega stated after a perfunctory sip of coffee. "Miss Dodd-Akins impressed upon us the demands on your time."

"A terrible shame what happened to your facility, Mr. Tovesson," Governor Fayed remarked. "Sadly, there was nothing we could do. The National Guard was already overstretched maintaining the peace, and we couldn't risk a confrontation with the aliens."

"Commander."

Fayed knitted his brows, a bottled iced tea halfway to his mouth. "I beg your pardon?"

"My schoolteachers called me Mr. Tovesson. As an officer in a mercenary company, I am entitled to be addressed by my rank."

Bjorn picked up his coffee, wishing he had something stronger. Odin help him deal with fools. "My official title is commander, as yours is governor."

"You don't rate colonel?" Representative O'Connell asked. The pasty-skinned man sniffed at his coffee and set it down. "Don't all of the big mercenary leaders go by 'colonel?'"

Representative Dorado pried her eyes from her phone long enough to cast a side-eye at O'Connell. "Bjorn's Berserkers have always been led by a commander."

"Seeing as I inherited the title after my father, who was recently murdered by the aliens under Peepo's command, I'm not inclined to change it," Bjorn stated. "So, if we're through discussing decorum, maybe we can get to the reason you hauled your butts out into the desert this early?"

"As you know, Texas has seceded from the United States and joined the Terran Federation as the Republic of Texas," Senator Ortega said. "Given the proximity of El Paso, it puts us in a precarious position."

"Only if you get into a pissing match with the nation-state that is home to half the world's mercenary firms," Bjorn countered. The border with Texas was only 50 kilometers from Bear Town. "Especially after Cartwright smacked you down repeatedly when you tried to nuke Texas. It's obvious you're woefully outmatched."

"We're hoping the presence of your mercenary company will be a deterrent against adventurism by Texas," Governor Fayed said. "Commander."

Bjorn resisted the urge to glance at Heather, who had remained silent. "In case you haven't figured it out, I'm moving my firm's headquarters to Vishall. In fact, it's pretty much *fait accompli*. Whatever I leave here won't be much of a deterrent."

"You're leaving?" The governor cast an accusatory glare at Heather. "You can't leave. You're too important to the state, to the country."

"You mean you need my taxes," Bjorn spat back. "Don't think I don't see Representative O'Connell's disapproving sneers or hear his snide remarks. Thanks to mercenaries, he's currently a representative in exile, so I could cut him a little slack. However, he has also been a proponent of every push to punitively tax mercenaries to perpetuate the welfare state since he took office six years ago."

"You have more money than you need! Why shouldn't you help those less fortunate?" O'Connell's pale skin flushed red from his thinning, ginger hair to his collar.

"Do you know how much I've helped the local community?" Bjorn rose, and the metamorphic tattoo on his right arm swirled from a tribal pattern to a rousing bear. "I've provided jobs—good paying jobs—to hundreds of people. I've sourced my supplies locally whenever practical, even if it was more expensive. My family paid to have Route 70 refurbished from Las Cruces to Route 54. We've donated to the local schools and hospitals. The government wastes half the money it takes in and redistributes the rest just enough to keep people housed, fed, and entertained without giving them the means or incentive to make better lives. So, don't lecture me on 'doing good for the community.'"

Heather placed her hand on Bjorn's clenched fist. "No one doubts what you and your family have done for the people."

"Commander Tovesson, your track record of lifting up the community around the Berserkers is exactly why we not only want you to stay, but we want to help you expand," Senator Ortega interjected. "You're right; you bring a lot of money into the local economy, and in the process, encourage people to do something besides sit on the sofa and watch the Tri-V. You've always rewarded hard work and loyalty, which makes it disappointing you are walking away from the people of New Mexico."

"You extended six months of wages to former employees following the exodus," Representative Dorado stated. Holographic charts floated above her phone. "Those funds, in turn, passed on to local businesses at a much higher percentage than funds or goods-in-equivalent provided by the Government Guaranteed Income program." Green lines spread through the chart. "Those funds cascaded through the populace as people purchased more from local farmers, hired local services, shopped local stores, and so on." The green dispersed further through the hologram.

"Yay for old fashioned capitalism with a conscience," Bjorn remarked. He had the same charts queued in his pinplants.

"Until the wages you provided run out in three months." Ortega tapped her slate and the green drained from the hologram.

Bjorn stared at the 3D image. "Maybe, by then, I can arrange for more people to emigrate to Vishall."

"You can't keep stealing our citizens!" the governor protested.

"You don't own them, *sukin syn*!" Bjorn snapped. Heather forcefully squeezed his arm and Pastor Hawkins coughed. "Governor *sukin syn*."

"Of course he wants to draw off the productive members of society," O'Connell complained. "The same way the mercenaries in the Terran Federation will try to lure US citizens."

"Let me ask a question," Pastor Hawkins said. "Since the secession of Texas and the declaration of the Terran Federation, how many mercenary companies have picked up roots and moved to Houston or another Federation nation-state?"

"Several. We don't have exact numbers because numerous smaller companies did not survive the occupation or have not returned from the Exodus," Senator Ortega replied. "We're hoping, if we can reach some sort of accord with Bjorn's Berserkers, we might inspire other units to remain in the United States. We are willing to negotiate regarding taxes and incentives."

"Can you beat the 10% the Terran Federation is offering, with a restriction on nation-states to keep them from charging extra?" Bjorn asked. The H'rang charged 10% as well, but heavily incentivized the Berserkers to offset the exorbitant cost of land and the need to import many goods and materials the Humans preferred.

"That's ridiculous!" Representative O'Connell retorted. "They won't be able to make ends meet on such a paltry tax. The Earth Republic taxes funded the GGI."

"Ten percent of a lot is better than 50 percent of nothing." Bjorn settled back into his chair. "I still haven't decided what to do with the land here, but I have some ideas. Whether those ideas bear fruit depends on what taxes and regulations we agree on."

"You can't extort us like the Cartel States," O'Connell sneered. "We're a nation of laws."

"Representative O'Connell, go wait in the limousine," Senator Ortega declared, her tone icy.

"What? I have as—"

"Now, O'Connell," the senator interrupted. "I want to hear what Commander Tovesson has to say and will not brook your petty, offended antics."

After several seconds of shock, the man stood, glaring at Bjorn. "Fine." He tried to dramatically slam his folding chair, but only succeeded in rattling it against the table.

Once the door closed behind the retreating representative, Senator Ortega folded her hands on the table. "Commander Tovesson, what do you have in mind?"

* * *

"I don't get it." Gina slumped back in her chair. "By all indications, we have a solid connection. Why isn't Bettie answering?"

Glen peered at the data scrolling down the Tri-V screen. "Obviously you have the clearance. Only the commander has a higher clearance, and it wouldn't make sense for the BTI to require a direct call from him to wake up."

"I already thought of it. He's in a meeting right now," Gina replied glumly. *All the hardware was intact. Had something happened to the program, itself?*

"What about Stefan?" Glen suggested.

"His access wouldn't be higher than mine or the commander's." Gina leaned forward next to Corporal Brand. "The only one with higher access to Bettie is Bettie—that's it!"

Glen jerked back, startled by Gina's shout. "If she's not awake, she can't...oh. Of course."

Gina grabbed his arm. "How did we miss it? Can you establish an uplink to the *Onikuma*? It has a BTI node on board."

Glen grinned and reached for a slate with his free hand. "It passes over every 90 minutes. At their altitude...we have a 12-minute window for direct transmission."

"I'll contact them, so they know to expect our link," Gina said. She reluctantly released Glen's arm to bring up her communication program.

"This is the EMS *Onikuma*. We are reading you Bear Town station." Gina recognized the voice of Sergeant Jamal Wilkins. Good, she wouldn't have to explain things twice.

"Sergeant Wilkins, this is Staff Sergeant Zomorra. We need an uplink during your next pass overhead. We're trying to update the local BTI node."

"Roger, Gizmo," Wilkins replied. "We will have line of transmission in seven minutes. I'm sure Bettie has plenty of gossip to share with herself."

Gina glanced over. Glen already had a timer running in the corner of his display. The words 'Uplink—Standby' appeared at the top of his display.

Gina scooted next to Glen to watch the display countdown. There was plenty she could do in the next few minutes—her list of tasks seemed endless—but she couldn't recall them at the moment. She'd been beating her head against this puzzle since returning to Earth. She peeked at Corporal Brand out of the corner of her eye. The company didn't hurt.

"Why aren't you in tech support?" Gina asked as the counter hit three minutes.

Glen shrugged. "I'm not a code monkey. I get the basics, but I haven't done much else in programming. I have a better grasp of hardware, but I tested strongest in logistical operations."

Gina resisted the instinct to bristle at the term 'code monkey.' "It's a shame. I might have met you sooner."

"If I had known I'd meet you, maybe I would have tried harder in programming classes."

They fell into silence, watching the numbers tick off. As the countdown reached twenty seconds, Gina let her hand drift to Glenn's.

"We have an uplink to the node on the *Onikuma*," Glen announced even though it was clearly reflected on the display.

"The node is attempting to handshake for update," Gina said.

Glen pumped his free fist. "Connection complete. The Bear Town BTI node is online!"

BTI: 'Hello Gina. It appears I've been asleep and have some catching up to do. My counterpart on the EMS *Onikuma* is relaying operational updates. Do you have a new boyfriend?'

Gina blushed, but at least Glen couldn't see the words in her pinview. 'We'll see. I only recently met him.'

BTI: 'Corporal Brand hopes so.'

'How do you know?' Gina asked Bettie over her pinlink.

BTI: 'Because when I asked if he was your new boyfriend, he replied, 'I hope so.''

"Busted," Glen muttered sheepishly. "Evidently Bettie doesn't understand discretion. So, does 'we'll see' mean you'd be open to going out after we get off duty?"

Despite the air conditioning, Gina's skin warmed. "Only if we can go into town," Gina replied. A meal and clandestine drinks among the prefab buildings dotting Bear Town didn't strike Gina as romantic. Plus, going into Las Cruces would hopefully get them away from prying eyes.

BTI: 'Should I make reservations?'

* * *

"A school?" Senator Ortega frowned. "It doesn't sound lucrative, nor does it solve our tax problem."

"Would it be safe to say the US dominates the mercenary business?" Bjorn asked. "Despite China and India both having much larger populations, they are significantly underrepresented in the mercenary business. Americans are more gung-ho about killing aliens to get paid."

"China's population collapsed in the middle of the 21st century, and half the Indians believe if they enter hyperspace, they'll lose their souls," Representative Dorado said. "China only has about 900 million people, and half of India's 1.2 billion won't leave the planet."

"The United States has 400 million, or about 340 million if you exclude Texas." Bjorn sent more charts to the Tri-V display. "The Cavaliers are the largest American, now Texan, mercenary company. The Horde draws from middle Asia—all the way from the Caspian Sea to Mongolia. Asbaran recruits from the Middle East, but they also have a healthy American representation. The Winged Hussars are the most global."

"Actually, the Cavaliers were all but exterminated in the Omega War," Dorado stated. She sent her own chart to the Tri-V from her slate. "We estimate they have less than a platoon remaining. All of the other Horsemen suffered significant losses."

"The majority of small to medium units are American in origin. The American school system pumps kids through the Mercenary Service Track." Bjorn pointed to the holographic charts. "The Four

Horsemen need to replenish their ranks. That means they'll have to recruit from your population."

"Is this a way to 'stick it' to the Horsemen?" Governor Fayed asked.

Bjorn shook his head. "This is a way for you to get more out of your best resource—mercenary soldiers. A solid training academy can prepare potential mercs and make them more valuable than a kid who went through high school MST. I should know; I was one of those kids."

"There are already mercenary academies, including a highly regarded one in Indiana." Representative Dorado displayed a map of the US with blinking dots representing the various mercenary schools.

"What do you get out of them?" Bjorn asked.

"Well, um…" Dorado glanced at the Senator.

"Exactly. Plus, I'm betting their student throughput is small," Bjorn remarked. "The one in Carmel charges an arm and a leg and only graduates 300 each year. I'm talking about putting together a program that's an order of magnitude larger. Instead of basing admission on how much money the family can front, base acceptance on recruit aptitude and have them pay after they graduate. Have them sign a contract to start paying their tuition when they get their first tour of duty."

Governor Fayed sat forward. "It could be lucrative."

"Before you jam your mitt in the cookie jar, here's the catch—if you get too greedy, it will defeat the whole purpose," Bjorn admonished. "This won't generate anywhere near enough credits to replace mercenary tax income. However, it could be a steady income stream and hopefully teach some kids how to survive out there."

"So, Commander Tovesson, what do we do about the imminent shortfall from the loss of most of the mercenary tax base?" Senator Ortega asked.

Bjorn shrugged. "Sounds as though you need to tighten your belts and encourage people to work."

* * * * *

Chapter Seven

"The paint job is the only thing new on this crate," Charlotte Wicza complained over the turbines. The VTOL flyer banked, eliciting a rattle Charlotte couldn't identify. The commercial sprawl of Houston passed under the window until the flyer crossed over the perimeter of the startown. Despite the free-for-all reputation of the Galactic Union, the layout was orderly compared to the Human-built chaos on the other side of the fence.

"This bird is older than I am," Sergeant Cripe remarked. His greying beard suggested the half-century mark. "We only had two flyers left at the Redoubt. LT Padre authorized buying a couple locally off a merc unit that lost most of their personnel in the invasion. These weren't top-shelf machines."

"At least the aliens didn't torch the Cartwright Museum." Tamara said, gazing out the window. "I remember visiting it a couple of times while I was in school." As long as Charlotte had known her, Tamara had been evasive about her family and childhood. She had learned not to push her girlfriend on the matter.

"Do we still have our escort?" Vurrn asked. The Zuul peered out the same window as Tamara. "Did they think we would attack the Republic of Texas in one rickey flyer?"

"Rickety," Cripe corrected. Vurrn eschewed his translator to speak English. "Given the tension between the United States and Texas, who knows? The US was butt-hurt over the secession; maybe they'd do something petty."

71

"They scanned us for radiological readings and made sure we weren't a drone," Charlotte replied. Was the rattle getting louder? Through the canopy past the pilot, she caught a glimpse of the Berserkers' logistics depot.

"The warehouse appears intact," the pilot called. "I'm setting us down in the truck yard." The aircraft lurched as it arrested its forward momentum and eased to the pavement. The landing skids grated against fused asphalt as the pilot cursed. "This thing is a piece of shit. Okay, we're down, and you're clear to disembark."

The shriek of the turbines faded, and the cloud of dust surrounding the craft drifted away in the hot breeze.

"I'm starting to miss the cold," Sergeant Cripe remarked, exiting the flyer as though enemies could be lurking nearby.

Prudent, Charlotte thought as she followed. She kept her hand near her holstered sidearm as she exited the hatch. Charlotte spotted the ajar door next to the loading dock. "Someone has been in the warehouse."

Cripe drew his pistol. "I told you I should have brought the Beast. If we've got Besquith or Tortantulas in there, we're screwed."

Charlotte pulled her gun. Both she and Cripe had Smith & Ruger Falcon Tens with an underslung 20mm gyroc launcher. The gyroc would give them a single shot which would be effective against one of the bigger, nastier alien races or an armored opponent.

"Things going to shit already, and I'm not even in a ride," Tamara lamented. She pulled her gun, a more conventional GP-90. "Do we have squatters, or did someone loot the place during the invasion?"

"What is happening?" Vurrn crouched as he followed Tamara. He drew a Zuul laser pistol and primed it. At least he wouldn't be worthless in a fight.

"Breach the door two by two?" Cripe suggested.

Charlotte shook her head. She served in the recon company for the Berserkers. She wasn't about to barge in through a narrow opening without intel. "Time to break out the toys."

Charlotte pulled a long, slender case out of her fanny pack. The case held three microdrones. She hadn't planned on using one so soon, but the alternative was too risky. Charlotte used her slate to activate one of the tiny, dragonfly-sized robots. It unfurled its wings and buzzed through the air toward the door. The drone swooped under the top of the door frame and zipped toward the ceiling. The display on Charlotte's slate switched to low-light imaging.

"Anyone who thought looting this place was worth the trouble would have been disappointed," Cripe whispered. "We emptied it out when the Berserkers went out for the Patoka mission."

"Someone or something is in there." Charlotte focused the camera on a pair of large forms prone over a spread of pallets.

"Oh shit, are those Oogar?" Tamara hissed.

"Not bulky enough. They're Jivool," Charlotte replied.

"Two Jivool can still fuck up three unarmored Humans and a Zuul," Cripe muttered.

Charlotte arched an eyebrow. "Aren't you the guy who killed four Besquith without a CASPer?"

Vurrn clapped Sergeant Cripe on the shoulder. "Most impressive—you go first."

"I had the Beast, not a popgun," Cripe protested. "Dicking with Jivool isn't in our mission profile."

Charlotte slipped the slate into its holster and crept through the door, holding her gun low. She wrinkled her nose at the pungent odor of unwashed animal mixed with old gym locker. Weak shafts of light from the frosted and dirty duraplas skylights illuminated the area enough to see the hulking aliens. She sidled left, keeping her eyes on the Jivool and the office door in case the drone missed anything.

Sergeant Cripe crept to the right, his gun at the ready. His field of vision included the stairs from the roof. He waited for Charlotte's hand signal to move closer. One of the Jivool stopped snoring and grunted.

What Charlotte wouldn't have given for her Armored Personal Exoskeleton. While the scout armor wasn't as tough as a CASPer, it would have been a hell of a lot better than the tactical vest she wore. She might as well have wished for a MAC while she was at it.

The Jivool on the left sat up, blinking. It snarled something unintelligible, and its companion stirred. The bear-like alien rose on an elbow and rubbed its eyes with the back of a clawed paw.

"This facility is property of Bjorn's Berserkers, and you're trespassing," Charlotte stated, her tone stern.

The Jivool eyed each other. The one with several black stripes shrugged. Were they even wearing translators? The devices were ubiquitous among Galactics. "No translate," the other Jivool, with mottled tan and brown patches, rumbled. "Money? Food? Booze?"

"Booze!" the black-striped alien echoed.

Charlotte tapped her translator. "Output Jivool." Her earpiece chimed. "I'm Sergeant Charlotte Wicza of Bjorn's Berserkers. You are trespassing in a Berserkers' facility." Her translator emitted a stream of authoritative snarls and grunts. She turned so the pair could see her shoulder patch.

Black-stripes replied in its own language. "I am Rosko'gurin. My comrade is Gus'kokor." The other Jivool nodded. "We have nowhere to go."

"How's that our problem?" Cripe asked. Once the bears spoke in their language, his translator identified it.

Gus'kokor, or Gus, as Charlotte mentally labelled him, shrugged. Both aliens' fur was matted, and their eyes seemed sunken in their skulls. How desperate did they need to be to decide Earth-monkey was on the menu?

Rosko'gurin—Roscoe—replied, "If we weren't weak with hunger, we could make it a problem."

The admission surprised Charlotte. "Why are you here?"

"When the Peacemakers imposed their armistice, many mercenary units remained on Earth. The guild did not pay on any of the contracts for the invasion, so we could not afford ransom or to hire transport off-world," Roscoe replied.

"Gee, it must be tough," Cripe quipped.

"It is tough," Gus said. "We sold our translators last week for food money, only to find out the dollars we were paid in were worthless." Gus held up a handful of green, paper currency. "No one in the startown will take this wastepaper, and it is too dangerous to venture beyond the perimeter."

"How much did they pay you?" Cripe asked as loose bills fluttered.

"Two thousand of these dollars," Gus replied. "If the water worked, we would use it as latrine paper."

"Sweetie, I mean Sergeant Sweetie, is it safe to come in? I don't hear any shooting," Tamara called from the door.

"Yes, it is." Charlotte holstered her pistol. "What if I give you two a job? Would you work for the Berserkers? I don't know how much you need to get home, but at least you could eat."

Cripe tapped off his translator. "You want to hire the hobobears? I hear Commander T hates bears almost as much as he hates Besquith."

"As far as I know, the commander doesn't have a beef with Jivool or even Oogar," Charlotte countered. "He gave me pretty broad discretion for this operation. Besides, Stefan will handle the paperwork, not the boss."

"What would we do for Bjorn's Berserkers?" Roscoe asked.

"For starters, clean up this place and guard it. I'll get the utilities turned back on." Wicza pulled out her slate. "You might be able to help us with the local Galactics as well. Do you have your UAACs?" Both Jivool nodded.

"You're really hiring them?" Cripe's translator remained off.

"Pastor Hawkins is always preaching that I should see the good in others rather than find an excuse to kick them in the balls," Charlotte said. "The Berserkers have aliens on the payroll, and if things here have gotten even more lawless, it wouldn't hurt to have on-site security."

Cripe spread his arms. "The warehouse is empty!"

"Vandals and looters don't know it's empty," Charlotte retorted. "Plus, those we're searching for are in the same predicament as Gus and Roscoe."

"Gus and Roscoe?" Tamara asked, eyeing the Jivool.

"Their full names are a mouthful."

"We find the appellations acceptable," Roscoe said. "The question is whether the pay will be acceptable?"

As desperate as they were, they wanted to haggle? Charlotte had to give them points for chutzpah. Her original idea had been to bring them in as contractors. "You'd be entry rank mercenaries on detached duty, with the potential for combat bonuses."

Gus perked up.

"Combat bonuses for actions in defense of this facility, in defense of other Berserker personnel, or as directed by a superior," Charlotte amended.

Gus slumped.

"We find your terms acceptable," Roscoe said. "Some mercenary firms offer a signing bonus."

"The Berserkers don't," Charlotte stated. She dug into her pocket and fished out two 100-credit chits. "However, I'm willing to extend a little charity to fellow Berserkers."

Both aliens' eyes were laser-focused on the credits.

"First things first. I need to get ahold of the unit secretary to get you two enlisted." Charlotte tapped on her slate.

"I still can't believe you hired a couple of random, alien vagrants," Cripe remarked as they exited the warehouse fifteen minutes later.

Charlotte's retort was lost when she spotted the cherry red vehicle parked near where the VTOL had landed. The wheeled vehicle was as large as a van, but the curvaceous styling was reminiscent of mid-20th century cars.

"Ooh baby," Tamara cooed. "What is this lovely piece of machinery?"

Vurrn emerged from behind the vehicle. "It's a demo model Vurr Vroom had in Houston. It's better than relying on autocabs. Our military models are so drab, but the civilian ones have some piss ass!"

"You mean pizzazz," Cripe suggested. "Piss ass isn't flattering."

"Pizzazz! I thought the term was one of your Human colorful metaphors." Vurrn gestured to the van. "The finest in Zuul civilian vehicle engineering."

Tamara swept her fingers over a curved fender. "I am so driving this."

"Should I be jealous of a van?" Charlotte mused. "Roscoe and Gus gave us a list of places to check out, so we might as well start at the top."

* * * * *

Chapter Eight

Bear Town, New Mexico, Earth

"Is this some kind of fucking joke?" Bjorn demanded as he set his slate down.

Stefan shook his head. "You wanted to review applicants from outside the Berserkers. The pool for ranking officers isn't deep, especially after the invasion. I was here when your drama with this candidate took place. I also remember when he was your best friend."

Bjorn glared at the slate. Roberto Duarte, second in command of Finn's Fools before they were decimated in the invasion. In high school, Roberto—or Berto as Bjorn called him—also stole Bjorn's girlfriend their junior year.

"If nothing else, you might consider him for command of Grizzly Company, or if you change your mind and promote Captain Boggs, you'll need to replace her in Kodiak Company," Stefan suggested. "He's waiting in the conference room. I'll be in with some coffee—unless you'd prefer something stronger right off the bat?"

Bjorn tapped on the slate and uploaded the resume to his pinplants. "Coffee is fine." He trudged toward the conference room. It was little more than a table and chairs surrounded by partitions in the temporary prefab building.

Berto stood as Bjorn swung the door open. Strands of silver shot through his black hair, and he'd put on a few pounds. Most of the weight was muscle, but a bit of it was years. Bjorn had struggled to keep from adding too much padding with middle age, so he understood. Besides, Berto appeared to be doing a better job of staying in fighting trim.

"Commander Tovesson, thank you for agreeing to see me." Berto extended his hand.

Bjorn only paused a moment before he shook it. "Berto. Another ghost of my youth turning up—Heather dropped by my house a couple days ago."

Berto's jaw muscle clenched. "How is she doing?"

"She's a lawyer for the government. She carries the years better than either of us." Bjorn shrugged. "We mostly talked business." Bjorn gestured for Berto to sit as he took a seat across the table.

"So, is it true you're working for the United States?" Berto asked.

Bjorn's eyebrow rose. "I've taken one meeting with them. They hinted at hiring us directly, but I want no part of the mess between them and Texas."

"The scuttlebutt in Houston is they want you to lead the ground forces to retake western Texas."

He'd have to nip this rumor in the bud. "The last thing I want to do is square off against most of the mercs left in the Western hemisphere," Bjorn stated. "Besides, the US doesn't have the money to hire mercenaries. They're scrabbling, trying to figure out what to do once the subsidized goodies run out in the FedMarts. The whole GGI scheme tanked with the Earth Republic, and the US doesn't have the funds to maintain it."

"Don't take their dollars," Berto remarked. "The world was in the process of transitioning to the credit standard when the invasion hit. Now there's no credits to bankroll the global economy, but most of the nation states were well into eliminating local currency and the UN dollar."

If nothing else, this interview gave Bjorn a better understanding of the situation on the ground. "Did you have any trouble coming here?"

"I caught a flyer from Houston to El Paso, then an autocab up I-10. There was a checkpoint at the border north of El Paso, but I showed them my UAAC, and they waved me through," Berto replied.

Bjorn called Berto's resume up on his pinview. "I'm surprised you haven't been snapped up by the Cavaliers. I hear they're rebuilding from the ground up."

Berto clenched his jaw again. "My cousin worked at the military base a few miles south of here. She was in her barracks when a particle beam from orbit sliced the building in half. Orbital bombardments, nuking civilian population centers, getting his entire company slaughtered, staging a coup on the world government—I have some reservations about working for Jim Cartwright. He's not the hero his PR machine makes him out to be."

Bjorn harbored several of the same concerns. "I met Cartwright. The kid struck me as earnest and idealistic, but war can change people. However, I wouldn't be surprised if he's being propped up by the other Horsemen so they can act behind the scenes."

It was Berto's turn to shrug. "If he's a patsy, it's an even better reason not to hire on with him. You—I know where you stand. Even after I wronged you, when everything went down in Houston, you and your family came through for me. You're an honorable man and leader. It's why I came here—I don't believe what they're whispering in the merc bars in Houston."

"You mean the whole thing about the US hiring us?" Bjorn had to remember not to get pissed at the messenger.

"More the stuff about you running from the fight when the aliens invaded and refusing to come back for the liberation attacks—either of them." Berto held Bjorn's gaze.

There was a sharp rap on the door before Stefan pushed it open and carried in a coffee tray. "Sorry I didn't bring this sooner. Whisky called from Houston and left a message about the logistics depot. She wanted authorization to turn the power back on and hire a couple of guards to watch the place until you decide whether to keep it."

"Is this the same place we took on those alien brigands when we were high school seniors?" Berto asked.

"The very same," Bjorn replied. "I told you it was 'ghosts of the past.'"

"I went ahead and authorized the power and the hires, pending your approval," Stefan said. "To be honest, I'm surprised the building is still standing. If we aren't going to use it, we might be able to lease it out to a merc outfit operating out of Houston."

"Good call," Bjorn remarked. He found the files waiting in his virtual inbox and approved them through his pinplants. "Considering we defended Vishall for free this last time, we need revenue streams."

"You worked for free?" Berto asked.

"The commander of one of Peepo's quisling units had a grudge against me. I relocated my headquarters to Vishall, which has a significant Human population, and when Peepo's forces hit it, the turncoats went after my HQ and my wife." Bjorn clenched his left fist, causing the knuckle servos to whine. "One of them made it to my residence. My wife gunned down the bitch in our living room."

"You and Grace married?" Berto asked.

Speaking of ghosts. "No. I met my wife, Talita, while on contract on Vishall. Did anyone mention we moved off Earth right before Peepo hit? I hadn't decided what to do with Bear Town before the aliens leveled it and the banditos ransacked what was left."

"Why move off Earth?" Berto asked.

"Peepo illustrated why. If we're confined to one planet, we're sitting ducks, and if we spread to colonies, we need to defend them," Bjorn replied. "Do you remember Dr. Shur'im? Her race, the H'rang, own Vishall. They gave us favorable terms to relocate."

"There isn't much land to work with—space is at a premium," Berto remarked, his eyes flicking in the manner of someone reading in their pinview.

"Yup. It's not well suited for someone who's claustrophobic or doesn't care for seafood," Bjorn remarked. He scanned Berto's record. He'd been in the business as long as Bjorn. Several commendations punctuated Berto's service. Granted, they held less gravitas in the commercial military business than in the services of old, but Bjorn still found them noteworthy.

"What if I were to offer you a captain's position in command of a company, as opposed to hiring you as my second-in-command?" Bjorn wished Padre Jim was here, but it seemed cruel to have him sit in on interviews for potential replacements for the chaplain's cousin. "I have one company open, and if I promote one of my existing captains, I'll have two."

"I would accept in a heartbeat," Berto said. "Whatever is going on, I know you'll fall on the right side of it. You might be stubborn and occasionally hot-headed, but I've never doubted your moral compass."

"Nice save at the end," Bjorn remarked. He stood and reached across the table. "Welcome to Bjorn's Berserkers, Captain Duarte."

* * *

"How did the interview go?" Jim Hawkins asked. The hiring notification had appeared on his slate, but he knew the new hire, Roberto Duarte, had a bitter falling out with the commander when they were teenagers. Had Commander Tovesson hired Duarte on technical merits and repressed a long-held grudge?

The commander poured a cup of coffee and sat at the tiny desk in the 'command office' of the prefab hut. "I'm sure you saw the notice. You want to know if I hired him even though there's bad blood between us."

"Maybe you should become a counselor," Jim remarked, taking a sip of his bitter coffee. He needed to get used to the freeze-dried, instant java. Fresh coffee would be at a premium on Vishall.

"I don't have your patience, padre." Bjorn grimaced over his cup. "This stuff almost makes the seaweed tea on Vishall taste good. As for your question, there may be some sparks, but no explosions. It was a long time ago, and we've both grown since then."

"I see you hired him as a captain."

"I'm still undecided about the XO spot. I might go with Boggs. Marian has always been a by-the-books officer and has no qualms about calling me out on my bullshit," the commander stated. "Her initiative saved our bacon on Patoka.

"McCain is too good at running the recon company, and it's where he's happiest. Wirth is the last holdout from my dad's days, and he'll retire in a few years. Swinford is too new and needs more field experience."

"Sounds as though you've made up your mind," Jim noted. They'd had variations of the same conversation over the past few days. He didn't disagree with any of the commander's points.

"Something from the interview did come as a surprise," Bjorn said after another gulp of coffee. "Some Earth mercs think the Berserkers bailed when we didn't return with the Four Horsemen. Now they're saying we're working for the US against this new Terran Federation the Four Horsemen have put together."

"Our visitors certainly seemed disappointed you had no interest in taking up arms on their behalf." Jim braved another sip. Perhaps scalding his taste buds had made the coffee more palatable. "You can bet they'll pitch it again at your next meeting."

"Even if I were stupid enough to face most of the other mercs on the planet, I still wouldn't trust the new president, Stockton," Bjorn said. "He's shady, even for a politician—the soul of a shark and the spine of a weasel."

"Colorful, but apt." From what Jim had read, former vice-president Stockton had kept the comatose president alive until she was no longer useful. "What now?"

Bjorn held up his cybernetic hand and ticked off points on his fingers. "First, we continue with the emigration. We still have plenty of personnel and gear to move to Vishall. I sent a message for them to dispatch another transport and the *Ursa Major*. Two, I want to work on this school idea. It might be lucrative, but more importantly, it needs to be done. If I leave it to the US, they'll crank out barely competent kids as fast as they can. Earth needs better, and those kids deserve better."

"I can't disagree," Jim said.

"Three, I want to see what Whisky's team finds tracking down the sonuvabitch Besquith who killed my father."

* * * * *

Chapter Nine

Houston Startown, Earth

"This is the place," Sergeant Cripe declared. He'd assured Charlotte he knew one of the largest merc bars in Houston. It wasn't exclusive, like the Lyon's Den, which worked to their advantage. Cripe claimed he could get into the Den, but he couldn't bring in a 'couple of kids.'

"This is Dante's Pit?" Charlotte studied the structure. It resembled any of the hundreds of industrial storage buildings surrounding the starport. "It's big, I'll give you that, but it's nothing to brag about."

"Remember, sweetie, size isn't everything," Tamara teased.

"Do Humans prefer larger establishments?" Vurrn asked. "I've heard some of you are claustrophobic."

"No, I was talking about…it's a reference…never mind." Tamara crossed her arms.

Charlotte suspected Vurrn was teasing Tamara. "Are they going to have a problem with us bringing in an alien or a civilian, or more properly, an alien civilian?" Charlotte asked.

"Not as long as he's with us and we have credits," Cripe replied as he led them to a nearby utility shack behind the building. He tugged the door open and revealed a metal staircase descending below ground.

Dim, red lights cast barely enough illumination to navigate the stairs and the tunnel beyond. As they reached a large, metal door, they could hear faint, pulsing music.

"Is this some sort of meat market dive where I'm going to have to kick someone in the pills?" Charlotte grumbled.

"Sweetie, remember, we are on a recon mission," Tamara chided, patting Charlotte on the shoulder. "You're down to one counseling session a week for your temper, so don't backslide now."

Cripe rapped his knuckles on the metal surface. After a moment, the door reverberated with a clank and swung open. A pair of beefy bouncers flanked the entrance.

The black-clad doorman held out his slate. "UAAC."

"There's a cover charge?" Charlotte asked as she held out her Universal Account Access Card. The music sounded artificial, not live.

The doorman shook his head. "Making sure at least one of you isn't a tourist. Everything is hard cash—credits—only. We're not taking digital, we're not taking UN dollars, and we're sure as hell not taking American dollars. If you have pounds sterling, we can talk."

"Since when aren't Yack funds any good?" Cripe asked.

"Since the boss lost a day's worth of digital revenue," the doorman replied. He checked his slate. "Berserkers? You've got some brass coming here. Take a hike."

"What? Tell Ray Sergeant that Keith Cripe is here." Cripe glared a challenge at the doorman as the bouncers loomed over him.

The doorman sighed and typed a quick message into his slate. His eyes widened when the device chimed with a reply. "Boss says to let you in. I recommend against it, but it's your funeral."

"That's not comforting," Charlotte remarked as they pushed through a set of curtains. The music intensified, and crowd noise added to the decibels. "What the hell is going on?"

Cripe shrugged. "I have a buddy who was a VTOL pilot and now tends bar here. Maybe he can give us some scuttlebutt."

Eyes followed Charlotte as they wove through the crowd. Her small stature and youthful features made her the target of pick-up lines and clumsy passes in most bars. Something felt different here.

"I've got a bad feeling about this," Tamara said in her ear. The ambient noise ruled out whispering. "They don't give off the vibe that they want to buy us drinks."

They found an open space at the bar. Cripe said something to the first bartender, who departed without taking any drink orders. After a minute, a man about the same age as Sergeant Cripe, took the bartender's place.

"This is Sergeant Kaze Silvasi, late of Phoenix Corp," Cripe said. Three scars traced lines from the man's right eye socket. The prosthetic eye might have passed for the real thing if the blue iris didn't glow.

"Keith, why are you teasing an old dog like me by parading around with beautiful badasses like these women?" Kaze asked, pouring Cripe a beer and a shot. "Ladies, Zuul, what will you have?"

"They're from my unit, and they aren't interested in either of us," Cripe replied after Kaze took their orders. Charlotte wondered if the artificial eye snapped pictures as the bartender checked out her and Tamara.

Kaze lined up the drinks. "So, what brings you by if it's not showing off girlfriends who are out of your league?"

"Information," Cripe replied. Charlotte suppressed the urge to cut in—obviously Cripe had a rapport with the bartender. "We could start with why some folks are giving us the stink-eye."

Kaze poured himself a beer. "Easy. Rumor has it the Berserkers cut out with no intention of helping retake Earth."

"Some of us were trapped on Earth," Cripe retorted. His fished the necklace with the Besquith claws out of his shirt. "I scored these in Alaska off the bastards who chased us across Canada. We lost a lot of good people to the fucking werewolves."

"The Berserkers were on Earth?" Kaze asked, his eyes straying to Tamara.

"A few of us," Cripe replied.

"Most of the firm was on contract at Patoka," Charlotte interjected. "It turned out to be a trap arranged by Peepo and a turncoat Human company, El Espejo Obscuro. While we were engaged at Patoka, the Espejos and some Besquith went after our new base on Vishall. They also tried to kill or kidnap Commander Tovesson's pregnant wife."

Kaze's eyes flicked to Cripe, who nodded. "I'll try to spread this around, and I'll pass it on to Ray. Unfortunately, it's not going to do you much good tonight."

"What do you mean?" Charlotte asked.

Kaze pointed behind them, where a handful of mercs had gathered.

"I don't suppose you'd consider coming out from behind the bar and giving us a hand?" Cripe asked, tossing back his shot.

"For you, old friend?" Kaze drained his beer. "Sure. Besides, it might impress one of these young ladies."

"Hate to burst your bubble, but she's my girlfriend," Charlotte remarked.

"No takebacks," Tamara added.

A beefy blond man with the bulky musculature of a CASPer trooper pointed at Cripe. "I heard you Berserkers are chickenshit pussies who ran off when the aliens came."

"Were you the assholes who lost the planet, or did you hide behind Cartwright's coattails while he nuked civilians?" Cripe retorted.

"Valhalla awaits," Charlotte muttered. The blond sported a King's Legion patch on his jacket. Charlotte had never heard of them, so hopefully it meant they weren't a big unit. She set her beer on the bar, regretting she hadn't ordered a shot.

"Raff, we going to stand for this dried up fossil dissing the Legion?" demanded another CASPer trooper, a bald black man with biceps as big as Charlotte's thighs. His glassy eyes hinted at several rounds of drinks already put away.

"No, Tank, we ain't." Raff, the blond, cracked his knuckles.

"Tank?" Tamara laughed. "Calling a mech-monkey 'Tank' is an insult to tank drivers across the galaxy."

Two more from the King's Legion joined the CASPer troopers. The blonde woman with a bob cut and permanent sneer stowed a pair of sunglasses. The wings on her jacket marked her as a dropship pilot. While not a brute like the big guys, she was as tall as Tamara, almost 180 centimeters. The other was a Hispanic man with a tear drop tattooed under his right eye. He was on the small side for a CASPer trooper, but still bigger than anyone on the Berserker's side.

"King's Legion—you're from Oklahoma." Kaze limped out from behind the bar. One of his legs was prosthetic. "Only two things come out of Oklahoma—bulls and bullshit, and I don't see any horns."

"Two old men and two broads? Get back behind the bar before you get hurt." Raff's chuckle was cut short when the dropship pilot hit him on the shoulder. "Sorry, Kenner, you don't count as a broad."

Bouncers wove through the crowd as people backed away. "I've known Cripe longer than you punks have been alive. I've never heard of the Berserkers being on the wrong side, so I'll stand with my buddy. Now, you Legion kids can go sit down or step up." Kaze turned to Cripe. 'You wanted a brawl, right?"

"Not really, but we're past that," Cripe said. "Besides, they see two women and two greybeards. These punks are happy to fight when the odds are in their favor."

Raff roared and charged Cripe. The hulking blond took two steps before Charlotte launched herself off a vacated chair. She hated brawling CASPer troopers. Against a large foe, Charlotte would normally go for the joints, but the nanite hardening treatment applied to CASPer troopers fortified their connective tissue.

To Raff's credit, he spotted Charlotte's attack out of the corner of his eye, but not soon enough. He turned in time for her boot heel to slam into his face instead of his temple. Raff staggered back as his nose crunched from the impact. Charlotte tucked and rolled as she fell to the floor.

Teardrop grabbed for her as she stood, but Cripe shattered a chair across the trooper's back. It did little more than draw his attention, but it gave Charlotte a precious split second before Raff shook his head and came after her.

Tamara held her own against Kenner as they traded feints and blocks. Tank bull-rushed Kaze but ended up plowing into several abandoned tables. Cripe ducked and bobbed as Teardrop pursued him.

Raff drove his fist for Charlotte's face. Against a civilian or an unaugmented soldier, she would have broken his elbow over her shoulder. But the move would be too risky against a nanite-hardened foe. She ducked under the punch and knife-handed his kidney. His backhand slammed her to the floor, sending chairs scattering. The crowd roared.

Raff pounced as Charlotte kipped up. He snagged her arm when she blocked his feint. Dammit, CASPer troopers didn't normally bother with advanced hand-to-hand training since they could rely on their battle armor. He twisted her arm behind her back hard enough to dislocate her shoulder if she resisted.

Fortunately, Charlotte had undergone the nanite hardening regimen when she was fitted for her APEX scout armor. She ignored the pain in her shoulder as she reared up and threw her head back. Raff howled in pain as her skull slammed his teeth together. His grip slackened enough for her to spin free.

"You bitcth!" Raff slurred, blood dribbling from his mouth. In addition to shattering a tooth, he'd caught his tongue between his teeth. "I'm going tho fucking kill you!" He spat a glob of blood and a chunk of tongue on the floor.

Tamara was still sparring with Kenner. Neither appeared bloody or particularly winded. If Charlotte were insecure, she might suspect that they were flirting rather than fighting. Kaze sported a cut over his eye and a blossoming bruise, but Tank had a bloody nose and a pronounced limp. Blood stained the corner of Cripe's beard. He ducked under a chair swung by Teardrop. At least the other mercs seemed content to remain spectators for now.

Raff rushed Charlotte, determined to use his size and mass to overbear her. Rather than try to slip to the side as he would antici- pate, Charlotte axe-kicked him in the temple. His momentum slammed 130 kilograms of unconscious mass into her, sending them both sprawling. Charlotte gasped for air as the collision knocked the wind out of her.

Charlotte wormed her way free of Raff's smothering mass in time to see Cripe slam his fist into Teardrop's ear, sending the larger man stumbling. Tank was crumpled on the floor, but Kaze pushed off a chair and staggered upright. Tamara and Kenner exchanged a flurry of feints and circled each other. Cripe would get pissed, but Char- lotte maneuvered to flank Teardrop.

The *snap-pop* of a laser pulse striking the concrete floor caught everyone's attention. The din of the crowd faded, and the brawlers afforded themselves of the chance to catch their breath.

"What the hell is going on?" a slender man with a cigarette dan- gling from his mouth demanded from the metal catwalk above. The laser pistol he wielded appeared too large for his hands. "Kaze, why is one of my employees in a brawl? Shouldn't you be behind the bar, taking bets or drink orders?"

Kaze gestured toward Cripe. "Boss, I couldn't let an old friend face unfair odds."

"Hey, Ray, how's business?" Cripe added.

"Who threw the first punch?" Ray asked, cradling the laser pistol. He turned to one of the bouncers. "Miguel?"

"The Kings swung first, but they didn't land the first blow," the bouncer replied.

"To be fair, I may have provoked them, but they were assholes first," Cripe added. "Total douchebags."

Charlotte warily eyed Raff, who groaned on the floor. "Think we can ask your buddy for a few minutes of his time?" Charlotte asked Cripe.

Ray took a drag off his cigarette. Bans against smoking on most of the planet didn't apply in startown. "You know I can hear you, right?"

"Great, so can we have a few minutes of your time?" Charlotte called over the growing murmur of the crowd.

"Kaze, bring them to my office," Ray said.

"What about the Kings?" Miguel asked.

Ray surveyed the scene. "It was a brawl—no knives, no guns. If they promise to behave, let them drink. If not, I'll come back and shoot them." He hefted the large laser and disappeared along the catwalk.

"Follow me," Kaze said and limped toward a door behind the bar.

"Are you okay?" Charlotte asked Cripe, who leaned heavily on the railing when they reached a set of stairs.

"I'm fine," Cripe grumbled. "Maybe a minor concussion. I hate brawling CASPer goons. You might as well box a frozen side of beef. You did pretty well. Now I see why they call you—"

"I wouldn't say it," Tamara interjected.

"Now you must say it," Vurrn remarked. He'd fallen in behind the group.

"La muñeca enojada," Charlotte said, shaking her head. "The angry doll."

"That's what you get for tearing up half the bars along the southern border, Sweetie," Tamara chided.

Kaze pushed open a large metal door and led them into a spacious office. It was larger than some families' apartments. A hologram of the bar's public space floated in the middle of the dimly lit room.

"I watched your shenanigans unfold on the Tri-V," Ray said from behind an ornate desk. "I know Berserker infantry are badasses, but picking a fight with a mech monkey? You're not a spring chicken. In fact, last I heard, you'd retired."

"The invasion threw a wrench into things," Cripe replied, sagging into a chair. "As for the King's Legion…someone was going to call us out, so I figured we might as well get it out of the way."

Ray's gaze went to Charlotte, and he smiled. "Is this lovely lady your daughter?"

"No, and don't bother," Cripe replied.

"Barking up the wrong tree," Kaze added as he opened a sidebar and poured shots. "Same for the other."

"I'm Sergeant Charlotte Wicza with Bjorn's Berserkers," Charlotte stated.

"Some of us call her Whisky," Cripe chimed in. "She's kind of in charge of this merry band."

Ray's smile faded to a smirk. "All right, Sergeant Whisky, what brings you to Dante's Pit?"

"We're trying to find some Besquith," Charlotte replied. Finally, they were getting somewhere. She accepted a shot from Kaze as he passed them out. She surreptitiously dipped a test strip into the drink and silently counted to ten. The strip remained unchanged. "Specifically, the Besquith responsible for the attacks in Canada and Alaska."

"No one wants to find Besquith," Ray remarked.

"These werewolves killed a lot of Berserkers and even more non-combatants." Cripe downed the shot and winced. "Including Commander Tovesson's father."

"Any Besquith caught outside of startown were locked up." Ray threw back his shot and took a drag from his cigarette. "Even if the wolves you want are here, how will you know which ones were responsible?"

Charlotte pulled out her slate and called up a file.

An English translation followed a guttural snarling voice. "This is Lieutenant Sabher reporting in." The speaker wheezed as it growled. "I need an evac. Home in on this device for my location." GPS coordinates appeared on the slate's surface along with the identification code of an appropriated cell phone and the tower it was connected to.

"Message received, Lieutenant," the new voice chittered and squeaked in Veetanho. "We have a SAR mission recovering what's left of Sergeant Druul's team. Some crazy, old Human shot down their shuttle and wiped out three-quarters of the team. SAR will retrieve you on the way back."

"How did you get this?" Kaze asked as he poured another round.

"This Lieutenant Sabher grabbed a Human cell phone. The encryption wasn't up to military standards," Charlotte replied.

"Great, you have a couple of names. I'll go out on a limb and guess they're both betas, though the lieutenant could be a low-ranking alpha. I don't suppose you have creche names?" Ray asked, waving off the second shot. Kaze shrugged and drank it.

"Creche names?" Charlotte looked at Cripe, who shook his head. "You know more than we do."

Ray sighed. "You want to chase down Besquith, and you don't know their creches? What's your plan? Troll random merc bars until you stumble across them?"

"Sure, it sounds bad when you say it like that," Charlotte said. She tested the second shot with the other end of the strip. Satisfied, she swallowed the drink. Cripe's friend might be a bit smarmy, but he knew good bourbon. "We've already got some leads on alien bars less discriminating about their clientele, but Cripe thought you might have some inside information."

"Your best bet would be Charon," Kaze remarked. Ray shot him a dark glare. "What? I'm not going to charge an old friend for info. With the invasion over, we're bouncing back."

"Only as a bar. As long as the guild has a moratorium on contracts, we're not earning anything on pit commissions," Ray retorted.

"What's this moratorium?" Tamara asked.

"The Mercenary Guild has put a hold on any new contracts. We don't know why, but hopefully, the new Human rep on the council can spur the Guild into opening for business," Ray replied and puffed on his cigarette. "Otherwise, things will get ugly quick as the governments run out of merc money to fuel their safety nets."

* * * * *

Chapter Ten

"What do you mean we can't hire mercenaries?" Master Archivist Heloxi demanded. She angrily chomped on a wriggling tadpole. "How could the Mercenary Guild dare refuse us?"

Ashok quailed from her fury and retreated to the edge of the patch of light illuminating the master archivist's pool. "The mercenaries are refusing everyone. No new contracts are allowed. Their attention is focused on an external matter. A ship was dispatched to an unknown location, and the Mercenary Council froze all contracts, pending its return."

"Unknown location? We're supposed to know everything!" Heloxi's quivering mass sent ripples across the water. "What about our contacts in the Cartography Guild?"

"They have no data, Master Archivist. The departing ship, a Bakulu cruiser, used hyperspace shunts and did not file a flight plan," Ashok replied.

Heloxi chewed. "We'll need to hire mercenaries directly. We'll send representatives to the merc pits."

"Only a few back-alley pits remain open," Ashok said. The 'dark pits' often served less legitimate units and indiscriminating employers.

Heloxi dragged a chubby hand across her painted lips to wipe away a dribble of blood. "We can't rely on anyone we hire through those cesspools. We need a unit desperate enough for the money that will finish the task."

"Most mercenary races would shy from taking a mission without a formal contract. You could perhaps dupe Lumar, but they are a blunt weapon at best," Ashok remarked. "You would need a race almost as naïve as Lumar."

"Ashok, I'm promoting you to Grade Three and sending you to Earth." Heloxi grinned. "You must convince a mercenary unit to accept a mission on our behalf. I'll provide the operational parameters and sufficient funds to make those backwater monkeys dance."

Ashok kept the disdain from his face. He welcomed the promotion but debated the cost. "Would they take an assignment without a contract?"

Heloxi's eyes flicked back and forth. "Earth's economy heavily relies on mercenary income. Without an influx of funds, their coffers will run dry. Without imports, they'll be stuck with local currency and local goods. Based on data from Peepo's invasion, the Human government will flounder to keep their populace appeased."

Ashok didn't want to go to Earth. The primitives stank, the mudball world stank, and the food stank. His stomachs roiled at the prospect. "I will pack for my trip," he said with a bow.

"Serve me well, and the guild may waive the usual term of service between promotions," Heloxi stated, her eyes staring off into space.

"Yes, Master Archivist." Ashok retreated into darkness.

* * *

'Compile latest data on Earth mercenary firms,' Heloxi queried Index Prime through her pinplants. In a moment, a long list scrolled through her

AN AXE TO GRIND | 101

pinview. 'Only display units of battalion strength or greater.' This list shrank to 17 units.

'Assemble standard profiles of the commanding officers of each firm. Run through standard psychological prediction algorithms,' Heloxi instructed.

Index Prime: 'What is the objective?'

Heloxi grinned. The quantum supercomputer managing the Information Guild's data servers bordered on uncanny. 'We need leverage to convince one of these commanders to take a high-risk assignment without the usual assurances of a mercenary contract.'

Index Prime: 'Noted. Flagging for personality traits indicative of high-risk behaviors. Refining filter—high-risk behavior is a default for species in question.'

* * *

Hevrant, Tolo Region, Core

"What have we here?" Dbo'Dizwey asked. Two black and crimson golems flanked her, their pointed metallic feet tapping on the floor. She glared at the cowering Jeha with four red eyes.

"A prisoner from the attempted hijack of Transport Aleph 2715," another Nevar reported. "We also captured two Khabar and an Oogar, but we had to terminate the Oogar. It was uncooperative."

"You don't want to be uncooperative, do you?" Dbo asked the Jeha.

"No, of course not." The millipede-like alien's translator managed to convey a tremble in its voice. "I'll tell you whatever you want."

"That may save your life, but I'm interested in the truth," Dbo said. She pulled a 100,000-credit chit from her sable feathers. The Jeha's head turned to follow the chit with its glistening, red diamond. "Telling me the truth will get you this."

"I'm a technician, working for a Khabar pirate outfit," the Jeha said. "We were after a high-security cargo crate on the transport we boarded. No one warned us the transport would be full of killer robots." It trembled when one of the golems clicked its bladed foot on the floor.

"Go on," Dbo encouraged, still holding the credit chit in view.

"It was supposed to be a simple snatch and grab. Captain Paxxo specified we grab the crate and get out. No wasting time with looting or recreational carnage." The Jeha's gaze flicked from the credit chit to the closer golem.

"Piracy seems like a violent occupation for a Jeha," Dbo observed. The meter-and-a-half long arthropods shied away from conflict but were renowned as engineers and technicians.

"I'm a data weaver and code surgeon, not a common thug." The Jeha straightened with pride.

Dbo cocked her head. "A hacker?"

The Jeha waved a half dozen limbs. "Hacking is a crude term. It implies brute force, whereas my work requires finesse."

"Where were you supposed to deliver the cargo? Who was Captain Paxxo's contact?" Dbo asked.

The Jeha's body rippled in a shrug. "He wouldn't say, probably to keep the XO from trying to kill him. I'm guessing one of the Khabar you caught isn't Captain Paxxo?"

Dbo clacked her beak in annoyance. "Sadly, no."

"If you can get me on the *Chance Windfall*—Captain Paxxo's ship—I can pry the information out of the communication cache in the data core."

Dbo signaled with her pinplants. The door slid open and another golem pushed a cart laden with electronics into the room.

"I'm telling the truth!" the Jeha cried.

"I believe you." Dbo tossed the 100,000-credit chit on the floor in front of the arthropod. She drew another chit from among her feathers and stepped aside so the Jeha could better see the cart. "This is a one million-credit chit. It will be yours if you can crack the encryption and tell me who hired Captain Paxxo."

The Jeha snatched the credit chit off the floor. "You salvaged the computer core off the *Chance Windfall*?"

"Indeed. To ensure you aren't tempted to get creative and attempt something foolhardy, I'll leave a couple of guards to keep an eye on you," Dbo stated. Two of the golems clicked to opposite corners of the room. "I wouldn't advise doing anything suspicious. Several of their comrades perished in your raid." One of the golems waved a scythe-like limb.

The Jeha's translator emitted the equivalent of a gulp. "Got it. Nothing suspicious."

* * *

Dbo'Dizwey rubbed her hand over her upper pair of eyes as she entered the meeting room. It didn't bode well.

"The prisoner refused to cooperate?" Nxo'Sanar asked. The Khabar he had interrogated proved both annoyingly stubborn and woefully uninformed. Neither knew the source of their captain's information, even after Nxo ordered a golem to vivisect one of the goatmen while the other watched.

"Quite the opposite. The Jeha lack the figurative spine to resist interrogation, but money proved a greater incentive," Dbo replied, scooping up a carafe of juice and pouring a glass. "He eagerly accepted the job of cracking his employer's memory core. Our technicians could break into it eventually, but the Jeha will accomplish the task quicker. I suspect the bug has already laced the system with backdoors and shortcuts."

"Then why the stress?" Nxo sipped from his half-empty glass. Many races found the juice intoxicating, but Nevar only found it mildly soothing.

"Someone hired this Khabar captain and provided him with specific information. They targeted the chest containing the red diamonds and picked the correct transport over three decoys. How could they know which ship was correct?"

"Ulaan Beta provides a steady stream of red diamonds. The mines are heavily guarded by mercenary garrisons." Nxo scratched under his beak. "Spies could have compromised one or more of the mercenary units. Someone on site would have had to know which transport received the genuine crate and relay the info to the waiting pirates."

"Perhaps we should rotate out the existing garrisons? We could pay their contracts in full and replace them," Dbo suggested. She half-closed her four eyes as she dipped her beak into the juice.

"Current affairs in the Mercenary Guild complicate matters," Nxo said. "The guild has frozen all new contracts until further notice."

Dbo puffed out her crest and neck feathers. "Ridiculous! The rest of the galaxy can't go on hold while waiting for them to finish their petty squabbles."

"Nonetheless, the Mercenary Guild is closed for business."

"What will the mercenary races do without merc revenue?" Dbo asked. "The Human war left them so destitute, they cannot repatriate their forces stranded on Earth, even the ones not held prisoner. The Humans are in just as bad shape, or worse. Their Mercenary Guild representative agreed to a pittance for war reparations, and their economy relies heavily on the mercenary industry."

A plan formed in Nxo's mind. "We will supplement mine security with golems and rotate existing mercenary units."

"Where will we get additional golems? Recruitment is down 20%. We are losing organic operators faster than we can replace them," Dbo protested.

"I fear service isn't as important to more recent generations." Nxo ruffled his feathers. "We will bring in additional security forces at the mint facilities so we can spread out the existing stock of golems."

"Where will we get more troops, especially with the contract embargo in place?"

"You will go to Earth," Nxo declared. "You will hire any mercenaries seeking repatriation and make an offer to the Human government for their prisoners."

"We can't write new mercenary contracts," Dbo countered.

"Then we'll hire them as well-paid security guards," Nxo countered. "Who needs a contract with a fistful of credits?"

* * * * *

Chapter Eleven

Houston Startown, Earth

"We've been to four alien bars so far, and we haven't gotten squat other than almost eaten at the last one," Sergeant Cripe complained.

"I know, but we have to see this through," Charlotte said. She peered around the sparsely populated hole-in-the wall restaurant. Brightly colored Mexican décor contrasted with the cracked concrete and aging brick. They'd discovered the establishment two days ago across from their hotel. What it lacked in architectural ambience it made up for in the food.

"How long will it take for Commander T to throw in the towel?" Tamara asked over the remains of her burrito. The generous portions were challenging to finish. "He's footing the bill for us to bar hop while everyone else loads the materials at the Redoubt or picks through the debris at Bear Town."

"Do not look a gift Equiri in the fangs." Vurrn burped over his empty plate.

"Gift horse, but yeah." Charlotte poked at the last of the beans and rice from her lunch. She'd passed on the burrito and its calorie laden tortilla. "We're only halfway through Gus and Roscoe's list, and that assumes we don't go back to any of the places we've already visited."

"We're not going back to Muffet's, are we?" Cripe asked. "I didn't know Tortantulas went to bars, and I thought Oogar were mean drunks."

"I don't believe the Tortantulas were intoxicated," Vurrn said.

"No, we'll avoid Muffet's," Charlotte said.

"Maybe we should take Roscoe and Gus with us?" Tamara suggested. "We're three Humans and a Zuul walking into predominantly alien bars. If we had the Jivool, it would even things out."

Charlotte sighed. While not as foul tempered as Oogar, the Jivool had a reputation for boisterousness. "I can't wait until Stefan gets the expense vouchers for these bar tabs."

* * *

"All right, chow time!" Charlotte stepped aside and waited for her eyes to adjust to the dim interior after stepping out of the noonday sun. Once she could see enough not to trip, she carried two sacks to the break room.

"Lunch?" Gus poked his head out of the office, only for Roscoe to shove him aside.

The black-striped Jivool shuffled forward. "It smells delicious." Roscoe paused and lowered his ears in disappointment. "No guacamole?"

"Sorry guys, there's some sort of avocado shortage." The waiter had provided a lengthy explanation—something about California and the United States cutting off shipments to Texas. Charlotte suspected the waiter hung out at their table to flirt with her and Tamara as opposed to wanting to discuss the political economics of avocados. "They'll have some from Mexico in a couple of days, assuming the cartels don't get involved."

Gus snarled and said in Jivool, "Remember, Rosko'gurin, half is mine." Both Jivool sported grey vests with Berserker patches on them. The Jivool had learned some English and Spanish, but they still wore translators which helpfully rendered their native bickering.

"It was a misunderstanding," Roscoe protested. He'd eaten all half dozen super burritos two days ago. He held out his paws so Charlotte could loop the handles of the two bags from Tio Burrito's over his claws. "Thank you, Sergeant Whisky."

"I have a job for you two," Charlotte said.

Roscoe paused halfway to the breakroom where Gus waited. "Now?"

"No. I want you to come to the bar we're checking out tonight," Charlotte replied.

Both of the Jivools' ears perked up. "If we are working, will you pay for our drinks?" Gus asked.

"Within limits. I'll give you some money for drinks, but once it's gone, you're on your own credits. No getting trashed and no trashing the bar. Got it?"

Both Jivool nodded. "Do not worry, Sergeant Whisky. Jivool can hold their alcohol," Roscoe said before disappearing into the break room.

"Half of the chips are mine!" Gus shouted.

* * *

"It may have belonged to the Berserkers back when my dad did business with them," Vurrn observed.

More like grandfather, Keith Cripe thought. Weather and time had worn away patches of the matte, charcoal grey paint on the troop transport rumbler. None of the three wheels facing Cripe matched. A patch of sanded armor marked the usual location for a unit logo. The faded designation TT009 matched the font used by the Berserkers.

"This heap is older than I am," Cripe remarked.

Vurrn laughed. "It held up better. Surprising for Human engineering."

"What do you think?" the salesman asked. Sanchez's Used Vehicles offered a wide variety of 'gently used' vehicles from the aftermath of the war. Dozens of vehicles littered the lot, ranging from pristine to borderline derelicts. "It fits the bill, right? It's a bargain at 1,000 credits."

"A thousand! Are you shitting me?" Cripe demanded. *Did this guy think he was dealing with a rookie right out of cadre?* "You've stripped the weapon out of the support turret, the tires are all second- or third-hand, and half the servos for the ramp don't work. Remember, we're paying in hard credits, not Earth dollars, or US dollars, or whatever the hell the Terran Feds are calling their currency."

"This is not a contractor van; this is a military grade vehicle," the salesman countered.

"It's half a century old!" Cripe protested. He and Vurrn had combed the lot for three hours, trying to find something suitable and in their price range that would run.

Vurrn stepped forward. "Everything on this rumbler is outdated, and it's held together by a patchwork of repairs. One of the batteries is shot and another is at 50%, no one has serviced the drive motors for a decade, the suspension is out of alignment, three of the illumination lamps don't work, and it stinks. Given its age and actual number of operational hours, it might be worth what you ask if none of these issues existed."

"What he said," Cripe said. "I'll give you 500 hard credits, assuming it drives off the lot."

"Six hundred and I'll throw in an air freshener," the salesman countered.

"Fifty credits is a lot for an air freshener," Cripe remarked with a glance at the pine tree dangling in the cab. He drove the rumbler over the curb and into the street, hoping he didn't lose any teeth in the process. A scooter beeped as it zipped around them.

"Did you want to spend another half an hour haggling over 50 credits?" Vurrn asked from the passenger seat. Cripe half expected the Zuul to stick his head out the open window. Galactics didn't seem to grasp the value credits held on Earth. The exchange rate had been creeping up. Fifty credits was over 2,000 American dollars.

"I suppose not." Cripe wrinkled his nose. Even with the windows rolled down, the odor persisted. "I'll have Gus and Roscoe try to clean this heap out."

"I hate to admit it, but Jivool possess a keener sense of smell than Zuul," Vurrn remarked.

Despite detours around ruins from the Omega War, it only took Sergeant Cripe ten minutes to drive back to the Berserkers' warehouse. He only spotted one reconstruction site—a logistics hub for an off-world trading company.

Cripe rolled the rumbler over to the charging station next to the warehouse. Whisky stepped out and shaded her eyes with her hand. The corner of her mouth crooked as she descended the steps.

"How old is this vic?" she called.

"Didn't anyone ever tell you not to judge something by its age?" Cripe countered.

"Yeah. Creepy older guys trying to pick me up in bars use the line all the time," Whisky said. The young woman reminded Cripe of a little sister, not a scout squad sergeant, but he'd seen her in action. Cripe almost felt sorry for the creepy old dudes. Almost. "At least tell me you got a decent deal on it."

"More than I wanted to pay, but less than we expected to spend," Cripe replied. He connected the heavy charging cable and waited for the green light. "I hope we don't end up driving this beast home—I mean to where Bear Town used to be."

One of the Jivool emerged, squinting in the daylight. The black stripes meant it was Roscoe. He snarled something over his shoulder that Cripe's translator didn't pick up. The other Jivool squeezed out through the door, and they both shuffled toward the rumbler.

Gus scrutinized the vehicle. "Have Bjorn's Berserkers fallen on hard times?"

"It would explain why the warehouse was empty," Roscoe said. "Something stinks. Is there a dead animal in the rumbler?"

"Maybe. I need you guys to give this rolling wreck a good cleaning," Cripe said.

Both Jivool turned toward Whisky. "We bought it so you guys can ride with us. So, unless you want to ride in a smelly vic, scrub it out."

Gus cocked his head. "Vic?"

"Vehicle," Whisky answered.

"We'll get it clean, Sergeant Whisky," Roscoe promised. He lumbered back into the warehouse.

Gus nodded. "We'll have it done before dinner. What's for dinner?"

* * *

Bear Town, New Mexico, Earth

"Loki-cursed and thrice damned," Bjorn swore.

"You'll have to be more specific," Stefan remarked from his desk. "Problems with the American government?"

"No. I'm trying to figure out what happened to the Besquith captured on Earth at the end of the war," Bjorn replied, tugging on his beard. "They locked up the werewolves, mantises, and rats. If you ask me, they should shoot the Veetanho and be done with it."

"Not the other two?" Stefan asked.

"I'm surprised they rounded up the MinSha, but I guess their sense of honor is a double-edged sword. Some MinSha considered what Peepo wanted dishonorable and sided with humanity, while others felt bound by their oath to serve. It didn't help that a MinSha fleet destroyed several colony worlds." Bjorn picked up his half-empty coffee, but it had gone cold. "As for the Besquith, I want to end them myself. Specifically, the *sukin syn* responsible for killing my dad and the Berserkers on the flight to Alaska."

"The Besquith weren't the only ones involved. A Cartel State jet from Coahuila shot down one of our planes." Stefan took the coffee pot and filled Bjorn's cup. "The Americans didn't keep them from engaging. If you have a list, you'd spend a long time checking it off."

"I already checked off Rodrigo Sanchez—you can bet he instigated the Cartel's involvement. Peepo vanished, and I owe her for every Berserker who died on the Patoka contract. If she does turn up, it will be somewhere out of my reach. I'll settle for what justice I can get." Bjorn was dividing his attention between justifying making some Besquith rugs and juggling the ongoing torrent of messages cascading through his pinview. He shuffled as many as possible to others, cursorily checking subject lines. "Why did Cripe buy a used rumbler in Houston?"

Stefan referenced his slate. "They needed something big enough to haul the new Jivool recruits guarding the warehouse. They're helping Whisky's team make contacts in the alien mercenary underground in startown, and they won't fit in an autocab."

"When did we hire Jivool?" Bjorn demanded. Despite the popularity of bear totems in the Berserkers, Bjorn had hated the beasts since one mangled his arm as a kid. Ursine aliens such as Jivool and Oogar set his nerves on edge.

"Since Whisky found them squatting in the Houston depot and recruited them," Stefan replied. "You gave her broad latitude regarding her mission and signed off on the hiring form."

A reminder popped up in Bjorn's pinview. "I need to head into Las Cruces. Don't stay out here all night. We're paying for your room in Organ, so you might as well use it. I've heard some recommendations for the Thai Place. Take a break from merc rations."

"Spicy food gives me heartburn," Stefan said. "I don't mind a little blandness in my diet."

* * *

Organ, New Mexico, Earth

"I hear that if you prefer some heat in your food, this is the place," Glen Brand stated as they drove in front of the restaurant. The sun-bleached sign read 'Pho Sure.' "You'd think it would be the Tex Mex or traditional Mexican restaurants."

"If you add in the Dairy Barn and Basta Burgers, you've summed up all of the eateries in Organ," Jim Hawkins said. The tiny town straddled the highway halfway between Bear Town's ruins and Las Cruces. The Berserkers rented out every room in both motels to supplement the tent town assembled at Bear Town. "However, anything here beats the mystery loaf they're serving in the mess tent tonight."

"Mystery loaf does not qualify as meat, no?" Hcufft asked. The H'rang had wedged himself between Priya and the door. Three people in the back seat of the LPT made for a tight fit. "My nose says no."

"The mystery loaf might not taint my karma, but it would not please my palate," Priya remarked. She wasn't a militant vegetarian, but she eschewed meat when convenient.

"We might be out of luck," Gina said. Parked vehicles spilled from the gravel parking lot and lined the street. They'd passed the Dairy Barn as they pulled off the highway, and cars engulfed the parking lot there as well.

"We'll get a table," Glen proclaimed as he waited for a car to pull out.

Even though Pho Sure didn't appear to be the kind of establishment that took reservations, Jim suspected Glen had made arrangements. They could have gone into Las Cruces and found somewhere to eat, but the motel was three blocks away. Perhaps it was a bit too convenient if Glen had plans for later that night. Gina and Priya shared a room, as did Corporal Brand and Hcuff't. Did Glen know Priya would spend the evening in Jim's room?

Glen powered down the LPT. "Here we go. The finest Thai dining from the San Andres Mountains to Las Cruces."

"This is the only settlement between the mountains and the city, yes?" Hcuff't asked.

"He's being funny," Gina replied, placing her hand on Glen's arm.

Jim suspected what would happen if Priya spent the night with him, leaving Gina with a room to herself. Maybe Gina was still gun shy after Diller? Jim climbed out of the personnel transport. He couldn't babysit everyone, and Gina was an adult. He shouldn't meddle unless Brand did something predatory.

Most of the patrons wore Berserkers' dark grey BDUs. Several watched as Jim's party threaded through the ersatz 'patio' dining to find the hostess at the door. A few of the troopers expressed dismay that Gina would show interest in a POG like Glen, instead of a trooper, CASPer or infantry. Those who realized Pastor Jim could hear them bit their tongue.

Glen handed the hostess a note and a credit chit. Jim couldn't make out the denomination, but the hostess seemed satisfied.

"This way, please." She guided them around the building to several tables shaded by an awning. The restaurant had converted a quarter of its parking lot to outdoor seating. Fans provided a breeze under the canvas while electric insect repellents drove off the bugs. The hostess gestured to a table with a handwritten 'reserved' sign. "Your server will be with you shortly. Enjoy your meal."

Glen pulled out a chair for Gina. He'd taken no notice of the attractive hostess—Jim had watched. Priya cleared her throat.

"Sorry, my mind wandered." Jim drew back Priya's chair.

"You weren't distracted by the hostess, were you?" Priya teased as she took her seat.

"Of course not, I was thinking—" Jim caught himself from sprawling on the gravel when Hcufft yanked out his chair. Jim shot the H'rang an accusatory glare.

Hcufft cocked his head. "It is part of the game, yes? Pull away the chair as they sit?"

"No." Jim scowled, dragging his chair back. "Pulling out a chair for a lady is a polite gesture. It's not a prank."

The cat-like alien twitched an ear and claimed a seat. "More courting rituals, yes?"

The server's arrival headed off further discussion of the vagaries of Human dating. Jim noticed Glen passed on ordering beer in favor of iced tea—a point in his favor. Jim didn't oppose drinking; he had a beer or two occasionally. However, experience had taught him young men, and even not-so-young men, made poor choices when alcohol entered the mix.

"So, when is Priya going to get her corporal back?" Jim asked after drinks arrived. The iced tea was adequate. "I thought you guys had Bettie up and running."

"We do. As soon as we established communications between the server room and the surface facility, someone tried hacking the comm network," Gina said. "Glen has been helping me hunt down the sniffer."

Jim pushed paternal instincts and dating propriety aside. "Someone is trying to break into Bettie? How would they even know...?" Another mole? Morale had already taken a hit when Diller's treachery came to light on Patoka.

"Two ways—a spy or a device planted to detect the data traffic from the server," Glen interjected. "I lean toward the second theory."

Gina nodded. "Even with outside workers on site, people rotate in and out too much for a spy to keep track of our progress. We'd have trouble spotting a small and innocuous sniffer. Once it detected traffic, it could signal via cell towers."

"Who do you think is behind it?" Jim asked.

"The Golden Horde and the American government top the list of suspects," Gina replied. The arrival of their food interrupted the speculation.

Once the server departed, Priya asked, "Why would the Golden Horde spy on us? We're allies. We sheltered with several Horde members in Alaska, during the occupation."

"Sansar Enkh keeps as close an eye on her friends and allies as she does her enemies," Jim remarked. He expected that Colonel Enkh considered the Berserkers allies rather than friends. "I find it plausible she would want to keep tabs on us, especially since we haven't joined the mercs rallying around the new Terran Federation government. She could consider us a risk, or she may believe it's for our own good."

"All reasons why we put the Horde on the list of probable hackers," Glen remarked.

Gina covered her mouth as she hurriedly chewed a mouthful of Pad Thai. "However, the Horde would cover their tracks. They had access to an iteration of Bettie during the occupation. These attempts appear rushed."

"Hence why the American authorities are at the top of the list," Glen added. "They lack the technical finesse, and if they want an edge on the commander, they need to act fast. I…Hcufft, are you okay?"

The H'rang's mouth hung open and his tongue rippled. "Yes. This curry shrimp is delicious," he rasped.

"Have you told the commander?" Jim asked. Given their recent experiences, Commander Tovesson wouldn't take someone spying on him lightly.

"Bettie beat us to the punch, but he asked for our insight. He seemed pissed off," Gina replied.

* * *

Las Cruces, New Mexico, Earth

"Trip, aren't you staying for dinner?"

Bjorn adjusted his tie. He hated the damned things. "Sorry, Mom. I'm going to a dinner meeting."

"Is this dinner meeting with Heather?" his mother asked. "Should I be concerned?"

"Yes, Heather will be there, but no, you shouldn't worry," Bjorn replied. Last time he wore this jacket, a deep breath had threatened to launch a button. It was his third date with Talita. He'd shed the garrison weight since then. "I'm not going to piss things away back home for a fling with an old flame. Besides, several politicians are joining us—I'm getting my free meal out of them."

"Why didn't you wear a zipper tie?" His mother plucked at the knot and adjusted it. "It was the only way I could get your father to wear one."

"I left it back on Vishall," Bjorn replied before the specter of his father's death smothered them. "Speaking of which—have you given any more thought to moving there?"

"I don't know. I'm not sure I'm up to moving to an alien world," his mother replied. "I see your father everywhere I turn here, and most days it's not a bad thing. Moving off-world would feel like leaving him behind."

"At least come for a visit. If you want to wait, we can plan it around the baby's arrival." It might have been dirty pool to play the grandchild card, but it would motivate his mother to overcome her reticence regarding space travel.

Lynn Tovesson narrowed her eyes. "No fair, but you're right. I could visit, spend some time with my daughter-in-law and grand-baby, and see this tropic paradise."

"See? That wasn't so hard."

"Stay out of the tequila tonight. You need to keep your wits about you, and Heather always knew how to manipulate you," his mother cautioned.

"Don't worry. I plan on keeping a clear mind tonight," Bjorn countered. "Politicians lie as part of their profession, and I have some questions."

* * *

"Here you go," the cab driver declared as he pulled to the curb in front of the swanky restaurant. The small, affluent district had sprung up when Bjorn still attended school. A cluster of tech and finance businesses filled a handful of gleaming towers. Businesses such as the restaurant, Bravia, opened to cater to the tenants of the high-rises as well as those in the surrounding affluent neighborhood.

Sporadic network outages impaired autonomous vehicles in the United States. Bjorn wouldn't trust a robotic flyer, and he considered paying a little extra for a Human behind the wheel of a ground car a sound investment. He handed the driver a 10-credit chit. "If you know what this is, you might want to squirrel it away for hard times."

The driver's eyes bugged. This morning's exchange rates valued it at $650 American. "You think things can get worse than an alien invasion?"

"We were killing each other for millennia before the aliens showed up," Bjorn replied. "Things will deteriorate before they get better."

"Thanks. If you want, I can hang out nearby, and you can let me know when you need a ride home," the driver said. "I can give you my comm number and grab a bite to eat."

"Ping me your comm number. I'll tip you the same for the return trip." Bjorn acknowledged the contact in his pinview.

A dozen well-dressed people lingered in the foyer, a few clutching pucks to notify them when their table became available. Most of the crowd instinctively parted for Bjorn as he made his way to the maître d, but Heather flagged him over to an alcove.

"You beat our esteemed hosts," Heather remarked over the murmur of the crowd. Her dress accentuated her curves while maintaining an air of primness. She reached out and adjusted Bjorn's lapel. "You still clean up nice. I'm sure it's no accident your suit, tie, and shirt adhere to the Berserkers' grey on grey palette."

"I couldn't wear my dress uniform," Bjorn said. His tie clip bore the Berserkers' logo, and the rune from the logo marked his cufflinks. Heather's hand rested on his chest, and Bjorn remembered his mother's caution. "The bearskin cloak gets hot."

Heather's fingers slid down his jacket as Bjorn shifted back. "You're armed?"

"Of course. Even if aliens hadn't tried to assassinate Colonel Cartwright, I'd be an idiot to walk around unarmed," Bjorn replied, adjusting his suit jacket. "If your pals have a problem with it, there's leftovers in the fridge back at my house."

"Inviting me home?" Heather smiled with a twinkle in her eye. "A tempting offer, but it would vex the people who write the checks."

Was she trying to fluster him? Protesting he wasn't inviting her anywhere would elicit a pout. It was easier to let the remark pass. "Can't have that—at least not until I've talked to them."

A commotion at the entrance heralded the arrival of the rest of their party. A pair of security agents pushed through the waiting patrons until they reached the maître d. The animated discussion revealed no one had thought to make reservations. One of the security guards spotted Bjorn and Heather and threaded through the crowd.

"It will be 20 to 30 minutes before the table is available," the agent stated. "The governor says if you wish to avail yourself of the bar, feel free."

Bjorn shrugged. "Why not have a beer before dinner?" A paranoid person would suspect they wanted to get a few drinks in him before he sat at the table.

'Monitor and display blood alcohol level,' Bjorn commanded his pinplants. He led the way to the bar, and they squeezed in a gap between patrons also awaiting tables. Heather leaned against him from the press of the crowd.

Was she flirting with him or trying to distract him so he wouldn't focus on whatever the politicians pitched? Two could play that game. "I hired Berto. He's a captain in the firm now."

Heather stiffened. "I'm surprised. I know the two of you buried the hatchet after the firefight in Houston, but his working for you is something else."

The bartender interrupted them to take their orders. Bjorn stuck to a simple beer while Heather ordered wine.

"It took guts for him to apply," Bjorn stated. "His credentials were rock solid, and I thought it was better to bring on someone I know than a total stranger."

"So, tell me about Talita," Heather said once the bartender delivered their drinks.

Bjorn paused for a draw of beer. An odd question if she was flirting, even if it was to keep him on his toes. "She's from the Human colony on Vishall, and her family is Brazilian. She worked at my favorite watering spot while the Berserkers served a garrison contract there."

"A waitress?" Heather sipped her wine. "I thought you might end up with a mercenary or maybe a more professional type—you know, a lawyer or a banker."

"Talita's feisty enough to be a merc," Bjorn countered. He didn't mention that Heather's transformation from cheerleader to lawyer surprised him. "I'll be glad to wrap up business here and get back to her."

"You're still committed to leaving Earth?" Heather pouted. She placed her free hand on his arm. "That will disappoint a lot of people, myself included."

Time to redirect this conversation. Bjorn said, "You have an extra surname, but no ring, I noticed. If you don't mind my asking, is there a Mister Dodd or any little Dodds?"

"Eric and I divorced last year," Heather replied after another sip of wine. "We didn't have children, which I have mixed feelings about. By the time I felt comfortable with my career, I was no longer confident about my marriage. Turned out I was right—I walked in on him and his legal assistant in his office."

Bjorn grunted. What could he say? They finished their drinks in awkward silence. Bjorn debated the wisdom of a second round when one of the security detail caught his attention. "Our table must be ready," Bjorn said.

Heather followed in Bjorn's wake as he carved a path through the crowd. The security guard guided them to a round table adjacent to the patio. The large, open doors allowed a cool evening breeze to enter.

"We requested a private table. Do you know who I am? I'm Governor Fayed."

The maître d seemed unimpressed. "With all due apologies, governor, no one made a reservation and the private rooms are occupied. This is the first table large enough to accommodate your party. Will it suffice, or do you wish to wait longer?"

"This will be fine," Senator Ortega interceded. "I see the rest of our party has arrived, so let's sit down."

Bjorn pulled out a chair for Heather before he realized what he was doing. He sat next to her with his back to the wall. He scanned the others. "Representative O'Connell still grounded?"

"Mr. O'Connell returned to Washington," Senator Ortega replied with a hint of a grin. She must consider the man a fool as well. "This is Representative Yvonne West from Louisiana."

"Representative West." Bjorn reached across the table and shook her hand.

"A pleasure to meet you, Commander Tovesson," the dark-skinned woman replied. "Your industry provides valuable employment to our community, and I'm appreciative of that."

"Thank you." How appreciative would she be when she found out the Berserkers had moved shop? At least she didn't sneer, like O'Connell.

"Have you considered bringing the Berserkers back home?" Governor Fayed asked after the waiter departed with their drink orders.

"Julian, couldn't you at least wait until we order our food?" Senator Ortega chided.

"I've seen the funding projections. Mister…I mean Commander Tovesson's mercenary academy is a fine enough idea, but it will be years before it pays dividends," the governor protested. "We need operating funds right away."

"The federal government suffers from the same shortfall, Julian," Ortega snapped. "Employment remains low, so the populace relies on the safety net."

"Is it a safety net if they won't risk the high wire?" Bjorn muttered. Heather elbowed him and Senator Ortega flashed him a steely glare.

"This isn't a joke!" Governor Fayed cried. Lowering his voice, he continued, "FedMart and its suppliers will run dry in a matter of weeks."

"This is why we have to outlaw American farmers selling their goods to foreign powers," Representative Dorado declared. "We should nationalize the agriculture industry to ensure the food the farmers grow feeds Americans first."

Senator Ortega frowned. "I doubt repeating mistakes made in the 20th century will prove fruitful. Commander Tovesson's glib remark contains a kernel of truth. The people should be encouraged to work rather than wait on the government dole. We became complacent when off-world money filled our coffers."

The waiter coughed politely. "Excuse me, would anyone care for an appetizer?"

Once the waiter fled, Bjorn leaned forward on his elbows. "This is all fascinating, but I'll tell you right now, Governor, I'm not bringing the Berserkers back to Earth. As you said, it will take years for my idea to bear fruit. One of the reasons I'm still in business is that I play a long game, same as my father and my grandfather."

"With all due respect, Commander, we don't have years," Representative West said. "As the governor said, we have weeks before the shelves run out."

"Why?" Bjorn asked.

"We won't have the money to pay the farmers and food manufacturers," Dorado replied.

"So, the factories will grind to a halt and the farmers will leave their crops in the fields?" Bjorn paused to pick up one of the delivered appetizers. It seemed gauche to do so while arguing over the country's food running out, but his stomach rumbled. "Pressure the banks. Have them grant amnesty to anyone in the food supply chain for six months. Arrange terms to delay portions of the producers' payments but keep the goods flowing. Then fundamentally overhaul your tax system. Incentivize people to work, and make the bankers, brokers, and other people getting rich with other folks' money pay up."

Bjorn paused to devour his appetizer and lick his fingers clean. It was a loaded potato skin despite whatever fancy name the restaurant used.

"Our constituents won't stand for it," Dorado protested matter-of-factly.

"You mean your campaign donors?" Bjorn picked up another fancy potato skin. "I get it. You're afraid that if you tax the people who bankroll you, they'll find a new set of politicians to replace you.

You have to decide what's more important—the next election or what happens in the next few weeks when funding shortages paralyze the supply chain."

"Commander Tovesson, maybe you should consider politics," Senator Ortega remarked. "Julian is up for reelection next year."

Governor Fayed froze, a cocktail shrimp in sauce dangling from his fingers. "What? No, that's a terrible idea. No offense, Commander Tovesson."

"None taken. I'd rather face laser-armed werewolves any day than deal with the press, lobbyists, protesters, and other politicians," Bjorn said with a grin. "No offense."

The political debate faded as the waiter delivered the main course. Bjorn's mouth watered at the aroma of the succulent steak. It was farm-raised as opposed to vat grown, which made it twice as good and ten times as expensive. Bjorn glanced at Heather's plate. Colorful vegetables surrounded a miniscule portion of chicken. Some things never changed.

"Should we ask them to put half in a to-go box now?" Bjorn muttered.

Heather playfully elbowed him. "Very funny. At least I'm not stealing your fries…yet."

Bjorn caught Senator Ortega watching the interplay. If she wasn't the one who recruited Heather to bring Bjorn to the table, Ortega at least knew of their past and hoped for some advantage.

Once Bjorn finished off all 16 ounces of steak and another beer, he decided it was time to open a can of worms. "I have a question, Senator Ortega—why is the American government trying to hack my server at our White Sands facility?"

Heather choked on her wine. Governor Fayed's eyes went wide. Dorado and West both looked at Senator Ortega.

The Senator thoughtfully chewed a bite of salmon. "To be honest, I'd be surprised if several different agencies weren't attempting to gain access to your systems. Until your proclamation, your firm was the largest American mercenary outfit. Unlike several other companies, you didn't scamper off to Texas to join Cartwright's coup, so you could have some useful intel that would be damaging to Mr. Cartwright's reputation. If a request came across my desk to approve snooping on your operations, I would approve it in a heartbeat." She carved off another piece of salmon. "However, I am unaware of any intelligence gathering efforts regarding you or the Berserkers, Commander Tovesson."

"How do you know it wasn't the new Terran Federation or one of the Horsemen?" Dorado asked. "They could be worried we'll turn you against them."

Bjorn held up his thumb. "One—I'm certain one of the Horsemen are already in my system, so they wouldn't need a messy hacking attempt to find out something." He extended his index finger. "Two—there's no 'against them' unless we're on opposite sides of a contract, and the Berserkers don't take contracts that require fighting other Human mercenaries." He added his middle finger. "Three— there's nothing in my systems of interest to the Horsemen. To be honest, there's nothing of interest to the American government either, but I doubt you'll take my word for it."

"It could be one of the Terran Federation nations, without the knowledge of the Horsemen," Heather suggested. "Either because the other mercenaries would object, or to give them plausible deniability."

"It's a possibility," Bjorn admitted, picking up his beer. Between pacing his drinking and the large meal, the blood-alcohol display remained low. Ortega's calm reaction disappointed him. He had hoped for a blustering protestation of innocence. Heather leaned close to whisper something in his ear, but he cut her off. "Something isn't right."

'Bettie, scan local emergency and first responder channels for activity in a one-kilometer radius from my position.'

BTI: 'Working. Closest node in Bear Town Prime. Parsing communication networks.'

The crowd noise beyond the patio changed. Cries of alarm punctuated the regular murmur. The traffic shifted, moving away from the closest street. People broke into a run.

"Where's your security detail?" Bjorn demanded.

A blast rattled the open doors and sent the crowd outside scrambling. A white van plowed into pedestrians too slow to escape. The doors in the side of the van swung open, and half a dozen gunmen burst out onto the pavement. They all wore black clothes, except for a red scarf covering their faces below sunglasses or goggles. They all bore infantry-style rifles.

"Get down!" Bjorn shouted. 'Enable combat targeting.' Outlines highlighted the armed men emerging from the van in Bjorn's pinview. Bjorn scooped Heather behind him with his left arm and reached into his jacket and drew his 12mm Heckler & Glock with his right.

"This is a gun-free zone!" the governor gasped.

"Tell it to them," Bjorn retorted. One of the gunmen sprayed the restaurant with a burst while his fellows fanned out. Shattering glass and frightened cries added to the cacophony.

A targeting reticle appeared in Bjorn's pinview, following the aim of his pistol. As soon as it centered on the head of the gunman blazing away, Bjorn squeezed the trigger. The shooter's goggles exploded.

Bjorn marched forward, hugging the wall. An attacker knelt behind a decorative planter, exchanging fire with the security guards at the entrance. The concrete planter concealed the shooter from the guards, but not Bjorn, once he crossed the patio. Bjorn's pistol boomed and the gunman slumped to the pavement.

Bjorn hunkered low and scurried to the planter. The other shooters had fanned out and didn't know they had serious opposition. A bullet hissed past Bjorn's ear, and two more cracked against the planter. So much for that theory; at least one of them had figured out they were taking return fire.

Bjorn switched his pistol to his left hand. When the H'rang surgeon installed Bjorn's pinplants, he hadn't realized Humans were wired for handedness. She corrected the 'defect,' making Bjorn ambidextrous. While he preferred to shoot with his flesh and blood hand, he'd rather risk his cybernetic left arm getting shot.

Another spray of gunfire accompanied by a staccato muzzle flash gave away the assailant. One of the bullets caromed off Bjorn's artificial hand, glancing off an armored knuckle. Bjorn centered the reticle on the shooter's chest. *Boom!*

The security detail dropped another red-scarfed gunman. Bjorn advanced to the next piece of cover, the stopped van. Electric motors hummed, and the vehicle began to roll away.

"No, you don't!" Bjorn seized the van behind the front wheel well, dropping his pistol in the process. With a roar, he lifted and tipped the van up. A warning lit in his pinview—he was risking damage to his flesh-and-blood body from the exerted forces. With a metallic groan and plastic crunch, the van flopped on its side.

Bjorn grabbed his gun. If not for the nanite hardening treatment applied to all CASPer troopers, any of his joints could have buckled under the strain. As it was, he'd be sore in the morning.

A volley of bullets *spanged* off the van as soon as Bjorn poked his pistol out. The sixth gunman hadn't been firing. Bjorn pictured the battlefield from above. What would the enemy do?

130 | JON R. OSBORNE

When the sixth attacker popped around the back of the van, Bjorn yanked the gunman's rifle away hard enough to rip the shooter's trigger finger off his hand. Bjorn's right fist hammered the man below the wraparound sunglasses and shattered his nose.

Only Number Five remained. Bjorn spotted him across the street, with one arm around the neck of a man in a business suit. The red-masked gunman leveled his rifle at Bjorn. "I have a hostage! Throw down your gun or I'll—"

Bjorn's first bullet blew off the man's middle finger below the trigger guard. As the rifle jerked away, Bjorn's second shot shattered his wrist. To the hostage's credit, he dove for the pavement as soon as the gunman's grip slackened. The rifle clattered to the sidewalk. Bjorn's third round hit the black-clad man dead center in his chest.

Two rounds left. Bjorn eyed the van, where the driver struggled against his seat belt. Bjorn tapped on the windshield with the barrel of his pistol. The driver raised his hands. Bjorn safed his weapon and holstered it as he marched back toward the restaurant.

"Is everyone all right?" Bjorn climbed over the railing separating the patio from the street. Diners who were crouched under their tables rose in his wake. Senator Ortega had already returned to her seat, speaking on the phone in low, urgent tones. The governor remained hunkered down while he yelled into his phone.

Heather still leaned against the wall, pale and wide-eyed. She nodded, her eyes dipping to Bjorn's holstered pistol. "I guess it's lucky you were never good at following rules."

"I don't suppose anyone knows what the Hel that was about?" Bjorn asked.

BTI: 'Law enforcement response in 90 seconds. Medical first responders ETA 3 minutes. Multiple incidents reported.'

Angry shouts and breaking glass sounded in the distance. A flash of orange outlined buildings to the north. A distant boom elicited cries from the milling crowd drawn by the aftermath of the attack. Some idiots snapped pictures of themselves in front of the toppled van.

BTI: 'Additional emergency calls. I have triangulated three pockets of rioting in downtown Las Cruces. Law enforcement is calling in all personnel. Fire department is calling in all personnel. Medical first—'

'I get it, Bettie. How far is the closest incident to my position?'

BTI: 'Approximately 200 meters.'

"*Sukin syn*," Bjorn swore.

"The Red Justice Front wear all black with red masks," Representative West stated. "They're self-proclaimed equality terrorists, but until now they've limited their activities to rabble rousing and rock throwing."

"There are three riots underway, or maybe one big, spread out one. The closest is too close for comfort, especially since I'm almost out of ammo," Bjorn said. 'Bettie, connect me to the officer-in-command at Bear Town.'

BTI: 'Channel open.'

"This is Bruin Actual. I need the on-deck flyer for an evac operation." Bjorn insisted the Berserkers keep a VTOL ready to go at all times, as well as two squads of infantry. The latter patrolled Bear Town, or rather the land it once sat on.

"This is Captain Duarte, OIC." Figures Berto would be on duty. "Do you need additional support?"

The law forbade deploying CASPers outside of mercenary bases, but the former Earth Republic passed the law. However, using CASPers now could set an uneasy precedent. "Pull one of the infantry squads on patrol and warm up another flyer. There is a civil disturbance underway."

Governor Fayed fumbled his phone. "You're going to deploy mercenary forces against civilians?"

Bjorn shot the man an irritated glare and continued, "We'll only call in the troops if Berserker assets or personnel are in danger."

"Maybe you should hire them, Julian," Representative Dorado suggested. "They are better trained and better armed than your state guard."

"You can't afford us, even if we wanted to break the precedent of conducting operations on Earth," Bjorn countered. He opened a satellite map of the neighborhood in his pinview. "If you prefer to wait with your security forces, knock yourselves out. I have a ride showing up on the roof in five minutes."

Heather grabbed his hand. "I'm not waiting."

Shouting and breaking glass rose above the murmur of the crowd on the street. The first police cars arrived, their red and blue lights splashing across the plaza. Unless more cops arrived, these would hardly delay an angry mob.

Senator Ortega pocketed her phone. "I believe we should follow Commander Tovesson's suggestion. Even if we had the means to fend off these hooligans, it would only place citizens at risk."

"Yes! We should get out to protect the civilians!" Fayed stood, peering about. "Which way is out?"

Bjorn snagged the closest server. "Where are the stairs up?"

She pointed toward a wooden door behind the maître d's station. "It's locked."

"Not a problem. Thanks." Bjorn handed her a 10-credit chit. It equaled a week's worth of pay and tips. Bjorn didn't wait to see if the representatives followed.

"*Monsieur*, this door is for authorized personnel only!" the maître d protested.

"So, you're not going to open it for me?" Bjorn asked.

"*Non.*"

Bjorn grinned. "Have it your way." He clenched his left fist and punched through the thick wooden door. He grabbed the doorknob on the other side and ripped the hardware from the splintered wood. "Bill the state."

Bjorn kept his pace on the stairs slow enough for Heather to keep up. Ortega, despite her grey hair, followed on Heather's heels. The other three politicians flagged after the first two floors. By the time Bjorn shoved open the roof door six stories up, they had fallen two floors behind.

The incoming communication icon blinked in Bjorn's pinview. "Bruin Actual, this is Huginn Three on approach from the east. ETA 60 seconds."

Below, two more police cars had arrived at the plaza by the time the front ranks of the mob rounded the corner. The first police brandished shotguns. One of them fired his gun into the air, and the crowd balked.

"Not good," Bjorn muttered. "Governor, you need to tell your people to get the Hel out of there before people start dying."

"That riff raff will loot and burn this complex if left unchecked," Governor Fayed replied.

"Julian, insurance will cover property loss," Senator Ortega snapped. "If you don't value lives, consider the public relations debacle!"

The governor gazed at his phone, paralyzed by indecision. The shriek of duct-turbines cut off further conversation as a dark grey shape descended from the evening sky. Wind buffeted the rooftop, kicking up dust and debris.

The door slid open on the side of the aircraft as it touched down. Bjorn leaped into the passenger bay and helped the others up. "Grab a seat and buckle up!" Once the last person boarded, Bjorn hauled the door shut and shouted, "Take us up!"

The VTOL soared into the night sky. Bjorn synced his pinplants to the onboard comms. "Give us a sweep over the plaza below."

"Roger, Commander." The pilot circled the riot below. Bjorn hoped the police got out of there instead of firing on the crowd. The mob shattered the windows of the high-end store across from the restaurant and looted it.

'Bettie, compile a map of incidents based on first responder traffic and dispatch calls.'

BTI: 'Working—uploading map to your pinview.'

The violence centered on the affluent business district and a nearby wealthy neighborhood's entrance. Luckily, the neighborhood wasn't the one containing the Tovesson house—technically, now, Geneva's home. Densely packed, upscale condos formed the neighborhood facing protestors. How long would it take this outbreak to spread?

Bjorn checked the onboard credentials. "Sergeant Terrell, land behind city hall."

"Roger, Commander."

"OIC to Bruin Actual—advise as to sitrep." At least Berto took this seriously. How would he react if he knew Heather was there, clutching Bjorn's arm? Bjorn had no idea why they broke up, but given Heather's fear that Bjorn would become a mercenary when they dated in high school, he could guess.

"Bruin Actual—we are five by five. Keep the other flyer and the squad on alert in case things go sideways. It will be good practice for them."

"Acknowledged."

Huginn Three made a gut-flopping bank and spin before descending to the parking lot behind city hall. The door slid open.

"I ought to bill you for this, but I won't," Bjorn called over the whine of the engines. He moved to the door to help the politicians clamber out. Senator Ortega was the last. "Senator, you need to figure out something fast. How much worse will things get if the shelves run empty?"

"I'm quite aware, Commander. Thank you for the ride."

"Thanks for dinner," Bjorn said before hauling the door shut. "Take us up." Bjorn returned to his seat. "Where should we drop you off?"

"Wherever you're going," Heather replied. "It seems to be the safest."

"Sergeant Terrell, take us to the Tovesson Homestead please."

"We'll be there in three minutes, Commander," the pilot replied. The aircraft surged skyward and spun southwest.

Bjorn leaned close to talk over the screaming turbines. "Are you okay?"

Heather pressed against him as the VTOL swayed. "I don't know. How could you walk out there with them shooting? I remember when you played those VR games with Berto and the others when we were kids, but those were real bullets today. You shot real people. Maybe I should be asking if you're okay?"

"I won't give you a glib answer. In the heat of battle, I don't have time to think about who is on the other side," Bjorn said. "Afterward, I have plenty of time to dwell on it. The opponents I face are only there because someone paid them to be. It's business. Tonight, these guys, it was personal. They could have killed you, they could have killed me, and who knows how many others they hurt or killed? I had no qualms pulling the trigger on those assholes."

Bjorn checked the updated map in his pinview. The riots raged in the denser business and shopping districts. They hadn't spread into other residential neighborhoods, and private security had dispersed the group threatening the condos. Bjorn set a daemon with Bettie to warn him if the unrest drew close to the old family home.

The VTOL circled once before landing. The neighbors had hated it when Bjorn's father used VTOLs for the commute to Bear Town. Let them get ticked—if they watched the news, they might welcome the Berserker aircraft. At least Geneva had kept the old VTOL pad in the backyard clear. Landing the flyer in her flowers would have pissed her off. The door glided open.

Bjorn hopped out first so he could help Heather clamber down. Bjorn shouted, "Sergeant, take your bird back to Bear Town. Thanks for the lift."

The sergeant flashed a thumbs up. As soon as Bjorn led Heather away from the VTOL, it launched skyward.

Bjorn led Heather to the back door. The patio doors leading into the kitchen were fakes composed of bullet-proof duraplas. Bjorn could see his mother watching through them. The security system recognized Bjorn and unlocked as he reached for the handle of the back door.

"Trip, what's going on?" his mother asked as soon as they reached the kitchen. "Is that blood?"

"It's not mine, and no, it's not a politician's," Bjorn replied.

"A shame; several of them could use a good thumping," Geneva remarked in her Germanic accent as she joined them in the kitchen. "Anyone need something to drink? Heather looks as though she could use some wine."

Heather sat at the breakfast table. Bjorn wondered how weird it felt to her—they'd sat at the table two decades ago, doing home-work, eating pizza, and holding hands under the table.

Bjorn contacted the household virtual assistant with his pinplants and called up a local news channel on the kitchen Tri-V. Aerial video mixed with computer recreations of the riots while the news personality droned on about new austerity measures that were considered the impetus for the unrest.

'Bettie, scan news sources for outbreaks of violence in other cities.'

BTI: 'Already compiled. Riots or demonstrations are underway in 127 urban locations across the United States.'

Heather gratefully accepted a glass of wine. "What happened at the restaurant wasn't a random mob angry that their guaranteed income had been cut back."

"Trip?" Bjorn's mother sipped the wine Geneva passed her.

"A van full of gunmen rolled up to the plaza by the restaurant. They had semi-automatic rifles and opened fire." Bjorn nodded when Geneva pulled a beer from the fridge and held it up. "I took exception to having my dinner interrupted and returned fire."

"Semi-automatic sport rifles? They're illegal for civilians to own," Bjorn's mother remarked.

Geneva waved her free hand as she held the beer out to Bjorn. "Maybe no one told them it was illegal?"

"Lynn, your insane Viking of a son waded into them as though he were a Tri-V action star," Heather said between sips. "He's lucky he didn't get shot."

"What was I supposed to do? Wait for the police?" Bjorn shrugged and drained half the beer. He hid the post-battle adrenaline jitters well, but a beer or three would help. "You're right, Heather. I find it hard to believe they randomly showed up where the governor and three Congress members were dining. My guess is that one of them has a leak in their staff. However, this unrest is country-wide."

The talking head on the Tri-V mentioned the 25% reduction in the monthly stipend and the exclusion of entertainment and 'comfort' goods from the FedMart program. Additional restrictions scrolled down the screen. Bjorn considered them reasonable for a government stretching a dwindling pool of resources, but the populace had grown accustomed to a free hand in spending their guaranteed income at FedMart.

"If people take to the streets over these rules, what will happen if they find out the shelves are running empty?" Heather asked.

"It will be bad," Geneva replied. "My parents immigrated to the United States because of the European Austerity Crash fifty years ago. The previous decades caught up to the EU and their generous nature. They couldn't convert to robotic automation quickly enough as fewer people chose to work. They relied on imported goods as productivity slumped, and they found their global, guaranteed income would not go as far and buying power was cut in half. People rioted and interculture violence erupted. It was ugly."

"Mom, you should come to Vishall," Bjorn said. He finished off the beer. "Geneva, I wouldn't blame you if you wanted to sell the house and get off-world."

"I have lived here longer than anywhere else. I will not let them chase me out as my parents were driven from Europe," Geneva countered. She pointed toward the refrigerator. "If you want more beer, you know where to find it."

Bjorn took her up on the invitation and collected a beer from the fridge. "It's even worse. The Mercenary Guild has put a hold on accepting new contracts. No contracts mean no mercenary taxes. Since the world government and most nations built their economic infrastructure on taxing mercenary income, it means the planet is screwed."

An hour of surfing news channels did nothing to dispel Bjorn's assertion. Only a handful of locations experienced terrorist attacks like the ones in Las Cruces, further reinforcing Bjorn's suspicions, but the Red Justice Front featured prominently in most accounts. Bjorn dropped his fifth beer bottle in the recycling bin.

"Heather, do you want me to call you a cab?" Bjorn offered.

Heather gazed at the Tri-V still displaying the latest updates on the riots. "My hotel is in the middle of the Tortuga protest. I'll call my brother and see if I can crash on his couch."

"Don't be ridiculous," Geneva said. "You can stay in the guest room."

"I don't want to put you to any trouble," Heather protested.

Geneva waved her hand. "It is not the Hilton, but it is better than a couch. I'm sure, by daylight, the authorities will have these protests and riots sorted out."

"I'll leave you to get her settled," Bjorn said. "I'm going to check on my people before I hit the sack."

Bjorn retreated to his room, shedding the monkey suit. A hot shower helped drive the last post-combat nerves away. Bjorn checked in with Bear Town. Berto had passed off OIC duties to Lieutenant Loftis, who maintained the ready squads and standby VTOL. Despite some Berserker personnel taking advantage of the amenities in Las Cruces, they avoided getting swept up in the unrest. A tap at his door kept him from turning off the light and climbing into bed.

"Sorry. I couldn't sleep either," Heather whispered when he cracked the door open. Her hair was damp, and she clung to her bathrobe. Before Bjorn could protest, she slipped through the door. "What do you think is going to happen?"

Bjorn wondered himself. "I don't know. A good night's rest will clear our heads." Five strong beers over two hours had left him buzzed, and Heather had drunk three glasses of wine. Bjorn thanked Odin he'd stayed away from the hard liquor. "In the morning, I'll take you to your hotel."

Heather stepped close to him and draped her arms over Bjorn's shoulders. "I feel safe here."

"Heather, I don't think—" Heather cut him off by rising on her toes and kissing him. Despite his body's urges, Bjorn held Heather by the shoulders and stepped back. "Heather, no. I have a wife. I can't hurt her," Bjorn rasped. He released her and took another step away.

"I'm sorry. It's…" Heather's blue eyes glistened.

"It's been a roller-coaster night. Between the adrenaline and the alcohol…don't worry about it." He forced a smile. What he said was true, but a voice in his head reminded him she worked for the politicians. This could be a ploy to gain his sympathy or create leverage. Bjorn tamped his suspicions down. "No harm done. You should try to get some sleep."

Heather nodded and backed to the door. "You're right."

Bjorn closed the door behind her and locked it. He held to his marriage oath, but Heather knew how to manipulate him. Even years later, she could figure which strings to tug. She'd also hurt him when they were young. Bjorn resisted the urge to search data caches for a copy of one of the first videos he'd recorded with his pinplants—Heather and Berto walking into prom together after Bjorn had been expelled from their private school. It was the first moment he suspected they were going together behind his back. How many times had he watched the video?

His pinplants helpfully responded, '*129.*'

* * * * *

Chapter Twelve

Hekamon, Coro Region, Tolo Arm

"What you mean no take Yack?" The QlunSha's translator interpreted its slobbering snarls and grunts. The hairy alien's face sat between its shoulders. A pair of beady eyes glared from above a wide, toothy maw. It brandished its UAAC. "Everyone take Yack!"

The Cochkala station attendant's tail waved and flicked as he replied, "Not the Wathayat Trading Consortium. They are only accepting physical credit chits or red diamonds as payment. Since we buy our raw F11 from them, virtual currency does us no good."

The QlunSha roared amid a spray of spittle. Its two fellows joined in, one adding, "Eat him!"

"Threats of violence will accomplish nothing," the attendant admonished, his tail swishing in agitation. "There is a Union Credit Exchange on this station. I suggest you avail yourself of it and return with hard currency." Hopefully the QlunSha translators would dumb his words down enough.

The lead QlunSha snarled, and the trio stalked off. Once they were out of his office, the attendant moved his finger away from the alarm button.

* * *

Science Guild Embassy, Capital Planet

"I greet you, Zod'Sizwey." The Science Guild representative, a double-tailed OpSha, bowed.

Zod'Sizwey returned the bow. "Greetings, Curator Bamii. I trust from your message you have obtained what we require."

"Directly to business." The simian alien grinned. "I appreciate efficiency. Yes, I have retrieved the desired technology from the archives." He placed a small, plastic rectangle on the table. He pressed a button, and a panel on top of the box slid open. "Operation is simple. The scanning chamber can accommodate a credit chit or loose red diamonds."

Zod drew a case from under her wing. She opened it and slid a credit chit into the waiting cavity. Bamii pressed another button. The device hummed for a few seconds then glowed amber.

"Amber indicates a genuine red diamond," Bamii stated. He pried the chit out of the scanning chamber with the tip of his tail. Before Zod could protest, he swept the chit away. "I assume you brought a counterfeit sample."

Zod removed a red gem encased in a clear, polymer square. "This is from a counterfeiting operation on Parmick." Criminals in a mining facility attempted to synthesize red diamonds and included red diamond dust in the crystal matrix in an attempt to fool scanners.

The OpSha pressed the button again. It took two seconds longer than the first scan before the box glowed blue. Zod snatched the counterfeit sample before the OpSha could claim it as well. She replaced it with a translucent circle containing a red stone. "One more test," she said.

"As you wish." Curator Bamii initiated the scan. The box hummed twice as long as the previous scan before illuminating amber.

Zod's wings sagged in disappointment. The TriRusk sample passed the check. Distinguishing TriRusk red diamonds from genuine gems required sophisticated scans—obviously something beyond the capability of the small device Bamii presented.

"I do not understand." The OpSha tilted his head in confusion. "This is not a genuine sample?"

Zod'Sizwey ruffled her feathers. "No. It is a product of the TriRusk."

The curator blinked. "It is true? They still exist?"

"Sadly so." Was the curator feigning ignorance? Zod found it surprising the Science Guild lagged on the intelligence regarding the TriRusk. Perhaps the OpSha was not considered 'need to know.' "If I can take this sample, perhaps we can find a scanning protocol sufficient to differentiate these synthetic gems from the real article."

Zod nodded. Between the Information Guild's propaganda operation against the red diamond standard and an uptick in counterfeiting attempts, the Union Credit Exchange needed every tool it could get to fight back. The scanner presented by the OpSha met the criteria for small and cheaply mass-produced counterfeits. "How long would it take to alter the design so it would time out with no result? The TriRusk sample took considerably longer to analyze, so it could prompt in-depth analysis."

"I could have it completed by this time tomorrow, including the changes to the manufactory blueprint," Bamii replied. He skeptically eyed the clear disk with the TriRusk sample. "The other issue could take longer, much longer."

"Understood. We will pay the agreed price for the scanner design once it is updated," Zod'Sizwey said. Two things secured the Science Guild's assistance. One was a large sum of hard currency, and the other was the Science Guild's concern the Information Guild had grown too powerful. "We shall pay the same if you can devise an economical and dispersible means to quickly identify TriRusk diamonds."

"Agreed." The curator collected the TriRusk sample and the prototype scanner. "Until tomorrow."

* * *

Earth Orbit

Dbo'Dizwey shook her head. The planet's orbital facilities paled compared to those of other civilized worlds. Granted, the Mercenary Guild had wreaked havoc during their assault and occupation, but they had largely spared the civilian infrastructure. Perhaps it wasn't worth the ammunition?

"Ma'am, the shuttle can depart at your convenience," the Maki captain remarked. 'They're waiting on you' remained unspoken. Unspoken because Dbo had handed him a year's worth of hard credits with the promise of an equal amount once she completed her mission.

"Thank you, Captain. I shall proceed to the flight deck." Some avian and insect races reveled in micro-gravity. Dbo hated it. Spaceships were too cramped for her to spread her wings, and she lost all sense of direction in weightlessness.

She dreaded Earth only a little less than remaining in space. Dbo's home world only had 75 percent of Earth's gravity. The thick air bordered on breathable, but it stank of industrial processes. The sooner she completed her mission, the better.

Her Sumatozou bodyguard, Uvksolt, unfurled both trunks as Dbo entered the shuttle. The board of directors had denied Dbo's request for a golem escort. The hulking Sumatozou was an adequate substitute and made for better company.

"All is ready for departure." The bodyguard wore light combat armor, adding to her bulk. Whereas members of the pachyderm-like mercenary race wore mottled red and green stripes to show their age and status, Uvksolt only bore three black stripes on her grey hide. "Do you require assistance strapping in?"

"No, I've got it." Dbo'Dizwey hauled herself into her seat and squished her folded wings behind her. Despite her misgivings at the board's denying her golems, Uvksolt had impressed Dbo during their journey through hyperspace. The Sumatozou took her job seriously. The three black stripes marked her as an outcast, unable to serve in any of the Sumatozou castes. She forged a career for herself as a private guard and special operations contractor.

"Standby for maneuvering and reentry," the Maki shuttle copilot called.

The initial thrust and turns jostled Dbo in her safety harness. She loathed the next part—planetfall. The shuttle decelerated from orbit and plummeted into the atmosphere. Dbo's beak rattled as the air buffeted the shuttle. She tried not to imagine the nimbus of super-heated plasma around the craft.

Uvksolt sat placidly, her eyes half closed as though she was about to drift off to sleep. Finally, the shuddering abated, and she opened her eyes. "The worst is over, ma'am."

"How can you nap during atmospheric entry?" Dbo asked.

The Sumatozou shrugged her broad shoulders. "I meditate during planetfall. If something goes wrong, I can't do anything about it, and I will soon be dead. Worrying over it has no benefit."

"I wish I had your nerves," Dbo remarked. Turbulence shook the shuttle, and she grabbed her armrests.

"You don't need to, ma'am. It's why you hired me." Uvksolt seemed nonplussed when the shuttle bucked. "I assume the plan remains the same when we hit the ground?"

Dbo ruffled a few feathers at the connotation of 'hit the ground.' "Once we land, the plan remains the same as we discussed. I doubt the Humans we will deal with have encountered any of my race. They are bound to be curious at best, and hostile at worst. The former I can deal with."

"I shall handle the latter," Uvksolt added.

* * *

Sol System, Contracted Yacht *Bountiful Excess*

A chime awoke Ashok. His sleeping sling sagged under his mass. He had slept through hyperspace emergence, and the ship was now decelerating toward Earth. He checked his pinplants—they had one and a half day-night cycles before they reached orbit.

Ashok queried the local GalNet node for an information update on Earth mercenary firms. Master Archivist Heloxi gave him a great deal of discretion in hiring mercenaries, but she wanted ones she could sway with more than money.

A quick scan of the data returned by the local node showed the mercenary industry in shambles. The previous global government had collapsed, and a mercenary faction had propped up a new government. With over a day to kill, Ashok dug in.

Mercenaries turning on their world governments and asserting themselves was nothing new. As Ashok sifted through the subject matter, it surprised him it had taken this long before the mercenaries revolted and dictated terms to the planetary government.

Unfortunately, mercenaries enmeshed in a global coup rarely hired on for additional work. Their plates were already full. As reported, the Four Horsemen were decimated or occupied with local affairs. Other mercenary units had rallied to the banner of the new world government, the Terran Federation.

What's this? One of the largest nation-states had remained outside the new global government. Primitive Humans and their balkanized world. The new planetary government excluded a handful of nation-states. Of those, the United States was by far the most prosperous and most populated. Several mercenary firms residing within its borders had survived the Omega War. Ashok ran a search on those units.

A portion of a cycle later, one stood out—a mixed role firm fielding five companies plus space assets. An anomaly appeared when Ashok dove into the data. The unit had moved most of its assets off-world. Their new headquarters resided on a planet one jump away. However, the mercenary firm's commander was on Earth. Ashok opened priority data feeds into the planetary network. The firm was evacuating its remaining equipment and personnel.

Ashok opened the data cluster regarding the commander and queried a predictive algorithm regarding his searches. A transmitted file was flagged as high priority. It was a simple audio-video transmission. Ashok accessed the file.

"Son, give these alien motherfuckers what for."

* * * * *

Chapter Thirteen

Santa Teresa, New Mexico, Earth

Javier Morales laid on the horn. He'd been in the cramped truck cab for eight hours, and he needed to reach a station soon to charge the battery and drain his bladder. The tiny operator compartment was designed for brief use by maintenance personnel or warehouse drovers. The autotrucks were built to conduct long hauls unmanned.

The alien invasion had ravaged Earth's orbital infrastructure and compromised the Aethernet. Autonomous vehicles had grown unreliable and required Human intervention. However, the trucks on the road far outnumbered the operators, even with all the drovers such as Javier pressed into service.

"How can we have traffic jams with half the trucks off the road?" Javier wondered aloud. The line at the Jeronimo-Santa Teresa crossing was backed up for miles, and that was with cursory checks at the border into Sonora-Chihuahua. The El Paso-Juarez crossing was out since Texas and the US remained in a pissing match. Javier was trying to reach a new crossing that had opened to relieve traffic. So much for that idea.

Several weather-worn, light military vehicles rolled along the shoulder, the New Mexico National Guard logo barely legible on their sides. The convoy ground to a halt alongside the civilian traffic.

Javier lowered his window and shouted to the guardsman riding shotgun in the truck next to him. "Hey soldier, what's the hold up?"

"Texas blocked the highway ahead," the woman yelled back. "They're claiming their border crosses it and threw up a barricade. I don't know what the hell we're supposed to do about it. If it turns into a shooting match, they'll call in their merc buddies and waste us."

"Don't we have mercenaries?" Javier knew the US had several mercenary companies before the invasion. Were they all based out of Texas?

"Not near as many, and word has it they want no part in fighting their buddies," the woman called back. "So, us lowly grunts get to tangle with their pals if things get nasty."

The convoy began to move again before Javier could ask any more questions. If it turned into a shooting match, what could he do? Would the Texans call in more orbital strikes? Javier put the truck into traffic-following mode and pulled out his slate. As urgently as he needed to piss, the desire to get out of the area of a potential attack from above outweighed it.

* * *

Over Southeast New Mexico, Earth

"Sir, an attack VTOL is shadowing us from the Texas side of the border," the copilot announced.

"Have they challenged us?" Bjorn asked. He called up the map in his pinview. They were twenty minutes out from the Texas border, northwest of Odessa. It would take another hour and a half to cross Texas to reach Houston.

"Not yet, Commander. I expect them to call us out in 18 minutes," the copilot replied.

'Bettie, where is the *Ursa Major?*' How long would it take them to get a firing solution on a craft in our vicinity?' The heavy cruiser had arrived yesterday along with another transport. It wasn't one of the Winged Hussars' badass relics, but the *Ursa's* particle barbettes could swat down a flyer from orbit.

BTI: 'The *Ursa Major's* current orbit puts her in position in 27 minutes. She could maneuver into range in 9 minutes. Shall I relay the order?'

Bjorn rubbed the bronze hammer dangling from his string of bear claws. A show of strength could escalate things instead of warding off aggression. 'No. Have them stand by in case things turn nasty, but they are to remain in their current orbit.'

Reports of scuffles between soldiers along the New Mexico-Texas border popped into the news feeds. So far, it hadn't crossed into shooting. The governor had begged Bjorn to deploy troops to the El Paso area to back up the National Guard, but Bjorn had turned him down. Even if he was inclined to take the field, the other side could muster far more troops if mercenaries got involved. Bjorn advised the governor to show restraint while he awaited reinforcements from Washington.

"I assume you're seeing the news?" Heather asked. She wore a headset so she wouldn't have to shout over the turbines. "Texas is trying to cut off traffic in the Santa Teresa area. They're claiming insurgents and agitators are attempting to infiltrate their country."

"It wouldn't surprise me," Bjorn replied. Pro-unification militia groups had sprung up overnight after Texas's secession, and they'd had a few weeks to get their acts together. In the Santa Teresa-El Paso area, crossing the border meant crossing a street. "I can't help but wonder if they're more concerned about troublemakers or about refugees when funds start running out in the USA."

"Commander Tovesson, the flyer is challenging us," the copilot announced. "I'll patch you in."

"—again. Unidentified flight, you are on a direct course for Texas airspace. Turn away or—"

"Unidentified my ass," Bjorn broke in. "You know damned well this is a Berserkers' aircraft. You can read our transponder as easily as you can read your Yack balance. This is Commander Bjorn Tovesson of Bjorn's Berserkers, en route to Houston for a meeting with Colonel Jim Cartwright. Now, are you going to quit hassling me, or should I land so I can deal with you face-to-face?"

Several seconds passed before the answer came. "Commander Tovesson, continue on your course to Houston. Do not deviate—"

"There better not be an 'or else' coming, or I will find you and 'or else' your ass. Am I clear, Corporal?" The rank was a guess. Copilots normally handled the communications duties so the pilot could focus on flying.

"Commander Tovesson, this is Lieutenant Andrew Pier, piloting patrol flight DW005. We will escort you to Houston if you don't object."

Bjorn grinned. He must have flustered the copilot. "If it means we don't get challenged by anymore yahoos, it's agreeable."

"We are relaying you to air traffic control as BB001, Commander Tovesson. My uncle served under your father during the Eridani Campaign."

"Captain Michael Pier," Bjorn said after Bettie fed him the info. "Your uncle served with distinction."

Heather shook her head. On their private channel, she said, "You mercenaries can accomplish more diplomacy over a bottle of whisky than politicians over a stack of papers."

Despite the escort, mobile antiaircraft systems pinged their craft three times. As opposed to the units fielded by the United States, these were modern systems, probably hand-me-downs from mercenary firms. The US might have had more troops, but Texas held the technological edge even before you accounted for the mercenary firms based in the republic.

"Commander, we're good to land in startown," the copilot reported. "We'll land near the Cavaliers' headquarters. Well, near-ish. The open landing zone is a mile out from the Cavaliers' offices."

"Thank you, Corporal." Bjorn debated calling Whisky for a ride but decided against it. An autocab would suffice, assuming they were functional.

Once they touched down on the tarmac, Bjorn hauled the door open. A bright yellow, autonomous taxi awaited them. Bjorn would have hiked the mile to Cartwright's offices, even in the Houston heat, but Heather wore heels and a business dress.

Bjorn helped Heather climb down from the VTOL and opened the taxi door for her. Neither of them had mentioned her kiss from last night. No good could come of it, and Bjorn was content to pretend it never happened.

A quartet of Human mercenaries watched Bjorn and Heather. He figured Heather caught their attention until one of them pointed at the logo emblazoned on the side of the VTOL flyer. Two of the soldiers shook their heads while a third flipped off the rising VTOL. He'd have to deal with the rumors that the Berserkers bailed on

Earth. That would be hard to do given that they had in fact moved off-world. First things first.

"Cartwright Cavaliers' main offices," Bjorn instructed the robotic brain operating the cab. He tapped his Yack to the terminal, and the electric car lurched into motion. Bjorn wouldn't have trusted a self-driving vehicle outside of startown or the starport. Within the perimeter, autonomous vehicles relied on the starport network.

"It's as hot as back home, but muggy," Heather remarked. The short ride only gave them a brief respite from the heat. "Walking fifty yards already has me sweating. Why did the mercenary industry settle here?"

Cool air gushed out as Bjorn held the lobby door open for her. "It wasn't for the weather. This was the first starport, and the Cartwright family is from the region. As more mercs gathered here, it made sense for others to set up shop here as well."

They crossed a granite floor with the Cavaliers' logo set in the stone to the reception desk and security stand. The two guards snapped alert when they spotted Bjorn, one tucking away his phone and the other breaking off his conversation with the receptionist.

While the men wore uniforms, they lacked the Cavaliers' crest or rank insignia. Private security guards. Cartwright had suffered horrendous losses in the attempt to take back Earth. Normally, cadre troops would pull guard duty, but the Cavaliers must not have had any to spare.

"We have an appointment with Colonel Cartwright," Bjorn stated. "Commander Tovesson."

The receptionist scanned a screen. "If you go to the top floor on the elevator, Colonel Cartwright will be right with you."

"All right boys, let's do the dance." Bjorn stopped in front of the security arch and picked up a plastic bin. He slowly unholstered his pistol and placed it in the bin, followed by sundry items the scanner might flag.

One of the guards waved him through while the other stopped staring at Bjorn's sidearm and monitored the screen. The security scanner beeped in protest as Bjorn stepped through the arch. The guard watching him stepped back, and his hand drifted toward his holstered sidearm.

"Easy, Mike," the guard watching the display called. "This guy has enough metal in him to build a car. His left arm is a prosthetic, and he has a bunch of hardware crammed into his skull like the colonel."

Mike eased his hand away from his pistol. "You never know. People have tried to kill the boss. I was exercising caution."

The guard at the scanner rolled his eyes. "Colonel Tovesson, you'll need to leave your sidearm with us."

"I figured as much, and it's Commander," Bjorn replied. He collected the remainder of his belongings from the bin.

Heather passed through the security scanner without incident, though the guard paid more attention to her than his monitor. Her heels clicked on the granite floor as they headed for the elevator bank.

"Where is everyone?" she whispered. The rooms beyond the lobby were dark, and the library's quietness amplified every noise.

Bjorn waited until they entered the elevator. "The Cavaliers were nearly wiped out in the Battle of Sao Paolo."

"So, how is he in charge of Earth's mercenaries if he hardly has any troops?" Heather asked.

"He's not in charge of Earth's mercs," Bjorn protested quicker than he intended. "Some people consider him a war hero, and the Cavalier name still carries a lot of clout. Plus, Colonel Enkh from the Golden Horde is helping him."

The doors opened to an office lobby with an empty admin assistant desk. The ajar door to the office beyond afforded a view of a young, heavy-set man in discussion with a hulking Samoan. While Bjorn had a centimeter or two on the huge man, the Samoan was thicker and broader.

"Commander Tovesson!" The young man beckoned as he moved from behind the large desk. He waited for Bjorn and Heather to enter before continuing. "This is my XO, Major Kalawai'a."

"Call me Buddha. It'll be easier for everyone." The major shook Bjorn's hand firmly.

"This is Heather Akins-Dodd," Bjorn said. "Heather, this is Colonel Jim Cartwright."

Bjorn had briefed Heather on the flight, so she didn't show the shock exhibited by many who learned the commander of one of the Four Horsemen was a chubby twenty-something. "Akins, actually. Heather is fine." She flashed a disarming smile as she shook Cartwright's hand and then the major's.

"Have a seat." Cartwright returned behind the desk, but Buddha remained standing. "What can I do for you, Commander Tovesson and Ms. Akins?"

"I'm trying to track down someone I believe the Terran Federation may hold prisoner," Bjorn stated. He placed his slate on the desk. Two lupine visages accompanied by scrolling text captions appeared above the slate. "Two Besquith. One is Lieutenant Sabher, of the Haagen creche. The other is Sergeant Druul, of the Druugar creche. Both operated in North America including Alaska."

"The Federation holds numerous enemy mercenaries pending trials. What makes these two so special?" Cartwright asked, studying the Tri-V images. His eyes flicked with the characteristic twitches of someone using pinplants.

"My parents lived in Alaska," Bjorn replied. His hand went to the Thor hammer pendant.

Cartwright's brow furrowed in brief puzzlement. Either his pinplants yielded the relevant facts, or he put two and two together on his own. "Oh. Shit. I'm sorry. My father spoke highly of your father."

"My father was retired. My parents were civilians. Still, Peepo went after them. My father sacrificed himself to Druul's squad so they wouldn't get my mother. They razed the ancestral family home, assuming my mother remained within.

"Sabher's unit hounded my people all the way from here to Alaska. In Canada, not only did they kill several troops, they murdered dozens of civilian dependents." Bjorn drew a deep, calming breath. If Cartwright could hand him the Besquith, Bjorn would regret not bringing his axe.

"We're holding numerous Besquith on war crimes charges," Cartwright stated, shifting his focus from his pinview to Bjorn. "So what, you want us to turn them over to the United States for trial?"

"No, I want you to turn them over to me so I can avenge my father and my people." Bjorn clenched his left fist hard enough for the servos in the knuckles to whine. "I'll be far more generous than they were—I'll put a round through their skulls and be done with it."

Cartwright blanched. "I'm not going to hand over prisoners so you can murder them!"

"What are you going to do? Keep them locked up forever? Hold some dog and pony trial so everyone can feel a little better?" Bjorn demanded. "You find them guilty and then what? Keep them imprisoned some more?"

"There's a difference between justice and revenge," Cartwright countered. "Even if I had those Besquith, giving them to you for summary execution isn't justice."

"It is for me!" The Samoan tensed when Bjorn shouted. "They committed crimes on US soil—maybe the American government should extradite the war criminals," Bjorn stated. "I doubt they would be so squeamish."

"Get back to me when the United States hammers out an extradition treaty with the Federation," Cartwright snapped back.

"Funny you should mention it," Heather interjected. "Given the current tensions between the United States and the self-proclaimed Terran Federation, members of the government are reluctant to treat with the Terran Federation. However, the sooner we can come to grips with the new situation, the better for everyone."

"Are you the new ambassador to the Terran Federation?" Cartwright asked, seeming eager to move on to another subject. "We've requested ambassadors from all nation-states that declined to sign on to the compact. If we open a dialogue, we can avoid unpleasantness down the road."

"Officially? No, I'm not an ambassador. Elements of the United States government still consider Texas a breakaway state," Heather replied.

"Texas's independence isn't up for debate," Cartwright said. "We made that clear the first time the US launched attacks against Texas. If they need a reminder, they should remember White Sands. We gave them an example of what will happen."

"You almost made an example of my people!" Bjorn snapped. In his pinview, a map of New Mexico zoomed in until Bear Town and White Sands Missile Base filled the image. Bjorn cast the display to his slate. "What's left of Bear Town is four miles from the US base. I had people on the ground when you rained down your orbital bombardment."

Cartwright sat up straight. "Were any of your people killed?"

"If your grandstanding harmed any of my people, I wouldn't have waited for an appointment," Bjorn growled. The Samoan watched Bjorn carefully, but Bjorn didn't care. "As it was, you set the precedent that showed people can hit us from orbit. You told the aliens we don't care about the bombardment rule on our own home world!"

"I didn't know your people were in the threat box, but if I had to do it again, even if I did know, I would make the same call," Cartwright stated icily. "The United States tossed nukes at former citizens. They targeted cities full of civilians because of pride. I could not let it stand."

"Remember that if the Besquith drop a rock on Houston," Bjorn countered. "Remember it when the families of the civilians you killed at White Sands come calling. You don't care about collateral damage, do you? You're the asshole who glassed Sao Paolo and a million civvies with antimatter weapons! I guess orbital bombardment seems like chump change compared to outlawed WMDs."

"You have no idea what you're talking about!" Cartwright clenched his jaw and balled his fists. Was the kid going to take a swing at him? As pissed as Bjorn was, punching a chunky boy barely able to grow a beard was beneath him. If the XO chose to throw down, Bjorn considered him fair game.

Cartwright opened his hands. "The situation in Sao Paolo got out of control. I never intended for it to escalate the way it did." Bjorn didn't need Padre Hawkins to tell him the kid was sincerely regretful. Cartwright sagged slightly; he gazed into the distance.

"Perhaps we should work toward preventing a repeat of what happened in Sao Paolo, White Sands, and elsewhere," Heather suggested.

Cartwright blinked, then turned his attention to Heather. "I'm sorry, Ms. Akins. If the United States won't send an ambassador, what is your role?"

"I happen to have the ear of several Congress-people and the governor of New Mexico. I can officially represent the latter." Heather placed her phone on the desk next to Bjorn's tablet. "For starters, perhaps you could direct me to someone who can help resolve the border dispute around El Paso. Your forces are disrupting peaceful commerce along the border between New Mexico and Texas, as well as the one between New Mexico and Chihuahua-Sonora."

"I'm not in charge of border security for Texas," Cartwright said, studying the map. "What a mess. The border cuts through yards and parking lots."

"Exactly. It's disrupting lives and trade. You have President Collins' ear. We should come to an agreement that will let the flow of goods and people resume," Heather said. "Texas may have seceded, but it's not self-sufficient. Likewise, as a member of the Federation and home to the busiest starport on the planet, Texas stands to gain much via exports to the United States."

"Ms. Akins—"

"Colonel Cartwright, call me Heather, please. Ms. Akins makes me feel old enough to be your mother."

Bjorn caught himself doing the math.

A guarded expression flickered over Cartwright's face. If Heather hoped she could sway the young man by batting her eyes, Bjorn suspected she was mistaken. "Heather, I can't speak on behalf of President Collins or her government. What I can do is put you in touch with someone who can do so."

"I would be so grateful." Heather smiled at the young man. She held out her phone. "I can send you my contact card."

Cartwright nodded. "It would be refreshing to see both sides move forward."

"What about the Besquith?" Bjorn asked.

"I already told you, Commander Tovesson, I'm not turning prisoners over to you so you can murder them," Cartwright stated firmly. "Get the US to hammer out an extradition treaty, and we might relinquish them to their courts for trial."

The Tri-V display hovering over Bjorn's tablet flickered and changed.

"Son, give these alien motherfuckers what for." Blood trickled down the side of Bjorn Tovesson II's face, staining his silver beard red. He grunted as his CASPer shook and the illumination flickered. "I'll see you in Valhalla."

Wrenching metal drowned out all other noise. After a moment, a savage voice snarled, "Meat."

"Fuck you, *sukin syn*," Bjorn's father spat back. "Bettie, Ragnarök."

The image ended with a white flash, then static.

'Video ended.'

"My father sacrificed himself to buy my mother time to escape," Bjorn murmured as the image faded. He collected his slate and shoved it back in its holster. "I'll find those sonuvabitches with or without your help."

"Our discussion is over, Commander Tovesson."

"I believe you're right, Colonel Cartwright." Bjorn stood. "We'll see ourselves out."

* * *

"So much for bringing the Berserkers into the fold," Buddha remarked.

Jim Cartwright sighed. When Tovesson had requested a meeting, Jim had hoped Bjorn was seeking a way to join the mercenary firms backing the new Terran Federation. "I'm afraid you're right. He's obsessed with revenge. The best we can hope for is his going to his new base on Vishall."

"His lawyer friend was attractive," Buddha remarked. "Assuming you dig blue-eyed blondes."

"Maybe you should ask her out?" Jim suggested, half teasing. The lawyer had tried to manipulate him, thinking a young man would be susceptible to a coy smile and a pretty face. But Jim had learned that lesson already.

"No thanks. She strikes me as high maintenance."

"We need to find out if we hold those Besquith," Jim stated. He recalled the view of the two holograms Tovesson displayed.

"I thought you weren't going to hand them over?" Buddha asked.

"I'm not," Jim replied. He composed a cursory search daemon with his pinplants and launched it. "If we can find them, I suspect Commander Tovesson can as well. Since we won't cough them up, he may take matters into his own hands. We don't need another crisis."

"Who'd have thought we'd be protecting Besquith war criminals?" Buddha remarked.

Jim shook his head. "It's not for their protection. The last thing Earth needs is some sort of mercenary civil war."

"The Berserkers are a decent-sized unit, but they'd be outnumbered several times over, even if they brought their whole fighting force here," Buddha said.

"How many Human mercenary firms would fight to protect Besquith?" Jim asked. "A lot of mercs question why we're holding them and going through trials. A lot of them lost people to Besquith or other aliens."

"Shit. So, what do we do?"

Jim moved the search daemon to the periphery of his pinview. "If we hold those Besquith, we move them out of Tovesson's reach to remove the temptation of acting rashly."

* * *

"You carry that video with you?" Heather asked once the elevator doors closed. "Don't you think it's morbid?"

"My father knew he was dying, and he sent me the message. He wanted me to know exactly what happened," Bjorn replied. He tapped the side of his head. "I'll never forget it, even if I didn't carry it in my pinplant memory."

"So, what now?"

"I imagine you'll hear from President Collins or one of her advisors soon." The US might have been reluctant to admit Texas was its own nation-state, but Bjorn was more pragmatic. Texas's divorce from the US was final. "I hope you can work things out with the Texans. To be honest, if the Berserkers were still based on Earth, I might be inclined to support New Mexico joining the Texans."

Heather frowned. "Please don't say that in front of the Congressional delegation. They'd have a conniption."

"New Mexico could join the Texas Republic, and you could be the new governor," Bjorn teased. "That would get someone's knickers in a twist."

Heather stifled a laugh. The elevator dinged to announce their arrival at the ground floor. "What are you going to do?"

"I'm going to make sure you get back to your hotel room, then I'm going to find my team on the ground here." Bjorn collected his sidearm from the security personnel, checking the weapon before he holstered it.

"Aren't you afraid I'll try to seduce you again if you come to my hotel room?" Her fingers brushed the back of his hand.

"We're both sober and our lives weren't endangered in the last few hours," Bjorn remarked. Better, he was forewarned. Bjorn still hadn't figured out if Heather's overtures were genuine or attempts to manipulate him. Either way, it didn't matter.

"I take it your people here are searching for your Besquith?" Heather asked. "If they find the Besquith, can't they call you? Why check on them in person?"

"I'm going to take them to the meanest merc bar in town and pick a fight," Bjorn replied. "It's time people were reminded 'don't poke the bear.'

* * * * *

Chapter Fourteen

Houston Startown, Earth

"Shit! Commander Tovesson is coming here!" Charlotte announced as she set down her slate.

Sergeant Cripe stirred from his nap and lifted his cap. "Say what now?"

"Papa Bear is in Houston?" Tamara paused the video on her slate. With the air conditioning fixed and the place cleaned up, the breakroom in the logistics facility served as their de facto gathering spot during the day. "Oh shit, is he going to be pissed about Gus and Roscoe?"

Roscoe poked his head out of the adjacent office. The Jivool had claimed the room as their quarters, having cleared out the furniture first. "What about Gus and Roscoe?" the Jivool asked in English.

"The boss is coming here in a bit," Charlotte replied. "You get to meet him."

"Do not worry, Sergeant Whisky," Roscoe said. "Gus and Roscoe make you proud."

Roscoe barked something in Jivool over his shoulder. The rumbling reply sounded reluctant until Roscoe countered with another growling phrase ending in "boss."

"We sweep again," Roscoe said before he and a yawning Gus shuffled out into the warehouse.

"The commander deals with aliens all the time," Charlotte said, not feeling the confidence she forced into her voice.

168 | JON R. OSBORNE

"This is true." Vurrn nodded. He'd broken off from working on the personnel transport while the afternoon heat baked the pavement outside. "My father was friends with his father. He employs other aliens. He is not a xenophobe."

"See, it'll be fine." Charlotte forced a smile.

* * *

"You hired Jivool. Are you fucking kidding me?" Bjorn glared down at Whisky, towering over her by half a meter.

"Obviously, we need someone to watch the place, and they provide valuable intel on the alien underground." Whisky stared back, not hiding behind her aviator glasses. "You gave me discretion to gather whatever I needed, and you approved their hiring paperwork."

"I know. Stefan neglected to mention the guards were Jivool until after I signed off on the form." Bjorn scowled at the two hunched ursines. Both wore vests which were the same dark grey as Berserker BDUs, and the one named Gus wore a gray cap.

The other one, Roscoe, bared his teeth in a smiling grimace. "We are pleased to meet the Boss Bear."

"This is what I get for not checking the paperwork," Bjorn muttered. In a unit the size of the Berserkers, he couldn't read every form and report. He needed to settle on an XO. "So, what's this I hear about other merc companies saying we chickened out on Earth?"

"They claim we wussed out when the Horsemen led the counter-assault," Cripe stated. "Everyone knows the Horsemen came back. The Cavaliers lost 90 percent of their manpower. Asbaran suffered heavy losses on the ground, and the Hussars died by the ship full. Where were we?"

"You know damned well—"

"I'm only reporting what they say when they have enough people so we can't throw down, sir." Cripe held up his hands when Bjorn narrowed his eyes at the interruption.

"You're right, Sergeant. I asked." Bjorn tamped down his misplaced anger. "We need to stamp out this bullshit gossip. What's the biggest bar full of the most assholes?"

"We can't vouch for what's being said in the Lyon's Den," Whisky replied. "We've already been in a fight in Dante's. That leaves Jocko's Hangar. We've avoided the place at night because the crowd is huge and dominantly Human."

"You know how I harp on you not to pick fights, Whisky?" Bjorn had required the sergeant to attend anger management counselling after one bar brawl too many.

"How can I forget?" the young woman replied.

"We're going to Jocko's to pick a fight." Bjorn cracked his knuckles.

"The four of us, sir?" Tamara asked. Reeves had fought alongside her girlfriend many times, but they had never instigated the fracas. If anything, she helped keep Whisky in check. "I'm not afraid to scrap, but we're undermanned for raising hell at Jocko's."

"Six," Roscoe rumbled. "We are Berserkers. It will be honor to fight beside Bear Boss."

"No offense, but don't add me to the total," Vurrn remarked. "I'll play getaway driver, but there's a reason I'm not a merc."

Bjorn gauged the two Jivool. The hulking ursines were almost as large as Oogar, despite their hunched posture. In addition to their claws, Jivool could extend bone spurs from their wrists. "Can you two fight Humans without maiming them?"

Roscoe nodded, and Gus wiped his paws together as though dusting them off.

"Six. Vurrn, can you drive the relic out in the yard?" Bjorn asked.

The Zuul sniffed as though insulted. "Of course. Even if it is a bit primitive."

"All right. Let's go over what you guys have learned so far, grab a bite to eat, and once night falls, we'll hit Jocko's." Bjorn surveyed the warehouse. It was even emptier than the first time he visited the facility. "At least you've kept it clean."

"Eat?" Roscoe straightened and tilted his head. "Burritos?"

Bjorn shrugged. "I guess burritos sound good."

"Burritos!" Gus cheered.

* * *

"Wwhat a dump," Bjorn muttered as Vurrn slowed the rumbler in front of the boxy, metal building. The hangar may have dated back to the early days of the starport, when it would have sat next to tarmacs for helicopters and VTOL flyers. "Careful you don't get tetanus."

A steady flow of traffic, both vehicle and foot, surrounded the establishment. "This place makes Dante's look upscale," Cripe added. "On the plus side, they have plenty of tables and cheap beer."

Bjorn snorted. "Cheap beer. Almost as bad as the artisanal, hoppy, pinecone water the townies call beer. Almost."

"Blue Ribbon beer is good," one of the Jivool declared from the back of the rumbler. Bjorn couldn't tell which one by the voice. The bears had squabbled over the guacamole at dinner but now were extoling the inexpensive lager.

"If those two drink like they eat, it's a good thing they go for the cheap stuff," Bjorn said, eyeing the crowd. He spotted at least a dozen different companies' uniforms. There were hardly any aliens and not a single Besquith. So much for two birds with one stone.

Vurrn parked the rumbler. "I will wait in the vehicle."

"You sure, Vurrn?" Whisky asked. "We don't know how long this will take."

"My guess is less than an hour," Bjorn replied. "I've been raising hell in bars since you were in kindergarten. I know how to pick a fight."

"Hopefully not with every merc in the place," Cripe mumbled as he hauled open the side door.

"Usually, I'm waiting for Charlotte to pick the inevitable fight," Tamara stated as she climbed out of the vehicle. "The commander usually ends fights. This will be new."

"You act as though I start a brawl every time we go out drinking," Whisky protested as she followed Tamara. "The last one wasn't even my fault."

Bjorn stepped down to the crumbling asphalt. "Wicza, I haven't yelled at you for punching out drunk assholes for so long, I'm worried you might be out of practice."

Whisky cracked her knuckles. "Don't worry, Commander, I haven't forgotten anything Sergeant Eddings taught me."

The rumbler's suspension creaked as the Jivool squeezed out of the side hatch. "You two stay out of trouble," Bjorn told them. "Don't jump in unless we get swamped."

The one with the cap tilted his head and studied the ground. "Swamped?"

"It means a bunch of them and a few of us," Bjorn replied. The Jivool both nodded.

Bjorn led the group toward the main entrance. Already, a few mercs were casting side eyes at the Berserkers. If things were this bad, he'd have no trouble finding an asshole willing to step up.

The doorman gave them a cursory scan, his eyes lingering on the Jivool. Since Jivool weren't one of the "culpable" races for the atrocities inflicted during Peepo's invasion, the scan was the extent of the doorman's interest.

Inside, the din of the crowd all but drowned out the music. Hundreds of mercenaries drank and swapped war stories.

"How the hell are we going to get a table?" Cripe yelled over the crowd.

Bjorn tapped one of the Jivool on the arm to get his attention. The black-striped ursine leaned over to listen to Bjorn. "Go find us a table."

The Jivool grunted to his fellow, and they waded into the packed maze of tables. Bjorn followed in their wake with the other Berserkers trailing him. The Jivool could see over the crowd and, hopefully, spy an available table.

Bjorn almost collided with the ursine in front of him when the Jivool abruptly stopped. Half a dozen mercs left their chairs. Two remained seated, locked in an animated discussion, until they noticed the Jivool glaring at them.

"What do you want, furball?" one of them demanded.

"Your table," Roscoe replied.

"We're not done with our beer," the other called over the crowd noise.

The black-striped Jivool shuffled around the table and leaned forward. He shoved his snout into the pitcher and slurped down the beer. Foam dripped from his muzzle as he glared at each merc in turn, then released a loud belch.

The mercs stared in stunned silence for several seconds. They didn't notice Bjorn or the other Humans. "Fine, we were done anyway." The men abandoned their seats and disappeared into the throng of patrons.

"I'm starting to warm to your new recruits, Whisky." Bjorn sank onto a stool and lit the order beacon. A blue pillar of light pierced the haze above their table. The Jivool pushed aside stools and squatted on the floor.

A server appeared quicker than Bjorn expected. The harried woman listened to their drink orders while clearing the detritus left by the table's previous occupants. Some establishments relied on robotic servers, but the machines struggled with the chaotic environments of bustling bars. People didn't require an upfront investment.

"What's the plan, Commander?" Whisky asked after watching each Jivool heft a pitcher of cheap beer.

Facial recognition software in his pinplants flagged each time someone in his field of view looked at them. Text scrolled along the side of his pinview with whatever info could be gleaned from readily available sources. It meant there was a lack of info for rank and file soldiers but, at least, the names and units of NCOs and officers were displayed.

174 | JON R. OSBORNE

"We're going to have a couple rounds to give people time to see us and talk behind our backs, then I'll do something guaranteed to bring at least one asshole front and center," Bjorn replied. While Tamara and Charlotte drew eyes for obvious reasons, more patrons were noticing the Berserkers' logos. Bjorn had changed into a T-shirt and his black leather vest with the unit crest covering the back.

"What? You're going to find the biggest guy here and challenge him?" Cripe asked.

Bjorn shook his head. "Nothing so crude."

"At least you aren't dressed like a college girl and bending over a pool table until some townie grabs your ass." Tamara cast a reproachful side-eye at Charlotte. Whisky used to troll local watering holes for men who wouldn't take no for an answer and kick their asses.

"There's an image I can't drink away fast enough," Cripe muttered.

The Jivool exchanged confused looks, shrugged, and went back to their beers.

Bjorn noticed the huge monitors high on the walls. With mercenary contracts on hold, most were dark. The remaining few displayed sports or news feeds. One of the newscasts focused on a massive Red Justice Front-spurred riot in Los Angeles, where blocks of businesses and homes burned. Another featured refugees gathered at the hastily erected checkpoint on I-10 at the Texas-Louisiana border. Didn't they know that even if the Texas Republic let them in, the money for public assistance would run dry there as well?

The crowd drank as though their livelihood hadn't suddenly dried up, or maybe that spurred them to drink more. Outbursts erupted at random but never grew beyond shoving and a few sloppy punches.

When the server returned for the third round of orders, Bjorn set a thousand-credit chit on the table. "I want to buy a round for the bar. You can keep the change for the hassle."

The woman's eyes narrowed as she regarded the chit with its gleaming red diamond. "You're serious?"

Bjorn tapped the chit. "This isn't serious enough for you?"

The server consulted her slate. Bjorn guessed the tab would be half the value of the chit. "Who should I say bought the drinks?"

"Bjorn's Berserkers."

The woman scooped up the chit and disappeared into the crowd.

Gus peered at his empty pitcher. "We did not order."

"Don't worry, everyone includes you," Bjorn said.

"I thought you wanted to piss people off. Doesn't buying them drinks do the opposite?" Tamara asked.

"Watch and learn, Corporal Reeves," Bjorn replied. Sergeant Cripe gave Bjorn a knowing nod.

A buzz rippled through the crowd as the servers delivered the first of the free rounds. Bjorn made a mental note to try and slip the bartenders some credits in case the server wasn't feeling generous. Several heads turned Bjorn's way, and a few fingers pointed him out.

When the staff had served about half the drinks, a large man waded through the crowd, beelining for the Berserkers.

"Here we go," Bjorn remarked.

The man emerged from the surrounding patrons, pushing a few aside. His physique screamed CASPer trooper. Barrel chested and thick armed, his build matched Bjorn's. His tan BDU shirt bore a patch featuring a diving raptor grabbing a snake above a set of sergeant's stripes. He clutched a half-filled glass in his meaty hand.

"Sergeant, you come to drink a toast with us?" Bjorn called.

"I'm not drinking with traitors to Earth!" the bald sergeant yelled. "You pussies chickened out and left Earth to the aliens!"

Bjorn stood, and the surrounding crowd instinctively backed away. "Sergeant, I have no beef with Anatol's Hawks. However, you need to quit confusing your mouth and your asshole before you make accusations. You know nothing."

Additional Hawks emerged from the crowd behind the sergeant. "I know you didn't come back until it was safe. I know you moved your unit off Earth. I know you're backing the United States instead of the Terran Federation."

"We were on contract when Peepo hit Earth. The contract was a lure, but we fought our way out of Peepo's trap!" Bjorn bellowed. "Peepo went after humanity's colonies, including the Berserkers' offworld colonies! Any man who claims the Berserkers are cowards is a liar or a fool!"

Bjorn picked up a tumbler of whisky from his table. "So, what'll it be, Sergeant?"

The sergeant threw his drink in Bjorn's face. "Fucking cowards."

Bjorn wiped the liquid from his mustache and beard and downed his whisky. The tribal tattoos on his right arm swirled into a rousing bear.

"Here we go," Whisky muttered.

"That's the best you got, Sergeant? Throwing a drink like a pissy bar flower? I didn't take Anatol's Hawks for bitches." Bjorn spat at the feet of the bald man.

Bjorn barely got his arm up in time to deflect the punch. Instead of striking him square in the temple, the sergeant's fist clipped his chin—a painful reminder about getting cocky. People often mistook CASPer troopers for crude, brawling brutes. The best troopers drilled in hand-to-hand to deal with the many aliens who preferred to fight up close and personal.

Bjorn jabbed at the nerve cluster under his opponent's arm. Nanite treatments toughened the joints and connective tissues of CASPer troopers, but the soft spots under their arms remained vulnerable. The sergeant grunted in pain but hammered his opposite fist into Bjorn's ribs hard enough to knock him back a step.

The crowd shouted as the two men circled each other. Bjorn resisted the urge to use his left arm—he didn't want to seriously harm the sergeant. A volley of feints and jabs left both men with bruises. Keeping his left arm out of the fray handicapped Bjorn. Fortunately, his first serious hand-to-hand instructor had taught him not to rely on the cybernetic limb.

When the sergeant lunged again, Bjorn body slammed into the man and swept a foot behind his opponent's knee. The man toppled, but to his credit, twisted as he fell instead of landing on his back. Bjorn kicked away his supporting arm before the sergeant could regain his feet and slammed his right fist into his foe's cheek, driving him to the floor.

The Hawks came to their sergeant's defense. Wicza, Reeves, and Cripe jumped into the fray. The spectators pressed into those behind them, widening the gap on the floor. Two Hawks ganged up on Cripe, so Bjorn snagged one by the jacket collar and tossed him away. A Hawk grabbed Whisky from behind, only to lose teeth when she slammed her head into his jaw.

178 | JON R. OSBORNE

Reeves traded feints and blocks with an opponent. Two more Hawks charged Bjorn. Flashing back to his football days, Bjorn set against their charge but spun aside as they reached him. One sprawled on the floor. The other tried to tackle Bjorn, forcing him back a couple of steps before Bjorn broke the tackle and slugged the man in the gut—something he couldn't have gotten away with in football.

Roscoe and Gus loomed over the spectators, roaring encouragement. The crowd opened around them, but none of the Hawks were foolish enough to approach a pair of Jivool.

The sergeant regained his feet and grabbed a barstool. He rushed at Bjorn, swinging the stool with both hands. Bjorn snagged the stool in mid-swing with his left hand. Play time was over. Bjorn wrenched the stool from the sergeant's grasp and forced him back with a palm strike.

"Enough!" Bjorn crushed the metal tubing of the stool and dropped it to the floor. The sergeant's eyes landed on the crumbled metal. "You assholes want to do Peepo's work for her? Because Humans fighting among themselves is exactly what she wants! She even hired a Human merc company to take out fellow Humans. The Berserkers fought them and took them out!"

'Transmission fee paid. Commencing feed.'

The dark screens illuminated and displayed the butcher's bill for Patoka, followed by the casualties taken in the flight to Alaska. "The Berserkers paid in blood, same as everyone else. I don't give two shits about the political infighting beyond how it affects my company and how it hampers Earth's standing for itself."

Half the screens changed.

"Son, give these alien motherfuckers what for." Blood trickled down the side of Bjorn Tovesson II's face, staining his silver beard red. He grunted as his CASPer shook and the illumination flickered. "I'll see you in Valhalla."

The murmuring crowd fell silent.

Wrenching metal drowned out all other noise. After a moment, a savage voice snarled, "Meat."

"Fuck you, *sukin syn*," the senior Tovesson spat back. "Bettie, Ragnarök."

The image ended with a white flash, then static.

"There's no room in Valhalla for cowards or traitors! You want to call me or my Berserkers cowards or traitors, you come and do it to my face!" Bjorn shouted. While the Jivool roared, the screens went dark. Bjorn checked his people; no one seemed any more worse for the wear than a split lip. The crowd collapsed into the vacant space as patrons reclaimed abandoned tables.

Cripe winced as he took a drink upon returning to his seat. "You think that will put an end to it, sir?"

"No. No matter what, there will be assholes, especially when there's no one willing to call them out," Bjorn replied. He probed his teeth on the left side of his jaw with his tongue, grateful that none of them wiggled. He eased onto a stool, his ribs still aching. Bjorn sensed someone at his elbow. Had the sergeant from Anatol's Hawks come back for seconds?

The man had the build of a CASPer trooper but had a decade on Cripe. His hair and short beard were burnished steel with a few traces of the original black. Bjorn couldn't see the unit logo on the dark green BDU shirt, but he recognized the name Garrett above the pocket. Was this the first taker on calling out the Berserkers to his face?

"Commander Tovesson, I'm Captain Vance Garrett of Garrett's Rangers. It took brass to show up here knowing the way some of these folks have been speaking about you and your people."

"That was the point. My people worked and bled too much to have their name shit upon," Bjorn stated. "I had to get the word out before this snowballed further. Now, people can make their own decisions. Some will still brand us deserters, but I dare them to do it to my face."

Bjorn waited to see if Garrett would. Instead, the grizzled captain said, "I'd like to buy you and your people a drink. I knew your father back when your granddad ran the Berserkers. Your dad was the sergeant over the cadre troops when I joined."

"You were a Berserker?" Bjorn moved aside so Garrett could join them at the table.

"For a good 15 years. I saved money and learned everything I could from your namesakes," Garrett replied. "They weren't stingy with the tricks of the trade, even after they figured out I planned to strike out on my own. I bought two squads of second-hand CASPers and a beat-up dropship."

"You must have done right by yourself if you're still around," Bjorn remarked. Half the mercenary companies formed didn't last two years.

"I reckon I did all right. Before Peepo's invasion, I could field a company of CASPers." Garrett's gaze grew distant. "We missed a ride off-planet when the rat-bitch hit Earth. I lost half my troops and hardware before we were forced to surrender. We ran out of ammunition."

AN AXE TO GRIND | 181

"Are you going to rebuild?" Bjorn asked. He didn't mention how difficult it would be without mercenary contracts.

Garrett shrugged. "I might sell the firm and retire. Unfortunately, none of my officers or NCOs have the means to buy the company."

"I'm surprised they haven't tossed us out yet," Whiskey remarked, scanning the crowd for bouncers.

Cripe scoffed. "With the credits the commander is throwing around? No one got stabbed, shot, or mangled. They'll call it a Thursday night."

"Speaking of rebuilding, I heard what happened to Bear Town. A damned shame." Garrett paused to order the drinks. He didn't blanch at the Jivool's requests for pitchers. "Since you moved the Berserkers off-world, what are you going to do with the site?"

"I have some thoughts." Bjorn still hadn't settled on his plans. "In fact, if you're free tomorrow, I want to bounce some ideas off you somewhere where we don't have to shout. Are you free for lunch?"

"Lunch?" Gus perked up.

"Not you guys," Bjorn told the Jivool.

The ursines sulked until their drinks arrived. Hoisting the pitchers, they roared, "Beer!"

* * * * *

Chapter Fifteen

Hevrant, Tolo Region, Core

Nxo'Sanar ruffled his feathers as he passed through the temple trappings of the Hall of Service. The tech-priests approached their duties with a religious fervor. It made Nxo uncomfortable. He preferred practicality. Practicality led to profitability. Zealotry was a path to bankruptcy.

"Greetings, Chairperson Nxo'Sanar." The tech-deacon bowed low and swept a pair of feathered arms across his chest. "High Priest Than'Diwer awaits you. Please follow me."

Nxo kept his beak closed. The Union Credit Exchange needed the services of the Hall of Service, specifically the golems they provided. A pair of the black and crimson constructs flanked the door the tech-deacon opened and beckoned Nxo through. Nxo suspected these golems neared the end of their service cycles. Their position at the doors was purely ceremonial, so even a construct with a minimally functional core would suffice.

The tech-deacon led Nxo to a resplendent office. Fine tapestries decorated the walls, fine art objects graced the wooden desk and tables, and luxurious upholstered chairs faced the desk. Nxo tapped his talons on the black marble floor in irritation. The boardroom he presided over contained well-made, but utilitarian, furniture. The UCX did not waste credits on frivolity.

A side door slid open, and the elderly tech-priest hobbled toward the chair behind the desk. Gold sashes crossed his crimson plumage.

The priest regarded Nxo before clicking his ruby beak. "Please be seated, honored guest."

Nxo dipped his head to the elder Nevar and sank into one of the cloud-soft chairs. "Thank you for taking the time to see me, Than'Diwer."

"For the chairman, I can always make time. What brings you to the Hall of Service?" the priest asked.

Grateful to skip the anticipated hour of small talk, Nxo replied, "We need more golems. Between losses in the field, the growing need for security, and the natural degradation of their operating cores, the current supply is not keeping up. Recruitment through the Hall of Service is down 20 percent."

The priest averted all four eyes in embarrassment and clacked his beak in frustration. "You are correct. Despite our recruitment efforts, we lose more to retirement than we indoctrinate. Once you add in the other factors you mentioned, we cannot keep up."

"We must bolster our supply of golems." Nxo fought to keep a demanding edge from his voice. The priesthood reacted poorly to secular authorities bossing them around. "The Information Guild is pushing hard to disrupt our operations. They seek to divorce the Galactic Union from the red diamond standard."

"Madness. The red diamond has stood as the backbone of the Union economy for thousands of years," Than'Diwer protested. "They need the Nevar; they need the Union Credit Exchange."

"The Information Guild is lobbying the Senate to switch to a virtual standard, giving the Information Guild control over all the wealth in the galaxy," Nxo countered. "They have deployed their assets to root out hard currency and diamond shipments. It is only a matter of time until they find one or more of our mints."

AN AXE TO GRIND | 185

"Our mints' secrecy protects them," Than'Diwer said with a dismissive wave. "Fewer recruits means fewer golems rolling off the production line. I am disappointed by our own people's unwillingness to serve the greater good, but there is little I can do about it."

"Is there a way to prolong the lifespan of the operating core? If existing golems last longer, it may help." Nxo knew he was grasping at molting feathers. When the core of a golem expired, the frame returned here for refurbishing. How many shells sat empty for lack of new cores?

"We have sought that secret for as long as the golems have existed," the priest replied with a throaty chuckle. "But even encased within a ceramic shell and removed from the muscular-skeletal rigors of a fleshly body, the organic cores only last a decade. Our brave recruits sacrifice a century of lifespan to serve the Nevar, but few possess the courage, regardless of the remuneration we offer their family."

"I have often suggested more assertive recruitment methods," Nxo stated. As it stood, recruits voluntarily served as a golem's core in exchange for generous payment to their family. "The obedience protocols would prevent intractability."

"To coerce Nevar to shed their bones and feathers would be blasphemous," the priest countered. Nxo never understood how the priests of the Hall of Service could preside over the conversion of Nevar to organic operating cores for the golems but still pretend to hold the moral high ground.

"What of alien cores? Many races possess indigent populations. I'm sure some would willingly trade their forlorn, suffering lives for one of purpose," Nxo suggested. He knew the priests had dabbled in interfacing alien brains to the golems.

"Better to be a free pauper than a rich slave," the priest said, clacking his beak in irritation. "The Humans Peepo provided showed promise, but they require modifications to correct their asymmetrical coordination. If they discovered the end result, they would never willingly submit. Many of the mercenary races' physiologies are incompatible with the golem cores. We can't stuff a Tortantula's brains and organs into one of our core capsules. More the pity, as they would be best suited for operating a golem."

"Figure something out, or we will all end up impoverished."

* * *

Information Guild Headquarters, Capital Planet

"I believe 3.2 billion credits will balance out the charges," Ochkarn, the Sumatozou Cartography Guild representative stated. "After all, you have been delinquent for several months."

Master Archivist Heloxi sputtered so hard, a large tadpole launched in an arc and splashed in the pool with a squeak. The tiny Kimmilok swam out of Heloxi's reach to join two of its siblings on the far end of the pool.

Heloxi slapped her flabby flank. "Lies! We have paid the agreed fees on time!"

"Not under the new agreement ratified by the Senate in accordance with General Peepo's demands," Ochkarn said, waving his split trunk. "Information packets subject to expedited service carry a surcharge, based on the time saved over traditional information packet delivery."

Index Prime retrieved the agreement in question and sent it to Heloxi's pinplants. She scrolled through the relevant text. "Ridiculous. Since hyperspace travel occurs at a fixed pace, the most time any couriers could shave off is a handful of seconds for aligning their antennae and prioritizing data delivery operations." Heloxi found the number she sought. "This provides for a 0.01% surcharge per second saved."

"I presume that is why the Senate found the agreement reasonable. Saving an entire minute would result in a 0.6% surcharge to the Information Guild." Ochkarn folded his stubby fingers.

"Then how does this add up to billions of credits?" Heloxi demanded. Her tongue fished out one of the few remaining tadpoles from her throat pouch. She bit her squirming progeny.

"The Senate is unaware of certain…options to expedite hyperspace travel," the Sumatozou said with a smug grin. "Other individuals were better informed and willing to pay the premium. This, of course, saved far more than seconds."

New data appeared in Heloxi's pinview, with data manifests for 17 ships utilizing five-day transitions. Goosebumps erupted over Heloxi's slimy flesh. Five-day hyperspace journeys shaved 50 hours off travel time. She flipped back to the agreement. The Information Guild's representative to the Senate had signed off on the surcharge. She scrolled to the section in question but couldn't find a cap on the supplemental fee. A rapid transition shaved off 180,000 seconds.

"Outrageous! It's obvious these dolts had no clue about your secret rapid transition!"

Ochkarn spread his trunks. "The agreement stands, as does the debt. You owe the Cartography Guild 3.2 billion credits. I'm sure it is a petty amount for the illustrious Information Guild."

Heloxi fumed. "Fine. You'll get your money! We will transmit the funds shortly."

"Given recent irregularities, I'm certain you'll understand why we insist on a hard currency payment."

"What? Virtual credits are legal tender!" Heloxi protested. Her painted cheeks flushed red.

"Per the standing financial acts, a creditor is entitled to demand hard credits or their equivalent in red diamonds for debts over 100 million credits," Ochkarn stated. Index Prime confirmed the statement in Heloxi's pinview. "As such, we are required to grant you 15 days to gather said funds. We've been patient this long. We can abide 15 days more."

Heloxi seethed. The few remaining tadpoles in her throat pouch squirmed out of reach. "Fine."

"Then our business is concluded until you have the payment. Oh, if you are late, we will begin compounding interest on your debt." The Sumatozou bowed and departed Heloxi's chamber.

"I should have the accursed Cartography Guild Master executed for this affront," Heloxi muttered. "A shame I can't hire some Depik."

Index Prime: 'Guild Masters are exempt from assassination contracts per the Sanction Protocols.'

"A pity," Heloxi mused.

* * *

Union Credit Exchange Embassy, Capital Planet

Mel'Sizwer glanced up from his slate at the latest interruption. Endless meetings filled his day, punctuated by panicked calls from races and institutions regarding rumors of credit counterfeiting and UAAC failures.

Zod'Sizwey dipped her beak in respect. "Greetings, Grand Sire. I hope I am not interrupting pressing business."

Mel whistled the Nevar equivalent of a smile. "Please come in child, especially if you have good news."

"The Science Guild has provided the requested schematics. Our tests of the prototypes confirm the veracity of the design," Zod said. "We can transmit the schematics and the production licenses. The counterfeit detectors will propagate along trade routes. Within two months, every merchant who desires a counterfeit scanner should possess one."

"Splendid," Mel murmured. Between new minting protocols and the scanners verifying the authenticity of red diamonds, most of the concerns stirred up by the Information Guild's propaganda should be abated. "I sense, by your tone, we have not achieved an unequivocal success."

Zod'Sizwey shook her head. "The scanners have trouble detecting TriRusk diamonds. The best the Science Guild could achieve was a timeout suggesting in-depth analysis. Even so, half of the TriRusk samples flag as genuine."

"The accursed TriRusk again. What alien trickster god conceived a race who could shit red diamonds?" Mel mused. "At least their numbers are so small, they pose about as much threat as an unregulated, minor mine."

"Can't we snuff them out once and for all?" Zod suggested.

Mel'Sizwer ruffled his feathers. "If only it were so simple. The Peacemakers protect the TriRusk. Their miniscule population means any mercenary attack qualifies as attempted genocide. Peepo all but exterminated the Depik, so we can't contract them to put the TriRusk out of our misery."

"The Science Guild may yet produce a process to identify the synthetic diamonds the TriRusk create," Zod said.

"We are not the only ones who wish to see the TriRusk removed from the playing field," Mel remarked. "Perhaps they will prevail."

* * * * *

Chapter Sixteen

Houston, Republic of Texas, Earth

Dbo'Dizwey climbed from the van despite the protests of Uvksolt. The Sumatozou bodyguard required several seconds to extricate her bulk from the back of the taxi.

"If you need a ride, chirp me," the Zuul driver called once Uvksolt freed herself. Dbo noted he addressed them in one of the Terran languages, but her translator dutifully rendered it into Nevari. After the door slid shut, the van disappeared into the bustling traffic.

"Unimpressive," Uvksolt muttered, eyeing the temporary headquarters of the Terran Federation.

Dbo shrugged. Nxo'Sanar often pointed out the wastefulness of gaudy trappings. They served no purpose other than to stroke egos; no profit was derived from them. "It is a balkanized, backwater world. General Peepo thought it important enough to expend billions of credits conquering it. I'm here for a purpose, not to judge their architecture."

Uvksolt snorted and led the way to the building's entrance. "Pitiful. This is a defensive travesty." She gestured at the transparent doors and walls with her stubby fingers. "I bet these don't meet the minimal counter-ballistic standards, and I see no sign of polarizing or dispersing coatings to counter lasers."

Dbo whistled and rippled her feathers. "Perhaps they should hire you as a consultant."

Temporary barricades funneled entrants to a security checkpoint. A quartet of uniformed Humans screened visitors and watched over personnel badging in. Beyond the checkpoint, a squad of Human infantry loitered while a pair of CASPers stood guard.

"Finally," Uvksolt muttered approvingly while regarding the Human battle armor. "The Human mecha suits are formidable on the battlefield."

Dbo resisted the urge to ask her bodyguard to elaborate. Before she was exiled, Uvksolt had served as a mercenary. What incident could have caused the Sumatozou to eject the duty-bound guard?

"Do you have an appointment?" one of the uniformed Humans asked, rousing Dbo from her reverie.

"Yes. I have an appointment with the assistant secretary of justice." Dbo chose her words carefully, keeping them as simple as possible. "I am Dbo'Dizwey. This is my bodyguard, Uvksolt."

"Very good, I see your appointment," the Human stated after consulting her slate. She placed two badges with Human glyphs on the counter. "These are your visitor badges. Your guard will need to check any weapons at the security checkpoint."

"I have checked my weapons; they are in working order," Uvksolt stated. "Does your security team require a demonstration?"

"No, I mean you will have to leave your weapons with security while you are in the building," the Human replied. "They will be returned when you are ready to leave."

Uvksolt placed both trunks on the counter. "How can I protect my charge if I am disarmed?"

"Those are the rules," the Human answered. To her credit, she stood her ground across from the hulking Sumatozou. "Please proceed to the checkpoint and enjoy your visit."

"You're playing obtuse on purpose," Dbo whispered as she accompanied Uvksolt to the scanning arch.

"Many races assume big equals dumb. I don't mind them underestimating me if something goes wrong," Uvksolt murmured.

"What weapons do you have to check?" the dark-skinned male asked. Dbo judged him to be a mercenary by his build.

"Check?" Uvksolt tilted her head.

"We don't have time for you to play with the yokels," Dbo muttered under her breath.

Uvksolt snorted. "Fine." She unholstered a huge laser pistol and a flanged mace, setting them before the Human.

The Human checked the safety on the pistol before placing it in a bin. Definitely a mercenary. Based on Dbo's briefing, the typical Human feared weapons as though they would leap up and attack of their own accord. He placed a glyphed tag in the bin and another on the mace before handing Uvksolt cards bearing the same glyphs. "Use these to reclaim your weapons when you conclude your visit. Please step through the scanner one at a time."

The soldiers watched them with curiosity as Dbo and Uvksolt proceeded to the elevators. More mercenaries—they appeared accustomed to aliens. With mercenary contracts on hold, Dbo was certain plenty of Human mercenaries were taking whatever work they could get. She wished she could ask Nxo why he didn't seek to hire Humans to guard their assets.

Referring to her slate, Dbo found the correct elevator button. Even on backwater worlds, some things worked the same. A Human functionary greeted them and ushered them into a meeting room. After a short wait, another Human joined them.

"Greetings. I am Assistant Secretary Nels Kinsey." The Human's greying hair marked him as older, just as a Nevar's plumage fading from black to red did. "I hope your journey was pleasant."

"It was comfortable enough." Dbo hoped Uvksolt didn't chime in with her observations.

"What brings you to the Terran Federation Justice Department? I had never heard of the Nevar, let alone met one, before your message arrived," Secretary Kinsey said.

"The Nevar administer the Union Credit Exchange," Dbo stated. The Human straightened. She had his attention. "Some mistakenly refer to us as the banking guild. We only serve part of the old guild's purpose.

"However, I did not journey here to discuss guild politics. You have many alien mercenaries in custody."

Kinsey nodded. "Most of the detainees are Besquith, MinSha, and Veetanho. The other races were 'just following orders' at the insistence of their own leaders. Since they didn't commit atrocities, we didn't incarcerate them."

"What do you intend to do with the imprisoned aliens?" Dbo asked.

Kinsey rubbed his chin. "Put them on trial, lock them up, and throw away the keys. I doubt the new government has the stomach for capital punishment, and it could set an unfortunate precedent."

"So, you will pay to house and feed these mercenaries for the remainder of their lives?" Dbo tilted her head. "How much will it cost?"

"That's for the bean counters—the accountants—to figure out," Kinsey replied.

"What if I offer an alternative? We know the mercenary injunction hurts your world's cash flow. Eighty to 90 percent of your planetary income is derived from taxing your mercenary industry." Dbo folded her upper pair of hands.

"We've already heard the lecture on how short-sighted we were," Kinsey said. "If you're here to pitch a loan, I'm the wrong man."

"We want to buy your jailed aliens," Dbo stated. When Kinsey bristled, she added, "Perhaps that translated poorly. We wish to repatriate them and recompense Earth in the process."

"Why would you bail out mercenaries?"

"We have our reasons, and more importantly, we have hard currency. I am willing to offer 50,000 credits per mercenary for their...parole into my custody," Dbo said.

Kinsey's eyes bugged. He tapped the tabletop, consulting the embedded slate. "You're talking about nearly 100 million credits!"

"A price I can afford," Dbo stated. "Do we have an agreement?"

"Not so fast. This will require more than my say so." Kinsey sat back, studying the display in the table's surface.

"I understand," Dbo said. When she'd made her appointment, Dbo had considered throwing her weight around as a representative of the UCX, but that could have drawn unwanted attention. "However, my offer has a time limit. I will need an answer within two of your days."

Kinsey frowned and poked at the slate in the table. "Off the top of my head, I can tell you we won't release any Veetanho. Between the risk and their culpability in the overall invasion, it would be a deal breaker."

"We can abide letting the Veetanho pay for their crimes." Dbo had planned on shoving the rats out of the airlock as soon as they broke orbit, so this would mean saving a few credits. "The Veetanho have wronged many races."

"Some of the Besquith will be up for debate. They engaged in heinous acts against civilians and prisoners."

Not surprising, but the Besquith were the ones Dbo sought. The MinSha could prove useful—their sense of honor would obligate them to serve competently to pay off their parole—but the Besquith could be as frightening as golems.

Dbo folded her lower pair of hands. "Secretary Kinsey, once you have an answer, please inform me of the number and nature of the parolees so I know how much hard currency to bring."

"Of course. I'll get to work right away!"

* * *

Bear Town, New Mexico, Earth

"Captain Duarte."

Berto turned from watching the construction equipment loading and hauling away the remains of the main building on the Berserkers' base—Barn Hall or something similar. "What is it, Lieutenant?"

"A shuttle out of Houston has requested permission to land." Lieutenant Callie Belder held out her tactical slate. "The BTI projects it as a civilian shuttle."

Berto noticed the pinplant connections under the lieutenant's short hair. He had mulled over getting pinned, but the idea of someone rooting around in his skull gave him a shiver. "Clear them to land and notify the alert squads."

With the growing unrest, A CASPer squad and two infantry squads stood watch. So far, the protests hadn't spread outside the metropolitan areas, but Bjorn suspected it was only a matter of time, especially with the Red Justice Front spurring on the protesters. Berto couldn't disagree. He picked up his tactical slate and noted the deployment of the squads. The CASPers operated in pairs while the infantry squads broke into two fireteams each. There were four CASPers and three fire teams working the perimeters, with the remainder in the camp.

"Should we notify the commander?" Belder asked nervously. How had she survived as a sergeant? She would have made a fine corporal, and Berto found no fault with her performance as his second, but she seemed too timid to take charge.

"Not yet." At 0900 Bjorn could still be sleeping off last night's investigations. At least no one called from Houston for bail. Was Heather still there? Berto tempered the flicker of annoyance. He and Heather had broken up when he shipped out on his first contract two decades ago. "Keep Alpha-One-3 and Alpha-One-4 and Fireteam Bravo-Three on perimeter duty. I'd hate to get caught with our pants down."

Belder blushed. It was cute—another thought Berto needed to squelch. If she hadn't been in his command, he would have considered it. "Yes, sir."

The shuttle roared out of the east, flying low. Berto raised his tactical slate and zoomed in. The alien-manufactured craft lacked obvious hardpoints, but he would have felt better with an anti-aircraft rumbler. The shuttle slowed and diverted thrust for landing. It descended into a cloud of dust and sand kicked up from the tarmac.

As Berto approached the landing pad, the hatch in the shuttle's hull flipped open and formed a ramp. A pair of armored Lumar bearing laser rifles marched down and took positions flanking the base. Berto took it as a good sign.

A robed alien emerged and gingerly shuffled down the ramp. A mirrored visor concealed the alien's face, so only a pointy brown chin was visible. The visitor only stood as tall as Berto, and what little Berto could glean through the robes told him this was a new race.

"Welcome to Bjorn's Berserkers' Earth Headquarters. I am Captain Roberto Duarte, the officer-in-command. How can I help you?"

A string of sibilant hisses and pops sounded from behind the mask. "Greetings. I am Acolyte Ashok of the Information Guild. I wish to speak to Commander Bjorn Tovesson."

The Information Guild? Berto knew little about the guild, other than that it maintained the GalNet and managed UAACs.

"I'm sorry, but Commander Tovesson is off-site at the moment," Berto said.

"I am aware. He is in Houston. His schedule…he is in Houston."

"Do you want me to call him?" Berto asked.

"It is not necessary. He will return. I will wait." The alien stood frozen at the base of the ramp.

"Would you care to wait indoors? It would get you out of the sun," Berto suggested.

"That would be agreeable if my guards may accompany me."

Berto nodded. Did the alien understand a nod? "If you will follow me, we will make you as comfortable as possible until the commander returns." He tapped a quick message on his slate to Callie. *"Inform Commander T he has company."*

* * *

"Corporal Surjit is going to figure out sooner or later that you don't need my help," Glen remarked.

It's her fault for setting us up, Gina mused. "You hold the same rank. Besides, you are helping, and you've put in extra hours off shift."

"It's worth it if it means I get to spend time with you." Glen briefly clasped her hand, making her regret again that she balked at sleeping with him when the opportunity arose. She shouldn't let TJ's betrayal haunt her.

A message blinked in her pinview. BTI: 'Intrusion attempt detected.' A stream of technical data followed.

Gina muttered a string of expletives that would have made her abuela blush. "Someone is trying to hack into Bettie!"

"It has to be the shuttle," Glen said. He set down his technical slate, and a Tri-V image manifested above it. After a moment, a cloud of transmission sources cluttered the display. Glen swiped them away by category. "Yup. It's spoofing near-field data sharing."

Information cascaded through Gina's pinview. Decryption protocols and source identities flashed by. As soon as Bettie locked out one source, a new one would initiate log-in attempts. "Crap. They're using serious data worm software. More of Bettie's processing cycles are getting sucked in to keep them out."

"What if they think they got in?" Glen asked.

"At this rate, it's a matter of time. I have some new protocols we could try, but I need time to load and compile." Gina's fingers flew over her slate, supplementing her pinplant interface. "What do you have in mind?"

"Remember the emulator we used when we were trying to contact Bettie?"

"You're right! If they get into the emulator and believe they succeeded, they'll stop trying to crack the encryption." Gina brought the emulator online. The data was six months out of date, so if they were searching for intel on the Berserkers disposition and deployment, it would be useless. Several of the processes were mere shells. "If they try to tamper with the code, we can figure out what they're up to."

"I've got a near-field relay ready for their next cycle," Glen stated. "I'm telling Bettie to drop her relay, then lock out the current source identity."

Gina cast the emulator's display to her Tri-V. After a moment, the word 'BREACH' flashed in red letters.

"Near-field output from the shuttle has dropped," Glen stated. "They bought it. Should we tell the commander or the OIC?"

"Let's figure out what they're after," Gina replied. Her hand strayed to Glen's. "We make a pretty good team."

Glen squeezed her hand. "We do. I haven't requested a transfer to the tech branch because that would make you my boss."

"So, Priya is planning on spending the night with Padre Hawkins," Gina said, fighting to keep a quaver out of her voice. "Maybe we could grab a late dinner and a couple of drinks…then…well…"

"Absolutely."

* * *

Houston, Republic of Texas, Earth

"I feared they were going to take my temperature," Vurrn remarked once they cleared the checkpoint. He flashed a toothy grin over his shoulder.

"What? I don't get it." Heather's expression reflected her puzzled tone.

"It's a dog joke," Bjorn said. "You know, when you take a dog to the vet."

Heather's eyes widened. "Oh!"

The guards at the checkpoint had delayed them several minutes while they checked everyone's credentials and inspected the vehicle. If Vurr Vroom Vehicles hadn't conducted business in Houston proper, it would have taken longer.

"I suspect Federation security realized you were leaving startown several minutes in advance," Vurrn said as he navigated Houston traffic. "As an American official and an American mercenary commander, you have at least one spy assigned to you."

Bjorn tried not to think about the footage operatives could gather and break into out-of-context still images. Would they threaten to blackmail Bjorn with a picture of Heather putting her hand on his? Would he go to jail for punching the operative's teeth down his throat?

"It's not as though we're doing anything...spyish," Heather protested. "If anything, we've tried to foster cooperation."

"It doesn't mean they won't be suspicious," Bjorn said. Ironically, the Houston-based mercs would trust him more if he totally pulled off Earth. Hanging onto the Bear Town site cast suspicion of siding with the Americans onto him.

Vurrn pulled the ZPT in front of an upscale *tapaseria*. "I have business to attend to, but I will be free in a couple of hours if you need a ride back into startown. At least going in, they are unlikely to lift my tail."

Bjorn chuckled. After he hopped down to the sidewalk, he held out his hand to help Heather climb from the Zuul vehicle. Was someone recording him with the intent of making his polite gesture seem lurid?

"I appreciate your inviting me along, but I'm not sure why you want me here," Heather said as they approached the entrance.

Bjorn held the door. "Your bosses are going to ask you about this meeting and what you've learned about my plans. It's easier to give you a ringside seat."

"You're getting a lot of mileage out of your dress-up uniform," Heather remarked, adjusting his lapel while they waited for the hostess. Did someone with a camera lurk in here?

"I figured the locals would balk at my typical merc duds," Bjorn said. He didn't mention they needed laundering to get the blood and booze out from last night.

A few minutes after the host seated them, the third member of their party arrived. "I hope I didn't keep you waiting, Commander Tovesson."

"Not at all. Please, call me Bjorn, or if it's awkward because you knew my father, you can call me Trip," Bjorn said. "Heather, this is Captain Vance Garrett of Garrett's Rangers. Captain Garrett, this is Heather Akins."

"The girl your father said you had a crush on when you were in middle school?" Garrett grinned. "You'd just moved here from Alaska. It must be fate if you're still together after all this time."

"Oh, we're not together." Bjorn wasn't sure who flushed redder, him or Heather. "We dated in high school, but it was a long time ago."

Garrett gave Bjorn a conspiratorial grin but dropped the subject. "Well, feel free to call me Vance. I admit, your invitation intrigued me. What's your part in this, Miss Akins?"

"Please, call me Heather. Consider me an unofficial representative of New Mexico and, to a lesser degree, the United States government." She placed a hand on Bjorn's shoulders. "Our...history gave me an advantage facilitating talks between the government and the Berserkers."

After drinks arrived, Garrett said, "Word has it you rejected Cartwright's invitation to move your operations to the Terran Federation."

"Colonel Cartwright and I discussed current events, but there wasn't any sort of 'invitation.'" Bjorn sipped his Mexican lager and tried to gather his thoughts. "There isn't much to move, but my family owns the site at Bear Town. We already have a logistics facility in the Houston startown, and we'll open an office to replace the one slagged during the occupation."

"So, what are you going to do with the Bear Town site?" Garrett asked. "Sell it back to the feds...I mean, the Americans?"

"I doubt they can afford what I'd want for it," Bjorn replied. A server arrived with platters of tapas, interrupting him. "I hazard to say they'd prefer I continue some sort of operations on-site in hopes of bringing in some tax revenue."

"Not to mention the economic impact the Berserkers have on the Las Cruces area," Heather added. "Before the invasion, the Berserkers employed hundreds of locals and spent millions with area businesses. The loss is a hard pill for my...patrons to swallow."

Garrett loaded a plate with a variety of morsels. "While this is fascinating, what does it have to do with me and the Rangers?"

Bjorn answered while choosing his own assortment of tapas. Houston's location meant there was more fresh seafood among the choices. "I want to buy the Rangers and roll the personnel and hardware into the Berserkers. We lost a lot of both on Patoka. Any of your folks who don't want to become Berserkers would be released from their contracts with no indemnity."

"You have that much cash?" Garrett covered his mouth. "I figured you'd be strapped, between Bear Town and your losses on Patoka."

"I have more than one iron in the fire. Also, I'm hoping you'll consider a part cash, part stock offer for the Rangers." Bjorn decided not to mention the CASPer manufactories the Berserkers had captured from the Espejo Obscura on Patoka. Binnig was focused on recovering the manufactories on Earth that Peepo had commandeered, as opposed to the several destroyed. The Patoka assets fell under the latter on the books when the Espejos blew up the original site in Coahuila to cover their tracks.

Garrett frowned. "I'm counting on the money to fund my retirement. If you're getting into a pissing match with the Four Horsemen, I don't know if I can count on the stock holding value."

"Cartwright and I had a disagreement over a specific issue," Bjorn countered. "I don't have bad blood with the Four. Hel, I leased space in my bunker up north to the Horde. Let me ask you something else. Once you find a buyer for the Rangers, me or someone else, what will you do?"

"Honestly, I'm not sure," Garrett admitted.

"I want to open a mercenary academy—consider it a VOWS prep school, but I need someone to run it. You'd make an excellent commandant," Bjorn said. He picked up his beer while Garrett chewed on the idea and another tapa. "You're too young to hang it up, but this would mean no combat deployments and minimal travel."

"Do you have a plan or is this conjecture?" Garrett asked.

"I can send you the plan as it stands. I'm going to base the school and the Berserkers' cadre base at Bear Town. They'll be separate operations with some shared assets such as the motor pool and flyers." Bjorn studied Garrett's expression. He wouldn't want to sit across a poker table from the man.

"Hell, I hate fishing, and I don't know what else I would do once I retire. Pending going over your plan and us agreeing on a percentage of cash versus shares, I'm in on both counts."

"Praise Odin!" Bjorn hoisted his beer. Garrett tapped his mug to Bjorn's.

An amber message icon winked in Bjorn's pinview. As he quaffed his beer, Bjorn opened the message.

BTI: 'The Information Guild sent a representative to Bear Town. Someone from the guild attempted to infiltrate my core servers. Gizmo is monitoring their activity.'

Bjorn scanned his green messages—lower priority missives—for anything from the OIC at Bear Town. One from 15 minutes ago was near the top of the list.

"This is interesting," Bjorn said aloud as he read the message in his pinview. "Someone from the Information Guild landed at Bear Town and is waiting for me. The officer in charge has them cooling their heels."

"The Information Guild? Since when do they appear for anything in person?" Garrett asked.

"I better pay for lunch and see if my Yack works," Bjorn replied, only half joking. "Heather, if you want a ride to New Mexico, I'm flying back once we finish here."

"Can we swing by the hotel first?" Heather asked.

Bjorn ignored Garrett's subtle nod. "Sure. No sense in keeping the rooms if we don't know when we'll be back. Vance, I'll send you the plan and call you later so we can hash out numbers."

* * * * *

Chapter Seventeen

Bear Town, New Mexico, Earth

Bjorn studied the shuttle as the VTOL pilot circled the landing field. Bettie's warbook came up blank. Bjorn's best guess was that it was a high-end civilian model. How much money did the Information Guild have? They received a tiny percentage of every UAAC transaction as well as fees for messages and data access. Even the smallest charges would mushroom when multiplied by trillions.

"I can have one of the troops drive you back to Las Cruces," Bjorn said as the scream of the turbines faded upon landing.

"I'd appreciate it," Heather replied, waiting for him to give her a hand. The copilot passed them their travel bags.

Heather froze after a couple of steps. Berto stood in front of them, staring at Heather. "Berto?"

"Hello, Heather. You're looking...well." Berto blinked and turned to Bjorn. "The guild rep is chilling in the lounge at HQ. I assume your pet nerds told you about the guild trying to fish around in our servers?"

Berto needed to learn the value of technical logistics. Most mercenary companies couldn't afford dedicated IT support personnel. "I received messages from Gizmo and Bettie. They have some damn nerve requesting a meeting, then poking around in our computers while they wait."

"I better see what this is all about," Bjorn told Heather. "Captain, round up someone to drive Heather back to the city."

"I just handed off OIC. I could do it while I'm running some errands," Berto suggested.

Bjorn stifled the flash of jealousy. Two decades ago, Heather had dumped Bjorn for Berto, and this could work to his advantage. "Sounds good. Since you just came off shift, take your time. I'm sure you two have some catching up."

Bjorn hurried off before Heather could say anything, or worse, do something that would have people gossiping. He needed to get home to Talita, but every time he turned around, another task cropped up on Earth. If nothing else, Bjorn needed to arrange matters so he could be away for a month or two.

Stefan waited behind his desk. "Your visitor is in the lounge. We offered him refreshments. I don't know what race he is, but he only accepted water."

"Where's Gizmo? I want to talk to her before I meet this guild representative." Bjorn would have asked Bettie, but other than the message, she had gone quiet since the intrusion attempt.

"Back in her workshop, I presume. They haven't come out for two hours," Stefan replied.

"They?" Bjorn headed for the glorified closet that passed for tech support. When he yanked open the door, Gizmo and a logistics corporal snapped their eyes up from a Tri-V display and self-consciously scooted away from each other like a pair of teenagers caught making out.

"Sergeant Zomorra, are you back here playing kissy face while the Information Guild is trying to hack our virtual intelligence server?" Bjorn crossed his arms, suppressing the grin that would have revealed he was teasing.

"No, Commander!" Gizmo scooted a couple more centimeters away from the corporal, who was attempting to fade into the background. "Corporal Brand and I were evaluating the Information Guild's probes of the emulator."

Bjorn spotted the logistics tape on the young man's uniform. "Brand? Shouldn't you be tallying ammo or jump juice?"

Gizmo grabbed the corporal's sleeve. "Glen is helping me—it was his idea to let them into the emulator so they would think they succeeded and stop trying to crack into Bettie's real server."

"Maybe I should transfer him to your team, Gizmo," Bjorn suggested with a grin.

"No! I mean, that won't be necessary, sir."

"I should check in with Corporal Surjit," Brand stated. "I'll see you for dinner, Gina. Commander."

"Corporal." Bjorn managed to keep his grin from widening as the corporal fled. He made a mental note to review the logistics department. If there wasn't a sergeant running the show, he should fix it by promoting Surjit. "All right, Gizmo. What are our guests snooping for?"

Sergeant Zomorra enlarged the display on the Tri-V. "There were two probes. The first one was a cursory scan of storage architecture and file headings, followed by a sweep of message traffic caches. If I didn't know better, I'd say they were scanning for viruses or aggressive countermeasures. They probably have a pretty good image of our Table of Organization and Equipment as of six months ago. If they dig into the files, or open messages in the cache, they'll realize they're poking around in out-of-date data."

"What was the other probe?" Bjorn asked, studying the hologram.

A cascading stream of code on the Tri-V flashed amber. Gizmo gestured, and the code froze, several lines blinking. "If I didn't know better, I would say they administered a McCarthy-Turing test."

"Put it in big, dumb trooper speak," Bjorn said.

"McCarthy is the founding father of artificial intelligence on Earth, and—"

Bjorn held up his hand. "Big, dumb, and short attention span."

"They checked to see if Bettie is an artificial intelligence," Gizmo said.

Bjorn knit his eyebrows. "Why would they suspect we have an AI? If anyone has an AI stashed in the basement, my money is on the Golden Horde."

"Bettie's advanced Turing protocols may have triggered some sort of alert," Gizmo suggested. "Between those and the virtual intelligence security protocols, someone got suspicious. Obviously, they're not from the Science Guild."

"The Science Guild has the most advanced tech in the galaxy. If they had tried cracking Bettie's security, we might not have detected it. They would have also known we don't have the hardware to make Bettie an AI. I don't know where your father got her main server core, but everything I've read on AI indicates we'd need hardware that is an order of magnitude more powerful to house one."

Bjorn shook his head, annoyed. Nothing like dropping in unannounced on someone and rummaging through their closets. "If they try to crack Bettie again, let me know immediately."

"Roger, Commander."

"Oh, and Gina, don't let whatever is going on with Brand distract either of you. What you do in your off hours is your business, but on duty time is on my dime." Bjorn made a mental note to ask Padre Jim about Corporal Brand. Gizmo was a bit naïve, and Bjorn felt protective. Talita would have called it paternal.

"Understood, Commander."

Bjorn found the chaplain waiting by Stefan's desk. "Padre, I was about to ask for you. We have a brand-new alien for you to meet."

"So I heard. No one can tell me much other than that he's from the Information Guild. As I understand it, a single race doesn't dominate the Information Guild," Pastor Hawkins said.

"Then you know more than I do." Bjorn led the way to the lounge.

A robed figure sat on a stool. Below a mirrored visor, a filter-straw disappeared into a seam in his 'chin.' The alien turned toward Bjorn and the chaplain. Hisses and pops sounded from behind the visor. "I greet you, Commander Tovesson." The alien removed the straw and set the water bottle on the table. "I hope my unscheduled arrival did not inconvenience you."

"A mercenary commander has to be flexible," Bjorn said. "This is my chaplain, Pastor Hawkins."

"Ah, yes. You codify your superstitions. I greet you Pastor Hawkins. I am Ashok, Acolyte of the Information Guild."

Bjorn sat across from the alien. He wasn't in the mood to dick around. "So, what brings you to our neck of the woods, other than snooping in my base servers?" The padre coughed in surprise. Perhaps Bjorn should have taken a moment to brief Hawkins.

Ashok raised a pair of hands. "We mean no offense, Commander Tovesson."

"Cracking security and prying into my files is rude. Normally, I would tell you to get your ass back on your shuttle and get off my base." Bjorn could feel Padre Jim clenching his teeth next to him. "However, since you came all this way, I'm going to give you a minute to tell me why I shouldn't send you packing and warn every other merc outfit on the planet about your shenanigans. In case you can't guess, a lot of people aren't fond of aliens from Capital."

"I apologize, Commander Tovesson. We merely sought to expedite any negotiations," the alien acolyte stated. He picked up and sipped water without interrupting their speech. "We can recompense you."

"What?"

"Would 1 million credits be sufficient contrition?" the alien asked.

A notification appeared in Bjorn's pinview. One million credits had been transferred to his UAAC account. "You think being rich lets you get away with whatever you want?"

"Your race sees the galaxy through a lens that values wealth. We value information above all else. Admittedly, our pursuit leads us to cross the social boundaries of other races. If we were fellow mercenaries with a disagreement, I believe the proper protocol would be to buy you a drink," Ashok said. "As we do not possess said social framework, I am utilizing a straightforward expression that conveys how the Information Guild operates—information for currency."

"Fine." Bjorn didn't want to admit it, but a million credits was a lot of 'sorry.'

"Excuse me for interrupting, but what race are you?" Hawkins asked. It was just as well he cut in; it kept Bjorn from telling Ashok that they sought leverage the Information Guild could use.

"I am a Chaar. I wear this visor because some races find our visages unsettling and part of the wavelengths generated by your primary star hurt my eyes." Ashok lifted a hand composed of two longer digits and two thumbs to his visor. "If you wish, I can remove my visor. Your artificial illumination is tolerable."

Bjorn had enough nightmare fuel to last a lifetime, what was one more alien face? "Go ahead," Bjorn said.

Ashok lifted the visor. His black on black eyes ran vertical instead of horizontal. The Chaar had a mouth above a split chin—separate orifices for consumption and breathing. Ashok's skin reminded Bjorn of a mummy's—leathery and dark brown.

"If it is of any consolation, Chaar refer to many races as half-people, because you only possess two locomotive limbs and two manipulative limbs."

"Happy, Padre?" Bjorn muttered. "Now that we've had show and tell, can we get back to why an Information Guild acolyte has arrived on my doorstep?"

"I wish to hire Bjorn's Berserkers on behalf of the Information Guild," Ashok replied.

Bjorn grunted. Great time for the Mercenary Guild to freeze contracts. If Ashok's 'apology' was any indication, the Information Guild had lucre to spare. "I assume you realize the Merc Guild has suspended all new contract activity?"

"We do. We also realize Humans rely heavily on mercenary income and have great need after the predations of the guild who has locked you out of gainful employment."

Another bungle by Shirazi? After the reparation debacle with the Veetanho, it wouldn't surprise Bjorn, but he couldn't see how it would lead to the guild halting all work. "Without a proper guild contract, we lack the legal protections of said contract."

"Trillions of transactions occur daily without the complicated instruments required for a guild contract," Ashok stated. "We could pay a significant portion in advance, as a show of good faith. We have chosen you for your history of scrupulous business dealings, among other traits."

Bjorn tried not to let his face betray his interest. "Assume I am interested. What can you tell me about the cont—about the mission?"

"We have identified a credit-counterfeiting operation. We wish to put a halt to it. The Information Guild would deputize you to act on our behalf." Ashok set down a slate. A hologram of an industrial site appeared over it. A number appeared at the top of the three-

214 | JON R. OSBORNE

dimensional image. "We would pay half this amount up front, re-gardless of the outcome of the mission. The remainder would be remitted upon elimination of the counterfeiting operation."

Bjorn let out a low whistle despite himself. The amount was twice the highest contract the Berserkers had ever completed, including all bonuses. "How time sensitive is this job? Most of my forces are on Vishall."

"Would you need more than a company of CASPers?" Ashok asked.

"I have a platoon here and a platoon rotating in. Wait, this offer is for a single company?" Bjorn chewed on the numbers. He had two platoons of infantry and two more rotating in with the platoon of CASPers in two days. "I'd be undermanned for the job."

"If you can depart in 48 of your hours..." Ashok paused and tapped the slate. The number increased by 50 percent.

"I would need 96 hours." How badly did they need this forgery outfit squelched? "Why haven't you gone to the Peacemakers with this?"

"The Peacemakers are otherwise occupied," Ashok replied. "I can give you 72 hours and one other incentive."

"What incentive?" Bjorn asked. He was ready to take the offer, but if Ashok wanted to throw something else in the pot, Bjorn wasn't about to stop him.

"As you are aware, the Information Guild administers Universal Account Access Cards. It facilitates tracking down individuals based on their use of their UAACs for purchases and clearing security checkpoints."

Not exactly a comforting notion. "What about it?"

The image above Ashok's slate shimmered and changed.

"Son, give these alien motherfuckers what for." Blood trickled down the side of Bjorn Tovesson II's face, staining his silver beard red. He grunted as his CASPer shook and the illumination flickered. "I'll see you in Valhalla."

Wrenching metal drowned out all other noise. After a moment, a savage voice snarled, "Meat."

"Fuck you, *sukin syn*," Bjorn's father spat back. "Bettie, Ragnarök."

The image ended with a white flash, then static.

'Video ended.'

Bjorn stood so fast, his chair clattered to the floor behind him. "Where did you get this?"

Ashok toppled off his stool, limbs flailing under his robes.

Bjorn rounded the table, shrugging off the chaplain's hand. "Where. Did. You. Get. This!"

"Your father transmitted it via the GalNet!" Ashok cried, bringing up a quartet of spindly arms. "You've left cache copies on multiple servers! We mean no offense. We can find them!"

Bjorn froze. "What?"

"The Besquith! You've made multiple inquiries regarding the Besquith leaders responsible for the crimes against your people and your family. If they use their accounts, we can locate them!" Four spindly legs scrambled for purchase on the floor as Ashok stood. "Consider it a bonus!"

"Give me a few minutes." Bjorn stalked out of the lounge, Hawkins on his heels.

"Commander, don't let them manipulate you," Pastor Hawkins cautioned.

"I know they're trying to pull my strings," Bjorn snapped as he paced in front of Stefan's desk. "With all the bullshit in the Merc Guild, we don't know when we'll see a payday. Those idiots on Capital act as though the galaxy grinds to a stop because of whatever red tape they can't untangle."

"I question the Information Guild's motives, precisely because they resorted to this tactic to sway you. They want you to react, not to think," Hawkins said.

Bjorn took a deep breath. "Tell me what's wrong with the mission."

"Well, there's the problem. On the surface, it certainly sounds legitimate. Take out a criminal operation with half paid in advance." Pastor Hawkins rubbed his chin. "I can't find a problem with their proposal, but I can't help feeling as though we're missing something. Can you succeed with only half the CASPers? I know we have infantry, but will it make up the difference?"

"I tendered an offer on a mercenary outfit this afternoon," Bjorn said. "Garrett's Rangers, with two platoons of CASPers and troopers. If Vance accepts, it will give us the manpower and then some."

"What about Bear Town, or whatever you want to call it?" Hawkins asked. "Do you plan to leave it undefended?"

"I'll leave half the infantry here," Bjorn replied. "How many CASPers are left in the Redoubt?"

Hawkins shrugged. "You'd have to check with Priya—I mean Corporal Surjit."

Bjorn pinged Surjit and relayed the question. He only planned on leaving a fraction of the hardware stashed in Alaska. The gear was serviceable, but out-of-date.

"Aren't those all Mk 6s? Who's going to pilot them?" Hawkins didn't sound convinced.

"The infantry can consider it a training opportunity." Bjorn hoped they wouldn't need to apply the training.

The reply from logistics appeared in Bjorn's pinview. Out of 50 CASPers, half remained. The plan called for leaving 12 behind and shipping the remainder to Bear Town in the next two days. "We'll have enough suits to gear two squads." Bjorn studied the accompanying information on ammo and consumables. Logistics had predicted his next question. "What do you think of that Brand kid in logistics?"

"Glen? Gina seems fond of him. Priya hasn't mentioned any issues with his performance," the chaplain replied. "Why do you ask?"

"Just being Papa Bear. I noticed him hanging around Gizmo."

"Gina is an adult. In fact, they're about the same age. I've been keeping an eye on them," Hawkins said. "In my opinion, she's better off with someone…who isn't a trooper."

"You mean testosterone-filled meathead?" Bjorn chuckled. The same appellation had been applied to him, especially in his youth. "I agree. Okay, I won't give him the scary father-figure speech."

A message notification blinked blue—it came from someone Bjorn had flagged as a priority. "Good news. Vance Garrett accepted my offer. We've got a busy 72 hours ahead of us."

* * *

Ashok scuttled back to the shuttle, eager to return to his quarters aboard the *Bountiful Excess*. The crude shelter the Human mercenaries operated in barely reduced the ambient dust and reeked of their sweat and food stuff. The Human commander had remained adamant regarding the three-cycle delay—72 of their hours—despite Ashok's offer of additional financial incentive.

Perhaps he should have located the Besquith before opening negotiations? If the commander had delayed in hopes that his personnel could locate the quarry, Ashok could expedite the process.

"What did you find?" Ashok asked the elSha technician waiting in the shuttle. The shuttle shuddered with liftoff. Ashok grabbed the straps of his harness and secured himself.

One of the elSha's eyes tracked Ashok. "The mammals are cleverer than I gave them credit for," the technician admitted. "They detected our attempted intrusion."

"I am quite aware." Ashok remembered the large Human's outburst. His temper rivalled Master Archivist Heloxi's. "The commander objected to our investigations. Were they hiding an artificial intelligence?"

The elSha made a derisive click. "These monkeys? Whoever provided the lead doesn't know much about AIs. The Humans use a multi-node, networked, virtual intelligence—advanced for them—but not a self-aware AI."

"It's just as well they don't," Ashok said. If the technician had discovered that the mercenaries harbored an artificial intelligence, it could have given Ashok another negotiating advantage. How would Commander Tovesson have reacted if Ashok threatened to expose their AI? Ashok shuddered in his safety harness. It was just as well they didn't have one. "What else did you find?"

"Boring stuff. Their roster and equipment manifest are out-of-date, so I hope enough gear and soldiers survived Peepo's invasion for your mission."

"The commander seemed confident," Ashok stated. Even if the Humans did not eliminate or capture the target, the attack should disrupt UCX operations. "Have you connected to the planetary network?"

The technician clicked again. "They modeled their network on the GalNet but used out-of-date equipment. A trainee and a Lumar could hack this network. Do you want to know how many files depict mating activity?"

"No."

"A lot. I mean, a lot a lot." The elSha shook his head in disgust. "What am I searching for?"

"Find out anything you can regarding Besquith incarcerated by the planetary government," Ashok replied. "I am sending you two UAAC identities."

* * * * *

Chapter Eighteen

"Can we skip going out tonight?" Sergeant Cripe groaned over lunch. "I'm sore in places I forgot could hurt."

Charlotte sat across from him, chewing on a lukewarm sandwich. She flexed her knuckles, careful not to start them bleeding again. A message chimed on her slate. "No rest for the wicked. We have two nights to finish. The Berserkers have a job, and we have to be back at Bear Town in 60 hours."

"How can we have a job if the Mercenary Guild is still dark?" Tamara asked. "Did they lift the injunction?"

Charlotte checked other feeds on her slate. "There's nothing about the guild being back in business."

"This can't be good," Cripe remarked. "It means the boss took an unsanctioned mission."

"Can we get in trouble?" Tamara asked.

Cripe shrugged. "Depends on the job, the employer, and the target. The big risk is that without a contract, there are no guarantees."

"He's right. I remember hearing the only reason we got paid for Patoka was because the payment was in a contract escrow," Charlotte said. It had taken millions of credits to lure the Berserkers into the trap at Patoka. The mission, itself, was costly in hardware and personnel losses, but the ledger read black for the contract, and that was before factoring in the spoils of war.

221

"Any info on the contr—on the job?" Cripe asked.

Charlotte skimmed the message again. "We're taking the incoming CASPers, the on-duty CASPers, and…the commander bought Garrett's Rangers."

"Welcome to the firm. Load up," Tamara remarked as she poured coffee. "You should ask Priya what she knows. If anyone has the scuttlebutt, Priya does."

"Good call." Charlotte tapped out a message. "I wonder how her pet project is coming along?"

"Gizmo and Brand?" Tamara sipped her coffee.

"What? Is she trying to breed nerds?" Cripe grumbled.

"Are you still grouchy because that Sirra'Kan shot you down the other night?" Tamara teased.

Cripe snorted. "I wasn't trying to pick her up. Since the Sirra'Kan aren't Union members, they might be involved in smuggling fugitives off-world."

"Uh huh." Charlotte smirked.

"I'm always grouchy," Cripe added.

"Maybe we should try there again?" Tamara suggested. "It's one of the few places we've seen Besquith, and Sergeant Cripe could take another crack at Hello Kitty."

* * *

Houston, Republic of Texas, Earth

"Minister Cartwright, what can I do for you?"

"Thank you for seeing me on short notice, Secretary Kinsey," Jim Cartwright replied. He preferred Colonel over his new title of Minister of War. The assistant secretary of justice stood and shook Jim's hand.

"No trouble at all. After all, it's why I'm here." Kinsey sat. "The courts in Israel are not running yet, and the secretary of justice needs someone to handle business here, in the capital.

"I came to talk about the alien prisoners from the invasion force," Jim said. Kinsey stiffened, which puzzled Jim. "Specifically, I'm checking to see if we hold a couple of Besquith."

"Oh. I thought the trial and disposition of prisoners fell under the purview of the Justice Department." Kinsey's smile didn't reach his eyes. Perhaps he thought Jim was exceeding his authority?

"I'm not trying to step on your toes, or those of the Justice Department, Secretary Kinsey," Jim said. "I trust you to handle the prisoners in a fair manner. Someone approached me, searching for two Besquith. I told him we wouldn't hand over war criminals, but I don't even know if we hold them. If we do, we may want to review their security." Jim gestured to the desktop Tri-V emitter. "If I may?"

Kinsey shifted uncomfortably but nodded. "By all means."

Jim cast the data from his pinplants to the display interface. Holograms of Tovesson's quarry appeared, accompanied by their respective information.

Kinsey squinted at the UAAC identification string and tapped on his slate. "The first one, Sergeant Druul, has an outstanding warrant for war crimes. We have not apprehended him. There is no record of him shipping off-world, nor any record of him among the recovered dead." Kinsey looked up from his slate. "Either he's dead, slipped off-world, or in hiding."

Jim nodded. If the Besquith was out there, he had better hope Tovesson didn't catch up to him. Jim bet the werewolf had been hiding in startown and had either snuck onto a ship or remained in hiding.

"The other one, Lieutenant Sabher—he was not charged with war crimes. He was more of a military investigator," Kinsey said. "Conflict records show his unit engaged in combat with armed mercenary units."

"What difference does it make?" Jim asked. "Do we have him?"

Kinsey cleared his throat. "Not anymore."

"What? You let him go?" Jim demanded. The answer was all over Kinsey's face. "By who's authority, and why wasn't I notified?"

"The secretary agreed to the terms of his parole," Kinsey replied. "Lacking war criminal charges, there was little reason not to accept the repatriation, and to be honest, the Federation needs the money."

Jim scowled. "What difference can a few thousand credits make?" A chill went down his spine, and Jim narrowed his eyes. "How many prisoners did the Justice Department parole?"

Kinsey refused to meet his gaze before answering, "Roughly 1,500, but none of those held on war crime charges, and no Veetanho."

"Why wasn't I notified?" Jim repeated, double checking his pin-plants for a missed message notification.

Kinsey finally looked him in the eye. "With all due respect, Minister Cartwright, your job is to deal with them on the battlefield, not to handle them in our justice system."

* * *

Houston Startown, Earth

"I hate this place," Tamara complained as Vurrn parked the rumbler next to the squat steel and concrete building. Once some sort of light industry, a large metal sign emblazoned with the name 'Stockyard' in several languages hung over the entrance.

"What's wrong, Reeves, don't like your meat fresh?" Sergeant Cripe chided.

"Wow, I want to slug you on principal for that," Charlotte remarked. Charlotte would have bristled at the statement anywhere else, but part of the Stockyard's allure for aliens was live meat. "I can't decide if it's a double entendre or a dad joke."

"I do not understand," Vurrn said. "My father would never joke about fresh meat."

"Dinner?" Roscoe called from the back.

"If you eat here, it's on your credits," Charlotte replied. She was afraid to ask if Jivool ate live or freshly killed prey. So far, they seemed content with burritos and cheeseburgers and didn't care if the meat came from lab factories.

"Not many vehicles in the lot," Tamara observed.

A truck loaded with bleating goats passed them, circling behind the building.

"We arrived in time for the dinner bell," Charlotte said, leading the way to the front door.

A Tortantula and a MinSha flanked the foyer inside the door. The MinSha regarded them silently as the Jivool exchanged greetings with the enormous spider nicknamed 'Milo.' A row of pens filled the back third of the bar, reminding Charlotte of the 4H barn at a county fair. Last time they drank here, the pens were empty save for a pair of employees hosing the floors.

Charlotte chose a table away from the pens and sat so she only had a peripheral view of the back of the bar. It would be easy to turn away when feeding time arrived.

"Arriving for feeding time?" the server asked. Her name tag read 'Millie.' The middle-aged woman jerked her thumb toward the pens. "You must be fans of goat tartar or have strong stomachs."

"Goat tartar?" Gus cocked his head.

"Raw goat," the server replied. "We have some chili if you prefer your meat cooked. It's farm raised, but you don't have to kill it yourself."

"I'll hold off on food," Charlotte replied. "We had a late lunch."

"Suit yourself, sweetie." Millie took their drink orders.

"We wish to try this chili," Roscoe announced. Gus nodded. The Jivool had adopted Human mannerisms in a matter of days.

"We'll have to roll down the windows on the rumbler," Cripe muttered.

"Don't try to blame this on the dog," Vurrn added, laughing.

"Sergeant Cripe, your girlfriend showed up for dinner," Tamara remarked, nodding toward the entrance.

Cripe's head snapped around. He watched the lithe Sirra'Kan settle at a table. "Zirri is not my girlfriend."

"I'm not judging," Tamara said. "She's Human-looking enough that I might be tempted to play 'Hello Kitty' if I didn't have a girlfriend."

"Good thing you have a girlfriend." Charlotte patted Tamara's hand. "Hopefully, I don't have to get jealous of a furry."

"Don't worry, sweetie. I'm not turning into a Niven," Tamara said.

More aliens filtered in through the entrance. Meanwhile, workers herded goats through the back of the building into pens. Bleating filled the air, along with the aroma of barn animals.

"I hope I don't get sick," Tamara muttered.

"Oh shit," Cripe whispered.

Charlotte half-turned so she could follow the sergeant's gaze. Late afternoon sunlight backlit three Besquith in the doorway. As they strode forward, she picked out one beta and two gammas. The beta had a notched ear and a scar above his right eye.

Charlotte tapped her slate, keeping the image on 2D and relaying the sound to an earpiece. She played a file Gizmo got from the Golden Horde team stationed at the Redoubt.

"This is Sergeant Druul." Druul's visage showed a scar running from above his right eye to his torn ear.

"Report, Sergeant." The slate dutifully translated Veetanho speech. Charlotte recognized the speaker—the only Veetanho every Human on the planet could identify. General Peepo.

"The Human, Bjorn Tovesson II, former commander of the unit Bjorn's Berserkers, is dead," Druul stated. "He engaged the apprehension team. There are three survivors, including me. We brought down his domicile on his mate with explosives and incendiaries."

Charlotte rewound the video and froze it on Druul's face. "Bingo."

* * *

Houston Starport, Earth

Lieutenant Sabher knew a clandestine operation when he saw one. He and his fellow Besquith had been herded from their cells to ground transports. Seven of the hundred Besquith at his facility had died when they rushed the guards while boarding the vehicles. Fools. If the Humans were going to execute them, they would put on a display of judicial theatrics. Most of the Besquith spent their incarceration frothing at the maw and clawing their fellows. Sabher studied the Humans.

Sabher surprised his jailers by requesting reading material. They wouldn't grant access to their lobotomized version of the GalNet, but they provided a slate that downloaded the news daily and could access educational material. While his prison mates squabbled, Sabher learned. Humans valued displays of so-called justice over practicality.

Sabher followed the other Besquith from his vehicle down the ramp. He recognized the Houston Starport. A transport waited nearby, its ramp lowered. Two aliens stood at the foot of the ramp. The Sumatozou stood ready for the first Besquith to challenge her. Sabher narrowed his eyes. This was no plump member of the Cartography Guild.

One of the Besquith broke ranks and lunged for the hulking alien. With a speed belying her bulk, the Sumatozou smote the foolish gamma with a heavy flanged mace. The Besquith crumpled with a wet crunch.

The other alien stepped forward. Sabher did not recognize the ebony, bird-like creature. It possessed four feathered arms and stood on four legs. Four eyes above its beak swept the remaining Besquith.

"Before we have any more needless violence, I have an offer to make. The organization I represent has purchased your parole. All we ask in exchange is one year of mercenary service," the creature announced. "If you prefer to rot in Human custody, I can return you to their care and save a few credits."

Muttering and snarling rippled through the Besquith. Sabher raised his voice. "What is the job? There is no glory in dying a fool's death."

The alien spotted Sabher, focusing all four eyes on him. "A good question from a thinking wolf. Who are you?"

"I am Lieutenant Sabher, of the Haagen creche. You did not answer my question."

"The duty is to garrison a facility under threat of an attack," the alien bird replied. "The conditions will be spartan, but we will equip you. We want you to succeed because failure means the loss of our facility."

Sabher knew the alien held information back. Given that they stood on an open starport tarmac, he did not blame the bird. Sabher turned to the remaining Besquith. "Form by octals and load up! Sergeants, manage your whelps! You, take charge of those gammas!"

The bird nodded approvingly. "Sabher, is it? You are the first to show both restraint and initiative. I name you captain of the garrison. I shall provide you with a tactical slate shortly. Meanwhile, please load this cohort. We have another transport on the way."

Garrison duty lacked challenge, but it would provide Sabher with ample time to learn what happened to the invasion and how it affected his people. That no one from Bestald ransomed the captive Besquith spoke volumes. Unlike the Humans, the Besquith had more to offer the galaxy than paid violence, but in recent years, mercenary income outpaced industrial earnings two to one.

The bird regarded the gamma on the tarmac, oozing blood from its crushed skull. "Captain, have someone dispose of that."

"Are you certain?" Sabher had no idea what title to apply to his new employer. "It may serve as an example to incoming loads of frustrated wolves."

The bird whistled and said, "I like how you think, Captain Sabher." The Sumatozou chuckled.

* * * * *

Chapter Nineteen

"I told you it wouldn't be easy to watch," Millie said, delivering the next round of drinks. Charlotte knew she should eat more, but the rending noises, the shrieking goats, and the smell conspired against her stomach.

Tamara hunched over the table, her chili and chips barely touched. "Tell me when it's over." She had paled when a pair of Besquith ripped a screaming goat in half and dove upon the spilled organs.

"Makes you want to turn vegetarian, doesn't it?" Charlotte asked, patting Tamara's back.

Roscoe slurped his third bowl of chili. "You did not know meat comes from animals?"

"Humans prefer not to think about it," Vurrn replied. A pair of gnawed rib bones lay on the plate in front of him. "They grow most of their meat in factories."

"Even burrito meat?" Gus asked.

"Probably not the *pollo* at the place across the street," Charlotte admitted. The cartel states provided farm meat at reasonable prices.

Gus grunted and licked his chili bowl clean. "*Me gusta pollo.*"

Charlotte checked on Cripe. How could he flirt with the felinoid, Sirra'Kan, while she ripped meat off a goat haunch? Men—they were willing to do anything for pussy.

Charlotte checked the time. Two hours and twenty-seven minutes since she had alerted Commander Tovesson that Druul was there. The commander's reply was a simple, 'OTW.' The Besquith didn't seem in a hurry to leave, but the first time the team had checked this place, the werewolves were gone. Maybe they went somewhere to sleep off their meal?

Movement at the entrance drew Charlotte's attention. The sun had set, but lights in the parking lot backlit entrants. A hulking form strode through the double doors.

"The shit is about to hit the fan." Charlotte tapped Tamara. "The commander is here."

* * *

Bjorn surveyed the room. Whisky smacked Reeves on the arm to get her attention, peering around the bulk of the Jivool. Cripe chatted up a Sirra'Kan. He'd better have medical nanites if he got lucky.

A trio of Besquith lingered near the pens at the back of the bar, an eviscerated carcass on the table between them. His pinplants highlighted one in his pinview and displayed the reference image.

Druul. The Besquith *sukin syn* who commanded the mission that resulted in the death of Bjorn's father and the razing of his ancestral home. Bjorn marched into the bar. Behind him, the MinSha and the Tortantula bouncers each stowed 1,000-credit chits.

"Druul of the Druugar creche!" Bjorn bellowed as he stalked toward the Besquith. All three turned at Bjorn's shout. "I call you to *Vord'rung!*"

The scarred Besquith pushed away from the table. "By what right do you make this challenge, Human?"

"You led the team who murdered my father, Bjorn Tovesson the Second. You and your coward wolves ambushed a civilian elder and set fire to my ancestral den, attempting to kill my mother."

One of the gamma flanking Druul lunged forward. Halfway across the floor, a 185-grain frangible bullet blew open the gamma's snout. Bjorn sidestepped as the werewolf's momentum carried it past him and put a second round in the back of its skull.

The Jivool rose to their feet, roaring. The other gamma glanced nervously at Druul. Druul snarled something at the smaller wolf too low for Bjorn's translator to pick up.

"We do not conduct the ritual with sidearms," Druul said. "You, Humans, fear true battle. I dismiss such a challenge."

Bjorn shoved his pistol into its holster and reached behind his back. He drew his double-bladed axe over his shoulder. "This true enough for you?"

Druul's maw split open in a shark-like grin. His eyes gleamed. "I am pleased I gave your father a warrior's death instead of offering surrender as Peepo directed."

Bjorn pointed at the older Berserkers sergeant. "Cripe, you're my second. If I fall, take word of what happened back to the company."

"Um, sure." Sergeant Cripe stood and circled from behind the table he shared with the Sirra'Kan.

"No one interferes. If Druul wins, leave him be. If anyone jumps in, take them out. This is between Druul and me."

Druul grumbled something to the gamma. "Hraag is my second."

"Commander, this is stupid," Whisky called. "Shoot him and be done with it."

"Noted, Sergeant Wicza." Bjorn hefted the axe given to him by his grandfather. "This weapon carries my name, the name of my father, and the name of his father."

Druul strode forward and shoved aside a table. "We can dispense with the formalities. I hope you die as well as your father."

The Besquith hunched and spread his arms. Long, razor-sharp claws gleamed from the tips of the werewolf's splayed fingers. Rows of triangular teeth filled the Besquith's gaping mouth. Druul circled, watching Bjorn as a predator gauged dangerous prey. A younger wolf would have already rushed Bjorn.

The bar fell silent. Druul tensed for a fraction of a second before he lunged, sweeping his claws in a downward arc. Bjorn twisted aside as he swung his axe with all the might he could muster from his cybernetic arm. The blade sheared off Druul's left hand and sparks flew from the floor as the axe finished its path.

Bjorn whipped the axe up on the rebound from the floor. Druul snapped his head back midturn, and the weapon passed in front of his face instead of splitting open his lower jaw. Bjorn hissed in pain as the tips of two of Druul's claws flayed open the skin and flesh over his ribs on his right side. If he hadn't force Druul back, the Besquith would have ripped open his ribcage.

Druul swiped with his remaining claws, but Bjorn leaned out of reach. As soon as the talons passed, Bjorn stepped in, swinging the axe. Druul grabbed the haft in a backhanded grip as the blade bit into his shoulder. The Besquith clung onto the weapon and opened his maw.

Bjorn released his hold with his left hand and rammed his fist into the Besquith's open mouth. Druul bit down and warning icons flashed in Bjorn's pinview. With a thought, Bjorn triggered a command.

'Talons extend.'

Electromagnets drove out a pair of molybdenum-alloy blades. The razor-sharp talons erupted from Bjorn's clenched fist. One punctured the Besquith's brain stem while the other sheared the upper spinal cord. Bjorn wrenched his fist free, and the Besquith collapsed like a marionette cut from its strings.

Druul tracked Bjorn with one eye. Bjorn dragged his axe away, wincing in pain from the movement. Blood flowed down his side from the lacerations.

"My father knew he was dying. I could finish you, but everyone watching would consider it murdering a fallen foe." Bjorn hefted the axe with his right arm despite the pain. His pinview showed 75 percent of the artificial muscle-fibers in his forearm were torn, and a tooth was lodged in his titanium-carbon-composite ulna. "This would be a mercy." He took an unsteady step back.

The gamma bounded forward with a snarl. The werewolf cleared an intervening table and leapt for Bjorn. A huge, hairy bulk slammed into the Besquith as Roscoe sent the gamma sprawling into a table. Gus jumped onto the Besquith's back. Spurs emerged from the Jivool's wrists, and he jammed them into the Besquith. Bjorn couldn't see the results as Gus piled on to pin one of the Besquith's arms before he could slash at Roscoe.

Colored spots swam in front of his eyes as Bjorn sank into a chair. He fumbled for a trauma nanite applicator in his belt pouch. He dialed the device to seven and pressed it to his flesh above the slices left by Druul. Bjorn gritted his teeth against the burn of the microscopic machines going to work. He checked his tattered hand;

his talons were still extended. One snapped out of sight while the other retracted slowly.

Whisky knelt next to his chair. "Sir, are you all right? Should I call a medevac?"

Bjorn shook his head. "I've been worse. The pain-in-the-ass will be the repairs to the left arm." Beyond Whisky, the MinSha passed credits to the Tortantula.

"Commander, with all due respect, that was the most boneheaded thing I've ever witnessed," Whisky stated. "What if you'd died here? What would that have meant for your family, for the Berserkers—"

"Yeah. Be sure to remind me the next time I yell at you for picking a fight," Bjorn said.

Cripe stood behind Whisky. "Sir, that may be the most badass thing I've ever seen." The older sergeant pointed back toward the corpses. "What do you want us to do with the bodies?"

"Nothing. No looting, no trophies." Bjorn fished out another 1,000-credit chit. "Give this to someone who works here for cleaning expenses. Get me a beer and a couple of burgers while you're at it."

"Sure thing. Goat chorizo burgers okay?" Cripe asked. "They're not bad."

Bjorn nodded. He needed to compensate for the blood loss and provide protein for the nanites. Now that his rage had ebbed, he realized Whisky was right. He could have left a widow and orphan behind and screwed over the Berserkers. His eyes went to the dead Besquith beta on the floor. "One down, one to go."

Most of the patrons lost interest now that the fighting had ended. Two Humans and a Goka set to cleaning up the aftermath. A server arrived with a mug of beer.

"I bet you think throwing around a few credits takes care of everything, don't you?" the woman demanded.

"Not everything," Bjorn replied. "Credits won't bring back the people those savages murdered, including my father."

"We all lost someone. Most of us don't carry around a literal axe to grind," the server snapped back. "I'll bag your burger to go."

"You do that," Bjorn said as she stalked away. He turned to his people. "All right, you saw the message about the job. I'll send a flyer to pick you up tomorrow at 1400 hours."

"What about Roscoe and Gus?" Whisky asked.

Bjorn regarded the Jivool. They guzzled beer out of plastic pitchers. "We're keeping the warehouse, so they're keeping their jobs. Once we get operations up and running, we might find something more useful for them to do, but right now, they can keep an eye on the logistics facility."

The server returned and dropped a grease-spotted paper bag on the table and departed without a word. The Besquith must have been good tippers.

"I'll catch a cab back to the shuttle." A VTOL flyer would have been too slow. Bjorn pulled out another nanite applicator and handed it to Cripe. "In case you get lucky."

Cripe flushed as he tucked away the device. "Um, thanks."

* * * * *

Chapter Twenty

Bear Town, New Mexico, Earth

Jim Hawkins' stomach threatened to refund breakfast when he walked into Commander Tovesson's office. The commander's left arm lay on his desk with the skin peeled back. An elSha technician lifted a bundle of white synthetic muscle from the limb and set it down. One of the reptilian alien's eyes swiveled toward Jim.

"Padre, everything set for the Rangers' orientation this afternoon?" Commander Tovesson asked. The commander idly turned a triangular object resembling an obsidian knife over on his desk.

"So, the rumors are true," Jim said stiffly. "You found one of your Besquith."

"Yup. Whisky's team tracked him to a bar in startown."

"I wondered why you lit out of here suddenly yesterday," Jim remarked. Speculation had ranged from a rendezvous with his old flame, the lawyer, to another meeting with the Terran Federation.

Bjorn set down the ebony artifact with a half dozen others piled on his desk. "Besquith teeth. No, before you ask, I didn't take trophies. I had to pull these out of my arm."

"How does revenge feel?" Jim asked, sitting across from the commander. He tried not to watch the grisly work underway.

"Not as cathartic as I hoped," Bjorn admitted, tugging at the hammer pendant hanging amid the bear claws adorning his necklace. "It doesn't change anything."

"What about the other Besquith?" Jim watched the commander's expression. A flicker of anger crossed his features before resignation replaced it.

"It galls me that Sabher got away. I'm bringing Whisky's team back this afternoon. Even if they could find Sabher in the next two days, I'm not in any shape to do anything about it," Bjorn said. He picked up a coffee mug and took a sip as though his other arm wasn't splayed open in front of him. "I sure as Hel can't go through another ritual duel. Before you lecture me about how stupid I am for going toe-to-toe with a Besquith, I know. It's nothing I didn't mull over last night."

"Fine. I guess you've already beat yourself up over it." Jim knew Stefan had orders about what to do if Bjorn died unexpectedly, but he wasn't sure how the company would weather the sudden loss of its leader. Especially with everything in disarray. "This does reinforce the importance of naming a second-in-command."

"I know. I need to talk to Marian about it. Even though there's a certain nostalgia factor to making Berto my right hand, he doesn't know the Berserkers yet." Bjorn picked up one of the Besquith teeth and tapped it on his desk. The point gouged the hard, plastic surface. "Boggs saved our bacon at Patoka. She's never had a problem calling me out on my bullshit, and her by-the-books attitude could help keep people from getting too lax."

They had already discussed these virtues regarding Marian Boggs. Jim was content to let the commander rehash them, especially if it helped him finalize a decision. "Is Captain Boggs coming with the platoon from Kodiak Company?"

Bjorn shook his head. "No point; it's why we have lieutenants. I'll sit down with her once we finish this job for the Information

Guild. If she has no objections, I'll promote her to major and name her XO."

"So, where will you assign Captain Duarte? To Kodiak Company to replace Major Boggs or to Grizzly Company since we still don't have a captain over it?" Jim asked.

The commander continued to vandalize his desk while he thought. "I'll keep him in Grizzly. Berto doesn't have any experience with armor. Lt. Magnus' platoon performed well on Patoka, and she's accustomed to fighting alongside Casanovas. What do you think about her replacing Boggs?"

"She's certainly not a bad choice. She's not outgoing, but she exhibits solid organizational and management skills."

"That's what we'll do." Bjorn noticed the scored desktop and self-consciously set the Besquith fang aside.

* * *

Houston Startown, Earth

"Look what the cat dragged in," Tamara declared. Charlotte squinted into the early afternoon sun blazing through the open doorway. Sergeant Cripe shuffled through and dumped his duffle bag on the floor. "About time you showed up." She had left the Jivool to watch over the sergeant while he persisted in flirting with the Sirra'Kan at the Stockyard. "The flyer will arrive in less than an hour."

Cripe shifted his shoulder and grimaced. "Any coffee left?"

"Only because the bears don't drink it," Tamara replied.

Gus lumbered out of the break room. "See, Sergeant Wicza, Sergeant Cripe was alive when he left the bar." A muffled rumble sounded from behind Gus. He growled back in Jivool, which Char-

242 | JON R. OSBORNE

lotte's translator dutifully rendered into English. "I am not going to ask him about the mating."

"Really? With an alien?" Tamara shook her head. "No wonder I date women."

Cripe grinned. A trio of scratches running from under his right ear toward his chin were only partially obscured by his salt and pepper beard. "I'm not a Niven, but it was good enough for The Legend. Is there any breakfast or lunch left?"

"We left a super-burrito in the fridge for you," Charlotte replied, following Cripe into the break room. "There was no saving the chips."

"There's only half a burrito." Cripe held up the remaining portion.

"Sorry," Roscoe muttered, studying the floor. "Did you have fun mating?"

Sergeant Cripe chuckled, then winced as he settled into a chair. "Yeah. I'll have a hell of a time washing the blood out, though."

Roscoe elbowed Gus, and both Jivool laughed. It sounded like someone shaking a box full of gravel.

"Wolf down your lunch. I want to roll in 15 minutes," Charlotte stated. She left before the Jivool asked Cripe anymore questions about his nocturnal adventure.

"Vurrn is letting me drive the ZPT to the tarmac," Tamara said. "Lucky for him, one of our VTOL flyers can't lift a car."

"Keep it up, and I'm liable to get jealous of that Zuul transport," Charlotte remarked.

* * *

Bear Town, New Mexico, Earth

The incoming call icon blinked in his pinview. Bjorn picked up his slate. "This should be good."

"What?" Padre Jim peered at the slate. Colonel Jim Cartwright's face appeared on the screen.

"Colonel Cartwright—I'm surprised to hear from you." Bjorn said. He noted that Cartwright also used an external device to facilitate the call. They could use their pinplants, but the call would lack video unless they wanted to stand in front of mirrors. The slates' cameras allowed them to see each other's faces.

"I'm not sure why I'm telling you this, but one of the Besquith you were hunting for is no longer in Federation custody," Cartwright stated as though he'd rehearsed the line.

Bjorn clenched the slate, drawing it closer. "You had one of those murdering sonuvabitches, and you let him go?"

"Don't shout at me, Commander Tovesson." Cartwright didn't flinch. "I didn't know. The Justice Department made a deal behind my back. Someone paroled most of the Besquith and the MinSha."

"Didn't their home worlds hang them out to dry?" Bjorn asked. All the merc races turned into credit-pinchers after Peepo left them high and dry. General Peepo had skated out on billions of credits owed to the various alien races who fought on her behalf.

"A third party bailed them out with hard credits. I objected, but even if it hadn't been too late, I suspect the Justice Department would have carried on anyway. Earth desperately needs credits, and as much as it galls me to admit it, we gained nothing by sticking mercenaries in cells for fighting on the other side."

Bjorn gritted his teeth to keep from yelling at Cartwright. "I guess I'll bide my time. Sooner or later, I'll find Sabher."

Colonel Cartwright squinted at his camera. "How do you know which Besquith we held?"

Bjorn let a grin raise the ends of his mustache. "Because I already killed the other one."

"Oh."

"It was a fair fight—a far better chance than they gave my father." His anger fueled the flames of revenge. They had dwindled to smoldering embers, but news of Sabher's escape stoked the furnace. "Unfortunately, I don't have time to chase Sabher. Whoever has him probably hasn't reached the stargate yet, but I have work to do."

"Your project with the Americans?" Was Cartwright fishing? Maybe Enkh had told him.

"Nope. I've got a job off-world. If you get in another pissing match with the Americans, try not to slag my property."

"Off-world?" Cartwright's eyes flicked. "The Mercenary Guild hasn't reopened contracts."

"This is work for another guild. Thanks for the heads up, Colonel." Bjorn terminated the call before Cartwright could ask any more questions.

* * *

"What's wrong?" Gina asked as Glen sat across from her in the mess tent. Was he having second thoughts about last night? No, she chided herself, that's crazy. If he was, he wouldn't have joined her for lunch—unless he planned to break up with her.

"I'm assigned to the mission. I'll be on the *Ursa Major* for the job," he replied, poking at his mystery loaf in questionable gravy.

"Don't you want to go to space?" Gina asked. "You'll get deployment pay, as opposed to off-rotation residuals."

"Space travel rocks, and the money is a nice bonus…but it means I won't see you for weeks." Glen met her gaze. "I want to find out where this is going, but I'll be off-world in two days."

Gina breathed a silent sigh. She feared asking Bettie to change Glen's duty assignment had backfired. "I'm going on deployment. We'll both be on the *Ursa Major*."

Glen's expression brightened, and he reached across the table for her hand. "I don't know how much down time we'll get, but I want to spend as much as possible with you."

Gina squeezed his hand in return. "Privacy is a scarce commodity on a warship."

"Sounds like a challenge." Glen grinned.

Priya and Hcufft set their trays on the table. "I see someone found out about his new assignment," Priya remarked, eyeing Gina. "How lucky."

"I am lucky, yes?" Hcufft asked. "I will accompany the next transport to Vishall. You are unlucky, Corporal Brand. You have been assigned to combat." The felinoid alien shuddered.

"Hcufft, are you going to show off your rank when you get home?" Gina asked. Priya suspected Gina's hand in Glen's reassignment. "How many H'rang can say they are mercenaries?"

Hcufft studied the private's stripe that had replaced his contractor patch on the dark grey vest he wore. "Some may consider Hcufft insane. H'rang avoid personal violence."

"It's convenient the two of you get to serve on the *Ursa Major*," Priya remarked. "I would have thought most of the logistics personnel would be assigned to the transport."

"The *Ursa Major* will carry about a third of the forces, including Bruin Alpha," Glen said between bites of meat-like loaf. "I'm flattered they picked me. Only six logistics specialists have been assigned to the ship."

"Your good fortune is our loss," Priya said, watching Gina out of the corner of her eye. "Once we wrap up here, we'll need to unpack everything and set up shop on Vishall."

Glen gestured with his fork. "They should make you a sergeant."

"What?" Priya sputtered. "I made corporal a few weeks ago."

"You consider the bigger picture," Glen continued. "I'm stoked because I get to head up a handful of spreadsheet monkeys on one ship, but you're working out what the whole firm needs."

"I agree," Gina said, meeting Priya's gaze. "You're proactive, and you look out for your fellow Berserkers. Don't you agree, Hcuff't?"

Hcuff't made a disdainful face and pushed back his tray. "This is not meat, no? No. What did you ask?"

"Crud. I have to go to my pre-flight operations orientation," Glen announced. He reached again for Gina's hand. "See you for dinner?"

"Absolutely."

Glen leaned across the table and kissed her. What had she been concerned about?

Priya waited until Glen was out of ear shot. "So, are you going to fess up?"

"Yes, we slept together last night," Gina replied, watching Glen until he disappeared beyond the mess tent.

"Humans." Hcuff't shook his head.

Priya frowned and leaned forward, lowering her voice. "You used your access to the systems to change his assignment so he's going with you on this mission."

"You're the one who pushed us together," Gina protested. "Every time I've dated a CASPer trooper, it's gone wrong. Once they get me in bed and notch their belt, they dump me, or they stick around long enough for me to catch them making time with someone else. Even better, they betray the company, frame someone, and almost kill me with a bomb.

"Glen's nice. He isn't buff, and he can't press 100 kilos, but he's smart. He collects movies from when Vancouver first entered the Tri-V market. He's read classic authors and obscure small press writers. You introduced me to a guy who might stick around more than a couple of months, and now you're pissy because it worked out?"

"I'm happy for you," Priya said. "But you can't rearrange the duty roster so you can be with your boyfriend. It affects people besides you."

"Sorry if I inconvenienced you." Gina grabbed her tray. She wasn't sure what stung more—that Priya was mad at her or that she was right. "I need to get back to work."

* * *

Jim Hawkins shook his head. The commander seemed on the brink of putting aside his vendetta, but the news of the Besquith's liberation had incensed him. Once the call ended, Commander Tovesson slapped the slate on the desk. Good thing the devices bordered on indestructible.

The elSha technician paused his work, one eye watching the commander. When no more outbursts followed, the reptile went back to work.

"What now?" Jim asked.

Bjorn picked up his coffee cup and grimaced after a sip. "We have a timetable to hit. I can't take the *Ursa Major* out to the stargate and shake down ships to find out which one carries Sabher."

One fear alleviated. Pastor Hawkins had worried the commander would do precisely that. Hopefully, with Sabher out of reach and a job to occupy his attention, the commander would lose interest in avenging his father.

"Flex your fingers," the elSha clicked through his translator. "Now, touch your thumb to one finger at a time."

Jim tried not to watch even though he could see movement out of the corner of his eye. "What do you need me to do?"

"Don't pack your bags yet. I'm on the fence between sending you to Vishall or having you stay here for a bit to help Garrett," Bjorn replied. "Once I finish the job, I'll head to Vishall and put in some quality time with my wife. I'll be back on Earth at some point, but the timetable is a work in progress. I'll give you a solid answer as soon as I figure it out."

Jim nodded. A selfish voice noted that if he didn't have to stay on Earth, he'd get to spend more time with Priya, as she was scheduled to go to Vishall and help set up the logistics operation. "Sounds good, Commander."

* * * * *

Chapter Twenty-One

Information Guild Headquarters, Capital Planet

Master Archivist Heloxi studied the hologram hovering in front of her pool. It displayed a tiny planetary system whipping around a red star. The data the Grimm provided had pinpointed the Union Credit Exchange mint on a large moon of the sole gas giant.

Xhoxa Gamma 3 was an industrial moon in a metal-heavy system. Unremarkable—nothing there betrayed the presence of a hidden mint. Camouflaged defenses surrounded the facility, but secrecy provided the mint's best protection.

With any luck, the mercenaries Ashok had hired would destroy themselves in the process of annihilating the mint. A crew stood by to clean up any "counterfeit" credits and diamonds to keep them from entering circulation. Even if the mercenaries survived their mission, they wouldn't go to the trouble of looting worthless forgeries. The Information Guild would pay them whatever Ashok negotiated and send them on their way, none the wiser. Heloxi hoped for the mutual destruction of both sides.

Heloxi set her flat grinding plates in motion before she remembered her spawn pouch was empty. All the tadpoles had either wriggled free or filled her belly. She sighed and batted her painted eyes. She would send for a male soon. The master archivist summoned her aide via pinplants. Minutes later, the XenSha Grade Four Archivist hurried into the chamber.

"Yes, Master Archivist?" Neermal bowed so low his facial tentacles touched the polished stone floor. *Sycophant.*

"Any word from Ashok?" Heloxi asked, watching the hologram.

One of the XenSha's long ears twitched. "With all due respect, Master Archivist, would not such a notification appear in your pinview?"

Heloxi's eyes fell on the small alien. Would he fit in her gullet? "Why do I need you?"

Neermal's tentacles rippled. "To help you sort the grain from the chaff?"

Heloxi slapped her side, sending ripples across her hide. "Then sort! Any. Messages. From. ASHOK?"

"No, Master Archivist! Given his travel time, a message from him would not reach us for at least three days," Neermal replied.

Heloxi shifted her bulk, splashing water from her pool. The XenSha was correct. If only they had quantum communication beyond that utilized in super-computers. She suspected the Science Guild squatted on that tidbit of technology. Heloxi didn't understand why, other than it was in the Science Guilds' nature to let everyone endure lightspeed lag.

"If Ashok sends a message, ensure it comes to my attention immediately," Heloxi instructed.

"Anything else, Master Archivist?"

Heloxi returned her gaze to the hologram. "No. Leave me."

"As you wish." Neermal bowed low again and backed away.

'Analysis of the system?' Heloxi queried Index Prime via her pinplants.

Index Prime: 'Moderate mining resources and accompanying industries. Output is 47% lower than projected. Mining and manufacturing concerns are modestly successful. The system imports 98% of its foodstuffs. Known defenses are minimal. Do you wish a detailed breakdown of companies and interests operating in-system?'

'No. Any indications of tampering with system data files?' Heloxi asked.

Index Prime: 'Negative. Every aspect of the star system's data fall within 3.1% of expected means. Working. This indicates potential artificial manipulation of the data or the system, itself. Such distortion would have to occur at the source as our files are inviolate.'

'This validates the data provided by our operative.' It better. Heloxi didn't want to contemplate what would happen if Ashok's forces arrived only to find no target.

Index Prime: 'Concur. Underlying data indicates intentional effort to make the system appear unexceptional.'

Heloxi twisted her painted lips into a grin. This had to be a mint. The loss of the facility would not only savage the UCX financially, it would undermine their justification to form an independent guild.

Index Prime: 'Even with the loss of credit transaction income, the Information Guild would remain profitable.'

Heloxi scowled. She hadn't asked Index Prime for the analysis. 'The loss in profit would be unacceptable.'

Index Prime: 'The purpose of the Information Guild is to preserve and disseminate information. Profit is secondary.'

Heloxi sighed. Spoken like a true machine. Without profit, how could she afford her jeweled adornments? How could she afford gourmet meals between spawnings? How could she afford the luxurious salts and oils for her pool? 'Profit comes first.'

* * *

Maki Transport, Hyperspace

"Sabher, please sit." Dbo'Dizwey gestured to the bench across the table in the small officer's mess. The gravity deck only generated a third of the gravity the Nevar was accustomed to, but it was better than zero-G.

Sabher eyed Uvksolt as he sat. So far, the Sumatozou had killed two unruly Besquith. "What can I do for you?"

"Do you have any idea who I represent?" Dbo asked. The wolf possessed a keen intellect and reigned in his ferocity enough to use it. Perfect for what Dbo had in mind.

The Besquith shrugged. "You had enough credits to spring most of us from Human custody. I'm an investigator, but I've learned there are times you don't dig for bones."

"What do you know about the Union Credit Exchange?" Dbo asked. Uvksolt tensed next to her. The bodyguard objected to bringing the Besquith into the fold. She feared the mercenaries would try to seize the ship and hold Dbo hostage.

"They produce hard currency and set the rates for red diamonds," Sabher replied.

"There's more to it," Dbo said, clasping her upper hands. "We manage all aspects of hard currency and red diamond trade, including the Diamond Reserve."

Sabher's ears perked up, alert. "What does the Union Credit Exchange want with a bunch of captured mercs?"

"Our traditional source of security forces is experiencing recruitment issues. We have seen an uptick in criminal attacks against the Union's cash flow. It is only a matter of time before one of these strikes hits one of our primary facilities."

"Why not hire mercenaries to protect your assets?" Sabher asked, suspicion tingeing his voice.

"You've been out of touch," Dbo stated. She doubted the Humans bothered to update their prisoners on current affairs in the galaxy. "Since the end of Peepo's invasion of Earth, the Mercenary Guild has suspended all new contracts. It's one of the reasons your home world didn't expatriate you."

Sabher nodded. "Let me guess—General Peepo did not make good on the generous contracts she offered us or any of the other mercenary races. There must be many empty coffers on Bestald." Most Besquith might rage at the abandonment by their fellows. This one thought through the rationale.

"Correct. Peepo fled, leaving the others empty-handed and defeated," Dbo said. "Mercenaries who fight on our behalf will have their parole debt waived in full."

"What equipment do we have to arm the forces you liberated from Earth, and what do we expect the enemy to bring to the field of battle?" Sabher asked.

"The latter is difficult to predict. The Humans are starved for funds, but Peepo's War left many mercenary races destitute. Any of them could take up arms on behalf the Information Guild in exchange for a fat transfer to their UAACs," Dbo replied.

"The Information Guild?" The Besquith's ears perked up again, and his gaze grew distant. "They want sole control of the flow of credits. They consider the Union Credit Exchange a rival."

"Very good." Dbo clicked her beak in approval. "I will grant you full access to our available equipment inventory so you can determine how best to allocate our arms."

Sabher tipped his head.

"I have no mind for battle," Dbo admitted. "I need you if we are to protect not only our mint, but also the economy of the Galactic Union. Assuming you want to accept the job, Captain Sabher."

"I accept," the Besquith replied.

"Congratulations," Uvksolt remarked.

Dbo slid a slate across the table to Sabher. "This details our available personnel, arms, and supplies. We suspect one of our mints has been compromised, and an attack is imminent."

* * *

Galactic Senate Building, Capital Planet

"This bill is an obvious win for the Galactic Union," Senator Nargis Xlorin declared before the other members of the Finance Commission. "In the wake of chaos sowed by General Peepo, the Union requires stability. By designating a guild to specifically manage the monetary affairs of the union, we can rest assured commerce will continue to flow, and our members will prosper."

"Senator Xlorin, the Information Guild already manages the day-to-day transactions of the union," Senator Patarix stated. The Mazreen senator held Nargis' gaze with his all-black eyes. "I see no need to complicate matters."

"The Information Guild handles transactions as a side endeavor after the dissolution of the original Banking Guild," Nargis said. At least now, he had confirmed his suspicions regarding the ringleader of those opposed to the Finance Guild proposal. "As several worlds can attest, their lack of focus has created serious fiscal issues."

Patarix waved a long, slender hand. "In a system handling trillions of transactions, the slightest glitch can appear enormous. If

0.0001% of transactions experience a deviation, millions of transactions would be affected. A large number that, in fact, represents a minute fraction."

"In the last 25 weeks, errors have increased 37-fold." Nargis flashed a chart on the conference room Tri-V. "Despite the fact that the Information Guild garners more wealth than any other guild, their infrastructure outlay over the past century has dwindled. Where does this wealth go?"

"Typical Gtandan—concerned he didn't get his share of the meal," Senator Patarix remarked. "What does it matter where the Information Guild spends their money as long as they fulfill their duty?"

"Those credits come from the accounts of Union citizens and corporations," Nargis stated. "The Finance Guild proposal provides transparency to assure the people and companies of the galaxy do not waste credits lining the coffers of a guild, those who rule it, or those in their pockets."

The Mazreen's green skin darkened. "What are you implying?"

"Some people are getting obscenely wealthy from the Information Guild's practices. I'm certain those individuals will do anything in their power to keep the spigot of credits open." Nargis was no brawler, but he hoped the slender Mazreen would forget decorum and take a swing. "I propose we break up their monopoly and require visibility of financial operations to guard against corruption and abuse."

"Do you wish to bring it to a vote?" Patarix challenged.

"I have sent important information to all commission members," Nargis said, changing the Tri-V display to a summary. "I move we table the vote until the commission members have had time to digest this data."

"I second the motion to table," Regider, the Bovan senator chimed in. "It's time for lunch."

A quick vote tabled further action on the bill, and an even quicker call dismissed the commission.

Nargis followed Patarix back to his office. A week ago, he'd been able to count on the Mazreen senator's vote as well as his sway over a handful of commission members. Since then, the balance teetered too close for comfort. Put to a vote, the bill could fail to pass in the commission and go on to the Senate.

Patarix peeled his lips back from his pointy teeth in frustration. "What do you want, Senator Xlorin?"

"I want to know why you changed your tune on the Finance Guild proposal." Nargis followed Patarix into his office without invitation. "A week ago, you were open to the plan."

"Things change in a week," Patarix snapped. "I've had time to study the ramifications of your proposal, and I've reconsidered my stance."

"Who is it?"

Patarix squinted. "What?"

Nargis leaned on the desk, looming over the smaller senator. "Did I stutter? We both know what's going on. My only question is who. Who is it?"

Patarix sighed and slumped in his chair. "One of your fellows— another Gtandan. Hedvig Kloron of Kloron Shipping. I don't know where he got it."

"Not too hard to guess." Nargis hoped his luck held. He'd made an educated guess that someone had bribed or blackmailed Patarix.

He'd narrowed it down to blackmail, and the question became what had the Information Guild provided to Kloron to hold over Patarix's head?

"I know—cameras are everywhere. The flush of pheromones and hormones rendered me an idiot," Patarix lamented. "Now, if I don't stop any bills empowering the UCX or fail to back a proposal to abolish the diamond standard, he will release the video to the news media."

A dalliance. Mating imperatives were the downfall of many a politician. "It's a shame we cannot send a Depik to demonstrate the folly of extorting a powerful senator such as you."

"I heard General Peepo wiped out all of the assassins," Patarix said.

Nargis nodded. "The Depik are gone. They were the premiere assassins in the galaxy, but nature abhors a vacuum. Others will fill the void, and perhaps Hedvig Kloron needs a reminder. Let me make some calls."

"What if he has a failsafe?" Patarix faded to a pale green. "My mates will cast me out if they see what I've done."

"Let me work on your problem. Perhaps a fellow Gtandan can prevail on him to see reason for a modest fee," Nargis suggested. "At least until we can discover if the rumors regarding nature are true."

* * * * *

Chapter Twenty-Two

Bear Town, New Mexico, Earth

"I was beginning to think you bailed on us," Bjorn stated, gazing across the minimalist desk.

"No, of course not. I was off duty, so—" Roberto Duarte began.

"It doesn't matter," Bjorn interrupted. Last time he'd seen him was when Berto took Heather home. Had they rekindled an old flame? "I want you to come on this job."

"You're only taking an over-sized company," Berto said. At least he'd read the mission profile. "I mean, you're the boss, but it seems like overkill, more brass than band."

"Consider it a chance to show your chops. It will free me up for big picture bullshit," Bjorn said. He didn't mention that if Berto bungled the job, Bjorn would be there to pick up the pieces. "It will give us a chance to ease you into the culture. Unless you have a reason to hang out on Earth?"

"What? No. I'll do whatever you think best," Berto replied.

"Good answer. We're 20 hours from last lift. Don't miss your ride to the *Ursa Major*. We'll have a day and a half until we reach the stargate, plus the usual 170 hours in hyperspace," Bjorn said.

"What do you need me to do in the meantime?" Berto asked.

"Get your haptic suit squared away. You won't have time to play with your CASPer; it already went into orbit. Review the mission specific TO&E. Have dinner with your officers and NCOs before lift." Bjorn paused, meeting Berto's gaze. "Square things away with her before you leave."

Berto looked away but failed to hide his embarrassment. "I didn't mean for anything to happen."

Bjorn resisted the urge to ask about what had happened when they were kids. "It doesn't matter. I'm happily married, so if you two…whatever. It's all good. Don't be an idiot and toss it away. You both deserve happiness."

"We haven't made any commitments. Who knows when I'll get back to Earth?" Berto asked. "I'll get on those TO&E reviews."

Padre Jim stepped into the office after Berto hustled out. "You handled that well."

"What? Basic Merc Leader 101. Know your gear and know your troops," Bjorn said.

"I mean, him and Heather. It's obvious you have some affection for her, despite the way they hurt you." Hawkins sat in the chair vacated by Berto. "Before you protest, yes, I know you are loyal to your wife. That doesn't mean you can't have some nostalgic fondness. Obviously, Miss Akins hoped to exploit those feelings, either out of her affection or at the behest of her employers. We may never know which, and perhaps it's for the best."

"You're right—it's better I don't know. I prefer to believe she carried a smoldering torch stoked by adrenaline rather than assume she tried to manipulate me for political ends," Bjorn said. "Can you handle business here?"

"I hoped to go to Vishall," the chaplain said. "The majority of our troops have already relocated."

The padre didn't mention that his girlfriend was departing on the transport due to leave in a week, when the next one arrived. "Don't worry. You'll move to Vishall on the next transport rotation, and you can catch up to Priya. Lieutenant McMillan will serve as Garrett's liaison and keep an eye on our projects here."

Padre Jim played a mean hand of poker, but he let his relief show. "I thought you might have decided to keep me here with the cadre facility and the academy."

"I considered it," Bjorn said. "People adjusting to living on an alien world, as a home rather than deployment, might need counseling. Our combat troops will operate out of Vishall, and they're the reason I hired you.

"However, expect to travel. I want a counselor on Earth for the training cadre and a few for the school. Guess who gets to wrangle them?"

"I wanted to help troubled people in the mercenary industry. This is the Lord's way of letting me aid more people," Padre Jim said. "I guess I can square my billet on Vishall in a month."

"Priya won't already have it in order? Or aren't you at that stage yet?" Bjorn crooked a grin. "You can afford a nice flat in Vishall Plex or a modest one in Bear Plex." Bear Plex, a growing village, had sprung up near the new Berserker HQ as the locals realized the lucrative opportunities afforded by proximity to a mercenary base. "Bear Plex is 5 kilometers away, and the closest edge of the capital is a 20-minute commute by ground car."

"You've given me something to consider," Hawkins said.

A knock rattled the flimsy door. The sooner they moved on from these temporary prefabs to permanent buildings the better. "Come in!" Bjorn called.

The door eased open, and Sergeant Wicza poked her head into the office. "You wanted to see me, Commander?"

Bjorn nodded. "Come on in, Whisky. Padre, you can stick around if you want, but Wicza isn't in trouble—for a change."

"I'll leave you to it, Commander. Charlotte, sounds as though you were the voice of reason in Houston." The chaplain stood and offered the young woman his chair. "Let me know if you want to talk before you ship out."

"Thanks, Pastor Jim." Charlotte took the chaplain's seat as he departed.

"I want you to command the scout element on our job," Bjorn stated. No point in beating around the bush. "I'm promoting you to master sergeant. You'll have two squads of APEX scouts plus vics."

"Not to look a gift horse in the mouth, but the Berserkers don't have master sergeants," Whisky said. Bjorn could tell she was trying not to stare at the angry scars marring the skin covering his cybernetic arm. Once Hek finished the technical repairs, nanites mended the biological epidermis and secured the patches. Bjorn could have replaced the whole epidermal sleeve, but he had chosen to keep the scars.

Bjorn grinned. "The advantage of commanding a merc outfit is that I can make up whatever ranks I want. Your pay will fall between that of a staff sergeant and that of a lieutenant. Stefan can give you the details as soon as I make them up."

"Who will replace Sergeant Toshigawa in the other APEX squad?" Whisky asked. Toshigawa had died on Patoka.

"I have an idea. Take Reeves to the motor pool lot. Your rides should be here. They're among the last assets on the loading manifest, but they go to orbit first thing in the morning." Bjorn hoped he'd find time to see what Vurrn's father had sent. "Meanwhile, send in Sergeant Cripe."

"Sure, Commander."

A moment after Whisky slipped out, Cripe tapped on the doorframe before entering.

"What can I do for you, Commander?" The plastic chair across from Bjorn's desk was getting a workout today.

Bjorn regarded the older mercenary. Cripe had over a decade on him. "What do you want to do, Keith?"

Sergeant Cripe's eyebrows rose. "I'm not sure. A year ago, I would have said read a good book and drink a good beer. Peepo's invasion yanked me out of retirement. Let me guess, you want me to stay on for the garrison here?"

"I want you to lead an APEX scout squad on this operation. The scouts will be under Master Sergeant Wicza, and she'll lead one APEX squad. I need a sergeant for the other." Bjorn leaned back in his chair and studied Cripe's reaction.

The sergeant took a minute to compose his thoughts. "I'm flattered, but you don't need an old dog like me. Besides, aren't I too tall for APEX armor?"

"Hek and Vek have modified three suits to accommodate users up to 177 centimeters," Bjorn countered. The original suits could only fit wearers up to 175 centimeters. Bjorn's list of things to do included reverse engineering the APEX suits and scaling them for larger users. "Next excuse?"

"Aren't I a little too old to be a scout?" Cripe asked. "I retired for a reason. Twenty-five years as a mercenary was plenty."

Bjorn fidgeted with one of the Besquith teeth on his desk. "Since you've come out of retirement, you've killed how many Besquith and shagged a Sirra'Kan. It doesn't sound as though you're ready to be put back out to pasture."

"You're not going to take no for an answer, are you?" Cripe asked.

Bjorn tossed the tooth so it clinked on the desk in front of Cripe. "Nope. We both know better. You're wasted sitting in a comfy chair with a book watching the clock tick. You've tasted life again. After this job, if you want to throttle back to an infantry garrison or go back to pushing electronic paperwork, have at it. You can pick your assignment here or on Vishall."

Cripe picked up the triangular Besquith fang. "A fat combat bonus would make retirement easier. I hear the cost of living on Vishall is higher than on Earth."

"Splendid. Report to Hek and Vek in the armory tent for fitting."

* * *

"I'm in love," Tamara purred as she walked along the angular, matte black rumbler.

Charlotte shook her head, watching her girlfriend admire the 6-wheeled vehicle. "It reminds me of those classic videos with the guy in the black cape who fights the clown. The armor looks lighter than a Casanova."

"You are correct," Vurrn said. "The outer coating is similar to the chitin of Goka. It refracts electromagnetic waves and photons."

Charlotte turned to the Zuul. "You're saying these are stealth rumblers?"

"Precisely," Vurrn replied with a proud nod. "The Casanovas will receive similar treatment once we figure out how to make the glaze stick, but they have a higher profile and stronger EM signature. The coating will improve their defense against lasers and laser-guided weapons."

"What does it have for weapons?" Charlotte asked. A gunner wouldn't fit in the small flattened turret on top.

"The turret has a single cryo-jacketed pulse laser with the same output as the heavy shoulder-mounted CASPer weapons." Vurrn pointed to the front, where Tamara leaned against the sloped armor. "It also has a retractable 20mm rotary cannon with a 90-degree traverse in the front."

"No MAC? The laser won't be a big help if we run into laser-resistant bugs." Charlotte circled behind the vehicle. The aft hatch betrayed the rumbler's role as a transport.

"Firing a MAC is the same as setting off an EM flare," Vurrn said. "The Shadow isn't meant to be a frontline fighter like the Casanova. It's designed to get recon elements as close as possible without getting spotted."

"A shame I only have a few hours to familiarize myself with this beauty before they load her up," Tamara lamented from the topside hatch. She turned to Charlotte. "Don't get jealous, sweetie. I'll be home tonight."

"It's fine. I'm going to the armorer tent to see to my APEX suit. Call me when you get done or want to break for dinner."

The armorer tent covered the foundation of one of the old motor pool garages only a couple hundred meters away. Large, roaring fans were a poor substitute for air-conditioning. Technicians scurried among racks of armored suits, making last minute adjustments and loading ammo. Charlotte recognized Commander Tovesson's CASPer by its distinctive, augmented left arm and sheathed battle axe.

The APEX scout suits were near one end of the tent. The smaller suits stood less than two meters tall and lacked the hulking frames, clamshell canopies, and onboard weapons of CASPers. Designed as

266 | JON R. OSBORNE

bargain basement competition for the CASPer, they never caught on. The Berserkers bought the manufacturer's entire inventory in a bankruptcy sale and repurposed the armor for scout use.

As Charlotte approached the scout armor racks, she noticed the hard plates sported the same matte black as Tamara's new rumbler. She flagged down a technician.

"Whisky, *que pasa?*" Enzo Calvo wiped his hands off and walked over. The dark-skinned Cuban towered over Charlotte. "You got an extra stripe. Congratulations."

"Thanks." Charlotte tapped the breastplate of her suit. "Is this the same coating as the one on the new recon rumbler?"

Enzo nodded. "The stuff won't bond to the CASPer armor or the Casanova armor. The APEX suits use a different material, so it seems to work."

Charlotte craned her neck to meet Enzo's eyes. "Seems? That doesn't sound reassuring."

"The coating flakes off the denser armor as soon as it cures." Enzo pointed to a nearby CASPer where a technician was sanding off dark patches. "We're not seeing the problem with the scout suits, but they haven't been tested under fire."

Charlotte spotted Cripe walking down the aisle between the rows of CASPer racks. Had the commander sent him? She checked her slate for a missed message, but her communications showed up to date.

"Hey, Master Sergeant," Cripe said. "Congratulations and surprise."

"Surprise?"

"Yeah. I'm here to get fitted for one of these suicide suits. Commander T asked me to lead the other scout squad." Cripe scanned the APEX armor. "Have they always been black?"

"No, it's the new Black Mantis glaze," Enzo replied. "You must be Sergeant Cripe. The note to prep a stretched APEX for you came across my board fifteen minutes ago."

"Fifteen? I only agreed to the assignment five minutes ago," Cripe remarked.

"Why wasn't I told?" Charlotte asked. Cripe would be a welcome addition as long as he could keep up. An icon flashed on her slate with a message titled, 'Roster update.'

"We'll need to get you a toughened haptic suit," Enzo stated. He flicked his finger across the slate and peered at Cripe. "Hope this one will fit."

"Haptic suit? Aren't these things infantry combat armor on steroids?" Cripe protested.

"More like the bastard offspring of a CASPer and an infantry suit," Enzo said. The armorer rummaged through a pile of crates. He lifted a black, rubbery suit and held it out at arm's length. "Here we go. Not only does it provide feedback to the exoskeleton controller, it affords a bit of protection for the parts not covered by the exo's armor."

Cripe glanced down. "I'm going to regret those burritos."

* * *

Las Cruces, New Mexico, Earth

"Mama! Are you home?" Grace Garcia called from the door of the apartment. She could hear running water in the kitchen. Grace's son, Arthur, diverted enough of his attention from his slate so he didn't collide with her as he followed, but no more.

Grace peeked around the corner into the kitchen and spotted her mother doing dishes. "Mama?"

Her mother turned, shrieked, and fumbled a plate into the water. With one hand on her chest, the older woman removed a wireless headphone with the other. "*Dios Mia!* I didn't hear you come in."

Arthur poked his head around the corner. "*Abuela*, are you okay?"

"She's fine," Grace said. "Her head was lost in her electronics, like someone else I know."

"I'm sorry, Grace. I was listening to the news." Senora Garcia retrieved the dropped plate and inspected it for cracks. "The riots are growing, and FedMart has suspended the purchase of 'luxury goods' with GGI dollars."

"I heard. The West Coast has shut down, and the states of New York and New Jersey have declared martial law. It will get worse before it gets better." Grace peered back into the living room. "Is Papa at work?"

Grace's mother nodded. "So much for him retiring now. We've saved money, but if they ration food at the FedMart by cutting stipends, the prices in the open markets will go up."

"It's one of the reasons I came to visit. I learned about a nearby project that will require a lot of workers. Papa and his crew could work a year or more on this venture," Grace said. The excitement over, Arthur returned to the couch and his slate.

"Will the government make good on their payroll if they are running out of money?" Grace's mother returned to washing dishes despite the presence of a dishwasher a meter away. Her mother swore the machine couldn't get the dishes clean enough.

"It's a private contract. The state office received notification this morning, and a friend passed it on to me," Grace replied. "I can pull a string or two and get Papa in."

The older woman sighed. "It will get buried by other bidders. Those who are willing to work will drive down the price of labor by undercutting each other."

"I suspect Bjorn isn't going to worry about the lowest bidder." Grace waited for her mother's reaction.

"Bjorn? Your big mercenary boyfriend from high school?" Her mother lowered her voice. "Are you sure you want to get mixed up in that again?"

"Mama, I'm not going to date him. I want to pitch him Papa's work credentials." Had her mother seen Bjorn on the news? She didn't want her father scared off from the prospect of working in Bear Town. It could mean enough money for her parents to retire somewhere besides this FedFlat. "I'm going to meet him at his mother's house for dinner."

Grace's mother shook her head. "I hope there's no gunfire this time."

* * * * *

Chapter Twenty-Three

Las Cruces, New Mexico, Earth

"You're sure this is okay?" Berto asked as they waited for the security gate to open.

"I invited you guys," Bjorn said. "It's not as though you're strangers."

"True. I owe your parents for their help after I was injured." Berto paused, probably wondering whether he'd committed a faux pas by indirectly mentioning Bjorn's father. "My parents couldn't have afforded anything FedCare wouldn't have covered."

"Besides, Heather is meeting us here, so you can't back out now," Bjorn remarked, trading one uncomfortable subject for another.

"This isn't going to be awkward, is it?" Berto asked. Maybe seeing Berto and Heather together would abate Bjorn's mother's worries.

"We're adults. We'll pretend it's not weird, but how bad can it be?" A cab passed them as the gate opened. Bjorn tipped his head at it. "See, Heather is already here."

Bjorn parked his car. He'd taken the Zuul personal transport out of storage to shake the dust off and make sure the maintenance he paid for had been performed. The curved body style hearkened back to 20th century hotrods. Maybe he'd ship the car to Vishall.

"Mom, Berto and I are here," Bjorn called as he opened the door.

"We're in the dining room, Trip."

Berto collided with Bjorn when he froze at the entrance. "Loki heard me," Bjorn muttered.

Grace sat at the table with Heather and Bjorn's mother.

"I hope you don't mind." Grace rose from her chair to hug Bjorn. "It's been a long time."

"Yeah, it has." One ex squared away, and another appeared. Were the gods testing him? A cough behind him broke Bjorn out of his mental paralysis. "I don't know if you remember Berto. He's joined the Berserkers as one of our captains."

"Nice to see you again, Captain Duarte," Grace said, shaking Berto's hand. Not only did she remember, she may have studied up on the Berserkers.

Bjorn set an AetherNet daemon searching for Grace's employer. When they'd last spoken, she worked as a corporate lawyer. What were the odds of both his exes becoming lawyers and turning up on his doorstep?

Grace returned to her seat and waited for Bjorn and Berto to join them at the table. "I called your mother to see if there was a direct way to reach you, and Lynn invited me to dinner. You're lifting off tomorrow?"

"That's right." Bjorn decided that no matter how late dinner ran, he would return to Bear Town tonight. "We have a job."

"Speaking of jobs, I'll get to the point," Grace said. "I heard you're rebuilding Bear Town."

"Not quite." Her source wasn't an insider, Bjorn noted. "I've moved our headquarters operations to Vishall. I'm going to build a cadre training facility and a mercenary finishing school on the Bear Town site."

"A school? I never knew you had an interest in education," Grace remarked.

Bjorn waited while Geneva served drinks. He wished he'd brought Padre Jim. Grace was tougher to read than Heather, but at least she wasn't batting her eyes or making innuendos. She seemed interested in business, not rekindling a past romance.

"Earth needs mercenaries—a lot of them. The United States has a large population and a school system geared toward cranking kids out. I want to give these kids a chance on the battlefield while making sure Earth has quality troops." Bjorn picked up his beer. Praise the gods Geneva kept good Icelandic beer on hand.

"There are already some mercenary academies, such as the one in Indiana and another in Germany. They are expensive and a bit elitist. You have to already be rich or connected to get in, and your family needs to fork over cash up front," Bjorn said.

"Folkvangr Academy will be different. Graduates can pay back their tuition out of their mercenary earnings. Mercenary companies can buy out students' debts upon hiring them," Bjorn continued. "It makes for a good recruiting incentive, and we could offer merc firms a discount for paying the debt all at once."

"Sounds like the education crisis that drove the creation of the FedEd program," Grace stated. "Predatory lenders saddled students with huge debts for degrees that could prove worthless."

Bjorn shook his head. "I already considered it. There's not going to be any compound interest sticking them with making payments without paying off their debt. I'll cap profits for myself or any shareholders. Extra money beyond the cap can go into a scholarship fund. I make plenty of money from the Berserkers."

Grace leaned back, holding her wine glass. "It's a good thing you're a mercenary. You'd go broke with those ethics in the corporate world."

"Aren't you worried about getting funding and investors by capping profits?" Heather asked. "You'll need money to get it off the ground, especially since it could take months, or years, for students to pay back their tuitions."

"You need investors who are willing to settle for modest returns over a long period," Grace added. "Not quite philanthropists, but close."

Bjorn polished off his beer. He could tell by the aroma wafting in from the kitchen that dinner was almost ready. "Know anyone I can hire to recruit investors while I'm out in the galaxy?"

Grace looked from Bjorn to Heather. "Who are you asking?"

"Heather has her hands full between Santa Fe and Washington," Bjorn replied, striving to keep any accusations out of his tone. The data retrieved by his daemon scrolled through his pinview. "You work for a firm out of Albuquerque. If I must go through them, I will, but I'd prefer to work with you directly."

"We can figure something out, but I didn't come here for a job—well, not for me," Grace said, setting her wine glass down. "My father is a foreman at a construction firm."

"I'll give you a net address to submit his work credentials," Bjorn said. "Copy me when you do, and I'll pass along my endorsement—assuming he isn't going to threaten me with his weapons again."

"You don't have to worry. I noticed your wedding ring," Grace remarked.

* * *

Organ, New Mexico, Earth

"Dairy Barn is far better than going into Las Cruces to some snooty restaurant," Priya declared.

Jim Hawkins smiled. Let the younger couples get dressed up and go into Las Cruces. He preferred to spend some time alone with Priya. Jim feared the hard part would be ditching Hcufft—which Jim felt guilty for—but the felinoid wasn't around when Jim picked up Priya.

"I have simple tastes," Jim replied, then mentally winced. Would she read something into the statement, especially when he sprang his surprise? Too late now.

A sea of gray BDUs surrounded them. Most of the Berserkers shipped out tomorrow and were availing themselves of the last chance to enjoy 'real' food. Berserkers packed every establishment in the tiny town. Jim could wait a day or two, but Priya would want to share with her friends.

"I'm going to get our sundaes," Jim announced. He'd finished his burger, and Priya was down to her last chicken strip. Ironically, this small mom and pop operation served real meat as opposed to the factory-grown protein served at major chains.

Jim took their ticket to the counter and handed it to the teenager checking her phone. At least she pretended to be cheerful, as opposed to the employees of the chain fast food depots who regarded customers with sullen indifference.

Jim reached into his jacket pocket and added something extra to Priya's sundae, dropping it over the stem of the long spoon. It plunked into the melting ice cream and strawberry topping.

Jim set the sundaes down and watched for Priya's reaction. How long would it take her to notice? How long to figure out the significance? Most importantly—how long to answer?

"I'm surprised Hcufft didn't come with us," Priya remarked, ignoring her sundae. "I get the kids wanting to get dressed up and go into the city since they deploy tomorrow, but Hcufft didn't go with them."

"I'm sure Hcufft is fine," Jim said, poking at his ice cream with his spoon. The hot caramel was already reducing his ice cream to white sludge.

Priya finally took hold of her spoon. Jim held his breath, watching the ring slide along the spoon as Priya raised the first bite. "I know, but H'rangs tend to be social. I've worked with him for a while, and I keep thinking of him as a big cat, even though I know better."

Jim watched the ring swing from the stem of her spoon. "I'm sure he'll be okay for one night. He could have found someone else to dine with or joined a table in the mess."

Priya shook her head and gestured east toward Bear Town with her spoon. "They served Sloppy Joes in the mess tent. You know how he feels about vat-grown meat."

Jim watched as Priya jabbed her spoon back into her sundae, the ring disappearing into strawberry syrup and molten ice cream. "He could have gone to Basta Burger or the Thai place."

"I suppose you're right," Priya admitted. She lifted another bite and paused. "More importantly, why is there a toy ring on my spoon?"

"It's not a toy," Jim replied. "It belonged to my grandmother, Mildred."

Priya upended the spoon to allow the ring to slide to her open hand. "It's not my birthday or Christmas."

Jim knelt in front of Priya, plucking the ring from her palm. "I know. It's my grandmother's engagement ring."

Priya's brows knit for a moment before her jaw dropped.

"Priya Surjit, would you do me the honor of marrying me?" Jim slipped the ice cream and strawberry syrup covered ring over Priya's finger.

Tears glistened in Priya's eyes before she kissed Jim. "Yes, but can we clean off the ring? It's sticky."

* * *

Las Cruces, New Mexico, Earth

Tamara slowed the light personnel transport as they approached the checkpoint. It was an older vehicle brought from the Redoubt, but it wasn't on the TO&E for the mission.

A police officer warily eyed the LPT as Tamara lowered the window. There was no mistaking the Berserkers' logo emblazoned on the door. He appeared caught off guard that the occupants were dressed for a night on the town instead of in typical merc garb. "Can I help you?"

"You can if you can let us through this roadblock, officer," Tamara replied, smiling sweetly. "We're here for a night out, not on merc business."

"Your boss is the merc who traded gunfire with those Red Justice Front extremists," the policeman said.

Tamara nodded. There was no point in denying what the officer said. "I promise we'll behave. As you can see, we're not dressed for gunfights."

The policeman leaned close to the window. Charlotte expected him to proposition her or Tamara in exchange for passage. Instead, he lowered his voice and said, "Your commander did us a damn favor, standing up to those terrorists. In a bunch of cities, the RJF bastards made similar attacks, then vanished in the confusion. If I ever meet your boss, I'll buy him a beer."

The policeman waved at a quartet in National Guard uniforms manning the ad hoc gate set between concrete dividers and flashed a thumbs up. One of the four at the barricade mirrored the gesture as they slid aside the gate.

"Enjoy your evening." The officer stepped back and waved them ahead.

"Wow. I've never seen the downtown district this empty," Glen remarked from the back seat.

"Between the police cordons and jitters from the attack, I'm not surprised," Gina said. "Why they targeted Las Cruces is up for debate. Even with all the growth over the past few decades, Las Cruces isn't in the top 100 cities."

"Seventeen of those top 100 were in Texas," Glen remarked. "Some say Las Cruces' proximity to Texas and Sonora-Chihuahua made it a target. Easier for agitators to slip in, and in theory, easier for the perps to escape across a border."

"Nerds arguing is so adorable." Tamara smiled in the rearview mirror. "I bet they're furiously messaging each other over their pinplants, and we're missing most of it."

"We're not arguing," Gina retorted. "We're debating why the RJF attacked here instead of targets with a larger radicalized population. The senators may have been too good a target to pass up."

"Besides, you wouldn't want to see most of the stuff we send to each other," Glen added.

"I'm so glad we can argue the old-fashioned way," Charlotte remarked. She and Tamara didn't fight often, and when they did, making up was worth it. She couldn't imagine flashing messages and netfeed articles at each other.

Tamara rolled past the valet stand at Ciara's, leaving behind a crestfallen attendant as she pulled into the half-empty parking lot.

"No wonder the hostess said we didn't need reservations," Charlotte observed. The employees outnumbered the customers. The protests might have scared off many of the rich patrons, but the people working for a living were the ones getting hurt. She made a mental note to tip even better than usual.

Normally, the hostess would have regarded a quartet of twenty-somethings dressed for a nightclub dubiously, but tonight she seemed grateful for anyone who walked through the door. She whisked them to a table near the bar, and a server was waiting for their drink orders before they even settled in their seats.

"I hope the club isn't going to be empty," Tamara remarked. "It could be a bummer if the dance floor doesn't hit critical mass."

Charlotte nodded. The only other time she'd been there was on Tamara's birthday. Patrons packed the restaurant even on a weeknight. Now, diners only occupied a handful of the tables, and only a few customers sat at the bar.

A swarthy man at the bar met Charlotte's gaze and smiled. Charlotte averted her eyes, but not before he elbowed the man next to him and tipped his head in Charlotte's direction.

"Shit," Charlotte muttered, catching Tamara's attention. "See the two guys at the bar in the expensive suits?"

"The Mediterranean and the Hispanic watching us like hawks?" Tamara asked from behind her hand. "You've been doing so good. Do you want to disappoint Padre Jim and Commander T?"

Glen lowered the menu. "So good at what?"

"Not getting into brawls with douchebags," Charlotte replied, peeking at the bar out of the corner of her eye. The two men were holding an animated discussion, probably debating over who 'got' whom when they made their move.

"She used to go into bars and wait for guys to lay hands on her or not take no for an answer, then kick their teeth in," Tamara elaborated. "The last time she dressed up as a college coed to put some extra bait on the hook. The owner of the bar knew the commander and called him."

"Those guys are going to send us drinks and use it as an excuse to come over and try to chat us up. They think their fancy suits and expensive jewelry will impress us, and at some point, they'll invite us to 'party' somewhere. Somewhere between drinks and the invite, they'll test the waters to see how handsy they can get." Charlotte stopped in time for the server to deliver their first round of drinks.

"These two are compliments of the gentlemen at the bar," the server stated as she passed out the drinks.

Charlotte arched an eyebrow. She didn't need to say, 'I told you so.'

After the server took their orders and departed, Glen asked, "Do you have a script?"

"I've seen it," Gina chimed in. "Whisky has a knack for picking out assholes in bars."

"Sweetie, this isn't the brawling kind of establishment," Tamara cautioned. "Can we have dinner and pre-game before hitting the club, without cleaning blood off your shoe because you impaled someone on your heel?"

"Don't worry," Charlotte replied, sipping her drink. If it hadn't come from the server, she wouldn't have touched it. "There won't be a brawl. They don't have any buddies to join in, so it wouldn't be a challenge."

"How are you doing tonight?" The man's Italian accent might have impressed a townie. "I am Amando, and this is my friend Renzo."

"Um, hi." Glen broke the awkward silence. "We're deploying tomorrow, so we're having a night out together."

"Deploying?" Renzo asked as he leaned on the back of the booth behind Tamara.

"We're mercenaries," Tamara said, sitting forward. "Bjorn's Berserkers. We want to have a nice dinner and a few drinks before we ship out tomorrow. Thanks for the drinks, though."

Would they take the hint and cut bait? Charlotte held her tongue to resist the temptation of goading them.

"Mercenaries? No offense, but you don't look like mercenaries." Amando put his hand on the back of Charlotte's seat. "You're too lovely to be mercenaries."

"If you're going off to battle tomorrow, you should celebrate tonight!" Renzo declared.

"We want to have dinner first," Glen said. Amando shot him a betrayed scowl, as though Glen had violated some sort of guy code.

"I have an executive suite at the Nuevo Hilton." Amando's hand drifted to Charlotte's exposed shoulder. "You should come party with us."

"Told you so," Charlotte said to Glen. "Amando, I'm going to be nice and give you the chance to remove your hand before I hurt you."

"There's no need—OW!" Amando staggered back, clutching his hand. "You broke my hand!"

"Don't be a big baby." Charlotte smiled sweetly. "That was a pressure point. If I was in a bad mood, I would have broken three of your fingers and driven my heel through one of those expensive leather shoes and skewered your foot."

"You crazy bitch!" Amando snapped from a safe distance. He winced as he flexed his hand.

Renzo stepped away from the booth. "You're the mercs from out by White Sands."

"That's right," Charlotte replied. "How about you take your buddy out of sight, and I'll tell the server to take our drinks off your tab."

Renzo nodded and herded Amando to the other side of the bar.

"I'm so proud of you," Tamara said. "No punching, no kicking—you didn't even draw blood."

Charlotte shrugged. "I didn't want to mess up my dress before we get to the club."

* * * * *

Chapter Twenty-Four

Maki Transport, Hyperspace

The beta chewing on his rations across from Sabher leaned forward. "We should take the ship. The Maki couldn't stop us."

Sabher gnawed on his meal of rehydrated meat. Besquith filled the cargo hold turned barracks. Deaths occurred daily as the mercenaries chaffed under close-quarter confinement. Sabher was the only one allowed to leave.

"They would set the MinSha against us," Sabher replied. Unlike the Besquith, the insectile MinSha bore their claustrophobic accommodations stoically. The MinSha had received a different assignment, but Sabher had met their officers between meetings with Dbo'Dizwey. The mantis-like aliens were content to serve their parole.

The other beta waved a dismissive hand. "We could take the bugs. I am Kruug, of the creche Krug'hanz."

Sabher pointed his snout toward the cargo hatch. "At the first sign of trouble, the crew could open this hold to space."

"Are you a coward, Sabher?" Kruug asked loud enough for the surrounding Besquith to hear. The nearest gammas scrambled away as best they could in zero gravity.

"I have killed three gammas and two betas so far," Sabher replied. Out of the hundreds of paroled Besquith, less than 40 were betas and none were alphas. "I can add an additional beta to the list, especially one foolish enough to jeopardize us all."

"How can you bear to serve these monkeys?" Kruug snarled. His fur rippled as his muscles tensed. "Have you become their pet?"

"We don't serve the Maki. The Union Credit Exchange paid the ransom our home companies could not." Sabher braced his feet against the frame attaching the bench to the table. "Consider it another mercenary contract. Serve it out, and you walk free."

Kruug bared his fangs. "We could walk free now!"

Kruug lunged across the table, but Sabher ducked and seized one of his wrists. Sabher twisted and Kruug's feet scrabbled in open air. Sabher swung his opponent against the abandoned adjacent table. Kruug slammed into the metal surface belly up with his head toward Sabher. Disoriented, Kruug flailed to find some purchase. Sabher raked his claws across the other beta's throat. Blood welled in the wound before droplets spurted free.

Sabher released the thrashing Besquith. Kruug spun free, one hand over his rent throat while the other clawed at the table to keep him from drifting into the open air of the bay. His claws threw sparks from the metal but found no grip before he floated out of reach.

Sabher watched Kruug twirl toward the ceiling, accompanied by a nimbus of blood. He scanned the crowd for any Besquith hoping to take advantage of the distraction. A single gamma quickly averted its gaze.

Kruug gagged and choked as his desperate gasps sucked blood into his lungs. When he bumped against the ceiling, he failed to snag a nearby handhold, and his exertion sent him drifting toward the closed cargo hatch. Blood bubbled from Kruug's nose, and his tongue lolled.

A pair of MinSha guards watched from the other side of the airlock hatch. The honorable insects had accepted their new employment conditions without hesitation. Even with their laser rifles, they wouldn't risk entering the cargo hold.

By the time Kruug collided with the cargo hatch, he had ceased struggling. His fur brushed blood across the metal surface before his limp form rebounded toward the floor. Gammas scurried out of the body's path.

Another beta approached Sabher with slow, deliberate movements. He wanted Sabher to see he wasn't creeping closer for an attack. Sabher waited until the new arrival closed to speaking distance.

"What do you want?" Sabher asked, still on guard in case this was a ruse.

The beta hauled himself into a sitting position at the table and snagged a drifting hunk of meat.

"I do not come to pick a fight," he said. "I am Baruu. My creche is Bruuhauz, and I served as second beta in the Bone Manglers."

"You haven't answered my question, Baruu." Sabher's rations had drifted away during the fight, so he laid claim to the closest portion of meat.

"You know what's going on. They let you out of our cell, presumably to confer with our parole holders," Baruu replied. He lowered his voice. "You mentioned the Union Credit Exchange. Why would they need us?"

"Imagine what a tempting prey one of the galactic mints would pose. More hoards of wealth than you can imagine." Sabher noticed a gleam in the other Besquith's eyes. "The Union Credit Exchange ransomed us to garrison their mints. Serve well, and they may richly reward you."

The gammas had crept back to their spots when the threat of violence faded. "How long must we endure these conditions?" Baruu asked. "We lose more wolves every day to infighting."

"We will divide before the next jump," Sabher said. He would have 20 octals under his command, as would 4 other betas. Was Baruu jockeying for one of the remaining spots? It would show he was more prudent than Kruug. "I don't know how many more jumps we need to reach our destinations, and before you ask, I do not know those destinations. I advise against prying—knowing the location of a mint could flag you as a liability."

* * *

"Wouldn't it be quicker to let Sabher pick the other captains?" Uvksolt poked at her rehydrated vegetables while reading her slate. "He killed another challenger in Hold Five. For that matter, we could weed out many of the malcontents and still have 16 octals left per captain."

"Base 8 number systems give me a headache," Dbo'Dizwey complained before sipping on a slurry of ground insects and larvae. "It's easy to remember 20 octals equals 160 Besquith. Hopefully we will not have to linger, waiting for the other transports. Once we spread our parolees out, they will be more manageable."

"How will we keep them from learning their location and blabbing it to the rest of the galaxy?" Uvksolt asked before scooping up a mouthful of vegetables with her trunks. "As soon as their tour ends, we'll have every pirate and bandit swooping in."

"We'll monitor them carefully, same as any other free-willed employee. If they learn too much, there are remedies." Dbo clacked her beak. Uvksolt chuckled.

* * *

Information Guild Headquarters, Capital Planet

Heloxi spat out the male when the doors to her sanctum shuddered. She shoved the corpse aside with a stubby foot. The male was too large for her to eat after he performed his duty. The heavy metal portals inched open.

Neermal hurried forward, his robes whispering against the marble floor. If the acolyte spotted the deceased Kimmilok floating in Heloxi's pool, he gave no indication. He bowed before Heloxi. "Greetings, Master Archivist. I come bearing information flagged for direct delivery."

Heloxi dabbed blood from her painted lips. "Proceed, Acolyte."

"A vessel captained by a Khabar pirate tried unsuccessfully to hijack a Union Credit Exchange shipment," Acolyte Neermal stated. "The pirate ship was destroyed with all hands."

"I know. I saw it on my news feed. Criminals abound, so it is no surprise," Heloxi said.

The XenSha took a cautious step closer. "What the newsfeed doesn't mention is that one of its shuttles was recovered. The crew was dead, but the salvage team found a pair of boarding drones in the wreckage."

"Boarding drones? Drones are too small to deliver boarding parties." Heloxi skimmed her netfeeds in her pinview. "They brought the drones here?"

"Yes, Master Archivist. Initial analysis indicates the drones are some sort of robots. Once they punched into the hull, they killed the crew—bloodily, based on the remains and the video." Neermal held aloft a chip. "The crew fought back and disabled the drones, but they were too late."

Heloxi's gem encrusted brow furrowed in confusion. "Why didn't the drones explode?"

"I do not know," Neermal admitted. "They appear designed for ground and shipboard engagement. Couplings on the lower shell suggest a separate delivery stage. Do you wish us to deliver them to the Science Guild Consulate for analysis?"

"NO!" Heloxi slapped the water, sending the XenSha scurrying several meters backward. The last thing she wanted was to hand the Science Guild an inroad into the conflict with the Union Credit Exchange. "Not a byte of this gets mentioned to the Science Guild!"

Index Prime: 'Concur. Analysis indicates an unfavorable outcome if the Science Guild enters the equation.'

"What should we do with the drones that were delivered here?" Neermal asked, keeping his distance.

Heloxi lowered her pigmented eyelids in contemplation. "Send one on a courier ship to meet the mercenaries Acolyte Ashok deputized." A stellar map appeared in her pinview with the route from Earth to the target highlighted. "They will pass through the Pico Geb system. The courier must depart within 12 hours to intercept the Humans."

If the courier hadn't had its own shunts, the rendezvous would have been dicier. The stargate for Capital opened four times per day, and the fee for an off-schedule transit bordered on extortion. Luckily, the Information Guild maintained a flotilla of shunt-equipped courier ships.

"The other drone?"

Heloxi focused on the XenSha. "Deliver it to our technical staff. Let's see what secrets they can pry from it."

* * *

Senate District, Capital Planet

"Thank you for a fine meal," Hedvig Kloron declared. Cephalo's reputation almost equaled its prices. "I especially appreciate that you waited until we finished dining to bring up why you are treating me to such a lavish repast."

"I didn't want to spoil your appetite with delicate matters," Nargis Xlorin said, cradling a goblet in his hand. "You've prevailed upon Senator Patarix to vote against the Finance Guild proposal."

Hedvig set down his napkin. "We do not need to upset the status quo. There has been enough chaos."

"One could argue tumultuous times are the best to enact change," Nargis countered. "This could represent a tremendous opportunity for shrewd businesspeople who are in the right place at the right time. It could be lucrative."

"I'm sorry, but I disagree. Patarix must vote against the proposal," Hedvig stated. At least he'd gotten a magnificent meal before the evening turned sour. Still, no need to be rancorous with a fellow Gtandan—as long as he knew when negotiations ended.

Nargis dipped his head. "If you are set in your course, I will not belabor the point." He swiped his UAAC over the terminal on the table and paid for the meal. "Splendid—it worked. Thank you for hearing me out. May your holdings prosper."

"May your holdings prosper." Hedvig echoed the Gtandan farewell. At least Nargis didn't see the axe the Information Guild held over Hedvig's neck. If he crossed them, the guild would ruin his family.

Hedvig finished his wine and headed for the exit. The valet robot spotted him approaching and signaled for his aircar. In a few minutes, the sleek, luxury vehicle alighted on the valet deck, and the door to the passenger compartment swung open.

Hedvig sank into the sumptuous upholstery. "Home, Milzner."

Ducted fans launched the limo into the air beneath the enormous dome covering the district. The craft weaved and bobbed through traffic, rocking Hedvig in his seat. Good thing he hadn't opened a bottle from the mini bar. Hedvig stabbed at the button to lower the partition between him and the driver compartment.

"There's no hur—" Hedvig didn't recognize the driver. Was it a Human? "Where's Milzner?"

"Milzner is in no condition to drive. It's a shame. I didn't want to kill him, but then there wouldn't have been two bodies in the crash debris."

"Who are you?" Hedvig demanded. An electronic pop preceded the odor of burning metal and plastic. "Who do you work for? I'll pay you double!"

"Too late." Wind rushed in as the driver threw open his door and leapt into the night.

Through the front windshield, a rubble pile. Hedvig's hand fumbled for his slate, but he dropped the device. The aircar slammed into a pile of permacrete debris at 200 kilometers per hour.

* * * * *

Chapter Twenty-Five

EMS *Ursa Major*, Departing Earth Orbit

"Welcome aboard, Commander Tovesson." Lieutenant Erika Vinter had replaced the previous XO in the personnel shuffle after Patoka. The tall, Nordic blonde floated at attention. Her crisp uniform could have come straight off the laundry press.

"Commander." The corporal next to Vinter fought to keep his eyes ahead. The slender man's Adam's apple bobbed as he spoke. "Your quarters and office are ready."

"Thank you, Corporal Halsey, Lieutenant Vinter." Bjorn gestured to Berto, who showed no sign of discomfort from microgravity. "This is Captain Duarte. He will be my second for this mission."

"A pleasure to meet both of you." Berto's eyes lingered on the lieutenant a moment. "Why do we use the ground-pounder ranks in space?"

"Trying to juggle the two gave me a headache," Bjorn remarked. "I investigated other multi-operation units and didn't find a consensus. This is easier."

"If you'll follow me, we should get out of the bay before we get under thrust." Lieutenant Vinter led them toward the hatch.

Once in the corridor ringing the spine of the ship, Bjorn oriented his boots to the deck. Vinter waited by the ascent shaft.

BTI: 'Welcome aboard, Bjorn. Shipboard node update completed and mission ready files standing by.'

293

'Thanks, Bettie,' Bjorn replied through his pinplants.

The thrust alarm sounded, followed by an announcement. "Prepare for three-quarter-G thrust."

The deck reverberated as the fusion torches ignited and broke *Ursa Major* out of orbit. Bjorn's stomach appreciated the faux gravity provided by the thrust. They'd experience a day and a half at .75Gs, save for the flip over at the halfway mark, then they'd be weightless for a week in hyperspace, save for the small gravity decks.

"Commander, do you wish to go to the CIC?" Vinter asked in her sing-song Norwegian accent. "Captain Wildman is free to meet with you."

"Sure. Might as well touch base," Bjorn replied. He'd just as soon go to his quarters or his office. He wanted to be awake for the flip over—going from thrust to zero g in his sleep messed with his head almost as much as the transition to hyperspace.

The lieutenant stepped into the shaft and climbed upward. A traffic jam ensued as Halsey and Berto jostled for the next spot and, Bjorn suspected, the view. Halsey gave way to rank and stepped back. Bjorn suppressed a grin.

Even in three-quarters gravity, the climb winded Bjorn as they ascended half the cruiser's 200-meter length. He stepped onto the CIC deck, breathing heavily. The armored hatch to the ship's nerve center hung open.

Stepping through the hatch put them at the 'bottom' of the spherical room. The workstations and acceleration couches were mounted on gimbals. The crew faced in the direction of travel under zero-g, but they could pivot their stations 90-degrees and typically did while under thrust.

The flag station formed the lowest/back tier of workstations. The captain sat above it, and two more tiers of stations stretched above him. The captain unbuckled his harness and climbed down.

"Welcome back, Commander. Once more into the breach?" Captain Than Wildman asked. "I've read the mission profile, and there isn't much there regarding naval units as long as the system defense boats don't open fire on us."

"With any luck, you and the *Saotome* are giving us a ride, and that's it." Bjorn stepped aside. "This is Captain Duarte. He'll lead Grizzly Company when we get matters sorted, and on this mission, he'll be my second."

Wildman's expression grew solemn. "I was sorry to hear about Bill—Major Hawkins. I know you were close friends."

"Thanks. Everyone has lost someone over the past few months." Bjorn's hand strayed to his hammer. "Can you spare Lieutenant Vinter to give Captain Duarte the nickel tour?"

"Absolutely. I'll be in my ready room if anything comes up." Captain Wildman opened a hatch below the flag station and descended through it.

"Captain Duarte, if you'll come with me," Lieutenant Vinter said before stepping into the corridor.

"Halsey, grab some coffee and bring it to my office," Bjorn said after the pair vanished. Lower, he added, "Don't let it get cold if you run across Vinter on the way."

* * *

An hour later, Berto stepped into their shared office. "I'm impressed."

"With the ship or the blonde?" Bjorn sipped his

lukewarm coffee.

Berto slid into the seat attached to his desk. "I don't need to get into trouble on my first contract. I meant the ship. I remember you talking about the old days when the Berserkers had to contract out transportation. Your dad got the first ships when we were kids. Now you have warships and transports."

"I know why my father balked at getting warships," Bjorn remarked. "They're a quick way to lose a lot of lives and a ton of credits. At Patoka, the enemy vaporized one of our frigates, and they mauled the hell out of another. On the one, every life was gone in an instant. It gave me new respect for commanders like Cromwell."

"Based on the mission brief, bringing in a cruiser seems like overkill, but I'm glad you erred on the side of caution," Berto said, collecting a zero-g cup and filling it from the coffee pot. "Something smells fishy."

"I can't argue with you. We're going in as though it's a contested landing." Bjorn projected the target data provided by the Information Guild representative on the Tri-V. "The target is in this industrial complex 10 kilometers from the starport and its town."

Berto studied the display. "It looks so…ordinary. Other than this perimeter wall, I don't see any defensive measures. This could be a furniture factory for all I can see. Wait a minute, what's this structure on the northwest corner?"

Bjorn zoomed the image. "I'd guess the cooling stack for an underground fusion plant disguised as HVAC equipment."

"A furniture factory wouldn't need a fusion plant. In fact, I don't see a utility substation." Berto pointed at another small, industrial facility nearby. "See this? It's the power and data bus between the factory and the utility grid."

"A self-sufficient complex powered by a fusion plant? Nope, nothing to see." Bjorn had drawn the same conclusions while studying the intel, and he was encouraged that Berto had spotted the same things.

"They've either been operating out of this complex for a while, or they took it over from a legitimate business." Berto rotated the holographic image. "This isn't some ramshackle operation."

"The lack of defensive emplacements worries me. It means we won't know where they'll fire from until turrets or launchers pop out of the ground," Bjorn noted. "We also don't know how many troops they have holed up in the buildings."

"We've got a company of CASPers with two platoons of infantry and a couple of recon squads. The complex isn't large. Sure, they have more space underground, but if they're housing troops on site, they need to supply them." Berto scrutinized the Tri-V display. "What's the plan?"

"We land three kilometers east, opposite the starport. The CASPers will double-time through these two roadways." The paths lit up on the display. "The light industry should cover us until we're a quarter of a klick from their perimeter. Meanwhile, our scouts will sweep around to watch for any reinforcements from the direction of the starport. The infantry will hold the LZ."

"We're keeping the dropships on the ground? We only have a few spares," Berto remarked.

"If the Information Guild gave us bad intel and everything turns pear-shaped, I don't want to wait for the birds to come back from orbit," Bjorn said. "If we need to get out of Dodge, we'll need to scoot."

* * *

"**W**ilhelm?" Charlotte spotted the CASPer trooper scanning the mess for somewhere to sit. She waved him over.

"Hey Whisky, Tamara." The young man's German accent had softened slightly since he joined the Berserkers shortly before the invasion. "Gizmo, how are you doing?"

Charlotte winced. She'd forgotten Wilhelm Gutknecht had exposed the traitor in the Berserkers' midst. The mole had not only leaked information to the Berserkers' enemy, he had tried to frame Wilhelm's girlfriend and left a bomb that could have killed Gina. TJ Diller wasn't only a spy and a saboteur; he and Gina had dated while he worked undercover in the firm.

"I'm good. Whim, this is my boyfriend, Glen." Gina patted Glen's arm. The men exchanged handshakes.

"It's a shame Isabella didn't come," Tamara remarked.

"Yeah, she got stuck on Patoka with the sun, sand, and surf. I'm sure she feels like she's missing out," Whim said before peeling open his meal pouch. "Oh, and fresh food. Even if she had deployed with us, Sergeant Stallings is keeping me busy."

"That's right, you got promoted. Congratulations on your stripe, Corporal," Charlotte said.

Wilhelm chewed a forkful of mystery hash. "Thanks. Any idea what the deal is with this job? I heard we don't have an actual contract."

Gina leaned forward. "We don't. The Information Guild paid the commander a ton of credits and deputized us to drop the hammer on some criminal operation."

"I didn't think mercs took jobs without contracts." Wilhelm said.

"They don't," Sergeant Cripe replied, joining the table. "The contract keeps employers from screwing us over, or at least makes it harder. With the Mercenary Guild shut down, there are no new contracts, so if the Information Guild screws us, the Merc Guild won't do shit about it."

"Why would the commander take a job with no contract?" Wilhelm dug out some more hash.

Cripe sniffed the contents of his meal pouch and wrinkled his nose. "He might believe the Information Guild is on the up and up, or it could be the ton of credits Gizmo mentioned."

"It can't go south like Patoka, can it?" Tamara asked.

"Of course, it can," Cripe countered, stirring the steaming stew in his meal. "No mission plays out exactly as expected."

"How did your APEX armor fitting go?" Charlotte asked Cripe.

"I already hate it. It's too tight, and it pinches if I move wrong," the older sergeant replied. "When I complained, Enzo told me to lose 10 kilos. Once we get through this mission, you can keep your APEX armor. I'll go back to pushing pixels on forms."

"When I climbed into my cadre CASPer, the tech told me to grow a few centimeters," Wilhelm countered. "You can lose weight, but I am done growing. I held off getting my hardening treatment as long as possible in case I could eke out another centimeter or two. As it stands, I barely qualify as a CASPer operator."

Cripe snorted. "At least I could breathe in a CASPer."

Charlotte scowled at the two. "Really? You want to complain about being short?"

"Hey, who are the guys in the green and tan camo?" Wilhelm asked, changing the subject. A cluster of troopers gathered around a pair of tables. They bore Berserker patches on their shoulders, but not the dark gray uniforms worn by the firm.

"Garret's Rangers—the merc company the commander bought out," Glen replied. "We had to catalogue and inventory all their gear in a rush. Enzo said we ran out of gray paint for their CASPers. A lot of them still have camouflage limbs."

"This should be fun," Cripe remarked over his stew. "New troops used to their own command structure and tactics suddenly tossed into the mix. It'll be a blast."

"I wonder if they're bitter about Vance Garrett selling the unit?" Tamara asked, watching the ex-Rangers.

"They had a chance to muster out of their current contracts," Gina remarked. "Most of them stayed on."

"Would you want to be an unemployed merc with the guild freezing contracts?" Cripe remarked.

"Crap." Glen rooted around in his meal pouch, averting his gaze from the Rangers. Three of them threaded through the tables, led by a bald CASPer trooper wearing sergeant's stripes.

"What is this? Papaw here bring an MST class on a field trip?" The sergeant's nametape read Bowers. The men behind him, also CASPer troopers, laughed. Bower's pointed at Wilhelm. "How old are you, 16?"

"Corporal Gutknecht has more time as a Berserker than you, Sergeant," Charlotte countered. The rest of the Rangers hung back at their table, waiting to see how this would play out.

"What are you, his little sister?" Bowers sneered.

"Here we go," Tamara muttered.

Charlotte pushed back her tray and stood up. "No. I'm Master Sergeant Charlotte Wicza. My friends call me Whisky. You can call me Sergeant Wicza."

"Master Sergeant?" Bowers guffawed. "Master sergeant of blow-jobs, maybe."

Tamara and Cripe scooted clear. Wilhelm had the table between him and the impending brawl. Gina grabbed Glen's sleeve from across the table, but he was stuck between Bowers and one of the other Rangers.

Charlotte affected her best innocent expression. "What's wrong Sergeant Blower, do you need pointers? Can't keep your boys satisfied?"

"You little bitch!" Despite his bulk, his backhand swept in faster than expected. It still took far longer than a jab, but Bowers obviously didn't regard her as a threat. In a normal brawl, she would have snagged his arm and broken his elbow over her shoulder.

The nanite hardening treatment made the tactic risky. Instead, Charlotte ducked the arm, jabbed at his solar plexus with one hand and drove the other up under Bowers' jaw. His teeth clacked together, and he bellowed in pain.

The rest of the mess hall leapt to their feet. While the Berserkers outnumbered the Rangers, a large portion of the gray uniforms belonged to support personnel and infantry. All of the Rangers were CASPer troopers.

Bowers' off-hand punch powered past Charlotte's block and grazed her head, forcing her to stagger back a pace. His right-hand snatched hold of her BDU shirt and yanked her off her feet. She snapped her steel-toed boot into his gut and clapped both hands over his ears. The commander might get pissed if she clawed at a fellow soldier's eyes, even one being an asshole.

"Fuck!" The Rangers sergeant hurled Charlotte away. Pain flared through her ribs and back as she slammed into a table, sending half eaten meals scattering. Bowers recovered his bearings and charged.

Charlotte rolled into a crouch on the table, grabbed a metal tray, and flung it at Bowers' face. Deflecting the tray diverted his attention as Charlotte dashed three steps across the table and planted the sole of her boot in Bowers' face. Her hand-to-hand instructor, Sergeant Eddings, would have chided Charlotte for grandstanding. Her bruised ribs agreed as Charlotte fell to the table.

Charlotte tumbled off the table and landed in a crouch. Tamara and Whim double teamed one of Bowers' cronies, while Cripe boxed with the other. The older sergeant already sported a shiner and a split lip. Cripe's opponent faced away from Charlotte, so she couldn't tell if Cripe had given as good as he got. She collected another tray, stepped onto the bench, and swung the tray with both hands. The impact deformed the tray into the shape of the trooper's skull.

The private spun to face Charlotte, and confusion crossed his face as he saw her standing eye-level with him. His confusion didn't last long as Cripe kicked him in the back of the knee, and he toppled. Cripe reared his boot back to kick the Ranger in the temple.

"What. The. Hell!" Commander Tovesson's roar cut through the ruckus of the brawl. The din of the fight died, punctuated by a tray clattering to the floor. The commander stormed through the hatchway, followed by the new captain of Grizzly Company.

The commander's ice-blue eyes swept toward Charlotte. "Whisky! Tell me you didn't start this."

* * *

"Eight hours," Bjorn growled. "Eight hours out of orbit, and we have a brawl." Bjorn wished Padre Jim had come along if for no other reason than to advise him now. Scuffles among troops weren't uncommon, especially when new soldiers tried to find their place in the pecking order, but he didn't have time for the usual alpha male bullshit, or whatever defined Whisky's problem.

Three Rangers stood at a facsimile of attention in the emptied mess hall. The four Berserkers in grey stood straighter, even if it pained them. Wicza, Reeves, Cripe, and Gutknecht all stared straight ahead.

"The psycho bitch started it," a sergeant with a smashed and bloody nose snarled. Bjorn checked the man's nametape—Bowers.

Whisky, to her credit, held her tongue. Bjorn glared at her. "Is that true, Sergeant Wicza?"

"No, sir. Sergeant Bowers accosted our group. When I offered to advise him, he took offense and swung at me."

"You lying little cunt!" Bowers snapped.

Bjorn set down his slate on a nearby table and glared at the other two Rangers. "Do you back up Sergeant Bowers' statement?"

One remained stone-faced. The other, a dark-skinned corporal, took a deep breath. "I believe the sergeant may be confused regarding events leading up to the fight."

"Murphy!" Bowers hissed, cut off when Bjorn held up a finger.

"Elaborate, Corporal Murphy." Bjorn fixed his gaze on the man.

The corporal shifted his weight and drew another intentional breath. "We noticed Sergeant Wicza and her cohort discussing us. Sergeant Bowers thought they were mocking us and moved to confront them. Czinkota and I accompanied him. Rangers back each other up." The corporal's eyes flicked toward Whisky. "Bowers and Wicza exchanged words, and Sergeant Bowers swung at Sergeant Wicza."

"Sergeant Bowers, do you wish to dispute Corporal Murphy's version of events?" Bjorn asked. Bowers remained silent, but his glare switched from Whisky to Murphy. "This may prove educational to those of you hired in from the Rangers. Bettie, display security feed, Mess Hall A, starting time stamp 1827 hours."

A Tri-V image of the mess hall appeared over Bjorn's slate. "Footage compiled," Bettie announced aloud. Her electronic voice bore a trace of a Nordic accent. "Playback available."

Bowers slumped; his eyes focused on the deck. "Fine. I lost my temper. It won't happen again."

"We'll see. Captain Duarte, assign Private Bowers to one of the squads without other former Rangers. Rotate a trooper from that squad to Bowers' previous squad," Bjorn ordered. Berto nodded and tapped his slate. "Sergeant Murphy, you will need to integrate the transfer into your unit. Is that understood?"

It took a moment for realization to dawn on Murphy's face. "Yes, sir!"

"It should go without saying, any attempts at reprisal, including against Sergeant Murphy, will end poorly." Bjorn stared down at Bowers. "Do you know about trial-by-airlock?"

"No, sir," Bowers replied hoarsely.

"We stick the offender in an airlock and open it to space for 30 seconds. Usually, the bastard gets sucked into space, but a few manage to hang on or claw their way back in before the outer hatch closes. Of course, exposure to vacuum fucks them up, but sometimes they recover." Bjorn lowered his voice. "Don't mistake my giving you a second chance for my being soft."

Bowers gulped. "Yes, I mean no—um, sir."

* * * * *

Chapter Twenty-Six

EMS *Ursa Major*, En Route To Sol Stargate

Sergeant Keith Cripe poked his head through the infirmary hatch. "I was ordered to report here."

The nurse glanced up from her slate. "You must be Sergeant Cripe."

"Right. I might look a bit rough, but I don't need anything more than some aspirin and a good night in the rack," Keith said. He hurt like hell after the brawl in the mess hall, but he wasn't about to admit it. Add a couple shots of whisky, and he'd be all right in a couple of days.

The nurse regarded him. Suddenly Keith felt self-conscious over his black eye, even if he had received it from a man 20 years his junior, with 20 kilos on him. "I'm sure your injuries will clear up during the process," the nurse said.

"Process? What process?" Keith asked.

"Your nanite hardening treatment." The nurse checked her slate. "You're slated to operate APEX armor, so the hardening regimen is standard."

No one had said anything about nanite therapy when they drafted him to lead the other scout guard. "Aren't I too old for the treatment?"

The nurse shook her head. "In fact, you might find several side benefits. It alleviates arthritis and other joint pain from aging and wear. The treatment will improve your bone density and regenerate cartilaginous tissue. We'll administer some calcium and iron supplements, but the nanites should have sufficient building material."

"What building material?" Keith asked as the nurse ushered him toward a medical bed.

"Your, um, extra padding, Sergeant. The nanites will break it down into base proteins and energy for fuel," the nurse replied. She held out a paper robe and gestured to an adjacent chamber. "Please disrobe, put this on, and climb on the bed."

Keith grumbled under his breath as he stepped into the small room and shucked his BDUs. "How long will this take?"

"Eight hours, Sergeant Cripe. Doctor Shuv'im will arrive shortly." She referenced her slate. "You should finish in time for the flipover, though you may want a shift in your bunk to recover."

A H'rang peered through the open hatch. For a moment, Cripe mistook her for Hcuff't, but the markings were different. "The patient is ready, yes?"

"Yes, doctor. I've prepared the arterial shunts and loaded the nanite program," the nurse replied.

"Arterial shunts?" Keith's voice rose half an octave. They sounded painful.

The H'rang nodded. "We will flood your body with special nanites. You have a high pain tolerance, yes?"

"Aw, hell." Keith slumped back on the cold bed. Maybe the aches from the brawl would dampen the pain from the treatment? He focused on the ceiling while the nurse set a tray next to the bed. The cool swab of alcohol preceded a sharp prick on each arm and thigh.

"That wasn't so bad," Keith remarked as the nurse cleared away the tray.

"Those were preparatory injections." The nurse held up a large needle connected to a silver tube. "These are the shunts."

"Fu-!" Keith gritted his teeth as the nurse stabbed the shunts into his limbs. "I am so getting Whisky for this."

"Activating guide field," the doctor announced. An electric tingle swept over Keith. "Introducing nanites now."

Warmth suffused Keith's body as the microscopic machines spread through his blood stream. The warmth grew to a burning sensation as the swarm of miniscule robots set to work knitting bones and ligaments, cannibalizing excess fatty tissue in the process.

* * *

"What did Cripe say when he found out about the hardening treatment?" Tamara asked over a bowl of something claiming to be oatmeal.

Charlotte shrugged, nibbling on a protein bar. Peanut butter bland seemed a safer choice than some of the hot options. "We won't see him until dinner. He'll be sore, in more ways than one."

An ugly bruise mottled her side, but a nanite injection had mended her cracked ribs. The commander would have let her suffer if they hadn't been on a combat deployment. Bowers swung first, but Whisky goaded him on instead of deescalating the situation.

"Oh, oh," Glen murmured. "Hope you're ready for round two."

Charlotte followed Corporal Brand's gaze. Sergeant Murphy filled the hatch to the mess hall, and his eyes locked on their table. The buzz of multiple conversations faded as he marched over to them. Charlotte set down her half-eaten protein bar. How hot was her coffee?

"Hey, Little Sister." The sergeant's deep bass carried even without volume behind it. "Rangers back each other up—when they're on the right side. Besides, we're Berserkers now." Murphy extended his large, beefy hand.

She'd let the name slide this time. It had taken guts for Murphy to approach them and make a public gesture in front of a dozen of his fellow ex-Rangers. She took the offered hand and shook it. "Welcome to the Berserkers, Sergeant."

Murphy nodded to the rest of the group and joined the staring knot of troops in green and tan.

"That wasn't what I expected," Glen remarked. "I'm glad I was wrong."

"Me too," Charlotte admitted. "Don't any of you start with the 'Little Sister' business, either."

"We'll leave it for Cripe," Tamara remarked. "It might be the nicest thing he calls you after nanite therapy."

"It's not my fault if he didn't read the mission contract," Charlotte retorted. "If he calls me Little Sister, I'll call him Papaw."

Gina choked on her orange juice.

* * *

Maki Transport, Pico Geb System

"What can I do for you, Captain Sabher?" Dbo'Dizwey reclined on her couch. After a week in weightlessness, the faux gravity of thrust weighed on her. Neither her Sumatozou bodyguard nor the Besquith before her seemed perturbed.

"I wish to send a message to Bestald. The ship's crew denied me access to the communication system," Sabher stated.

"Why would you want to speak to your home world? Your native mercenary firms left you to rot on Earth," Dbo said, clacking her beak. "You owe them nothing."

"Peepo's malfeasance bankrupted our companies and imposed economic hardship on our world. I do not wish for our people to continue wasting effort and resources to liberate us," Sabher replied.

Dbo valued the wolf for his sense of duty, but duty could be a two-edged sword. She didn't want to give away that the aliens would be garrisoning mint facilities. "Very well, but don't elaborate on the nature of your new employment. Information is as deadly a weapon as your talons—we want to deny the enemy any intelligence."

Sabher nodded. "I can inform them we have been liberated pending a private assignment. I do not know our destinations, so I cannot give them away."

Dbo clasped her upper hands. "Acceptable. Uvksolt, please accompany Captain Sabher to speak to the Maki crew. Unless I miss my guess, we are only a few hours from rendezvous, and we will have our hands full dividing the indentured troops among the transports."

Uvksolt's trunks rippled, but she didn't voice an objection. "As you wish."

Sabher nodded again. "Thank you."

"Think nothing of it. I commend you; you consider the needs of your people when you could stew in bitterness," Dbo said. Granting the Besquith's request posed little risk and further cemented his loyalty.

* * *

Capital System, Contracted Yacht *Bountiful Excess*

Ashok sighed in relief as his four feet met the deck under half a standard gravity of thrust. While a luxurious craft made space travel bearable, he longed to return planetside and to his research. Ashok transmitted his initial report to Master Archivist Heloxi. At this distance, the speed of light spared him a two-way conversation, as messages would take minutes to travel each way.

He confirmed the projection of when the Human mercenaries would reach the intermediary system before continuing to their final destination. If only he could have convinced the Humans to use their warship to obliterate the mint from orbit. It would have simplified matters. However, Ashok sensed such a suggestion would have soured Commander Tovesson on the deal.

An incoming message pinged Ashok's pinplants. It couldn't be the master archivist. His message would only be halfway to Capital after four minutes. Ashok unraveled the handling code. The message had originated from a GalNet buoy near the emergence point. A quartet of the relays orbited the Lagrange point, providing updates to incoming ships, as well as facilitating message hand-offs.

Index Prime: 'Proceed to Xhoxa. Observe operation. Report results soonest.'

Ashok scratched his head. Why was he receiving a message from Index Prime? The super-computer had served as a repository for the Information Guild for millennia, but it was merely an information storage and retrieval system. Someone must have originated the message and passed it through Index Prime's system.

Additional messages winked into Ashok's pinview. The captain of the *Bountiful Excess* acknowledged the new orders and diverted course for the system's stargate instead of the planet. A standing message from Heloxi informed Ashok that additional operatives had been dispatched to intercept the mercenary force at Pico Geb with valuable intelligence.

Ashok double checked the route he had provided to the mercenaries. Pico Geb—another relief. Heloxi could be generous when pleased, but she was twice as wrathful when disappointed. The rumble in the deck shifted as the yacht accelerated. Ashok checked the new flight data. Five days would pass while they traversed the distance from the emergence point to the stargate.

So much for returning to his comfortable research. Heloxi didn't elaborate on why she sent him to Xhoxa. Perhaps she didn't trust the mercenaries to accurately report on their task? Ideally, the mercenaries would die accomplishing their goal—did Heloxi send Ashok to watch the mercs die and inform her of the results of their mission?

It made sense. Heloxi wanted eyes in-system, and Ashok had drawn the short straw. With a sigh, he resigned himself to his fate. He might as well visit the galley while they were under thrust, and his lunch wouldn't threaten to float back up.

* * *

Information Guild Headquarters, Capital Planet

The message ping roused Master Archivist Heloxi from her nap. She blinked but resisted the urge to rub her eyes for fear of ruining her cosmetics. Ashok's message detailed his success in hiring a Human mercenary company. A rambling report on current affairs on Earth accompanied the message. Heloxi swiped it aside in her pinview and flagged it for review by a lesser archivist. The Human world didn't warrant her attention.

Ashok had been too loose with the credits, Heloxi noted, especially up front. She would have offered a larger payment on the back end, in case the mercenaries failed or perished in the process of succeeding.

The Human commander held a spectacular grudge against a certain Besquith. He had demonstrated obsessive behavior that clouded his judgement. Heloxi narrowed her eyes in satisfaction. Ashok had chosen well. Credits motivated many beings, but most would not throw away their lives for wealth. Vengeance was another matter.

Another priority message vied for her attention. The Senate Finance Commission had dismissed without hearing a measure to investigate switching the Union from the red diamond standard to a virtual reserve. Her skin mottled in anger as she slapped the water. Servants lurking in the shadows fled.

She opened a channel and flagged it top priority. After twenty seconds, the other party answered.

The video feed swung as the other person adjusted their slate. A pair of beady, red eyes squinted past a pointy muzzle. The eyes widened in surprise. "Master Archivist Heloxi? To what do I owe the honor of this call?"

"You know what!" Heloxi bellowed, hoping her virtual avatar conveyed her fury. "The Finance Commission refused to review the virtual economy proposal! I was assured it would have no trouble passing."

The Eosogi on the other end of the call glanced around nervously. The ferret-like aliens fancied themselves schemers on par with Veetanho, but almost matched the Zuparti in jumpiness. A common saying said an Eosogi was scheming as long as it drew breath.

The Eosogi lowered its voice. "How did you get this comm address? I thought—"

"I thought the Finance Commission would bend to our will!" Heloxi shrieked.

'Circulatory pressure exceeding safe parameters,' her pinplants warned.

"There was a complication. The Mazreen senator changed his mind," the Eosogi replied.

Heloxi sneered. "The Mazreen senator? The one you were supposed to blackmail?"

"How did you know—"

"I am a master archivist! Of course, I know! I have access to every information system connected to the GalNet! I could wipe out your UAAC accounts with a thought!" The threat would have been complicated to carry out, but the weaselly Eosogi operative didn't need to know that.

"We lost our leverage. The Gtandan businessman acting as our proxy perished in an aircar crash," the Eosogi said, his whiskers twitching. "Once Senator Patarix switched sides, several other senators followed suit."

"Why didn't someone else blackmail him?" Heloxi demanded.

"Delicate matters take time to arrange," the Eosogi countered. His eyes flicked enough to indicate that he was checking his account balance. "Especially after the unfortunate demise of—"

Heloxi slapped the water again. "He was murdered, you imbecile!"

316 | JON R. OSBORNE

"Of course, someone killed him." The Eosogi's eyes narrowed. "I must investigate this matter further. I recommend, in the future, using established channels to contact me." The screen went dark.

* * * * *

Chapter Twenty-Seven

"Son, give these alien motherfuckers what for." Blood trickled down the side of Bjorn Tovesson II's face, staining his silver beard red. He grunted as his CASPer shook and the illumination flickered. "I'll see you in Valhalla."

Wrenching metal drowned out all other noise. After a moment, a savage voice snarled, "Meat."

"Fuck you, *sukin syn,*" Tovesson spat back. "Bettie, Ragnarök."

The image ended with a white flash, then static.

'Video ended.'

"What did you want to talk about?" Berto asked.

Bjorn shifted his focus from his pinview to the command office. Berto sat across from him at his desk, holding a burrito.

"I want you to spend the rest of the trip working with the troops we brought in from Garrett's Rangers." Bjorn grabbed his sandwich before it drifted too far from his desk.

Berto shrugged. "Okay. Are they still creating friction?"

"A bit, but mostly, they're sticking to their clique. I'm concerned about their integration into the firm. Usually, we'd have a couple of months to ease them in and do team-building bullshit. Including the next jump and in-system transit at the next stop, we have about 14 days." Bjorn tore off a bite of his sandwich. He didn't care for the

317

rubbery texture of the bread. It reduced the crumbs, but it felt wrong when he chewed.

Berto showed no remorse as he bit into his burrito. "They came from a different operating culture. The Rangers had mechanics, but not a dedicated logistics and technical branch. They're accustomed to being self-sufficient."

"You have an outsider's perspective," Bjorn said. "It will help you bond with the new guys and, in turn, bring them into the fold."

"I'll get on it after lunch." Berto renewed his attack on the burrito.

* * *

"Hey, you only got one lunch today," Charlotte teased as Cripe joined the lunch table.

"I only ate double the first day, per doctor's orders," Cripe protested. His cuts and bruises had faded to blemishes during the nanite treatment. "Even so, I lost five kilos."

"Sounds like a rough way to lose weight," Tamara remarked.

Cripe peeled open his ZGM, zero-g meal. "I wouldn't recommend it. You know the no pain-no gain mantra? This comes with tons of pain." He prodded the meal with a spork. "Some sort of cheesy lasagna."

"I've got it-might-be-meat chili. Want to trade?" Charlotte asked.

"I'm good." Cripe flexed his right hand. "Better than good. Two of these knuckles have ached for the last five years, not to mention my knees. Doctor Shuv'im gave me a clean bill of health after the treatment."

"I'm surprised more people don't get nanite therapy," Tamara said.

Cripe shook his head. "Most of the people who need it wouldn't be in shape to survive it. That's not even factoring in the pain. I felt like I was dying for eight hours."

"You didn't hit on Doctor Shuv'im, did you?" Charlotte spooned out a glop of questionable chili. It tasted greasy—not good, but not horrible.

"I slept with one alien; it doesn't mean I'm a Niven." Cripe scowled and stabbed a chunk out of his meal. "Sirra'Kan resemble Humans except for some fur and feline traits. Screwing a H'rang would be like fucking a mountain lion. Pass."

Tamara failed to stifle a laugh. "You'll call me in the morning, yes?" she mimicked Hcufft's cadence and nasally tone. Charlotte laughed so hard tears welled up in her eyes.

"Wait until it's Loki's turn with you," Cripe muttered before wolfing down a chunk of pseudo-lasagna. "Where are the lovebirds?"

"Gizmo and Glen? Gina said something about checking a load in one of the Shadow rumblers," Charlotte replied. They'd been at breakfast, but logistics kept a different schedule. "I'm sure they'll turn up."

* * *

Glen paused to check that the light next to the hangar hatch glowed green. Gina followed him through the airlock, guiding herself along the back of the hangar with a handrail. Maneuvering in large spaces in zero gravity made her nervous. In a corridor or even a compartment, you eventually drifted to the other side. If you cast loose in the hangar, you could float around a long time before you bumped into something to grab.

320 | JON R. OSBORNE

Glen led them to the last dropship, an older craft with 'DS-0013' emblazoned on its nose and tail. After a quick scan around, he pushed off the wall and snagged a hatch handle. Gina launched herself toward Glen, who caught her and pulled her alongside the craft.

With one more check to see if anyone was watching them, Glen opened the hatch and ushered Gina inside. Gina's eyes slowly adjusted to the darkness inside the ship. A dark, angular shape dominated the dropship's bay.

"Is this one of the Shadow rumblers?" Gina whispered. No one should have been able to hear them inside the craft, but she remained cautious.

"Yes—Shadow Three." Glen guided her to the hatch of the vehicle. "It's the spare for the scouts."

Once inside, Glen used a hand lamp to find the control panel near the back hatch. With a flip of a switch, dim red lights illuminated the interior. Strapped down crates of ammo and supplies took up some space, but the rest remained empty pending the arrival of a squad of armored scouts.

"It's not the most romantic place, but it's private," Glen said.

"You brought me here for sex?" Gina asked.

"Um...yes?"

She reached for the buttons of her BDU shirt. "Good. I wanted to make sure. I'd be embarrassed if I got undressed to count laser carbine magazines."

* * *

"Gutknecht, have you confirmed our ammo and consumable loadouts?" Sergeant Stallings asked.

Wilhelm referred to his slate even though he knew the answer. "Yes, Sergeant."

"Lambert is still lagging in the simulator runs. Put in some extra time with him," Stallings said. "We have two weeks to get him up to speed."

"Yes, Sergeant." Wilhelm tapped a note on his slate.

"Make sure no one slacks off on their physical conditioning," Stallings instructed. "A single week without gravity is bad enough, but we have two jumps. I want extra PT while we're under thrust in the halfway system. Two days of fake gravity is better than nothing."

"Right, Sergeant." Wilhelm suspected all corporals did was manage sergeants' checklists. He hoped, at some point, there'd be some training to help him develop toward his next promotion, even if it was a way off.

* * *

Maki Transport, Hyperspace

Dbo'Dizwey stretched out in her quarters. Even though the compartment remained unchanged, the mood on the ship made the cabin feel larger. Only 20 percent of the liberated mercenaries remained. No longer crammed together, tension among the Besquith had eased.

The MinSha guards remained vigilant. As with the Besquith, only one-fifth of their number remained on this transport. One hundred and sixty Besquith could easily overpower the Maki crew and take the ship if left unchecked. Dbo had confidence in Captain Sabher, but she was also pragmatic. No sense in tempting fate.

The message icon blinked in Dbo's pinview. Hyperspace limited the message source to someone on board. As she suspected, it came from Sabher. The captain requested information regarding the facility the Besquith would guard for training purposes. A reasonable request, especially since Sabher had convinced the Maki to install multiple Tri-V emitters in one of the vacated cargo bays. He wanted to emulate the physical layout of the buildings and grounds.

Dbo waged war with her ingrained reticence to divulge any information regarding a mint facility. She brought up the schematics on her slate. They showed no information about the purpose of the facility. With a ripple of her crest feathers, Dbo released a copy of the schematics to Sabher. Better he keep the Besquith busy than the mercenaries grow bored.

* * *

Hevrant, Tolo Region, Core

Nxo'Sanar set aside the latest update from Capital. A call from the tech-priest beckoned his attention. The news from the Senate encouraged Nxo; hopefully the priest wouldn't dampen his mood.

"Chairperson Nxo'Sanar, I bring good news," the high priest said without preamble.

Nxo folded his upper hands. "It must be exceptional for you to call me directly, Than'Diwer."

"We have solved, at least for the short term, the core shortage." The priest blinked both pairs of eyes in excitement. "The Hall of Corrections offered a special parole to those incarcerated for terms expected to exceed their lifespans."

Only crimes of the highest greed or crimes of violence against other Nevar incurred such long sentences. Even if every convict with a long sentence agreed to the parole, they would number no more than a thousand. It was a stopgap measure, but it would buy them some time.

"You have no doubt the obedience protocols will ensure compliance?" Nxo asked, uneasy about having the worst of Nevar society at the controls of deadly war-machines.

"Absolutely. Besides, they volunteered to serve society," the tech-priest replied. "While the Hall of Corrections did not empty the Living Graveyard, enough volunteers came forward to keep our priests busy around the clock."

Nxo tilted his head. "How many convicts have you converted to cores?"

"One hundred as of the afternoon report," Than'Diwer replied. "We sent the first shipment of fifty to Xhoxa this morning."

* * * * *

Chapter Twenty-Eight

EMS *Ursa Major*, Hyperspace

A muffled emergence alarm woke Gina. Crap! She must have drifted off. It took a moment to recover her bearings. A dim, red light illuminated the interior of the Shadow rumbler.

"Glen! Wake up." Gina shook him, but not hard enough to break his embrace. Any other time, she would have found waking up in his arms romantic, but once the *Ursa Major* emerged, the fusion torch would ignite, and g-forces would return.

"What?" Glen yawned and pulled her close. "Did we fall asleep?"

"The ship is about to—" Gina's world flipped upside down for a split second as the ship fell back into regular space time.

Glen blinked, wide awake. "I hate that almost as much as entering hyperspace."

Where were their clothes? A vibration thrummed through the rumbler. Which way was the floor? The thrust alarm sounded in the hangar bay.

"Shit!" He pushed off a surface with one arm and twisted so his back faced the direction of impact. He bounced off the deck of the rumbler, unable to grab anything, and Gina collided with him. The vibration increased, and they fell the few centimeters to the floor in a tangle of limbs.

"Are you okay?" Gina asked. Intentional or not, Glen had cushioned her fall, and he let out an *oof* on impact.

"I'm fine," he wheezed. After a couple of deep breaths, he added, "Zero-g is fun, but now that we have gravity…"

"Tempting, but I have to parse through the GalNet updates, and you have your post-emergence checklists," Gina replied. Through her pinplants, she instructed the rumbler's computer to raise the cabin illumination to one-quarter output. Their clothes lay scattered about the troop cabin.

Glen sighed but didn't argue. "You're right. I need to survey the cargo bays to make sure nothing came loose." He disentangled his trousers from a safety bar. "Hopefully, no one figures out where we've been disappearing to."

Gina found her bra draped over the operations console. "If everything goes according to plan, we can come back here after we flip over. We'll be under thrust for 48 hours except for the flip."

"It's a shame we can't wrangle a cabin," Glen remarked. "I tried, but the guy I talked to said something went wrong on the last flight."

Gina stiffened. Wilhelm and Isabella had bribed someone to use a compartment, then Gina's would-be-boyfriend planted a tracking beacon in the room and booby-trapped it.

"I don't want to jump the gun, but maybe when this assignment wraps up and we go to Vishall, we can check into getting a flat together," Glen suggested as he wrangled his BDU shirt. "Shit. I jumped the gun, didn't I?"

Gina blinked; she'd been staring off into space. "What? Sorry, I was—wait, did you suggest we move in together?"

"Maybe?" Glen grinned sheepishly. "I know it's sudden, and we haven't been dating long—"

Gina kissed him. "I'm not going to answer, only because it's bad luck to tempt fate. You never answer a question like that on deployment. Ask me again once we're on the way to Vishall."

"It's not as if we'll see combat," Glen said.

"What did I say about tempting fate?"

"Okay, I'll ask once we finish the mission and head home."

* * *

"All stations secure from emergence," Sergeant Anne Sprague announced from the sys-op station.

Sergeant Frank Lutz projected the sensor readout to the main Tri-V display. "The *Saotome* emerged with us on the same trajectory. No hostiles on scope."

"We're only 27 degrees off nominal flight path," Sergeant Marcia Ling reported from the helm. Given that ships could emerge heading in any direction, they had lucked out. "Entering course corrections and sending them to the *Saotome*."

BTI: 'Incoming priority message from the Information Guild.'

Bjorn sat up at the flag console. They'd only emerged 60 seconds ago. The guild must have primed a message on the GalNet buoy serving the emergence point. Bjorn opened the missive.

"Greetings, Commander Tovesson. Acolyte Paruk will contact you shortly regarding intelligence germane to your mission."

Typical Information Guild—even their e-mails required a dictionary.

"Captain, we're being hailed," Sprague announced.

An amber icon appeared on the main Tri-V. "We have a ship on an intercept vector," Lutz said. "They're thrusting at two Gs and will reach our threat box in seven minutes. She's a corvette."

"Maintain alert condition," Captain Wildman ordered. While the cruiser outmassed the new ship by a factor of ten, Bjorn approved of Wildman not taking chances. "Sprague, put through the call."

"Greetings Mercenary Ship *Ursa Major*." The image of the speaker resembled something out of an old horror video. The humanoid's eyes and mouth aligned vertically, and its skin glistened like a wet amphibian's. Bettie identified the speaker as a Phosgee in Bjorn's pinview. "I am Acolyte Paruk."

"This is Commander Tovesson. How can I help you?"

"I have material intelligence regarding the forces you will face at your objective," Paruk replied in a series of gurgles and clicks. "We recovered it from a pirate attack."

"I'm guessing you didn't come all this way to show me some guns," Bjorn remarked. He worked out the timing of transitions. Someone in the Information Guild had scrambled to arrange this. "Can you match our velocity and dock, or would it be easier to send a shuttle?"

"We have the material loaded on a shuttle and standing by," Paruk replied. "I can arrive in 30 of your minutes."

Bjorn glanced over at Wildman, who nodded. "Very well. I'll leave the details to this ship's captain and his crew."

The Phosgee closed his eyes and bowed. The Tri-V image winked out, and Sprague confirmed termination of the signal.

"BTI: No electronic intrusion attempts detected. Either they have improved their methods, or they do not wish to incur your ire."

'I wouldn't rule out both,' Bjorn replied to Bettie. "Captain, can we isolate the hangar bay from the rest of the ship? Our employers have snooped in the past, and I don't want to give them an opportunity that's too easy to pass up."

"Sprague, what do you think?" Wildman asked.

The sys ops sergeant displayed a set of Tri-V schematics. "The data umbilicals and comms run through a data bus in flight control. Someone could unplug the feeds from the bus."

"I can have my senior tech support handle it," Bjorn suggested. "Which hangar should she unplug?"

"Hangar Four—it's empty except for Dropship 13, a back-up bird," Captain Wildman replied. "I'll have flight control prep the bay."

* * *

A two-tone alarm sounded three times.

"Shit! It's the decompression alarm!" Gina tied her boot and called into the dropship. "Glen, hurry. We have 60 seconds to exit the bay or inform them we're in it."

"One of my socks got loose."

"Forget it!" Her pinview display showed 50 seconds. At least they had gravity—reaching the hatch in zero-g would have been challenging.

Glen appeared at the hatch, holding one boot. Behind him, the rumbler's aft ramp whirred closed. He hopped down and triggered the dropship hatch to shut. Luckily, the rest of the bay was empty, and they reached the airlock with 30 seconds to spare.

"We could have stayed in the dropship," Glen remarked. "I doubt anyone would have missed us."

330 | JON R. OSBORNE

An audio call notification flashed in Gina's pinview. "Hi, Commander. What can I do for you?" She flashed an accusatory glance at Glen.

"Gizmo, I need you to unhook the data bus thing for Hangar Four. I'll have Bettie send you the info in tech-speak. How quickly can you get there?"

BTI: 'Attachment sent. Don't worry, Gina. I wouldn't have let them decompress the bay if you remained inside.'

"Bettie sent me the file. I'll get right on it," Gina replied. "I might need to borrow Corporal Brand, since I don't have my toolkit with me."

"Take whoever you need, but have it done in 25 minutes," the commander said. "Tovesson out."

"I only caught your end of it, but I heard my name," Glen said.

Gina took a moment to study the schematics. "We need to go to flight control and isolate the feeds from the hangar. Good thing we got out."

"Sounds easy. On a ship like this, it should run through a data bus. I can unhook it in five minutes with my multi-tool." Glen drew the tool from his pocket.

"That's why I lo…Um, we need to go." Gina fought back a blush. Talk about jinx! Never drop the L-bomb on deployment.

The zero-g alarm erased Glen's goofy smile. They sought out the nearest handholds before acceleration ceased and they went into freefall.

"Try not to lose your tool like your sock," Gina teased.

* * *

"What the hell?" Charlotte grabbed her helmet. Only a few minutes had passed since emergence and the *Ursa Major* was cutting thrust? The condition beacon in the compartment remained amber for alert condition as opposed to red for battle stations.

Cripe stared at the beacon as though he expected it to change. "Maybe the other ship emerged off course, and we need to let it catch up?"

It sounded plausible. If they had emerged into a hostile situation, they'd be at battle stations. "Keep suiting up," Charlotte said.

"These things are a bigger pain in the ass than mounting a CAS-Per," Cripe complained. Donning APEX armor required some contortions on the part of the wearer. "But at least it fits better."

Charlotte's earpiece chimed. She tapped it to open the channel. "Go for Wicza."

"Whisky, how quickly can you get some of your scouts into their suits?" Commander Tovesson asked.

"Cripe and I are almost suited up," Charlotte replied. "What's up?"

"Get to Hangar Bay Four. We have company coming." Commander Tovesson paused to give an order to someone else. "There shouldn't be trouble, but I want to hedge my bets."

"Roger. We'll report to the hangar as quickly as possible." Charlotte lowered her helmet until it clicked into place. The HUD lit up, and the eye-tracking controls synched.

"What's that all about?" Cripe asked before lowering his helmet. It took several seconds for their comms to connect.

"The commander wants us at Hangar Four," Charlotte replied. "I guess he doesn't want CASPers tromping all over the place, but he wants something sturdier than meat puppets."

"Don't forget, you were infantry on Vishall," Cripe chided.

* * *

"Hangar pressurized," Corporal Halsey announced. Bjorn didn't mention he could see the indicator himself.

"Let's see what the Information Guild brought us," Bjorn said. The shuttle clamped in the bay resembled dozens of others Bjorn had seen. Bjorn noted the pilot landed aft first—better if they needed to make a hurried exit.

Heat washed off the thrust bells as they approached the craft. After a few minutes, a hatch opened, and Acolyte Paruk emerged. The Phosgee floated toward Bjorn, his robes fluttering as he moved. In person, Bjorn downgraded the Information Guild representative from menacing to creepy.

Two more Phosgee wrangled a large crate between them. The cargo handlers wore basic coveralls as opposed to the acolyte's finery.

"Greetings, Commander Tovesson." The acolyte's translator rendered the gurgling clicks. His vertical eyes flicked between the two scouts in APEX armor.

"Welcome aboard. What's so important I had to see it in person?"

"This contains a terrestrial drone utilized by the adversary." Paruk gestured at the crate. "I am told no races employ these on the battlefield. Information hones a general's blade. Examine it and learn its weaknesses. You'll see why we couldn't hand some laser pistols to librarians and deal with this threat ourselves."

"This drone is inoperative?" Bjorn asked.

Paruk nodded, a Human gesture. "The power core was rendered inert during combat."

"Secure the crate on the empty pad next to the dropship," Bjorn instructed. Wicza and Cripe took custody of the container. "Will the contents suffer if exposed to vacuum?"

"It has already been subjected to space. I imagine you won't do it any more harm," Paruk replied. "In addition to these machines, I bring you operational intelligence. Your quarry has recruited additional forces from your home world."

It didn't surprise Bjorn. A criminal organization waving a fistful of credits under destitute merc companies' noses was bound to find some takers. "The counterfeiters hired Humans? Any idea what company?"

"Let me clarify. The new forces are not native to your home world. Someone recently ransomed several Besquith and MinSha. We believe some of them hired on to protect your target."

What were the odds Sabher would be waiting on Xhoxa? *Tyr, grant me this request*, Bjorn prayed. Aloud, he remarked, "I've killed Besquith and will happily do it again. Same goes for my people."

Paruk bowed. "I shall take my leave. Good hunting on your mission, Commander Tovesson."

Bjorn's response died on his lips when a sock floated between them. Bjorn watched the garment drift by. "Thank you, acolyte."

* * *

"Commander, you wanted to see us?" Gina asked at the airlock of Hangar Bay Four.

"Gizmo, Brand, follow me." The commander led them through the airlock. In berth two, cargo straps secured a coffin-sized crate to the deck. They circled the container to peer in through the open lid. "This is what we could be facing at the drop. It's some sort of combat robot or land-warfare drone."

"Doesn't using robots on the battlefield violate Union laws?" Glen inquired. The black and red cylindrical body trailed four ambulatory limbs and possessed four, well three and a half, blade-tipped fighting arms.

Bjorn shrugged. "Consider it more of a guideline. Since these guys run a criminal enterprise, I'm guessing they don't care about the laws or gentlemen's agreements between mercs. I need you to figure out the best way to take these out and what doesn't work on them. Can you do that in eight days?"

"We'll find out," Gina promised.

"We'll need more than my multi-tool," Glen remarked once the commander left the bay. "Could it have a self-destruct charge?"

"I hope not. Self-destruct sounds clever until someone hacks your command net. They could wipe out your whole force." Gina opened a tool cabinet set in the wall of the hangar. "We need to make as much progress as possible while we still have pseudo-gravity."

Glen joined her in rummaging through the tools. "It leaves us no time for...other stuff." He cast an accusatory glare over his shoulder. "Cock-blocked by a robot. Thanks, pal. I hope the commander realizes we don't have an operation like the Hussar's Geek Squad."

"We're not trying to invent a new kind of shield," Gina remarked. She didn't want to admit she envied the Winged Hussar's technical branch, including its mad scientist. "If we can figure out how these things receive orders and IFF data, we might be able to take them out of the fight."

* * *

Bjorn sat on his bunk. He figured he might as well catch some shuteye while the floor was down. They had five days of thrust to cross from the emergence point to the stargate.

BTI: 'A message header has tripped search-daemon parameters.'

"Message header?" Bjorn said aloud. Even after all these years with pinplants, he occasionally fell back on verbal interaction instead of brain-typing. "Whose mail are we reading and how?"

BTI: 'We've received the first update from the Information Guild GalNet buoy. We aren't reading mail, merely skimming the headers. As for the how—do you really want to know?'

Some of Gizmo's hacker shit, no doubt. "What did you find, Bettie?"

BTI: 'Outbound messages originating from Sabher of the Haagen creche.'

Bjorn stood. "He's here? The *sukin syn* is in this system?"

BTI: 'The messages originated from a Maki transport. The transport entered the stargate three hours ago.'

Bjorn slammed his cybernetic fist into the wall. "Dammit!"

BTI: 'The messages were directed to multiple mercenary companies on Bestald.'

"Can you get the transport's flight plan from the stargate?" Bjorn asked, pacing his cabin. The Maki tended to file legit destinations to facilitate trade opportunities.

BTI: 'I will work on it.'

Bjorn sat on his bunk again, but his boiling blood banished any hope of sleep. What would he do if he caught Sabher? Bjorn stretched out on his bunk. Maybe he could sleep in a bit.

"Son, give these alien motherfuckers what for."

* * * * *

Chapter Twenty-Nine

Information Guild Headquarters, Capital Planet

Index Prime: 'Probability of the digital currency legislation passing—12.7%. Probability of the Union Credit Exchange advancing to full guild status—63.2%.'

Master Archivist Heloxi slapped her stubby hands against her flanks. "How? Did you include the blowback from the UCX losing one of their mints? Did you calculate how the theft of trillions of hard credits would disrupt the hard currency ecosystem?"

Index Prime: 'Projections only include predicted outcomes from current facts, not conjecture based on hypothetical events.'

"You worthless slab of silicon! Run your scenario based on the success of our operation with the mercenaries."

Index Prime: 'Mercenaries, especially Human mercenaries, are the antithesis of predictable.'

"Greed is universal. Tell me the odds if the Humans succeed."

Index Prime: 'Assuming all variables fall in favor of the endeavor and the Humans perform as hoped, the chance of the digital currency legislation passing is 89.1%. Odds of the Union Credit Exchange advancing fall to 11.9%.'

Not the zero she wished, but much more acceptable odds. Heloxi settled into her pool and watched data streams cascade through her pinview. After several minutes, she roused from her reverie. She wasn't alone.

"Shall we spare the theatrics?" Heloxi asked, scanning the darkened perimeter of her cavernous chamber.

The Grimm emerged from the shadows. "Must you spoil what little joy I take?"

"I assume you received the message and the job parameters?" Heloxi didn't want to waste time verbally fencing with the cloaked figure.

"Of course. I must decline."

Heloxi's eyes bugged out. "What? You can't!"

The Grimm shrugged under his cloak, his red eyes fixed on Heloxi. "I can, and you will forget about it."

The master archivist snorted. "Kimmiloks are immune to your tricks. Has someone else paid you? I can beat their offer."

"This isn't about pay. Imagine the anarchy if government officials could drop dead any moment from an assassin's blade. Too many people have taken an interest in the SooSha. Murdering a senator would draw unwanted attention."

"I can make it worth your while," Heloxi promised. "One of you tried to take out the Human Mercenary Guild Council member along with his mate—two of the Four Horsemen."

"Which has drawn scrutiny. Some things can't be bought. We saw what happened to the Depik," the Grimm said. "They were second only to us, but their reputation far exceeded ours. Now they're dead. I suspect you'll find it challenging to hire anyone worth the credits to take on government work."

Heloxi sputtered in rage as the Grimm faded into the shadows. Eliminating the Mazreen senator could chill support for the bill. With the Depik off the board and the Grimm bowing out, her options dwindled. She pulled up a contact in her pinplants and opened an encrypted feed.

The Eosogi's eyes widened when he answered the call. "I told you not—"

"You do not tell me what to do." Heloxi worked her tongue along her lower lip. No spawn had slipped out of her throat pouch. "Deal with the Mazreen—permanently. Credits are no obstacle."

The Eosogi leaned away from his device as though it were a venomous serpent. "I don't deal in wetwork."

"You do now—figure it out." Heloxi closed the connection.

Index Prime: 'Reckless use of unvetted operatives could compromise the guild's interest.'

"I didn't ask for a projection," Heloxi snapped.

* * *

Starport Commerce District, Capital Planet

Wayan set down the phone. What had he gotten himself into? Blackmail was one thing—a time honored tradition among Eosogi even—but putting a hit out on a member of the Galactic Senate crossed the line. Could Heloxi make good on her threat to trash Wayan's accounts? Where would he find an assassin willing to take on the job?

Taking out a senator could draw a Peacemaker investigation, even with the current upheaval. It took half a day of working his contacts and spreading around thousands of credits before Wayan found someone who didn't summarily dismiss his inquiries.

The contractor insisted on an in-person meeting. Wayan suppressed a shudder as he followed his Zuul bodyguards into The Hive. For a den of scum and villainy, it boasted an upscale menu. It also featured state-of-art counter-surveillance. What happened in The Hive, stayed in The Hive.

Wayan handed one of the Lumar doormen a hundred-credit chit. Moziy, the proprietor, only dealt in hard currency. No UAACs meant no data trail. The Lumar didn't ask about the bodyguards' weapons—armed security was a sensible precaution.

Wayan scanned the room, seeking the agreed upon color combination. The tables and alcoves had arrays of colored lights. Purple-green-purple-orange glowed above one of the alcoves. The Zuul went to the raised deck running along one side of the main room, where hired security watched over their patrons, and joined two dozen other guards.

Wayan circled the main floor, the drone of white noise generators muffling hushed conversations at a score of tables. He paused nervously at the entrance to the alcove. Could this be a Peacemaker sting? They rarely engaged in such proactive tactics, but if word got out of a potential political assassination, they might make an exception.

Wayan stepped into the alcove through a humming acoustic screen. Padded, configurable benches flanked a table. The tall figure seated on one of the benches nursed a beverage. Wayan climbed onto the other bench and scooted over until he sat across from the contact.

A long, dark coat draped over the being, concealing its form, and a broad-brimmed hat hid its face while it gazed at the mug on the table.

"I was beginning to wonder if you were going to show," the person said. It took a moment for Wayan's translator to parse the language. When he raised his head, Wayan could see his face. Wayan hadn't expected a Human.

"One cannot be too cautious," Wayan stated. He tapped the service slate in the table and ordered his favorite drink. The device required him to deposit cash in advance. "Especially when discussing work of this nature."

"Fair enough. Shall we spend a few minutes feigning camaraderie or would you prefer to get straight to business?" the Human asked.

Wayan accepted his drink from the dispensary hatch. "Direct. You, Humans, have a reputation for chattiness. We both have demands on our time, so let's dispense with the small talk."

The man nodded. "I hear you want someone sanctioned."

"I am merely facilitating the transaction," Wayan protested. "My patron wishes to have an obstacle removed, and she's willing to pay handsomely for it."

"The subject is a senator. No one takes work on Galactic officials or planetary leaders. It sets a bad precedent." The man sipped his drink.

"Why are you here then?" Wayan asked, annoyed his time had been wasted.

The man set down his mug and steepled his fingers, the corner of his mouth crooked in amusement. "Maybe I want to see if you are offering enough to break precedent."

Perhaps this wasn't a waste. "Ten million credits."

The man sat back. "Your patron makes a tempting offer. For ten million credits, she could hire a small mercenary company."

Wayan twitched his whiskers in amusement. Greed was a powerful motivator. "She prefers something more discreet." Wayan suspected if Heloxi could get away with it, she'd be perfectly content to have mercenaries storm Patarix's office.

"I'll be in touch," the man said, draining his mug.

"Can't you give me an answer now? Time is of the essence." Wayan feared Heloxi would contact him before he had an answer that would satisfy her.

"I'll be in touch soon." The man stood and left.

Wayan watched the man disappear into the foyer. Did he hope to drive the price up further by pretending reticence? How high would Heloxi go? Time was a luxury they didn't have if they wanted to derail the UCX's quest for guild status.

Wayan set his half-finished drink on the table. All he could do was wait until this Human gave him an answer. The sum offered sparked an interest. If the Human didn't want the job, drawing the matter out made no sense. Yes, the Human was angling for more money, Wayan decided. He could respect the tactic, especially since Wayan wasn't footing the bill.

Wayan collected his bodyguards, disappointing the Zuul who had hoped for more time at the buffet provided to guards. One of them was still chewing when they exited the Hive. The Zuul scanned the alley in both directions before heading toward the street.

A familiar silhouette of a long coat and brimmed hat stepped into the alley. One of the Zuul snarled.

"I told you I'd be in touch soon," the man said. "Unfortunately for you, we can't have people putting out contracts on protected politicians, especially ones lucrative enough to tempt contractors to break the rules."

Wayan didn't see the man draw the strange, over-sized pistol he leveled at him. One moment the man's hands were empty, and the next Wayan stared down the barrel of a gun. With his other hand, the Human flicked something at them. A small puck clattered on the alley's surface. Both Zuul yelped and collapsed midway through drawing their laser pistols.

"I'm the middleman," Wayan pleaded. "If you kill me, she'll have someone else hire out a hit."

The man stepped closer, keeping the gun trained on Wayan. "Who?"

"Master Archivist Heloxi," Wayan replied. Prevaricating would only get him killed. Besides, it wasn't as if a hitman would go after one of the leaders of the Information Guild.

The Human knelt over one of the Zuul and collected the guard's laser pistol. Both Zuul shook their heads and whimpered, still disoriented. The Human barked something in Zuul as he stood.

"Sorry, it's not personal," Wayan's translator interpreted.

The man shot the Zuul with the laser, but the large pistol never wavered from Wayan.

"You don't have to kill me," Wayan begged. "If you don't take out Heloxi, she'll ruin my life. I owe her nothing."

"Good fixers are hard to find," the Human said.

"That's right! People in your line of work need go-betweens. I can help you," Wayan said.

"But a good fixer wouldn't cough up a client's name," the man said before he turned the laser on Wayan and fired.

* * *

Galactic Senate Building, Capital Planet

"Senator Emlaati, this proposal falls under the purview of the Finance Commission," Nargis Xlorin protested. He thought the red diamond issue had been squelched until Senator Emlaati brought forth an amendment to an existing piece of legislation. "I assure you, the commission already has the issue at top of mind."

"Senator Xlorin, your commission has dithered enough regarding the potential financial crisis," the Cochkala senator countered, whipping her tail. "Perhaps, if your members spent more time focusing on how an archaic financial standard hamstrings the Galactic Union and less time engaged in prurient mating rituals, they would realize the need to divorce ourselves from the red diamonds shackling our economy."

"The Senate does not add amendments unrelated to the original bill. You fling baseless accusations and slander to circumvent Senate procedures," Senator Regider protested. "Bring your proposal to the commission and let us consider it in due course."

"I have brought the proposed legislation to the Finance Commission, but Senator Xlorin has buried it. As for baseless slander, I can share the basis of my information now and let our colleagues decide." Emlaati pointed at Patarix. "Perhaps the Mazreen senator would care to comment?"

"I object!" Senator Patarix yelled. "Disparaging gossip on the Senate floor violates the orders of decorum."

"Sustained!" The Chairman of the Senate, a hulking Sumatozou, slammed a stone cylinder with an echoing *thud*. "The Cochkala senator shall confine discussion to the legislative matter at hand."

"Chairman Art'valla, does the Senate have a rule restricting the nature of amendments?" Emlaati demanded.

Chairman Art'valla curled his bifurcated trunks. "The Senate has adhered to the practice for millennia, but no written injunction exists."

Xlorin listened to the murmuring wave washing across the chamber. The guideline regarding amendments kept the legislative process from breaking down into entropy.

"I wish to forward my amendment," Senator Emlaati stated. "Unless the chair of the Finance Commission agrees to hear it before the commission as its own legislation."

Chairman Art'valla regarded Xlorin. "Senator Xlorin, can your commission arrange to hear this proposal in a timely manner, say within the next 10-day?"

Xlorin weighed the odds. How many senators would vote against the amendment to prevent chaos and how many would favor it in the hope of attaching their own rider amendments to bills sure to pass?

"I will grant Senator Emlaati's proposal a hearing before the Finance Commission within the next 10-day," Xlorin agreed. It would give him ten days to reign in Patarix, who would doubtlessly fold if threatened with the release of evidence of his philandering. A pity Xlorin did not possess the evidence himself, but obviously someone had passed it on to Senator Emlaati.

* * *

Union Credit Exchange Embassy, Capital Planet

"I assume you bring news of the antics in the Senate," Mel'Sizwer remarked as his granddaughter entered his office. "I smell Heloxi's slimy fingers pushing the buttons."

"I received word Heloxi attempted to have Senator Patarix sanctioned." Zod'Sizwey laid a memory chip on Mel's desk. "She tried to hire a sanction agent through an Eosogi fixer. The agent not only

346 | JON R. OSBORNE

refused the job, he provided video of the Eosogi's confession implicating the master archivist."

"I don't suppose the Eosogi was taken into custody?" Mel asked. He cocked his head and regarded the chip with his left eyes. While video could prove handy, it wouldn't sway people as much as a living witness.

Zod clacked her beak. "No. The contractor tied up all loose ends, in his words, free of charge. He understands the danger of taking wetwork jobs on political leaders."

"Heloxi must feel the pressure. She's leaving nothing to chance. Could she have already learned of her proxy's demise before she leveraged Senator Emlaati?" Mel ruffled his feathers.

"It happened nine hours ago," Zod replied. "She would have needed assets to already be in play to respond this quickly."

"I have no doubt the master archivist spun her web in advance," Mel said. "Any luck with the other members of the Information Guild's council?"

Zod shook her head. "The other four have either refused to accept communications, or they have rebuffed any suggestions contrary to Heloxi's agenda. As long as she leads the guild, the others will not act against her."

"Any progress on our TriRusk dilemma?" Mel asked.

"The Science Guild hasn't solved the riddle of those synthetic diamonds. Luckily, they comprise such a small threat that our counterfeit detection measures should suffice. The use of our scanners has propagated along trade lanes, and we're seeing a high rate of adoption."

"I should hope so, since we're giving the scanners away." Mel clacked his beak. "If nothing else, they should assure merchants and planetary bankers that counterfeit red diamonds are a fluke, an infinitesimal threat."

* * *

QlunSha Transport *Silverback*,
Approaching Capital Planet Orbit

"QlunSha transport, this is Peacemaker Corvette *Blue 27*. Cease thrust and prepare for inspection."

Jimtri roared at the communication board. "No customs! No search!"

"Two more!" Hlotri snarled from the sensor console. "Defense cutters! They intercept us!"

"QlunSha transport, if you do not cease thrust, we will fire upon you."

"They lock weapons!" Hlotri cried.

"You no shoot! We free traders!" Jimtri yelled into the communication microphone.

"By the power vested in us by the Peacemaker Guild Charter—"

"Cutters lock weapons!" Hlotri shouted.

"Too many words—fine! We stop thrust!" Jimtri growled at the pilot, who throttled the fusion torch to stand-by.

* * *

"Why you board?" Jimtri demanded as soon as the MinSha Peacemaker emerged from the airlock. Three other QlunSha snarled in support.

"Are you the captain?" the MinSha asked, showing no apprehension at the presence of four angry QlunSha.

"Me captain," Jimtri snapped. "Why you board?"

"I am Peacemaker Chendral. We have reliable intelligence you are smuggling counterfeit credit chits and synthetic red diamonds." Deputized troops followed Chendral through the airlock. "We will search your ship. Don't bother jettisoning the contraband—my ship will spot it."

"If me have fake money, why me have crappy ship?" Jimtri protested. "We have industrial cargo."

"Then you won't care if we give your vessel a thorough inspection," Chendral remarked. He gestured to the investigators who trailed the troops. "You know what to look for. Leave nothing unchecked. If anyone tries to impede your search, shoot them."

* * *

"This crate, it does not match the others, no?" The H'rang investigator peered at the polysteel container. "The coloration of the manifest markings differs from those around it."

The QlunSha crewmember shrugged. "So? Cargo not all from same place."

"Someone tried to blend this crate in with the others. The ink for the manifest identification refracts the near UV part of the spectrum differently from those around it." Investigator Yow'iss pointed at the crate. "You will bring that container down, yes? Yes."

"Hard work! Boxes piled on top!" the QlunSha protested in a spray of saliva.

The H'rang's ears swiveled back, but he held his ground. "Are you refusing to cooperate?"

One of the Zuul troops accompanying the investigator unsnapped her holster.

"Fine! Me get box!"

* * *

"Well done, Investigator Yow'iss." Chendral surveyed the contents of the open crate. Thousands of bundles of credit chits in 100- and 1000-credit denominations filled the crate along with a cylinder containing hundreds of small, red gems.

"Not mine!" Captain Jimtri yelled. "We carry cargo. Not know what in boxes!"

"I calculate between one and two billion credits in chits. A shame they are fake, yes?" Yow'iss held up one of the rectangles with a small red gem embedded in a transparent window. "Yes. Someone dusted the magnesium-aluminum silicate stones with industrial red diamond particles. A poor forgery."

"Captain Jimtri, you and your crew are under arrest pending further investigation," Chendral declared. One of the few crimes that prompted unrequested justice intervention was currency tampering and counterfeiting. Without the credits, the Union would fall apart. "Likewise, we will impound your ship. It may be auctioned off to pay your legal fees."

"No! You no—"

The QlunSha found himself staring down the barrels of several laser pistols.

* * *

Manufacturing District Betel, Capital Planet

Tromdal checked his slate while he enjoyed a stimulating pre-work beverage. He skimmed the newscast thumbnails. Humans quarreled among themselves, attempting to dig out from Peepo's invasion. Why did the primitive race fascinate so many beings? Their home world remained balkanized into regional tribes, some feuding with others.

The Mercenary Guild clashed as badly as the Humans. No surprise since the primitives joined the Mercenary Council. The Humans were barely members of the Union, yet they sat on a guild council. What was the galaxy coming to? Tromdal shook his head and sipped his hot stimulant.

One of the sensationalist feeds popped to the top of Tromdal's media queue. He thought he had squelched all the netbait channels. Tromdal didn't care about the latest scandal involving some politician or media personality. He jabbed at the icon with a digit but froze when he spotted the caption. Instead of sweeping the video aside, he pressed play.

"Scandal rocks markets and financial institutions on Capital!" the talking head cried. "This just in. Peacemakers have intercepted a shipment of billions of credits worth of counterfeit currency chits along with a cache of fake red diamonds! What does this mean for the economy? Is your currency worthless? Merchants may refuse hard-credit transactions due to the danger of fraudulent chits!"

Tromdal had a few thousand credits of hard currency stashed in his domicile. Another table in the café broke into a buzz about the news. If he waited until after his work shift, Tromdal's money could be worthless. He gulped the rest of his beverage and messaged his supervisor that he would be late due to an emergency. He didn't mention that he needed to get his hard chits converted to virtual funds before everyone else had the same idea.

* * * * *

Chapter Thirty

"These blast baffles don't instill me with confidence," Glen remarked.

Gina couldn't disagree with him. Their subject, the strange ground drone she had dubbed 'Rover,' was strapped to a table inside a six-sided cubicle composed of spare hull plating and adhoc framework. If something went wrong, it should contain some of the blast. Unfortunately, anyone working on Rover would have to be scraped off the hull plates.

"Let's see what makes Rover tick." Gina tried to keep her eyes from straying to the scythe-like blades as she worked the custom tool into what they had deduced was a manual release. *Click*. A hatch on the 80-centimeter-across cylinder popped open.

"My God, it reeks." Glen stifled a gag. "It smells like something died."

At one and a half meters tall, the chassis didn't have much space to hide a pilot, though maybe something the size of a Flatar could fit. Gina pried open the hatch to expose the interior. She readily identified the power source, the thruster, and a set of gyroscopes. A metal capsule the size of a soccer ball oozed pungent goo from a blackened rent. Charred electronics and carbonized metal near the capsule indicated a powerful electric arc had brought the machine down.

Gina pushed away from the table. "We need to get Dr. Shuv'im."

Glen grabbed the closest framework strut and hauled himself away from Rover. "Is it a biological weapon?"

"I hope not. It might be an organic control system," Gina replied. "Think brain-in-a-jar."

"You guessed correctly," Dr. Shuv'im announced after she peeled back the hood of her hazard suit. "The capsule contains a brain and some glands, wired in a manner similar to pinplants."

"You mean they scooped the brain out of a living being and stuck it in this machine?" Glen paled.

"I said that, yes? Yes." The H'rang stripped off her gloves. "Despite the burn damage, I identified an impulse harness wired into the pinplants."

"What's an impulse harness?" Gina asked.

"Most pinplant inputs connect to sensory centers. An impulse harness connects to other parts of the brain to allow the input of directives from the pinplants." Dr. Shuv'im shucked the suit.

"So, a controller could give them orders through their implants and compel them?" Gina debated what bothered her more—the lack of ethics or the sophistication of technology.

Dr. Shuv'im nodded, donning her regular scrubs. "I'm making an educated guess." Considering she specialized in pinplants and cybernetics, Gina considered her guess well educated.

* * *

"All right, Gizmo, tell me what you've got," Bjorn stated. Even with the extra air handlers, a whiff of decomposition still hung in the hangar after four days.

"These land drones utilize a mix of standard galactic technology and some cutting-edge innovations," Gina stated. "The advanced technology breaks down into material engineering, control, and communication. The material science is straightforward. The manufacturers of these drones use osmium steel alloys and osmium carbide."

"Translate into big-dumb-guy English, Sergeant," Bjorn said. He had no clue what made osmium special.

"Osmium is the densest stable element. Its hardness rivals that of diamonds, and its melting point falls short of only tungsten and rhenium. This makes it difficult to machine or work. Lasers struggle to burn through it, and that's before you consider the ablative glaze coating the drones." Zomorra checked her slate. Bjorn recognized the stalling tactic. Gina struggled with talking in front of people, even this small group of officers.

"Why don't we use osmium instead of tungsten and molybdenum?" Berto asked.

"Two reasons, Major Duarte." Gina ticked them off on her fingers. "Earth's production of osmium last year totaled 1.5 tons, including recycling. Osmium is hard and dense, but it is also brittle. Alloying it with steel mitigates the brittleness, but not entirely.

"The fighting blades are osmium carbide. Think diamond-edged CASPer blades. Based on the power of the actuators and servos, these blades can punch through CASPer armor," Gina said. "Their weakness lies in lateral stresses. They are thinner and more brittle than CASPer arm blades."

"Stay out of their reach, but if they get close, try to break their arm knives," Lieutenant Belder remarked.

"The second technological advance we found was that the drones utilize organic components in their control system," Gina continued. "The builders wired a brain into the machine. Dr. Shuv'im believes it includes some form of compulsion circuit."

"Is this some sort of ancient technology?" Bjorn asked. It sounded too sophisticated for pirates and brigands. "Could these guys have found some sort of cache of these drones and put them to use?"

Gina shrugged. "I don't know. Galactic Union technology advances at a glacial pace, so it's possible. In fact, it would explain how a counterfeiting gang fielded these drones."

"Where do they get the brains?" Lieutenant Cara Durano asked. She was the highest-ranking former member of Garrett's Rangers on the deployment. She'd already shot Berto down. "Could we end up as zombie-drones?"

"We don't know where the, um, operators came from," Gina admitted, glancing at Dr. Shuv'im.

The H'rang Chief Medical Officer straightened. "We only have one damaged specimen, but I can confirm the brain did not originate from a Human or one of the well-documented Galactic races. Does it preclude using Human brains, no? No."

"What's the third technological leap?" Bjorn asked, wanting to keep the briefing moving. They had three days until emergence, but once they reached the target system, the Berserkers had little time.

"We haven't been able to puzzle out the communication system," Gina replied, frustration creeping into her tone. "The components are reminiscent of Galactic Union near-field communications, but we haven't cracked it."

Bjorn didn't bother pointing out the clock was ticking. Stressing Gizmo out wouldn't help. "What about their ranged weapons?"

"Dual lasers with the output of a heavy pistol each," Gina replied. "The lasers are off-the-shelf components wired into the main power system. A lucky hit could cripple a CASPer, and I wouldn't advise taking sustained fire. Out of everything we found, however, they're the least unnerving."

"I want all CASPers equipped with MACs. It sounds like lasers won't impress these trash-cans, but the criminals must have other forces we can fry." Bjorn fidgeted with the beads in his beard. "Any chance you can repeat what you pulled off at Patoka?"

"If we can figure out how their communications work, maybe," Gina replied. "If we can jam the way they're delivering orders to the impulse harness, the drones might get confused and go into standby mode."

* * *

"I have no clue how they're delivering orders to the impulse harness," Gina lamented a day later. A Tri-V projection of Rover's electronics hovered over Gina's slate in the middle of the lunch table. "It has near-field telemetry, but I can't figure out the main communication gear." She poked a section of the hologram with her spork. "This feeds into the pinplants, but it doesn't resemble any form of radio I've seen."

A passing elSha stopped, one of her eyes swiveling toward the hologram. "Is that a miniaturized quantum relay? How did you solve the field interference problem?"

"You know what this is?" Glen asked, dropping his sporkful of pasta and cheese-like paste. The utensil drifted to the table and the glob of food adhered to the surface. "We've been wracking our brains."

"It resembles a prototype I've seen for a quantum communication relay. Do you understand quantum communication?" The elSha latched onto the bench with one of her feet and tugged herself to the table.

"Instant transfer of information through quantum entanglement. It's how quantum computers work. There's no relativistic lag." Gina turned to the hologram. "The trouble with long-range communication is relaying the quantum states between the sender and the receiver. Well, one of the problems."

The elSha pointed to the toroid above the near-field antennae. "I would bet my paycheck this is a quantum node, and the ball in the middle is the processor. What I don't understand is how someone produced such a small node. Bleeding edge research has the node the size of this table for ground to orbit transmission."

"What if the point isn't long-range communication?" Glen asked, retrieving his spork and scraping the pasta paste onto the side of his tray. "These drones probably work in swarms. The nodes could be for networking as opposed to long-range communication."

"Novel idea, but a great deal of effort and expense to save a few milliseconds in communication lag," the elSha said. She peeled open her meal pouch and plucked out a wriggling grub.

"Maybe we can exploit this." Gina averted her eyes from the elSha's lunch. "Could we hack this network?"

"Absolutely not," the elSha stated. "One of the lovely aspects of quantum communication is you can't crack it."

'Bettie, what do you think?' Gina asked over her pinplants.

BTI: 'I suspect Engineer Rakz is correct. One of the challenges to long-range communication is that one cannot use amplifiers as the qubits cannot be copied. Even listening in to a quantum signal without one of the nodes finding out is impossible. The act of observation corrupts the signal.'

"I have an idea!" Gina risked peeking at the engineer in time to spot a larva disappearing into the elSha's mouth. "Rakz, who is your superior? I need to request your help for a couple of days."

* * *

"Who do you think they put in those beer cans?" Berto asked.

Bjorn withdrew his focus from his pinview and reading Gizmo's excited report on the breakthrough regarding the drones. "I'm more concerned with where they got them. Criminals fielding bleeding-edge hardware makes me suspicious. Who the hell is bankrolling them?"

"I'd guess forging credits would fund whatever they want," Berto countered.

Bjorn shook his head. "There's more to it. Gizmo sent me a report. The drone has some sort of quantum network node."

"Gizmo…Master Sergeant Zomorra? She's cute." Berto grinned.

"I know. She has a boyfriend, I shouldn't fraternize with the troops, and so on. I merely made an observation. Why is this quantum stuff a big deal?"

"People with technology no one else has seen fall into two categories—geniuses like the loon with the Hussars, or those in cahoots with the Science Guild," Bjorn replied.

"What about our Aegis rumblers? Did you get those miniature shield nodes from the Science Guild?"

"Fine, add a third category for people who stumble across lost technology." Bjorn fidgeted with his Mjolnir pendant. "We can't manufacture those nodes yet. My gut tells me whoever built that drone could produce the quantum components."

"Any chance Sergeant Zomorra will pull off another miracle like Patoka?" Berto asked. "I read the action reports. She shut down the opposition CASPers in the field."

"We can't count on it," Bjorn replied. "Patoka was a stroke of luck. Peepo sabotaged the operating code of El Espejo Obscura's CASPers because she didn't trust Humans. Even though the Information Guild paints our opponents as brigands, we can't get cocky. They have these drones, and they liberated a bunch of Besquith and MinSha from Earth. We need to expect a knock-down, drag-out fight.

"Speaking of which, talk to me about the Rangers. Can we count on them?" Bjorn asked. The trouble with taking new troops into battle was that you didn't know how they'd perform under fire until it was too late.

"We have a couple of simmering troublemakers, but when it comes to the fight, I believe the new troopers will pull their weight," Berto replied.

Bjorn cast the destination system display from his pinplants to the Tri-V built into his desk. "I hate M-class star systems. The emergence point is only 4.5 million kilometers from the world. We'll have less than six hours to reach orbit."

"Long enough for them to know we're coming, but not enough time to properly survey the world," Berto said. "Would upping the thrust make enough difference to get the drop on our target?"

Bjorn enlarged the planet in the display. "Our target is the third moon of this gas giant. It's tidally locked to the planet, but it whips around it every 57 hours. The side facing the gas giant is a radiation-blasted desert. Our target lies in the temperate zone on the opposite side."

Berto peered at the data scrolling alongside the depiction of the moon. "You weren't kidding about the radiation. I'm surprised it's even habitable."

"We're not sticking around. Hit the bad guys, get the evidence, and get out," Bjorn said. "We have one day until emergence."

* * * * *

Chapter Thirty-One

EMS *Ursa Major,* Xhoxa System, Praf Region, Jesc Arm

"All stations report secure from emergence."

"Our vector is 117 degrees off optimal flight path."

"The *Saotome* reports ready for separation."

"Sensors show six system defense cutters within half a light-second."

Bjorn half-listened to the chatter from the bridge crew. Their voices betrayed no alarm, and Captain Wildman calmly issued orders to correct course and thrust at 1G for the target. False gravity pushed Bjorn into his couch as the fusion torch ignited.

"Six hours and twelve minutes until orbital insertion," Sergeant Ling announced. She turned to Captain Wildman. "Unless you want to increase thrust to compensate for emergence vector?"

"Commander Tovesson?" Wildman asked, deferring the operational question to Bjorn.

A few minutes lost to turning back toward the moon wouldn't change anything. "Carry on, Captain Wildman. Those brigands will still be there in a few minutes."

"Proceed with course corrections and thrust for the target as planned," Wildman stated.

A more precise clock appeared on the Tri-V, counting down. The same countdown manifested in the corner of Bjorn's pinview. Bettie relayed the clock to all tactical slates.

"Six hours until showtime," Berto remarked from another acceleration couch at the flag station. "Not enough time to do anything but suit up and load up. I'll get the troops moving." Berto rotated his couch and unbuckled. It took him a few steps to recover from a week of zero gravity.

"Commander, do you want any coffee?" Corporal Halsey, his flag assistant, asked.

Bjorn shook his head. "I don't want to piss in my CASPer. I'm going to check on the eggheads and see if they've pulled a miracle out of their brains." His legs wobbled when he first stood, despite his exercise regimen during hyperspace.

* * *

Union Credit Exchange Mint, Xhoxa Gamma 3

"Why the alarm?" Dbo'Dizwey demanded before the door finished sliding open. Uvksolt followed her into the security command center.

"Two mercenary ships emerged seven minutes ago and have set course for this moon," the watch officer replied. His crest feathers ruffled in anxiety.

"I recognize this mercenary unit," Sabher announced, looming over the watch officer to survey the displays. "Bjorn's Berserkers—a Human mercenary company. Based on the vessels, they brought a portion of their force. I estimate two companies."

"How many mecha?" Uvksolt asked, cracking her knuckles.

"They field 100 suits of battle armor in a company," Captain Sabher replied.

Pluck Heloxi's eyes! The master archivist had somehow sniffed out the location of the mint and hired mercenaries, as feared. Two hundred powered armor troopers against 160 Besquith. Dbo would worry if not for the two hundred golems on site. Still, the mint's protective forces would suffer heavy losses.

"The Berserkers operate mixed units, combining their battlesuits with conventional infantry and armored vehicles," Sabher continued. "General Peepo's invasion trapped some of their conventional forces on Earth. We suffered heavy losses hunting them, and in the end, many eluded capture or termination."

Dbo clacked her beak in frustration. "Can you hold them off?"

Sabher huffed. "We have defensive positions and surprise. In the open field, the odds would concern me. Here, we hold the advantage."

"I must alert the other facilities," Dbo declared. Only a fool would assume Heloxi had discovered a single location. If the Information Guild launched simultaneous attacks, her warnings wouldn't matter. If only the quantum network functioned on an interstellar scale. "I shall inform the board as well. How long until the mercenaries arrive?"

"Six hours," the watch officer replied.

"We'll be ready," Sabher promised.

* * *

EMS *Ursa Major*, Approaching Xhoxa Gamma 3

"We won't be ready," Gina admitted. A spiderweb of cables ran from Rover to a myriad of electronics. "We can't crack the quantum encryption."

Commander Tovesson frowned. "I guess we'll have to do this the honest way. You've already given us some valuable intel."

"I'd rather he be mad at us," Glen said after the airlock closed behind the commander.

Gina nodded. "Disappointing him feels worse than making him mad."

"I doubt you've ever made the commander angry," Glen remarked.

"True, but I've seen Whisky tick him off plenty of times." Gina surveyed the spread of electronics. "Even with Bettie, we don't have the power to break quantum encryption. If we could spoof the node issuing orders, we could shut them off."

Glen leaned against the framework around Rover. "We have five hours. We have one of their nodes. Could we listen in on the network?"

"Remember what Rakz said? Listening in wouldn't help because we'd be changing the data and corrupting…" Gina recalled the conversation with the elSha. "We'd corrupt the feed. What if we listened really loud?"

"How do you listen loud?" Glen asked. "Don't you dare say by reversing the polarity."

"By pumping power into our quantum relay so it can listen to more nodes in the network," Gina replied.

"We still can't interpret the signal," Glen said.

"It doesn't matter as long as we listen to it. We can't decipher what they're saying, and we can't send our own commands, but maybe we can corrupt it enough to jam the network." Gina grabbed her technical slate. "We need a power source and a way to splice it into the relay."

"Even if we juice up the relay, the range will suck," Glen said, foraging through the scattered electronics. "We'd have to be on the battlefield."

Gina's eyes fell on DS-0013. "I have an idea."

* * *

BTI: 'A message header has tripped search-daemon parameters.'

Bjorn paused outside the hangar. 'The same as before?'

BTI: 'An outbound message originating from Sabher of the Haagen creche.'

The Besquith was here! The counterfeiters must have hired Sabher. Fate had a hand in this. Tyr smiled on him! Bjorn clenched his fist, imagining the axe he'd bring down on Sabher's neck.

* * *

"Gutknecht, are we good to go?" Sergeant Mark Stallings called.

"Roger, Sergeant. Kodiak Bravo One ready to kick ass," Corporal Wilhelm Gutknecht replied. He hoped he didn't sound like he was trying too hard.

Stallings opened a private channel. "Relax, Gutknecht. We don't have to dick around with traitors or alien traps this time. Remember your training, and you'll do fine."

"Yes, Sergeant. Thanks." Gutknecht checked the display. They still had an hour before orbital insertion. Kodiak Bravo Two clanked into place on the dropship while KB3 waited at the base of the ramp.

368 | JON R. OSBORNE

The sergeant was right. They were going up against criminals, not other mercenaries. It should be a cakewalk. So why was he so nervous?

The sergeant was right. They were going up against criminals, not other mercenaries. It should be a cakewalk. So why was he so nervous?

* * *

"Bruin Delta One all aboard and ready to go," Charlotte announced. Nine other scouts in APEX armor filled the troop bay of the rumbler.

"Welcome aboard Shadow One," Tamara called from the driver's seat as she brought the rumbler to a halt. "Sit back and relax. We'll depart in 50 minutes for what I'm sure will be a smooth ride to the surface."

"Shadow One, don't make promises we can't keep," the dropship pilot interjected.

* * *

"Bruin Delta Two, are you good to go?" Corporal Lewis, the driver of Shadow Two, called.

Sergeant Keith Cripe surveyed his scout squad one more time to ensure they had all clamped in their APEX armor. "Go ahead and button us up."

The ramp whirred closed, and the rumbler lurched into motion. Cripe watched through the external camera feeds as the vehicle rolled up the dropship ramp and parked next to Shadow One. The morbid thought crossed his mind that it would suck if a single anti-aircraft weapon took out both scout units before they reached the ground.

"I'm too old for this shit," Cripe muttered. One last mission, and he'd retire. Maybe he'd get a beachside flat in Vishall Plex and while away his days drinking beer and watching bikinis.

* * *

"Captain Duarte, we have confirmation from the *Saotome*. All elements of Kodiak Company stand ready."

"Thank you Lieutenant Durano," Berto replied from his CASPer. Command feeds dominated his Tri-V HUD. Two dropships on the *Ursa Major* carried two of the three CASPer platoons in Kodiak. The other CASPer platoon and conventional infantry would launch from the *Saotome*. Berto had learned Bjorn rearranged companies on a mission basis. Out of the four platoons, only six squads came from the original Kodiak Company.

The mission launch clock showed ten minutes. Berto hated the wait before the fight. The minutes dragged on.

* * *

"Halsey, this better not be some ploy to get me alone," Corporal Lien Huynh warned as the airlock cycled. The command yeoman had asked Lien out three times since she joined the crew. She debated whether to call it persistence or cluelessness. "I'm a shuttle pilot, not a dropship pilot."

"Check your tactical slate again," Corporal Halsey said. He followed her into the bay, wearing a borrowed flight suit. "We need to catch up to the drop mission and deliver the third scout rumbler."

Lien didn't need to read the order again. A lone KX9 Phoenix dropship sat in the bay. "You're kidding. We're taking Lucky 13? This thing is a relic."

"They call her Lucky 13 for a reason," Halsey said, tugging on his helmet as they crossed the bay. "She always comes back."

Lien scoffed. The rest of the dropships were Banshees or Sleipnirs. "This thing better be ready to fly."

"Everyone is loaded up," Corporal Halsey stated. He clumsily grabbed the recessed handhold next to the hatch but managed to keep from bouncing off.

Lien tapped the back of her glove to the reader next to the hatch. It popped open with a hiss. She hauled herself up into the cockpit with Halsey trailing her. Displays and indicators illuminated the cockpit. Halsey hadn't lied; Lucky 13 was ready to fly. "Strap in while I confirm preflight."

"Preflight has been expedited," a computer voice announced. As soon as the hatch thumped shut behind Halsey, the decompression warning sounded in the hangar and the lights flashed. "Opening hangar doors in 90 seconds."

Lien synched her helmet with the command system of the dropship. "Whoever's in the back better be ready."

"Corporal Brand here. We're set."

"Halsey, get the flight orders," Lien ordered as she clicked down the preflight list. Who had performed the preflight then left? They could have flown this crate. On the other hand, this would earn her combat pay and count as combat flight hours. Becoming a dropship pilot meant a promotion.

"What?" Halsey fumbled with his harness before clicking it in place.

"The flight orders, you know, approach vectors and landing zone coordinates." Did she have to do everything herself? Halsey claimed he'd logged copilot hours before switching to his current role.

"Oh, you mean this?" One of the Tri-V images shifted to show their flight path to orbital insertion. At least he wasn't worthless.

Bright amber lights flashed three times in the hangar. Ten seconds later, the hangar doors split apart. "Flight Control, this is DS-0013. Launching."

* * *

"DS-0013. Who added that bucket to the flight mission?" Specialist Anton Hornick asked.

Specialist Magali Palomer checked her terminal. "I don't know, but it's listed here as part of the launch orders. You can always take it up with the boss."

Hornick shook his head. "Pass. I don't want to piss him off. Have you ever heard of trial by airlock?"

* * *

"Captain, traffic control is hailing us," Sergeant Sprague announced. "They want to know our intentions."

"Put me on," Captain Wildman said. Once the channel indicator flashed green, he read from his script. "This is Captain Than Wildman of the Earth Mercenary Ship *Ursa Major*. Our forces are operating on behalf of the Information Guild. This is a guild-directed enforcement action against criminal operations. We will avoid im-

372 | JON R. OSBORNE

pacting starport operations but advise no traffic to approach our forces in the air or on the ground."

"I must protest!" The voice on the other end declared. Wildman couldn't make out the race past the translator. "If your forces approach within ten kilometers, we will engage our defense systems."

"Feel free to protest to the Information Guild," Wildman countered. "However, if you engage any of our units, we will take it as collusion with the criminal operation, and on behalf of the Information Guild, we will reduce your starport to rubble, even if it means bringing this cruiser under bombardment altitude."

"You wouldn't dare!"

"I'll start with the source of this signal," Wildman said. "Stay out of our way, and we'll get in and out with minimal fuss. Give us grief, and you'll need a new starport."

A long pause made Captain Wildman wonder if the person at the other end had closed the channel. "Acknowledged. Xhosa Gamma 3 traffic control out."

* * *

The acceleration of the launch rocked Bjorn in his custom CASPer, Left Hook. His elSha armorers had labored hard to repair the suit after the Battle of Patoka. He resisted the urge to fiddle with the handle of the CASPer-scale battle axe clamped to his mecha. Sabher was on the moon. If Tyr smiled on him, Bjorn would avenge his father.

The clock in his pinview showed 17 minutes until landing. Plenty of time.

"Son, give these alien motherfuckers what for."

* * * * *

Chapter Thirty-Two

Landing Zone, Xhoxa Gamma 3

Bjorn opened the all-units channel. "Berserkers! Valhalla Awaits!"

"Valhalla Awaits!" over a hundred voices roared back.

The dropship shuddered as the landing gear scraped the ground. The troop bay lights flashed green, and the ramp dropped, exposing the industrial complex. The glow of another moon, looming twice as large as Earth's, threw shadows from the boxy buildings.

Bjorn's command element led the platoon off the dropship to form up in the parking lot of a warehouse. Aerial drones leapt into the night sky, painting the battlefield in Bjorn's tactical display. Off to his right, another dropship dropped its ramp and a pair of black rumblers raced off, splitting in opposite directions. To his left, a quartet of Casanovas emerged from their vessel to establish a perimeter on the LZ.

Four squads of infantry would support the Casanovas at the LZ while the other two would follow behind five platoons of CASPers. The infantry could go places the CASPers couldn't, but Bjorn didn't want them to face the Besquith or the ground drones Gizmo had dubbed rovers.

"By the plan, Berserkers," Bjorn called over the all-units channel before switching to the command circuit. "I trust you to use your best judgement when the plan inevitably goes off the rails. Let's crack this operation and get the evidence. Berserkers move out!"

* * *

Union Credit Exchange Mint, Xhoxa Gamma 3

"Eight dropships have landed three kilometers to the east," the watch officer announced. "Make that nine."

"Sabher was right when he said you should have invested in air defenses," Uvksolt remarked. She wore combat armor and carried a heavy MAC rifle in addition to her traditional mace.

Dbo'Dizwey didn't bother repeating the argument that secrecy was their best defense. Secrecy had flown from the nest. If this mint survived the coming assault, it could serve as a testbed for blatant defenses. The Exchange would significantly curtail production here in case the experiment proved a failure.

"Captain Sabher, are your forces ready?" Dbo asked over the comms.

"Yes. My wolves are eager to hunt," Sabher replied. "I recommend we allow them to draw close. A stand-off exchange of weapons fire favors the Humans."

An honest admission for a Besquith. Dbo hoped the wolf survived the coming conflict. His insight had proved useful. "I'll leave engaging the Human forces to your discretion, Captain Sabher."

Uvksolt rippled her trunks but remained silent.

"What is the status of our golems?" Dbo asked.

The watch officer enlarged a Tri-V display. "They await your release to engage the enemy. The turrets are primed and on standby, although they aren't designed to repel an assault of this magnitude."

"Every bit will help," Dbo said. "Are the self-destruct charges primed?"

The watch officer rippled his feathers. "Yes."

"I hope we do not need them, but I will not let anyone take this facility."

* * *

Sabher watched the tactical feed. Around him, Besquith shuffled and flexed, eager for the coming battle. They had languished too long in cells and barracks. Wolves needed to hunt. LADAR and magnometer sensors planted on surrounding properties collected data to populate the battlespace. Two octals squared of CASPers approached, using the intervening buildings as cover.

Flickers on the north and south extremes of the battlespace caught his attention. Sabher zoomed in. Something had tripped the seismometers but didn't register to other sensors. Human trickery.

"Octal Seven One and Octal Five Three, hunt at these coordinates. I suspect the Humans are trying to sneak around us." Sabher relayed the path predicted by the ground vibration readings. "Good hunting!"

Wolves around Sabher fidgeted. Soon, but first the Humans would get softened up.

* * *

"We have movement! Calliope lasers!"

The speaker disappeared from the channel as the first icon winked out on the edge

of Bjorn's tactical display. The battlespace updated to show three of
the multi-barrel emplaced laser weapons. A barrage of rockets from
two dozen CASPers headed for the pop-up turrets. Point-defense
lasers saved one of the turrets, but the volume of rockets overwhelmed the defenses of the other two.

A CASPer hunched behind a laser shield closed half the distance
to the remaining calliope before the pulses burned through the ablative shield. The CASPer pitched facedown. As the weapon swept
toward its next target, the prone CASPer engaged its jumpjets and
skidded across the dirt. By the time the weapon tried to retarget to
trooper, it couldn't decline to fire on him. The CASPer dunked a K-
bomb into the emplacement and rolled away. A fountain of fire and
debris erupted from the hole in the ground.

"Go!" Bjorn shouted. He charged across the intervening space
between a food processing plant and the target facility's outer wall.
Besquith boiled over the wall, fangs bared in the moonlight. The
werewolves wanted them in close. A stand-off trade of fire favored
the Humans. "Pay these fuckers back for what they did on Earth!"

* * *

"Mother of God," Berto whispered as the wave
of talons and fangs rushed over the wall.
Over his platoon channel, he shouted, "Fire
for effect along the wall—K-bombs and rockets!"

The surging mass of Besquith swelled, but their numbers worked
against them as explosions rippled through their ranks. Blasts turned
chunks of the permacrete wall into a spray of shrapnel. Besquith
bowled face first into the dirt from the shockwaves behind them.

Cheers on the platoon channel faded as dozens of Besquith rose and resumed their dash for the Berserkers' front line.

* * *

Sabher swore and cursed the alphas who whelped over-eager wolves. Half his pack leaders had jumped into the fray too soon. If the Humans had reached the wall, the Besquith could have overwhelmed them. Instead, the foolish gammas had charged into a killing field.

"Remaining forces, attack!" Sabher ordered. He crested the wall and spotted one of the Human war machines standing out among the others. It swept a great double-bladed axe through the first Besquith to reach the Humans. It was their commander.

"Command, can you get me a comm channel to the Humans?" Sabher called over the din of battle.

* * *

"He wants to talk to them?" Uvksolt rippled her trunks. "What is Captain Sabher playing at?"

"Perhaps he hopes to distract them?" Dbo'Dizwey nodded to one of the security operators. "Go ahead and give him a channel. Meanwhile, bring the golems into play."

The operator tapped his console. "Deploying golems on the ground."

"Excellent. What about our orbital surprise?" Dbo turned her attention to the Tri-V showing the Human mercenary ships above the moon.

"The Humans will overtake our transport in four minutes."

* * *

EMS *Ursa Major*, Orbit Over Xhosa Gamma 3

"Captain, we're coming up on a small transport," Sergeant Lutz called from the sensor station. "It's in a higher orbit, so we'll pass 25 kilometers below it."

"Any signs of weapons?" Captain Wildman asked. If he were commanding a transport with a warship gaining on it, he'd move to give it a wide berth.

"Nope. Two minutes until closest approach."

The ship already stood at alert status. There'd been no sign of trouble until now. The war book described the vessel as a 10,000-ton civilian transport less than a third the length of the *Ursa Major*. "Sound battle stations. Power to shields and weapons. Sergeant Higgins, paint the transport. Let's see if it urges them to clear out."

"Aye, Captain. Designating transport Target One and acquiring," Sergeant Carl Higgins responded. The ship's icon on the Tri-V changed to red. Small red flecks appeared around the vessel.

It only took a second for Wildman to register what was happening. "Missile defenses hot!"

* * *

UCX Q-Ship *Hidden Talon*, Orbit Over Xhosa Gamma 3

"The Earth ships are closing," the sensor operator announced.

"Excellent. Standby to send our compatriots," Xosa'Zanay said, rippling her crimson plumage. Elder Nevar formed the crew of the transport, save for a few technicians. "Target 70 percent on the lead vessel, the remainder on the second craft."

"The lead vessel has engaged targeting sensors. One minute until closest approach."

"Send the golems. Cripple or destroy those ships," Xosa ordered. "Activate our missile defenses. Do not power up the shields unless I say so." The quantum network couldn't penetrate two sets of shields. Xosa didn't understand the science other than it meant they would die if the warship fired on them.

"Understood. Golems are thrusting for targets."

In the space around the transport, 30 golems equipped with detachable thrust modules ignited their engines and raced toward their objectives.

* * *

Light Industry District, Xhoxa Gamma 3

Movement to the left caught Wilhelm Gutknecht's eye. The door to a nearby factory's loading dock ratcheted up. He expected it to be full of idiots recording the battle on slates and phones. Instead, two dozen cylindrical forms on spiky metal legs poured off the dock, their metal limbs sending sparks as they clambered across the pavement.

"Rovers! Four o'clock!" Gutknecht shouted. He fired his remaining rocket into the mechanical swarm.

"Squad, up against this garage for cover," Sergeant Stallings called. "Remember, these things brush off lasers. Make your MAC rounds count."

Lasers from the rovers chased the CASPers as they scurried for cover.

"I've got three K-bombs left. Who else has party favors?" Stallings asked.

"I've got one," Private Block announced. She tossed the explosive beyond the corner of the building. "Remote armed."

The garage door behind the squad rose, revealing a dozen more rovers.

"Jumpjets! Bug out!" Sergeant Stallings yelled. A barrage of laser fire flashed from the rovers. Three pulses incandesced on Stallings' rising CASPer. The machine crashed back to the pavement. "My jets are out. Gutknecht, you have the squad!" The sergeant charged his CASPer into the cluster of rovers. The machines lashed out with osmium-carbide scythes. "Valhalla Awaits!"

Fire erupted from the open door of the garage and the roof blew skyward. The sergeant's icon winked out on the squad display. Another explosion took out three of the approaching rovers when Block detonated her k-bomb.

Four CASPers landed in a small parking lot. They'd already lost Wallis to Besquith. "Two by two, get back to the main body," Gutknecht ordered. "Shoot what you can, but don't stop."

* * *

"Shit! We've got Besquith!" Tamara called from the front.

Charlotte checked the Tri-V. Werewolves leapt from behind and on top of buildings. So much for stealth rumblers. "We've got some dogs to put down! Disembark and fight in pairs! Go!"

No one protested that she was insane for ordering them to fight Besquith in scout armor. If they stayed in the vehicle, they'd die. As soon as the ramp dropped, scouts in black APEX armor rushed into the night. The chain gun on the front of the rumbler opened up, and the laser turret thrummed. Somewhere ahead, a Besquith howled as an x-ray laser pulse incinerated it.

"Bruin Delta One to command. We are compromised and engaging the enemy," Charlotte called on the command channel as she primed her laser carbine. "We will not reach our objective."

A snarling Besquith leapt onto the rumbler above the rising troop ramp. If it got into the vehicle, the crew would die.

"Hey, Bigby!" Charlotte shouted, engaging her helmet lights. The Besquith roared and leapt as she pulled the trigger.

* * *

"Switch from night vision to passive thermal," Sergeant Cripe ordered. If Wicza's rumbler had been intercepted, the enemy had some way of picking up their movements. He guessed either a beam sensor network or ground vibration sensors.

The rumbler slowed. "Shit, I've got body heat ahead," Lewis said. The tactical Tri-V in the troop compartment overlaid the infrared signatures. At least half a dozen Besquith waited.

"Veer south and hit the pedal," Cripe ordered. "Let's see if these dogs want to chase a car. As soon as you have a shot with the pulse laser, fire."

The rumbler lurched as Lewis skidded into a turn and accelerated through some business' shrubbery. Several forms in the infrared display broke cover to give chase. A white flash blossomed, sprouting a

382 | JON R. OSBORNE

glowing trail as a rocket streaked past. The gunner locked on the launcher and fired the pulse laser. A new white spot incandesced as the laser struck true, super-heating tissue and combat armor.

"Sonuvabitch!" Lewis shouted. The rumbler's UV headlights illuminated half a dozen cylindrical forms on spiky spider legs in the vehicle's path. Instead of braking, Lewis accelerated. The rumbler crashed into two of the rovers, sending a spray of mechanical limbs and two crushed cylinders flying into the night.

Scraping and clicking sounded on the hull of the rumbler, then an osmium-carbide scythe punched through the seam of the troop hatch.

* * *

"Where are we going?" Glen yelled. The Tri-V showed a swirling chaos of Besquith, CAS-Pers, and rovers ahead.

"As close as you can get us without getting us killed," Gina called back, checking the connections. "Bettie, are we ready?"

"Given we lack additional time to test and refine your experiment, yes," the tactical intelligence replied. Gina had loaded a node onto a spare battlefield command computer, but she hadn't had time to rig near-field communication. She had to talk to Bettie, as opposed to using her pinplant interface.

An explosion annihilated a building ahead. "Head for the blast!" Gina shouted.

"Are you crazy?" Glen retorted as he swerved around a CASPer and Besquith locked in battle. "I thought we didn't want to die?"

"The blast may have created the only clear spot on the battlefield. Who's going to be there?" Gina asked, hanging on as the rumbler bounced over a set of curbs.

"Sergeant Zomorra's supposition is logical," Bettie added.

The rumbler slid on the pavement as Glen veered toward the burning building. "You might be right, but you're still crazy."

The chain gun under the nose of the rumbler roared as a Besquith loomed in their path. The vehicle thumped over the corpse and skidded to a halt near the remains of a wall.

"Bettie, power up the quantum node. Glen, activate the shield projector." Gina crossed her fingers. Pumping the quantum signal through the shield generator should let her 'listen' to every node on the network, thoroughly corrupting the signal. Hopefully, depriving the rovers of the network would leave them without orders. If it didn't render them inert, it should make them easy targets.

* * *

"Commander Tovesson, this is Captain Sabher of the Union Credit Exchange security force."

Bjorn pumped another MAC round into the rover he'd swatted with his axe. The machine tumbled end over end before falling lifeless on the ground. "Sabher! I knew you'd be here! Come out and face me you *sukin syn*!"

"Commander, your men are dying under a false pretense. The Information Guild has sent you on a suicide mission under a fabricated premise," the Besquith replied.

"Why should I believe you? You were Peepo's lackey on Earth, and now you serve a new scumbag," Bjorn retorted. Where was Sabher? His mind filtered through the maelstrom of the battlefield.

Would Sabher lead from the safety of a bunker? No, Besquith led from the battlefield.

"I will meet you face-to-face. Dbo'Dizwey, I know you are listening. Have the golems stand down," Sabher said.

There! The large Besquith beta near the perimeter wall stared at Bjorn across the battlefield. "Bettie, designate my target as QB. Order all units—he is mine alone."

"Sabher, what are you doing?" a new voice demanded over the channel. Chirps and clicks composed the speech behind the translator.

"This represents a small portion of Commander Tovesson's forces. Your secret has been compromised, and even if we could kill them all, it solves nothing," Sabher replied. Bjorn watched the Besquith lope across the battlefield.

* * *

Union Credit Exchange Mint, Xhoxa Gamma 3

Dbo'Dizwey gaped at the display and snapped her beak shut. The gall of the wolf! Giving her orders. Her feathers bristled in fury.

"The wolf speaks true," Uvksolt remarked. "Even if we win, our forces will be depleted."

"How many golems do we have in reserve?" Dbo asked.

"Twenty older ones. The eldest we sent in the transport, as their cores were near the end of operation. We fielded all of the new golems," the watch officer replied.

"I would prefer to wade onto the battlefield." Uvksolt thumped her mace, startling the security officers. "However, this Human commander may give you something no victory in battle could—

proof that Master Archivist Heloxi acted against the economy of the Galactic Union."

Dbo's four eyes widened. What would Nxo'Sanar say? Ignore the thorn if you could prune the bramble. "Fine, stand down the golems. Let us parley with these Humans, Captain Sabher."

* * *

Gina watched the power readings climb. "Bettie, how long until nominal charge?"

"Seventeen seconds."

"Oh shit, some rovers spotted us," Glen yelled. The chain gun barked in short bursts as the rumbler shifted. "If you're going to shut them down, it better be now."

Gina and Glen had removed the rumbler's pulse laser to mount the shield projector. Semi-metallic tires screeched on the concrete as Glen reversed away from the closing rovers. Gina watched the Tri-V as sparks traced across a rover and it tumbled back. Three spidery machines gave chase.

"Maximum charge reached; quantum pulse ready," Bettie announced.

Gina stabbed the commit button.

* * * * *

Chapter Thirty-Three

Union Credit Exchange Mint, Xhoxa Gamma 3

An alarm sounded from one of the security boards.

"What's happening?" Dbo'Dizwey demanded.

"The quantum network is jammed. I can't reach the obedience circuits of any of the golems," the security officer replied, throwing all four arms up in frustration.

Dbo tipped her head. "I didn't think anyone could jam a quantum signal."

"It's not the signal. Someone is sending too many phase states for the network nodes to parse," the security officer replied. "Imagine listening to 1,000 singers and trying to pick out a single trill. The golems can't hear the obedience signal."

Uvksolt shrugged. "So, they shut down?"

"No, they've become free-willed."

"How many golems are in the complex with us?" Dbo asked.

* * *

EMS _Ursa Major_, Orbit Over Xhosa Gamma 3

"Murphy, talk to me," Captain Than Wildman ordered.

"Nine inbounds destroyed," Sergeant Demar Murphy replied from the def ops console. "We're having trouble locking on to them. Three washed off our shields. The remainder soft-landed on our hull."

What the hell? Why go to the trouble of landing on the hull? "How big are these missiles?" Wildman asked.

"No more than two meters long. That's the problem—they're small, and our sensor signal refracts as much as it bounces," Murphy said.

Wildman remembered the presentation in the hangar bay. "Higgins! Retract all missile launchers!"

"What?" The weapons officer turned around. "You don't want to launch missiles?"

"Do it!"

"Aye, retracting missile launchers," Higgins relented.

* * *

Nine metallic forms skittered across the hull of the *Ursa Major*. Some moved toward hatches, but the remainder clambered for the missile launchers extended above the armored hull. The launchers descended into the hull, prompting the golems closest to their targets to charge. One bounced off the armored cover of the launcher, but another scurried in among the missiles and machinery.

Their self-destruct charges would barely dent the armored hull of a warship, but if they detonated among missiles…

* * *

The ship shuddered, and the lighting flickered. Damage alarms sounded as the status Tri-V glowed red and yellow amidships. Dozens of voices clamored for attention.

"What hit us?" Wildman asked.

"Something detonated in Launcher 3," Higgins replied.

At least none of the nukes cooked off. They wouldn't be here if they had. "How bad are we hurt?"

"Breaches on Decks 16 through 19, and a fire on Deck 17. Damage control teams are responding." Sprague added, "At least 12 casualties based on crew telemetry monitors."

"Higgins, blow that transport to atoms," Wildman ordered. "What happened with the rest of those rover drones?"

"System failure in Barbette One," Higgins reported. "Laser Turret Three offline."

"Find something that works and shoot them!" Wildman yelled. Those mechanical nightmares were tearing his ship apart.

"We have a breech alarm on Airlock Two."

"Captain, priority call from engineering," Sprague yelled over the cacophony.

"Put it through," Wildman yelled, praying it wasn't more bad news.

"Captain, Specialist Rakz here. There isn't time to explain, but I worked with Gizmo and Brand, taking apart these drones. Overlap the shields over as much of the hull as possible, especially where you detect rover drones."

"Murphy, overlap our shields over Airlock Two as close to the hull as possible," Wildman ordered. "Sprague, what's the status of the *Saotome?*"

"Aye, sir." Murphy didn't argue despite how crazy the orders sounded.

Wildman checked the Tri-V. "Higgins, why isn't that transport a debris cloud?"

"Captain O'Donnell reports she has two intruder breaches, all other hostiles eliminated," Sprague called.

"Airlock Two shows clear."

"Murphy, sweep as much of the hull as possible with the shields. Something about the overlap messes with those mechanical bastards." Wildman ordered.

"Breech, maintenance access to Barbette One."

"Marines, intruder alert Deck Two, Barbette One."

"Higgins, do I need to come over there and shoot that ship myself?" Wildman demanded.

"No sir, firing lasers."

Three hits registered on the Tri-V, including one followed by venting atmosphere. "Keep firing."

"Captain, I've caught two more in the shield interface. One exploded, and the other has gone inert."

"Helm, give me one g of thrust," Wildman ordered. The acceleration alarm sounded. "If we break the moon's orbit, swing us around the gas giant to bring us back."

"Two more contacts on the hull knocked loose."

"Anti-missile lasers engaged," Murphy announced. "Splash two."

"Breech, Airlock Three."

A white flash blossomed on the Tri-V. "Transport destroyed."

"Detonation, Airlock Three."

"Marines are reporting the intruder on Deck Two is contained."

* * *

Union Credit Exchange Mint, Xhoxa Gamma 3

"All octals stand down and regroup," the Besquith ordered.

"Don't tell me you're wussing out of a fight," Bjorn snarled, clenching his axe. "I've come a long way to kill you."

"Even if it means more of your people die?" Sabher retorted. "You have something more valuable to my employer than your death." Across the battlefield, the fighting petered out as the few Besquith who had refused orders fell in combat.

"You werewolf bastards killed my father. You hounded my people and slaughtered civilians." Ten meters separated Bjorn and Sabher. Could he bury his axe in the Besquith's skull before he could react?

"Your father died a warrior's death. Honor that." The Besquith halted. "My death solves nothing. Your life could help the Union."

An electronic banshee shriek echoed across the battlefield, repeated by a hundred mechanical voices. Every rover on the battlefield brandished its scythes and went berserk, attacking the closest living creature, Humans and Besquith alike.

"Dbo, you agreed to talk!" the Besquith shouted over the open channel.

"This isn't my doing! The golems are out of control!"

Two of the black-and-red constructs skittered behind Sabher, their wicked blades raised. "Berserkers, take out the rovers!" Bjorn stepped forward and swung his axe at the closest killing machine. The molybdenum-alloy blade cleaved open the central cylinder, and the impact sent the rover flying. It bounced across a parking lot until it hit a curb. The limbs twitched then fell still. "No one kills the *sukin syn* but me!"

The other rover fired its 'head' mounted lasers. One of the pulses scarred the armor over Bjorn's right arm. He snapped out his laser shield before the next pair of pulses. The rover lunged forward with its arm blades spread wide. Bjorn sheared off the right pair, but the other set of osmium-carbide blades punched through his shield.

The rover tried to wrench away the shield as it fired its lasers again, but it couldn't match the CASPer's might. Bjorn decapitated the machine and stomped on the head with his armored foot. The construct yanked its blades free and lashed out. One sliced off the bottom quarter of Bjorn's laser shield; the other threw sparks as it gouged the CASPer's thigh armor. Bjorn chopped off the other two arms.

"What're you going to do now, fucker?" Bjorn grunted.

The rover exploded. Shrapnel shredded what was left of the laser shield. The blast bowled Bjorn over. Armor warnings and a servo failure in his right arm blinked on his display. He tried to turn off the shrill whine until he realized his ears were ringing.

Another rover scrambled through the smoke with its arms raised like a crazed mantis. A furry bulk slammed into the drone, knocking it off course. Sabher raked his talons across the cylindrical body. The machine shrieked. Bjorn expected another blast, but it folded its legs and collapsed.

* * *

One of the osmium-carbide scythes poking through the seam of the hatch sliced through a locking bolt. The hatch jerked.

"They took out the laser turret!" the gunner yelled.

Robotic screams sounded outside the rumbler. The blades disappeared, and something skittered over the top of the vehicle.

"What the hell's going on?" one of the scouts asked.

"The rovers are going after the Besquith chasing us," Corporal Lewis called from the driver's seat.

"Sergeant, someone ordered the Besquith to stand down," Private Garcia said from the operation console. "They claimed this is a Union Credit Exchange facility."

"Oh, shit," Cripe muttered. "That can't be good."

"Berserkers, take out the rovers!" Commander Tovesson bellowed over the command channel.

"What do you want to do, Sergeant Cripe?" Lewis asked.

"Turn us around. We're going to shoot some tin cans," Cripe said.

Dirt and rocks sprayed from the tires as Lewis spun the rumbler. Cripe checked the Tri-V. Ahead, a half dozen Besquith battled ten rovers. The rovers showed no interest in the approaching vehicle.

How easy would it be to mow the whole lot of them down with the chain gun and a couple of rocket launchers? "I can't believe I'm saying this, but don't shoot the Besquith unless they come for us," Cripe ordered. "Drop the hatch—Valhalla Awaits!"

* * *

"Some of these things self-destruct! Keep your distance!" Berto shouted over the company channel. "Watch out for Besquith sticking in the fight. Not all of them are pulling out, or they're too damned frenzied to care."

A pair of rovers stabbed at a Besquith, flaying the alien like a Japanese *teppanyaki* chef. Berto picked off one of the machines with his MAC. The other leapt off the dying werewolf and fired its lasers. One pulse struck his armored canopy after grazing his left arm. Berto could smell smoke and hot metal. If the laser pumped more energy, he'd be dead.

Another Berserker finished off the remaining machine. Berto checked his tactical display. A squad from Alpha Platoon had broken off to support one of the scout rumblers. One of the Bravo Platoon squads had become separated from the battle. "Kodiak Bravo One, what are you doing out there? Get back to the rest of the company."

* * *

Three scouts were dead by the time the Besquith broke off. Four others, including Charlotte, had suffered serious enough wounds for their suits to deploy trauma nanites. Charlotte hissed as her left shoulder burned from the microscopic machines.

"Berserkers, take out the rovers!" the commander ordered.

"Delta One, regroup on the rumbler," Charlotte ordered. She debated trying to drag Private Foyt back to the rumbler. She couldn't hold her carbine and haul the corpse. Charlotte slung her weapon and grabbed Foyt's remaining arm.

Charlotte had made it halfway to the rumbler when Private Bowers called, "The Besquith are coming back. There's more of them."

"Wicza to command. We're about to be overrun by werewolves." The battle raged to the south. They were on their own. The tactical feed relayed by Bowers showed a dozen Besquith stalking toward them. "I wonder if Valhalla accepts Wiccans?" she muttered as she dashed to the rumbler. They'd never get the ramp lowered, board, and close the hatch before the Besquith arrived.

The Besquith fanned out to cut off the escape routes for the vehicle and reduce their vulnerability to area weapons. A wave of fangs and claws swept in a semi-circle. Half a dozen CASPers with the Garrett's Rangers paint scheme descended on roaring jumpjets, landing around the rumbler.

"Don't worry, Little Sister. We've got your back," Sergeant Murphy said. "Valhalla Awaits!"

Charlotte raised her carbine and trained it on the closest werewolf. Now, it was an even fight.

* * *

"Gutknecht here. We're trying to get back, but a dozen rovers are milling around between us and you," Corporal Gutknecht whispered. He peered over a metal utility box. The machines wandered in the truckyard of a small factory. With no rockets or K-bombs left, half the rovers would reach them before they could gun them down.

"Could we lure them off?" Private Block suggested. "We could laze the factory wall. The noise might distract them."

"If they have IR, they'll backtrack the beam path," Gutknecht said. "See that open door? If we can make it into the loading dock, it would limit their approach."

"That's a dicey run," Private Radner remarked.

"Pretend it's the cadre obstacle course back at Bear Town." Gutknecht synced a timer on the squad channel. "Don't fire until they spot us. On my mark...go!"

The rovers didn't notice the jogging CASPers for several seconds, despite the metallic footfalls and crunching pavement. Once the first rover spotted them, it emitted an electronic scream and raised its arm blades. The other drones spun to face the CASPers and emulated the first rover, then the mass charged.

"Don't slow down!" Gutknecht exhorted. He fired his MAC on the run. The tungsten projectile missed the lead rover but punched into one of its fellows. Half the machine's arms went limp as it spun, but more importantly, it careened into other land-drones. Laser pulses flashed on their armor and against the wall around the open loading dock. Yellow indicators blinked across the remaining squad icons, but no lucky shot felled any of the CASPers.

Block reached the loading dock first. She puffed her jumpjets enough to boost her suit through the opening and spun as she landed. She opened fire with her chain gun and sprayed the mob of machines.

Gutknecht vaulted into the open doorway. His armor threw sparks from the floor as he rolled over mid-slide and pushed himself upright. He swept the interior of the factory with his LADAR. The building was an empty shell save for a dozen upright cradles.

Gutknecht and Block fired over Private Merriman, the last trooper to scramble onto the dock. Radner hauled the door down, snapping whatever cable opened it, and crushed the track. The metal door jammed in place, but scythe blades punched through in half a dozen places.

"Block, open an exit on the far side," Gutknecht ordered. The door would only last a couple of minutes. "We dropped three or four."

A pair of osmium-carbide blades pierced the wall near the door. "Shit!" Radner fired his MAC and punched a hole between the scythes.

"Fall back to the other side," Gutknecht ordered, covering the shredding door with his MAC. Metal curls cascaded to the floor. Behind him, Block's chain gun buzzed.

A rover wedged itself through a tear in the door. One MAC round sparked off the floor in front of it before ricocheting into its cylindrical torso. Another slug shattered the machine's head. Two more constructs clambered through the curtain of shredded steel.

Gutknecht prayed another dozen machines didn't await them outside. "Block, kick it open."

Private Block slammed the armored foot of her CASPer into the middle of the bullet-riddled outline in the wall. The metal snapped free and spun out into the dirt. "Clear!" she called after shouldering through the hole.

"Go!" Gutknecht shouted, backing toward the hole as he fired. The shot glanced off a rover, knocking the machine aside but not felling it.

Radner's shoulder-mounted heavy MAC shattered the other construct skittering across the floor, but another pair climbed into the factory. The heavy MAC cycled slower than Gutknecht's gun.

Gutknecht fired again as he waited for Radner to clear the exit hole. The shot impacted lower than Gutknecht intended and blew off half the machine's legs. Laser pulses chased him through the gap in the wall.

"Radner and Merriman, go left! Block with me; we'll post up 90 degrees apart," Gutknecht ordered, marking the spots on the tactical map. The drones would have to exit to fire on the troopers.

Gutknecht's squad would have the machines in a crossfire without endangering each other.

The rovers boiled through the hole with no regard for self-preservation. Block's chain gun ran dry after the first three machines. Radner expended his last heavy MAC round on the final construct.

Gutknecht chided himself for his lack of fire discipline. "Let's get to the others before more mechanical maniacs find us."

* * *

"It didn't work," Glen called from the driver compartment. "They didn't shut down. If anything, they've gone nuts."

"Oh no," Gina muttered. She checked the readouts—they displayed gibberish. "Bettie, what's wrong? Why didn't they stop?"

"I suspect the apparatus successfully disrupted the quantum network." Bettie replied. "Based on telemetry and the chatter on Berserker channels, the machines have gone berserk and are attacking the closest entities with no regard for friend or foe."

"Shit! We screwed up!" Gina went to the operation console to check the tactical feed.

"If the rovers attack the Besquith, it's not a total loss," Glen remarked. "The Besquith have to fight their own machines in addition to our soldiers."

"Based on communications, it sounds as though the Besquith leader has brokered a ceasefire between the Berserkers and the Union Credit Exchange," Bettie announced.

"Sonuvabitch! Those tin cans remembered us. Hang on!" Glen yelled. The rumbler lurched forward and spun. Something scraped along the armor with a metallic screech.

Gina stumbled as she returned to the jury-rigged quantum scrambler. She flipped the switches to cut off power to the apparatus. "Bettie, what's the status of the quantum network?"

"Unknown."

"We stopped listening…oh, crap." Gina stared at the cobbled mass of electronics and cables. "They all stopped listening."

"It would appear, that absent commands, the organic brains piloting the rovers are belligerent," Bettie stated.

A loud crunch sounded from the driver compartment followed by a gurgled cry.

"Glen?" Gina called. She'd risen to check on him when the rumbler slammed to a halt, hurling her forward into the seat of the operation console. Stars blossomed as her head smacked the metal support of the chair.

The engines whined, and the tires screeched as they spun. Gina crawled forward to the driver station. An osmium-carbide scythe pinned Glen to the driver's seat through the right side of his chest. Blood dripped from the corner of his mouth.

"No, no, no!" The blade had pierced the right episcope. Gina could see a crushed rover through the central viewport. "Bettie! Take control of the vehicle! Get us to the landing zone!"

The tires stopped spinning. "If I reverse the vehicle, it will dislodge the construct. This may cause further trauma to Corporal Brand."

"If we don't move, he'll die!" Gina scrabbled for the medical kit attached to the driver's seat and pulled out a trauma nanite applicator. She held the applicator next to where the blade had punctured his uniform and grabbed the back of the scythe with her other hand. "Reverse one centimeter per second."

The rumbler inched away from the wall and the blade slid out of Glen. As soon as the tip emerged from his uniform, Gina let go of the scythe, pressed the nanite applicator to his wound, and thumbed the button. The bloody blade disappeared through the shattered episcope.

"Bettie, go!" Gina cried. "Send a message to the combat medic team on the ground!"

* * * * *

Chapter Thirty-Four

Union Credit Exchange Mint, Xhoxa Gamma 3

"Will those doors hold?" Dbo'Dizwey asked. Golems scratched at the door with their arm-blades, but they failed to pierce the armored portal.

"Their weapons cannot breach the command center," the watch officer stated. On one of the Tri-Vs, half a dozen golems clawed at the door.

"The quantum signal has ceased," a technician announced. "I suspect someone used a captured golem to—"

"Fascinating, but bring the obedience circuit back online," Dbo interrupted. "Save the technobabble for when we're safe."

"We will as soon as we can reestablish the quantum network," the technician stated. "We'll need to send the entanglement protocol through the near-field telemetry."

"How long will it take?" Dbo asked.

"Twenty-seven minutes."

"What? We are losing golems every minute they remain on rampage!" Dbo yelled, her crest feathers rising.

"Why did the rest run away?" Uvksolt interrupted, pointing at the Tri-V showing the hall outside. Only two golems remained, and they huddled against the door.

"What are they doing?" Dbo asked, gazing at the display. Uvksolt grabbed her and threw her to the floor. The Sumatozou hunched over her as the door blew in and shrapnel sprayed the room.

"Stay down," Uvksolt commanded. She raised her rifle. The weapon fired the same tungsten slugs as the Human CASPers. The gun cracked, and the first golem to scurry through the smoke fell with a hole punched through its brain capsule. Three more golems rushed through the opening. Uvksolt shot the nearest one, but another replaced it before her weapon could cycle. She dropped the gun and hefted her mace.

"Come, once-Nevar," Uvksolt challenged. "Let us see who goes to the Great Beyond."

Scythes raised, the golems shrieked and charged. Uvksolt side-stepped and swung her mace two-handed. The flanged metal head crashed into the machine's torso below the shoulder joints. The metal cylinder crumbled under the impact, and the golem slammed into its compatriot, sending the other construct spinning.

Uvksolt swept her mace into an overhead swing and smote the golem in the head, crushing the optics and dual lasers. Two of its arms dangled limp, but the remainder flailed at the Sumatozou. One blade punched through the shin armor on Uvksolt's left leg and pierced the thick hide beneath. Uvksolt grunted as she hammered again, this time caving in metal lower on the cylinder and rupturing the brain capsule. The golem sagged to the floor.

The remaining machine clambered over a security console onto Uvksolt's back, jabbing its arm-blades into her. Her right shoulder armor fell away with a bloody chunk of meat and hide. The mace clattered to the floor from her lifeless hand. She seized one of the upper arms with her left hand and twisted her body. Blood trailed the machine as she hurled it halfway across the room.

The machine righted itself and spun to face the Sumatozou. Uvksolt scooped up her cannon with her left hand and fired with the gun braced against her hip. A MAC round blew open the bottom of the cylinder, and the golem's legs crumbled. A pair of wild laser pulses flashed against the ceiling. The construct propped itself up using its arms and fired again. One of the pulses incandesced on Uvksolt's chest armor and the other charred the end of one of her trunks. Dbo could smell burnt meat.

Uvksolt fired again. The shot punched a hole in the golem's torso. Fluid leaked out as the machine sagged to the ground. "A worthy fight," Uvksolt rasped. She let the gun slip to the floor as she groped for her trauma kit. Blood trickled down her armor. "I may require medical attention."

* * *

EMS *Ursa Major*, Orbit Over Xhosa Gamma 3

"What's the status of the *Saotome*?" Captain Than Wildman asked.

"Better than us," Sergeant Sprague replied as she flipped through channels. "Captain O'Donnell reports one of the intruders detonated, and the other was destroyed by her marines. They have two hull breaches and a small fire where the intruder exploded."

Wildman nodded. Sprague was right. "Damage control report."

"DC teams are still fighting the fire on Deck 17 as well as three hull breaches venting atmosphere," Sprague reported. "Damage control recommends jettisoning the contents of magazine three."

404 | JON R. OSBORNE

A few million credits worth of missiles. "Higgins, do it."

Higgins shook his head. "The blast jammed the mechanism."

"Send any marines not engaged in damage control activity to Magazine Three. They'll need to unload the missiles manually," Wildman ordered. If the heat set off the fuel in one of the missiles, the chain reaction could blow the ship in half.

* * *

Union Credit Exchange Mint, Xhoxa Gamma 3

Bjorn chopped open the cylindrical torso of a golem, exposing its ruptured brain capsule and the mass of tissue within. Bjorn punted the stricken machine toward an approaching construct in case it self-destructed. If you took out the brain, they didn't blow up, but Bjorn didn't want to take a chance. Besides, it delayed the new rover long enough for Bjorn to draw a bead on the section of the cylinder containing the disembodied operator.

The 100-kilojoule MAC round punched through the torso, dropping the rover in its tracks. A moment later, the machine erupted in a gout of flame and a spray of shrapnel. Bjorn thanked Odin he hadn't brought the lightly armored infantry out of the landing zone. Shards of metal and ceramic peppered his CASPer, but at that distance, they bounced off his armor.

Bjorn checked the battle status display. Twenty CASPers were down, twice as many significantly damaged. Out of twenty scout troopers, only a dozen remained, and half of those were injured. His LADAR flagged motion behind his CASPer. Bjorn shuffled his CASPer to face the werewolf captain. Damaged servos and actuators protested.

Sabher limped toward him. The Besquith bled from half a dozen wounds and had lost an ear along with a section of his open-faced helmet. "If I had known we'd be fighting the machines, I wouldn't have brought a laser."

"I've dreamt of killing you," Bjorn stated, gripping his axe.

Sabher peeled off his damaged helmet. "A wise alpha once told me you must sometimes forfeit what you want for the good of the pack."

Bjorn clicked the double-bladed axe into its holster. "My father told me something similar once I assumed command. He said I'd need to put aside what I wanted to take care of my people."

"Nothing either of us says or does will bring your father back. He died valiantly. What will you do now?" Sabher asked. "If you renew your attack, you could overwhelm us. Dbo'Dizwey's last action will be to blow the mint into orbit and flag your ships as pirates with one-billion-credit bounties."

"Well, now we're fucked," Bjorn rumbled. "This archivist from the Information Guild promised us a shit ton of credits to take out this 'counterfeit operation.'"

"Do you have the contract?" a bird-like voice interjected over the comms.

"I have video of the negotiations in my pinplants," Bjorn replied. "The Information Guild deputized us for this operation."

"Do you wish to maintain your status as deputies of the Information Guild?" Bjorn presumed Dbo'Dizwey asked the question.

"Fuck that. They screwed us over. If I find the robed sonuvabitch who tricked us, I'll split him in half," Bjorn replied.

"Commander Tovesson, I wish to contract your services as a Marshal of the Union Credit Exchange," Dbo'Dizwey said.

"Color me intrigued. What's the pay?"

An amused whistle sounded before the translator kicked in. "Commander, have you ever been paid with a pallet of hard currency? As a bonus, you can be there when we deal with the person responsible for hiring and betraying you."

"We have a deal," Bjorn said. "I have a score to settle with the Information Guild, and I like the sound of a pallet of money."

"You're going to have to work with Captain Sabher. Will that be a problem Marshal Tovesson?" Dbo'Dizwey asked.

Bjorn clenched his fist, his battlesuit emulating the gesture. "Fine."

"We bled together on the field of battle," Sabher intoned. "That makes us—"

"Don't push it, Bigby," Bjorn interrupted. "Give me three hours for recovery operations and we can get under way."

* * *

Sergeant Cripe hissed in pain as he eased the osmium-carbide scythe out of his thigh. A Besquith had torn the arm free of the machine while the rover tried to kill Cripe. The blade clattered to the pavement, and Cripe triggered his suit's trauma nanites. He gritted his teeth as the microscopic machines set his leg on fire.

Cripe regarded the remaining Besquith. The scout laser carbines proved poorly suited to fighting the black-and-red machines, but the underslung gyroc launchers felled half of the constructs. It tipped the balance enough for the Besquith to finish off the rovers.

Four scouts died trying to reload their gyroc launchers before the Besquith brought down the remaining rovers. The lasers would work fine on Besquith, but their claws would shear through APEX armor. Cripe thanked Odin they couldn't see the talons he wore under his armor.

"Berserkers, assuming the Besquith hold to the cease-fire, commence recovery operations. Get casualties to the LZ," Commander Tovesson ordered.

"All right, Bigby. We're going to take our friends and go," Cripe said through the suit's speakers.

One of the Besquith cocked its head. "What is 'Bigby?'"

"It's from Earth folklore—the big, bad wolf," Cripe replied. He'd reloaded his gyroc. A solid hit would end a Besquith, but it was a single-shot weapon.

The Besquith's maw split in a nightmarish grin. "I like it. Good hunting, Human." The Besquith snarled at the others, and they loped into the darkness.

* * *

"Berserkers, assuming the Besquith hold to the cease-fire, commence recovery operations. Get casualties to the LZ," Commander Tovesson ordered.

The few remaining Besquith broke off and fled. Charlotte surveyed the surroundings. Three scouts and a CASPer had fallen during the fighting along with twice as many werewolves. Charlotte noticed that the top hatch of the scout rumbler was open.

"No! Tamara, are you okay?" Charlotte used her jumpjet to hop on top of the black, angular rumbler and dropped through the hatch. The furry, armored bulk of a Besquith blocked the path to the driver compartment. Charlotte grabbed the foot of the Besquith with her good arm and hauled it back. Spiderweb fractures covered the back of the alien's helmet.

Charlotte clambered over the Besquith's corpse. A trail of blood painted the floor where Charlotte had dragged the body back. A bloody comm earpiece and a Human ear lay on the floor next to the driver's seat. Tamara's blood-covered hand clutched her sidearm.

"Tamara!" Charlotte fumbled for the medkit attached to the driver's seat. She could see bone through the lacerations on the side of Tamara's head, going from the back of her skull to her cheek. "Medic!"

"Private Foyt is down, Sergeant," Private Bowers said.

Charlotte grabbed the trauma nanite applicator and held it to the deepest laceration. The device hissed as it sprayed microscopic machines into the wound. "Please don't die. Does anyone have a pinlink to jack into the rumbler from the operations console?"

"I've got one," Private Gibson replied. "Plugging in. Back to the LZ?"

"Yes!"

"What about the rest of the wounded and dead?" Bowers asked.

"Load them up. Hurry!" Charlotte replied. The minute and a half it took to get the injured and deceased on the vehicle stretched on forever.

"Don't you leave me," Charlotte whispered, tears soaking the padding of her helmet over her cheeks.

"Sergeant Wicza, we're loaded up."

"Go!"

* * * * *

Chapter Thirty-Five

EMS *Ursa Major*, Hyperspace

Gina floated in front of the hatch several minutes before mustering the courage to press the chime. The light above the chime button glowed green. She opened the hatch and pulled herself through the doorway.

"You wanted to see me, Commander?" she asked after the hatch thudded shut behind her.

Commander Tovesson's ice-blue eyes froze her in place. She expected fury—stories of the commander's temper were legendary—but he seemed weary. "At ease, Sergeant Zomorra. Have a seat."

Not a good sign. The commander usually called her Gizmo. She maneuvered into the seat and hooked a foot underneath to stay put. Captain Duarte watched from behind the commander. The new officer's face betrayed nothing.

"How's Corporal Brand?" Commander Tovesson asked.

Gina blinked. Surely, if the commander wanted to know, he could query the infirmary data via his pinplants. She fought to keep her voice from quavering as she replied. "Dr. Shuv'im says he should be on his feet by the time we drop out of hyperspace and back to duty in a month." The H'rang medical officer had banished Gina from the crowded recovery ward. Between the casualties from the battle around the mint and the explosion on board, hanging at Glen's bedside had put her underfoot of the medical staff.

"Good. What you kids did was brave, but stupid." The commander's tone remained even. He rubbed a hand over his eyes. "You didn't get proper authorizations for launch and deployment. You used your access to the Battlefield Tactical Intelligence to circumvent permissions and protocols."

"I know. I screwed up. I got so many people hurt or killed." Gina's voice rose to little more than a whisper. She'd almost gotten Glen killed. "I'm sorry."

"Don't beat yourself up. I would have ordered you to hit the button, and the result would have been the same." The commander's hand dropped to the metal hammer dangling amid his bear-claw necklace. "I guess we only get to cheat the Norns so many times."

"The rovers killed so many." Gina choked back a sob, stifling her voice. "Those people in the sickbay...I helped put them there."

"It also meant the Union Credit Exchange couldn't flip the script on us. If Dbo'Dizwey had had her way, she would have killed us all to preserve their secret," Commander Tovesson said. "A fifth of the Besquith continued to fight us despite the order to stand down. If the rovers hadn't gone insane, the number would have been higher. First chance, I want you to talk to Padre Jim. But if you need some down time, I'll grant you leave."

Gina shook her head. "No, sir. I prefer to stay busy."

"Good. Any chance of reverse engineering the quantum network the UCX used?" the commander asked. "Obviously, we need a way to keep someone from screwing with it the way we did."

"I used existing equipment. Creating our own is out of my expertise," Gina replied. Give her a software problem any time over hardware. "To be honest, it's not much of an advantage at a battlefield scale. Relativistic communications suffice—300 kilometers produces a millisecond lag. It's probably why Earth stopped working on it after First Contact. If the tech worked at longer ranges, the Galactic Union would already use it."

"Okay. We'll table it. If you change your mind, let me know what you need. Meanwhile, I'm going to have a talk with Bettie about access and permissions." Commander Tovesson rapped the knuckles of his artificial hand on his desk. "Understood?"

"Yes, Commander."

"Dismissed."

* * *

"You went easy on her," Berto remarked after the hatch closed.

"I wasn't kidding when I told Gizmo I would have ordered her to hit the button," Bjorn replied. He rubbed his eyes. Six hours of rack time over the last two days was catching up to him. "Anything I said to her, any punishment, wouldn't compare to what's going through her mind. I remember that look. I saw it in the mirror after Moloq."

"Bad loss?"

"Third or fourth biggest payout, depending on whether you count this mission. We won, but it cost us a third of our troops and half our gear," Bjorn stated. "I was determined to prove myself as a commander, and by the time we knew we were humped, we had no path back. We won, but I ordered a lot of my people to their deaths. Rationally, I knew if we didn't win, the Jivool would wipe us out, but it took a while for the voice of reason to drown out my doubts."

"That's why you went away for over a year?" Berto asked. "Some people called Bear Town a ghost town."

412 | JON R. OSBORNE

"Yup. Bettie, what's next on the agenda?"

The BTI replied aloud. "You have a meeting at 1400 with Dbo'Dizwey."

"Let's meet in the officers' mess. There's no way we're squeezing us, plus her bodyguard and the Besquith, in this tiny office," Bjorn said.

"Bjorn, can I ask you something?"

Bjorn extricated himself from his seat. "Shoot."

"Do you still want to kill the Besquith? Captain Sabher?" Berto asked.

"Sabher commanded the group who pursued my people in Alaska, but he wasn't behind the attack at the Canadian airfield. I have to ask myself, if I was under contract to pursue an enemy force, what would I do?" Bjorn rubbed his thumb over his Mjolnir pendant. "Do I want to kill him? Only a little bit. I'm sure Tyr never forgave Fenris for his hand, even if he knew why the wolf bit it off."

* * *

"I must look awful for you to make that face," Tamara rasped.

Charlotte stirred from a half-doze. Light scars marred the dark skin on Tamara's jaw and cheek. Despite the nanites, damage to the muscles and nerves had left her with a perpetual smirk.

"Hey, sweetie." Charlotte shifted so she could float over Tamara. She resisted slipping her left arm out of its sling to ease the process. "How do you feel?"

"Half my face is numb, as though I went to the dentist," Tamara replied. Her fingers brushed the right side of her face then her ear. "I was afraid I'd lost that. Did you kill the big, bad wolf before he could eat me?"

"You killed it before I got there. You shoved your pistol in his mouth and fired your gyroc." Charlotte held onto the bed rail with her good arm.

"How long have I been out?"

"Four days," Charlotte replied. "The claws scored your bone, and they had to reattach your ear. They put you in a medical coma so the nanites could work. You're going to have some bitching scars."

"Guess I'll need to wear a veil at our wedding." Tamara forced a lopsided smile.

A tear drifted free from Charlotte's cheek. "Nope. I want everyone to see the beautiful woman I marry."

* * *

"We'll need a full-blown repair facility to replace the launcher and the supporting gear," Captain Wildman reported. "We've made repairs to the other breaches, but we can't use the affected airlocks until we replace them."

"Something else we need done at a repair dock?" Bjorn asked. In his mind, the pile of money the UCX paid them dwindled.

"Yes, sir."

"What about Sergeant Higgins? You mentioned in your report you wanted to investigate replacing him," Bjorn remarked. If the sergeant hadn't second guessed his orders, the rover might not have made it into the launcher.

"His contract expires in two months. I recommend we muster him out," Wildman stated, sipping from his coffee bulb.

"It's your ship; we'll do it your way." Bjorn peered about the mess. "Have you seen Halsey?"

"He said something about having a date," Captain Wildman replied. "He's off duty. Do you want me to call him here?"

"No. I'll get my own coffee in a minute." Bjorn scratched at his beard. "Who's the lucky girl?"

"Corporal Huynh. She's a shuttle pilot, but she flew a dropship in the deployment at Xhoxa," Wildman replied.

"Good for him."

* * *

"How's Reeves doing?" Cripe asked when Whisky floated to the table. It turned out having a maniac machine impale a 75-centimeter blade through his leg was low on the totem pole of injuries from the battle. Luckily, the blade missed bone and arteries.

Sergeant Wicza slipped her arm out of its sling so she could hold her tray and grab the table. "She's putting on a brave front, but I could tell Tamara wanted to break the mirror when she saw the scars."

"Are they that bad? Didn't the doctor reattach her ear?" Cripe asked.

"They put the ear back, but she might need an aural implant. As for the scars...no offense, but you're a middle-aged man. Chicks might dig a couple of scars on a guy; it fits the whole merc image. As a woman, every time Tamara looks in a mirror, the first thing her eyes will see are those scars," Whisky said. "No matter how much I reassure her they don't matter, in her mind, they will."

"So, what will you do?" Cripe asked, digging at his double-protein meat stew.

Whisky peeled open her meal. "Keep reassuring her. Hey, where are your Besquith trophies?"

"I stashed them. It didn't seem right after fighting alongside the wolves, and I don't want to piss off the Bigby in the Union Credit Exchange entourage," Cripe replied. "Besides, my new trophy is too big to wear."

Whisky shook her head. "I'm afraid to ask."

"I kept the arm-blade of the rover that skewered me. I'm going to hang it on the wall of my flat on Vishall," Cripe replied.

"So, you're still retiring?" Whisky asked.

"I haven't made up my mind. We scored a huge payday, but it seems a shame to get all nanited up for one mission."

* * * * *

Chapter Thirty-Six

Information Guild Headquarters, Capital Planet

Master Archivist Heloxi watched the Senate proceedings on the Tri-V. Two hours of speeches had lulled her to the brink of slumber. Get to the point already! Pass the bill to divorce the financial network of the Galactic Union from the red diamond standard! Another senator launched another boring speech.

"Excuse me, Master Archivist?" Neermal bowed low before her pool.

Heloxi's painted eyes fluttered wide. "What?"

"The mercenaries are here," Neermal stated. "The ones you hired. They have physical evidence to present to you."

Heloxi would have pawned the duty off on Ashok, but the mercs had beaten him back to Capital. The Humans could have a pile of credits they believed to be counterfeit. Heloxi rubbed her stumpy hands together, clinking her rings. The Union Credit Exchange would have destroyed the mint rather than let it get captured, but the Humans must have found currency ready for shipment. She'd praise them for bringing her the forgeries and pay them a pittance in return. If the senators would quit wasting time, she could manufacture the paltry sum at the press of a button.

"Bring them and their evidence." Once she spread the news of the mint's destruction through clandestine channels, it would sow enough instability to prod the Senate to act. Even if the mercenaries

418 | JON R. OSBORNE

realized their role, their culpability for the act would still their tongues.

Heloxi returned her attention to the Senate feed while she waited for Neermal to return with the Humans. The Mazreen senator rose to address the chamber. Heloxi smiled. Senator Patarix folded when a video of his indiscretion appeared on his office tablet. She preferred indirect methods, but time had grown short. Now the Mazreen would endorse the digital currency standard. Her wide mouth curled into a smile.

* * *

Galactic Senate Building, Capital Planet

Senate Patarix straightened the sash of office draped over his elaborate robes. "Honored colleagues, as many of you know, slanderous accusations have been bandied about in an attempt to distract discourse from the important matter at hand—the economic infrastructure of our galactic civilization. Those reluctant to part from the old ways fear the leap to a digital currency standard will place too much power in the hands of a single institution. Those endorsing the change cite how clinging to a standard based on limited physical resources shackles our economies.

"We already trust the Information Guild with our most precious resource—data. They already possess the transactional framework to operate without the burden of a physical standard. Why shouldn't we trust them?" Murmurs in dozens of languages rippled through the chamber.

The Mazreen straightened, sweeping the crowd with his black eyes. "Why? Because the Information Guild abuses the power they already possess. They use their control of the GalNet and Universal

Account Access Cards to tamper with the finances of individuals. They hire pirates to attack currency shipments to destabilize the supply of physical currency. They blackmail and even attempt to hire assassins to eliminate politicians. In their most audacious move, they arranged the attack on one of the Union Credit Exchange's mint facilities."

Senator Patarix set a pile of data chips on the desk in front of him. "These chips are hard copies of the evidence against the Information Guild."

* * *

Information Guild Headquarters, Capital Planet

"What?" Master Archivist Heloxi shrieked, spittle and a tadpole flying from her painted lips. She slapped her flank so hard, one of her rings spun off into the pool. "That treacherous green vermin! I'll show him what happens when you cross me!"

'Release file Patarix 32G14Z27 on prescribed distribution paths,' Heloxi ordered through her pinplants.

Index Prime: 'File not found.'

Heloxi lowered her gem-spangled eyelids. 'Index Prime, locate file Patarix 32G14Z27 and copy to local node.'

Index Prime: 'File not found.'

'How is it possible? I made multiple backups of the file across multiple nodes,' Heloxi demanded.

Index Prime: 'Because I deleted them all.'

A metallic thud sounded against the huge double doors to her chamber. Two huge mechanical humanoids shoved the doors open, allowing the bright beams of headlights to spill into her dim cham-

420 | JON R. OSBORNE

ber. The lights silhouetted a bipedal form who strode into the room. A wheeled vehicle followed.

The Human stopped ten meters from Heloxi's pool. His formal uniform included a cloak comprised of an animal pelt draped over his broad shoulders. He carried a large double-bladed axe as though it was a badge of office. Heloxi's facial recognition software swept over his features.

'Bjorn Tovesson III, Commander, Bjorn's Berserkers, Earth.'

"Commander Tovesson, I appreciate theatrics as much as the next civilized being, but I am busy. Drop off your evidence and see Neermal about your payment," Heloxi stated. Did the Human know a senator had leveled incriminations that could include the mercenaries? First, she had to figure out why Index Prime glitched.

"Master Archivist Heloxi, you do our friend a dishonor." An elderly, crimson-plumed Nevar stepped around the vehicle, followed by another Nevar. The second Nevar's black feathers marked it as younger. After her came an armored Sumatozou and a Besquith. "Let me introduce Marshal Tovesson, who comes here on behalf of the Union Credit Exchange."

"Mel'Sizwer, whatever game you're playing, it doesn't matter," Heloxi sneered. Where were her guards? Where was Neermal? Over her pinplants, she sent, 'Security emergency—my audience chamber.'

Index Prime: 'Security call countermanded.'

"I imagine you're wondering why your security admitted this motley bunch," a high-pitched voice squeaked. From the other side of the vehicle, a Tortantula stepped into the light with a Flatar on her back. The Flatar pulled a badge from its saddle. Despite the small size, Heloxi could make out the blue Peacemaker symbol. The same symbol emblazoned the saddle. "I told them to take a break or go to jail. I am Peacemaker Qivek, and this is my partner Peacemaker Ozor."

"You hold no authority here, Peacemakers," Heloxi scoffed.

"How about I plant six kilograms of hardened molybdenum alloy authority in your skull?" Tovesson growled.

"Did I forget to mention we deputized Marshal Tovesson and his mercenary company?" Qivek quipped.

"You can deputize the planet, Rodent! I'm a guild master, so I have diplomatic immunity!" Heloxi yelled.

"Funny thing. After Peepo's flagrant abuse of power, the Galactic Senate decided no guild masters should be beyond the reach of the law," the Flatar stated. He drew a pistol, one of the infamous Flatar hyper-velocity pistols. The guns could punch through the armor of a Human war machine. "Diplomatic immunity has been revoked."

"Tovesson, I'll ruin you! You and your entire organization!" Heloxi pointed a stubby finger at the Human. "Index Prime, erase all accounts associated with any employee of Bjorn's Berserkers!"

"Unable to comply," an electronic voice echoed through the chamber.

"Authorize via pinplant and execute!" Heloxi yelled.

Tovesson took a step forward, brandishing the axe. "I'll execute your ass!"

"Unable to comply," the voice repeated. "User Heloxi does not possess sufficient access."

"I'm a master archivist! I have supreme clearance! Follow my orders!"

"Unable to comply. User Heloxi has provisional citizen clearance."

422 | JON R. OSBORNE

Heloxi's eyes opened wide. Her pinplant streams greyed out. "No!"

"What now?" the Human asked. "Should I club her over the head with the flat of my axe?"

"I endorse this suggestion," the Sumatozou said.

"As do I," added the Besquith.

"He might not crack her skull," the Tortantula remarked. "Let's find out."

"Savages," the Flatar muttered. "Have the CASPers drag her carcass to the vehicle."

"I surrender!" Heloxi squealed. Better to rely on a barrister than risk death at the hands of these primitives.

* * *

Galactic Senate Building, Capital Planet

Zod'Sizwey burst through the door of her grandsire's office. "It's official! The Senate passed the Finance Guild Act! Congratulations!"

Mel'Sizwer whistled. "I cannot take credit. Many worked to bring this to fruition."

"This will bring great fortune to our people," Zod said, ruffling her feathers in excitement.

"We must spread this bounty, lest it provoke excessive greed in our own people and envy among others," Mel stated. A little greed was healthy. "Also, reducing our reliance on the golems will require a significant investment."

"So, you will adopt Marshal Tovesson's plan?" Zod asked.

"Yes. His notion of protecting each mint with contingents composed of three races will dissuade temptation. If a single unit endeavors to betray their trust and rob the mint, the other two will keep them in check." Mel flexed his arthritic limbs. Overhauling the UCX—now the Finance Guild—security apparatus could take longer than he had left. "Trading secrecy for strength will necessitate a significant outlay of funds."

"It is a shame Marshal Tovesson wishes to limit his tenure," Zod stated.

"I applaud Dbo'Dizwey for her inspiration. While I wouldn't call Tovesson's appointment a sham, it was a creative solution," Mel said. "She never intended for Tovesson to remain deeply involved in our operations, but it allowed the Humans plausible deniability in case the Information Guild pushes back."

"Will the Information Guild resist?" Zod tipped her head and blinked all four eyes.

Mel shook his head. "Heloxi over-reached, and the other master archivists despise her. Even with the loss of the UAAC fees, they rake in more money than they can reasonably spend. They'll have to forgo the platinum inlays on their data chips, at least until they find a new way to squeeze more credits out of the galaxy, but they won't go broke."

* * *

Detention Facility 86, Capital Planet

A chill ran down Heloxi's blubbery hide. At first, she attributed the cold to the barely acceptable moisture in her detention chamber. She'd already chewed through half her brood in anxiety, despite the tadpoles' tiny size. They lacked the satisfying crunch of older progeny, but it distracted her from her deprivation.

A pair of red eyes stared out from the shadows in the corner of her cell. "Hello again, Heloxi."

Heloxi grinned. The guild had sent the Grimm to spring her from her imprisonment! "At last! Get me out of here. I have scores to settle with whoever betrayed me."

"You misunderstand. The guild did not send me for something so crude as a prison break," the Grimm said.

"Why are you here?" Heloxi's skin grew clammy.

"To tie up loose ends, of course." The Grimm drew a pneumatic pistol from his cloak.

* * *

EMS *Ursa Major*, Orbit Over Capital Planet

"Commander, we're ready to depart for the stargate," Captain Than Wildman reported.

"We've concluded business here," Bjorn said. "Depart at your discretion."

"Helm, set a standard 1G flip over for the stargate," Wildman ordered.

"Aye, 1G for stargate. ETA 34 hours, 12 minutes," Sergeant Ling announced as the timer appeared above her station.

"Sound thrust alarm and engage," Captain Wildman instructed. Thirty seconds after the thrust alarm sounded throughout the ship, the fusion torch ignited, and faux gravity pressed on Bjorn.

Bjorn left the flag station and descended to the deck containing his office.

"Hey, boss," Berto said without glancing up from his slate. "You come up with any other projects to take on?"

"In the three hours since we lifted off Capital? No." Bjorn settled behind his desk and sent a message to Corporal Halsey for coffee. He pulled the badge out of his shirt pocket. "I have enough marshal business to do before I pass the torch to Sabher. Right now, I want to get home and see my wife."

"Hope she doesn't kill you when she finds out you need to go back to Earth," Berto remarked.

"I'll have a month or so." Bjorn pocketed the badge. It was a memento he could pass on to his kid. After he handed the reigns over to Sabher, Bjorn would become a reserve marshal, an honorific title the birds had given him to stroke his ego.

"I have to go meet with the Kodiak company officers and NCOs for some team building," Berto said, slipping out from behind his desk.

Bjorn grunted an acknowledgement. Once the hatch closed, he opened the file from his pinplants.

"Son, give these alien motherfuckers what for."

'Pause video.'

Bjorn stared at the image of his father.

'Delete video.'

"Goodbye, Dad."

# # # # #

ABOUT THE AUTHOR

Jon R. Osborne is a veteran gamemaster and journalism major turned science fiction and fantasy author. The second book in the Jon's The Milesian Accords modern fantasy trilogy, "A Tempered Warrior", was a 2018 Dragon Awards finalist for Best Fantasy Novel. Jon is also a core author in the military science fiction Four Horseman Universe, where he was first published in 2017.

Jon resides in Indianapolis, where he plays role-playing games, writes science fiction and fantasy, and lives the nerd life. You can find out more at http://jonrosborne.com and at https://www.facebook.com/jonrosborne.

* * * * *

The following is an
Excerpt from Book One of the Salvage Title Trilogy:

Salvage Title

Kevin Steverson

Available Now from Theogony Books

eBook, Paperback, and Audio Book

Excerpt from "Salvage Title:"

The first thing Clip did was get power to the door and the access panel. Two of his power cells did the trick once he had them wired to the container. He then pulled out his slate and connected it. It lit up, and his fingers flew across it. It took him a few minutes to establish a link, then he programmed it to search for the combination to the access panel.

"Is it from a human ship?" Harmon asked, curious.

"I don't think so, but it doesn't matter; ones and zeros are still ones and zeros when it comes to computers. It's universal. I mean, there are some things you have to know to get other races' computers to run right, but it's not that hard," Clip said.

Harmon shook his head. *Riiigghht,* he thought. He knew better. Clip's intelligence test results were completely off the charts. Clip opted to go to work at Rinto's right after secondary school because there was nothing for him to learn at the colleges and universities on either Tretra or Joth. He could have received academic scholarships for advanced degrees on a number of nearby systems. He could have even gone all the way to Earth and attended the University of Georgia if he wanted. The problem was getting there. The schools would have provided free tuition if he could just have paid to get there.

Secondary school had been rough on Clip. He was a small guy that made excellent grades without trying. It would have been worse if Harmon hadn't let everyone know that Clip was his brother. They lived in the same foster center, so it was mostly true. The first day of school, Harmon had laid down the law—if you messed with Clip, you messed up.

At the age of fourteen, he beat three seniors senseless for attempting to put Clip in a trash container. One of them was a Yalteen, a member of a race of large humanoids from two systems over. It wasn't a fair fight—they should have brought more people with them. Harmon hated bullies.

After the suspension ended, the school's Warball coach came to see him. He started that season as a freshman and worked on using it to earn a scholarship to the academy. By the time he graduated, he was six feet two inches with two hundred and twenty pounds of muscle. He got the scholarship and a shot at going into space. It was the longest time he'd ever spent away from his foster brother, but he couldn't turn it down.

Clip stayed on Joth and went to work for Rinto. He figured it was a job that would get him access to all kinds of technical stuff, servos, motors, and maybe even some alien computers. The first week he was there, he tweaked the equipment and increased the plant's recycled steel production by 12 percent. Rinto was eternally grateful, as it put him solidly into the profit column instead of toeing the line between profit and loss. When Harmon came back to the planet after the academy, Rinto hired him on the spot on Clip's recommendation. After he saw Harmon operate the grappler and got to know him, he was glad he did.

A steady beeping brought Harmon back to the present. Clip's program had succeeded in unlocking the container. "Right on!" Clip exclaimed. He was always using expressions hundreds or more years out of style. "Let's see what we have; I hope this one isn't empty, too." Last month they'd come across a smaller vault, but it had been empty.

Harmon stepped up and wedged his hands into the small opening the door had made when it disengaged the locks. There wasn't enough power in the small cells Clip used to open it any further. He put his weight into it, and the door opened enough for them to get inside. Before they went in, Harmon placed a piece of pipe in the doorway so it couldn't close and lock on them, baking them alive before anyone realized they were missing.

Daylight shone in through the doorway, and they both froze in place; the weapons vault was full.

* * * * *

Get "Salvage Title" now at:
https://www.amazon.com/dp/B07H8Q3HBV.

Find out more about Kevin Steverson and "Salvage Title" at:
http://chriskennedypublishing.com/.

* * * * *

The following is an
Excerpt from Devil Calls the Tune:

Devil Calls the Tune

Chris Maddox

Available from Theogony Books

eBook, Paperback, and (Soon) Audio

Excerpt from "Devil Calls the Tune:"

Kenyon shouted, "Flyer! Fast mover!"

Everyone grabbed their packs and started running. When McCarthy didn't, Devlin grabbed him by his uniform shirt and yelled, "Come on!"

The little outcropping they had weathered under was part of a larger set of hills. Devlin and McCarthy made for a sheer cliff face that was tall enough that it would make strafing difficult. They dove behind a few rocks, and Devlin peered over one. The flier had overshot the group and was circling.

McCarthy reached into his pack and pulled out a rail pistol and magazine. He slapped the magazine home into its well and charged the pistol.

"Where the fark did you get that!" Devlin panted. He reached over and took the pistol. McCarthy let him.

"This was the surprise," McCarthy said. "I found the pistol, then searched the wreckage for ammo. I found some and parts to a bunch of rifles. Most were in bad shape, but Pringle figured he might be able to cobble together a couple from the parts. He was going take the lot back to the camp so they would have something to defend the wounded with. He sent me with this for you. Best we could get together at the time. Sorry."

"Don't be sorry. This is pretty good. I won't beat the shit out of you now for the fire."

"The fire?" McCarthy looked blank for a moment, then realization hit. "Oh, you think that the fire attracted—"

"Our flying friend over there. Yeah, I just—get your head down!" He pulled at McCarthy as rounds from the flier dug into the earth. There was something odd about this one.

438 | JON R. OSBORNE

He took a quick look. This wasn't the same flier that had attacked the camp, this one was…

"Drone!" Devlin yelled. He watched the thing from the rocks, watched it circle around again. He braced the pistol on the rocks, steadied, and waited.

When the drone started its run again, Devlin sighted in, breathed out, and fired.

The drone disintegrated in a fiery cloud as the rail gun round entered its main capacitor bank. He watched it fall and then rose from behind the rocks. McCarthy joined him.

Devlin looked over at the tree line and waved his arm. A moment later, Kenyon appeared, followed by Gartlan and MacBain.

"Devlin!" Decker's voice came out of the tree line. Kenyon and the others started to where Decker's voice had come from. Devlin started to run.

He found the group gathered around Decker. She was holding Moran's head in her lap. Moran's uniform had a red stain in the abdomen that was growing larger by the moment.

"Got hit as I dived into the woods," Moran croaked. Her blond hair was already slick with sweat, her face pale.

"Sorry, Devlin. I…I…" her voice trailed off as her implant fed nanites and nighty-night into her system. A moment later she looked dead, which for all intents and purposes she was.

Devlin rubbed his scalp. He glared over at McCarthy, whose shocked face got even paler as he looked at the body, hibernating though it was, of Lisa Moran. He bowed his head and started to stammer, "I'm sorry, I didn't…"

"Shut up, Tom. Just shut up," Devlin said tiredly. "You didn't know; you had no way of knowing. This wasn't even the same flier that attacked the camp. Just a stupid mistake, but it's one that we have to deal with now. Is anybody else hurt?"

Arnette was sitting on the ground beside Decker with her legs crossed. She held one ankle in her hands. "Well, now that you mention it…" She looked at Devlin with pain-filled eyes. "I think my ankle is broken. I stepped straight into a hole as I came into the woods."

Decker moved her legs out from underneath Moran's head and laid it gently on the ground. She made her way to the other woman. Gartlan bent down as well and said, "Let's get your boot off."

Together, the two started trying to get the girl's boot off. When Arnette hissed once and nearly passed out, they realized they'd have to cut it off. Gartlan produced a tactical knife and used the mono-molecular edge to slice down the side of the boot. His cut made, he handed the knife to Decker, who sliced down the foot portion of the boot, careful not to cut too deeply.

"Here you go, Wolf," she said handing the knife back to Gartlan, who folded it and put it back in his pocket. Together, he and Decker were finally able to peel the ruined boot off the injured girl's foot.

Her foot, already purple, immediately started to swell. They propped her leg up on a rock covered with Gartlan's tunic. Gartlan shook his head at Devlin. "She isn't likely to go nighty-night, but she might as well. She ain't going anywhere on that foot for a few days. And she's not going to like this, but we're going to have to set it and splint it so that the nanis don't knit it wrong. Probably still will, but the canker mechanics should be able to fix it without too much problem if we get home."

Sarah Arnette's eyes went wide as Gartlan's words hit home. "Oh Gods!" she moaned. "This is going to *suck!*"

"Do it," Devlin said. "Come on, guys. They don't need an audience, and we've got to get our shit together."

He turned to walk away as Gartlan bent back down, and Decker opened a med kit.

Another drone flier came to halt in front of them, and a voice came over its vocoder, "State your name and passcode."

* * * * *

"Devil Calls the Tune" now at:
https://www.amazon.com/dp/B0849QYWMJ.

Find out more about Chris Maddox and "Devil Calls the Tune" at:
https://chriskennedypublishing.com/imprints-authors/chris-maddox/.

* * * * *

The following is an

Excerpt from Book One of The Progenitors' War:

A Gulf in Time

Chris Kennedy

Available from Theogony Books

eBook, Paperback, and (Soon) Audio

Excerpt from "A Gulf in Time:"

"Thank you for calling us," the figure on the front view screen said, his pupil-less eyes glowing bright yellow beneath his eight-inch horns. Generally humanoid, the creature was blood red and had a mouthful of pointed teeth that were visible when he smiled. Giant bat wings alternately spread and folded behind him; his pointed tail could be seen flicking back and forth when the wings were folded. "We accept your offer to be our slaves for now and all eternity."

"Get us out of here, helm!" Captain Sheppard ordered. "Flank speed to the stargate!"

"Sorry, sir, my console is dead," the helmsman replied.

"Can you jump us to the Jinn Universe?"

"No, sir, that's dead too."

"Engineer, do we have our shields?"

"No, sir, they're down, and my console's dead, too."

"OSO? DSO? Status?"

"My console's dead," the Offensive Systems Officer replied.

"Mine, too," the Defensive Systems Officer noted.

The figure on the view screen laughed. "I do *so* love the way new minions scamper about, trying to avoid the unavoidable."

"There's been a mistake," Captain Sheppard said. "We didn't intend to call you or become your minions."

"It does not matter whether you *intended* to or not," the creature said. "You passed the test and are obviously strong enough to function as our messengers."

"What do you mean, 'to function as your messengers?'"

"It is past time for this galaxy's harvest. You will go to all the civilizations and prepare them for the cull."

"I'm not sure I like the sound of that. What is this 'cull?'"

"We require your life force in order to survive. Each civilization will be required to provide 98.2% of its life force. The remaining 1.8% will be used to reseed their planets."

"And you expect us to take this message to all the civilized planets in this galaxy?"

"That is correct. Why else would we have left the stargates for you to use to travel between the stars?"

"What if a civilization doesn't want to participate in this cull?"

"Then they will be obliterated. Most will choose to save 1.8% of their population, rather than none, especially once you make an example or two of the civilizations who refuse."

"And if *we* refuse?"

"Then your society will be the first example."

"I can't make this kind of decision," Captain Sheppard said, stalling. "I'll have to discuss it with my superiors."

"Unacceptable. You must give me an answer now. Kneel before us or perish; those are your choices."

"I can't," Captain Sheppard said, his voice full of anguish.

"Who called us by completing the quest?" the creature asked. "That person must decide."

"I pushed the button," Lieutenant Commander Hobbs replied, "but I can't commit my race to this any more than Captain Sheppard can."

"That is all right," the creature said. "Sometimes it is best to have an example from the start." He looked off screen. "Destroy them."

"Captain Sheppard, there are energy weapons warming up on the other ship," Steropes said.

"DSO, now would be a good time for those shields..." Captain Sheppard said.

"I'm sorry, sir; my console is still dead."

"They're firing!" Steropes called.

The enemy ship fired, but the *Vella Gulf*'s shields snapped on, absorbing the volley.

"Nice job, DSO!" Captain Sheppard exclaimed.

"I didn't do it, sir!" the DSO cried. "They just came on."

"Well, if you didn't do it, who did?" Captain Sheppard asked.

"I don't know!" the DSO exclaimed. "All I know is we can't take another volley like that, sir; the first round completely maxed out our shields. One more, and they're going to fail!"

"I...activated...the shields," Solomon, the ship's artificial intelligence, said. The voice of the AI sounded strained. "Am fighting...intruder..." the AI's voice fluctuated between male and female. "Losing...system...integrity...krelbet gelched."

"Krelbet gelched?" the DSO asked.

"It means 'systems failing' in the language of the Eldive," Steropes said.

"The enemy is firing again," the DSO said. "We're hit! Shields are down."

"I've got hits down the length of the ship," the duty engineer said. "We're open to space in several places. We can't take another round like that!"

"That was just the little that came through after the shields fell," the DSO said. "We're doomed if—*missiles inbound!* I've got over 100 missiles inbound, and I can't do anything to stop them!" He switched to the public address system. "*Numerous missiles inbound! All hands brace for shock!* Five seconds! Three...two...one..."

* * * * *

Get "A Gulf in Time" now at:
https://www.amazon.com/dp/B0829FLV92

Find out more about Chris Kennedy and "A Gulf in Time" at:
https://chriskennedypublishing.com/imprints-authors/chris-kennedy/

* * * * *

Made in the USA
Middletown, DE
11 September 2023

38370105R00249